INK, IRON, AND GLASS

INK, IRON, AND GLASS

GWENDOLYN CLARE

NEW YORK

[Imprint]
MAKE YOUR MARK

A part of Macmillan Publishing Group, LLC
175 Fifth Avenue, New York, NY 10010

Library of Congress Control Number: 2017945052

ISBN 978-1-250-11276-7 (hardcover) / ISBN 978-1-250-11275-0 (ebook)

Our books may be purchased in bulk for promotional, educational, or business use. Please
contact your local bookseller or the Macmillan Corporate and Premium Sales Department at
(800) 221-7945 ext. 5442 or by e-mail at MacmillanSpecialMarkets@macmillan.com.

Book design by Liz Dresner

Imprint logo designed by Amanda Spielman

First edition, 2018

1 3 5 7 9 10 8 6 4 2

fiercereads.com

Whosoever burns this book
Shall find that something precious is took
Thereafter living in sore deprive
Or altogether not alive

FOR ATHENA, WHO UNDERSTANDS
THAT REALITY IS HIGHLY OVERRATED

1

No great mind has ever existed
without a touch of madness.
—*Aristotle*

1891, THE SCRIBED WORLD OF VELDANA

Elsa crouched beside the tide pool, the hem of her skirt gathered over her arm to keep it off the algae-slick rocks. A new species of starfish had emerged, but whether it would persist in the world or not was an open question. Elsa pulled on her clockwork glove and activated the stability sensors in the fingertips, then gently lifted the starfish out of the water with her other hand.

The creature was quite lovely, orange and long-limbed and prickly against her skin, though Elsa tried not to get too attached just yet. New species sometimes destabilized and ceased to exist. She waved her hand over the starfish, and the mechanical innards of the glove buzzed against her palm, tiny gears whirring. After a minute, the indicator light on the back of the glove flicked on: green, for stable. Elsa let out the breath she'd been holding, relieved.

Then the starfish imploded in her hand, folding in on itself and disappearing with a soft *pop*.

Belatedly, the indicator light switched from green to red. Unstable.

"You don't say," she muttered to the glove. "Useless bit of scrap."

Elsa's mother would not be pleased—Jumi took special pride in the emergence of new species. She scowled at the glove as she pulled her hand out. It had never given her a false positive like this before, but a stable species should not cease to exist that quickly. She hoped it was a malfunction. The alternative would be much worse—if the problem wasn't the glove, then something had gone seriously wrong with the most recent expansions to their world.

The brass finger-joints of the glove had leaked lubricant onto her hand. She hung the glove from her belt and wiped her fingers on her apron, smudging greasy streaks down the pale cloth. Then she stood and hastily picked her way around the tide pools, the rocks rough against the bare soles of her feet, and she trudged up the narrow strip of sand between the sea and the shore cliffs.

After she retrieved her flat-soled leather shoes from where she'd left them at the trailhead, Elsa decided she should do a quick walk-through of the whole expansion before returning to the village to report to Jumi. She turned back to walk the length of the beach, which was longer than it used to be. Jumi had added a new section during her latest revisions to the world.

Perhaps a kilometer out to sea, the Edgemist hung like a gray curtain, running parallel to the shore. The Edgemist defined the boundaries of existence, and Elsa took comfort in the familiarity of its presence, even if it was farther away thanks to the most recent expansion. Veldana was a fabricated world, but it was Elsa's home, and she preferred the Edgemist to the endless horizons of Earth.

Up ahead, the cliffs curved outward and the Edgemist angled toward the shore. Though she couldn't see it from her vantage point on the beach, Elsa knew the two would meet somewhere, pinching off the sea. Along with the new cliffs there was a new trail, snaking up the side in a series of tight switchbacks. She was almost at the trailhead when the Edgemist, hanging close on her left, began to shift, and the movement caught her attention. She stopped short and whirled around to stare at it, a cold fear seeding in her stomach.

The mottled purple-gray patterns of the Edgemist, usually calm, now churned like angry storm clouds. Veldana only had mild rains, but Elsa had seen a real thunderstorm once in Paris, when she'd accompanied her mother on a trip to Earth. She remembered how the clouds hunkered low and menacing over the city, darkening the gaslit streets, and rain lashed the window-panes until they rattled in their casings. She'd been eight and ter-rified, and this was the feeling that welled up in her now, seeing the Edgemist writhe before her.

A breeze picked up, tossing strands of black hair across Elsa's face and carrying with it the salt-and-decay scent of low tide.

Could this be an aftereffect of the most recent changes? Had Jumi expanded Veldana too quickly and somehow destabilized the boundaries of the world?

The breeze shifted direction, carrying the muffled sound of

shouts from somewhere above. Could a person somehow be causing the disturbance? Elsa turned and ran to the trailhead, stopping only to shove her feet into her shoes before rushing up the switchbacks. The path wove between the narrow, twisted trunks of Aleppo pines and squat, thick holly oaks. She followed as it bent to the left, eventually spitting her out onto a long, grassy meadow bounded on one side by forest and on the other by the gray wall of the Edgemist.

The shouts belonged to a gaggle of boys from the village. They were throwing pebbles at the Edgemist, trying to see if they could penetrate the invisible force that held matter inside the world. Some of the pebbles rebounded off the Edgemist as if off a wall, landing in the grass, while others passed silently through and disappeared forever. Here, too, the Edgemist swirled like eddies in a fast-flowing river.

Elsa heaved an irritated sigh. Surely, this must be the cause. As Jumi always said, coincidence was the assumption of a lazy mind.

"Jumi just made those rocks," she said loudly in Veldanese.

The boys whirled around. One of the younger ones let out a frightened yelp, and another clapped a hand over his friend's mouth.

The eldest was her once-friend Revan, now too broad at the shoulders to really be called a boy. "What's the big deal? They're just pebbles."

"You're destroying part of the world. It's the principle of the thing." She turned her gaze on the younger ones. "Now run on home before I tell Jumi and she erases you out of the worldbook!"

The children squealed and ran for the trailhead. Revan folded his arms, annoyed. "You shouldn't scare them like that."

"Oh? How should I scare them?" Elsa said, eyebrows raised. "They need to learn to respect Veldana, and you're not helping any, encouraging these stupid games."

"While I'm sure you find Jumi's squirmy little sea creatures thoroughly enthralling, the rest of us have to make our own fun."

That was the way it was among the children: her versus the rest of them. Revan's mother, Baninu, was as close to a friend as Jumi had. Baninu hoped their children would someday marry, and this more than anything else had driven the wedge between Elsa and Revan, for she did not plan to marry. Ever.

"Just . . . find something else. Don't do this again," Elsa said coldly.

Revan stared at her like he was memorizing the face of a stranger. Elsa felt a sharp twinge of regret, but she turned away so he would not see it in her face.

The vanished starfish and the Edgemist's strange behavior still nagged at her. A few pebbles shouldn't have caused that instability all on their own. Best to rush straight home and consult Jumi.

The village lay nestled in a valley, bisected by a rocky-bottomed creek that emptied into the sea—now that there was a sea. The shallow banks were lined with moss, and Elsa's shoes sank into the springy stuff as she hurried upstream.

She crossed a little wooden bridge and wove her way between the scattered cottages with their dark thatched roofs and white-washed wattle-and-daub walls. Past the gentle slope of the hill was the cottage she shared with her mother. There was a vegetable garden along the side and a chicken coop behind, and as Elsa reached for the door she reminded herself that one needed weeding and the other needed sweeping.

The cottage itself had one large room on the ground floor and a loft for sleeping space. Hearing the door latch, Jumi glanced up from her writing table.

Looking at Jumi was like looking in a mirror that showed the future. Elsa's skin was a shade darker, bronze-brown to her mother's sienna tan, but they shared the black hair, clear green eyes, and even the shape of their faces: strong cheekbones sweeping low over an expressive mouth and sharp chin. Elsa took pride in the similarity, and if anyone saw parts of her father reflected in her, they did not dare to say. She herself had no idea what he had looked like when he was alive, and this was one of the few ignorances she felt no desire to correct.

"Elsa, dear. You're back early," Jumi observed.

"Afternoon, Mother."

Elsa came around the table to look at what her mother was working on. Jumi was scribing in a large worldbook—one that did not look familiar to Elsa, though she couldn't be sure since it was open to a mostly blank page.

"What's this?" Elsa said, curious.

"It's our freedom," Jumi said.

Elsa eyed her mother, wondering if she could press for a less cryptic answer. Veldana had been created by one of those self-superior European scriptologists, a man named Charles Montaigne, who had treated the Veldanese as subjects of an experiment. The damage he wrought to the Veldanese language alone had taken Jumi years to correct after she learned the scientific discipline of scriptology and negotiated Veldana's independence.

How, exactly, she had wrested control of the world from Montaigne was a subject Jumi always skirted around.

"What do you mean?" Elsa asked.

Jumi did not answer. Instead, she set her fountain pen aside and brushed her fingers across one thick off-white page, a soothing gesture, the way another person might stroke a nervous animal. "You'll be seventeen next month. A grown woman. I think it's time you have access to the Veldana worldbook. It will be your job to care for our world someday, and you're skilled enough now to take a more active role in the expansions."

Elsa felt a swell of pride. Nothing mattered more than being worthy of Jumi's approval, worthy of inheriting her role as caretaker of Veldana. "Thank you, Mother."

Jumi smiled one of her rare, soft smiles and put a hand to Elsa's cheek, a gesture of affection that would have been embarrassing if they hadn't been alone. "I could not have asked for better," she said.

Elsa covered Jumi's hand with her own, holding it against her face for a moment before letting it go. Flustered by her mother's praise, she wasn't sure what to say, so she changed the subject. "I think we might have a problem with the newest revisions. I'm not sure. . . ." Despite her earlier threats, Elsa found herself reluctant to betray the boys to Jumi. She decided to leave them out of the story. "The Edgemist was behaving strangely. It looked disturbed. And there was this starfish that seemed stable, then it up and vanished right out of my hand."

Jumi frowned. "I scribed the expansion hours ago. The Edgemist should have settled away to its new location by now."

"I know." Elsa shrugged. "Perhaps it was nothing, but—"

There was a loud crack, like the sound of a branch breaking.

The room began to fill with smoke, and Elsa covered her nose and mouth with her sleeve. A sickly-sweet smell crept through the fabric as she ran for the door, but she stepped on something and slipped, and the hard slate floor came up to meet her, knocking the wind from her lungs. The smoke was making her dizzy, too dizzy to get back up. Somewhere nearby Jumi coughed and wheezed, but Elsa couldn't catch sight of her through the smoke.

Her thoughts seemed to be slowing down, like her brain was turning sticky as honey, her skull heavy. Her head dropped and her eyelids closed.

On Earth, in the city of Pisa, Leo Trovatelli was dreaming.

In the dream he was on a walkway beside a canal with his brother, Aris. Mist clung to everything, the way it always had in the early mornings of Venetian winter. Aris flashed him a knowing grin, then spun around and sprinted off down the walkway. Leo tried desperately to catch up, but he was a child again, and his short legs weren't fast enough. Aris pulled farther and farther away, fading into the mist. The cobblestones beneath Leo's feet shook, throwing him off balance, and he fell over the edge into the black waters of the canal.

Leo jerked awake, but the shaking didn't stop. He was slouched awkwardly in the armchair in his bedroom; he'd meant to rest his eyes for only a minute and now the whole room was vibrating. An earthquake? He'd felt his share of earthquakes, and this was somehow softer and faster, more frenetic, as if it were tuned to a different wavelength.

Knickknacks jounced around on his shelves, clattering against the wood. Something fell to the floor and shattered. Through the half-open balcony doors, he heard someone shout in the cloister garden below.

After a moment the shaking stopped, but it left behind a sick, hollow feeling in his gut. Somewhere in the world, something had gone wrong.

He shook his head and pushed himself out of the chair. Aunt Rosalinda had always discouraged his superstitious feelings, and if she were here, she'd tell him it was nothing. Better to focus on the practicalities, like cleaning up whatever the earthquake had broken.

He knelt beside the shattered ceramic. There were so many pieces he didn't recognize it at first, but then he found part of the eye socket and realized: it was the *carnevale* mask, one of the few possessions he'd brought with him from Venezia. From his childhood with Aris.

This wasn't a sign, he told himself. *This wasn't a sign of anything.*

2

Reading Shelley's _Frankenstein_, I have to wonder:
Am I not the villain of Montaigne's story? Am I
not his monster? Or am I real enough for
this to be my story, and he the villain?
—*personal notes of Jumi da Veldana, 1886*

Elsa swam her way back to consciousness through a honey-thick sea of heavy dreams. When she finally forced her eyelids to peel themselves open, she was greeted by a splitting headache and a unique perspective on the underside of Jumi's writing table.

"Ugh," she said, lifting a shaky hand to press against her temple. "Mother, what happened?"

No one answered.

"Mother?" Elsa pushed herself up to a sitting position. The writing chair was knocked over, and her mother's favorite fountain pen had rolled across the slate flooring, leaking a thin trail of blue-black ink.

Fear tightened her chest, but she had to keep a level head and figure out what was going on. *Think, think!* Elsa groped on the floor for the object she'd slipped on and came up with a small metal cylinder of some kind. She lifted it and sniffed carefully, confirming it as the origin of the sweet smoke. Some kind of gaseous chemical designed to induce sleep?

This was no accident. Someone had abducted her mother.

A thread of panic laced through Elsa, quickening her breath. She struggled to her feet, grabbing the edge of the writing desk to pull herself up. Gone, too, was the worldbook her mother had been scribing in. What did that mean? Was it valuable? Who could have taken her mother, and why?

Elsa bent over, hands on knees, breathing too fast. She was unaccustomed to the sensation of helplessness. She needed to figure out what to do; there had to be something she could do. Gather information, focus on the details, employ rational evaluation—this was the methodology Jumi had taught her, and so she forced herself to look up and observe.

Sunlight still filtered through the windows. How long had she been unconscious? Elsa scrambled for the door, her legs feeling wobbly and loose-jointed, and she peered outside to judge the time by the angle of the shadows. An hour, perhaps.

She might still be able to catch up with them. A portal from Veldana could only transport someone to the location on Earth where the Veldana worldbook was kept: the home of Charles Montaigne, the scriptologist who'd created her world. They could open a portal in the Edgemist anywhere along the boundaries of Veldana, but they could only arrive in Paris, France, inside Montaigne's study.

They'd taken Jumi's portal device, which had been sitting out on the writing table. Elsa clattered up the ladder to the loft, opened her mother's clothing chest, scooped out all the clothes, and lifted the false bottom. Jumi was nothing if not dedicated to precautionary measures.

Elsa reached into the chest to take out the spare portal device and slipped it into a pouch on her belt. Next she lifted the revolver, shook six bullets out of the ammunition box, and loaded the revolver. She threaded the holster onto her belt and settled the revolver snugly into it. They were all Earth objects; Veldana had no infrastructure for manufacturing. The revolver had been a gift from Alek de Vries, a scriptologist who had mentored Jumi. Elsa knew how to operate the gun but had never pointed it at anything alive; the thought that she might have to, now, gave her a queasy feeling.

Last, Elsa lifted out a small book, its leather cover no larger than her hand. It contained her most ambitious scriptology project, and the only one in recent years for which she'd needed Jumi's advice—her doorbook. Deciding it might be useful, Elsa took the book, along with a pen and a little bottle of scriptology ink. Through the glass the midnight-blue ink gave off an iridescent sheen, as if swirled with quicksilver. There, that was everything.

Rushing from the cottage, Elsa lifted her skirt and ran along a narrow path that followed the creek upstream and out of the valley. There was a shortcut halfway up, a little-used trail so steep Elsa had to grab at tree trunks to lever herself or crawl on all fours over the rocks, but every step was familiar and she could fly up the slope much faster than a stranger might.

Her heart hammered against her ribs. The interlopers didn't know Veldana like she did, and carrying Jumi's weight would slow them down, but they had a whole hour's head start. They might have already reached the Edgemist—they might be dialing their portal device for the return trip even now.

The Edgemist . . . of course! The disturbance she'd observed had had nothing to do with a fault in her mother's alterations to the worldbook. These invaders must have opened a portal while Veldana was still adjusting to the expansions—even a single person coming through at the wrong time would be enough mass to destabilize the Edgemist temporarily.

Elsa flushed hot with panic and guilt. If only she had thought of that explanation before, there might have been time to prepare, time to fend them off. How could she have been so stupid?

She scrambled up the last section of the slope, and then it was a straight shot through the forest to reach the Edgemist. She took it at a run, her legs burning, the hard leather pouches that hung from her belt banging against her thighs. The forest opened up into a narrow strip of meadow separating the trees from the Edgemist, and Elsa stumbled to a stop. Her breath still hitching, she fished the portal device from its belt pouch.

Elsa knew the coordinates for Earth by heart, and she twisted the little brass knobs to the correct settings. The memory rose, unbidden, of the first time Jumi had let her work the portal device—she had been six, and the device had felt unwieldy in her small hands, requiring all her concentration. But she'd had plenty of practice since then, and despite the superior attitudes of European scriptologists like Montaigne, Elsa had taken to the science as if she were born for it. By now the controls were so familiar, she could have dialed the settings with her eyes closed.

The coordinates set, Elsa flipped the stiff brass switch in the center with her thumb. A small black dot appeared in the Edgemist before her, the mist spiraling around it as if it were the eye of a storm. The black eye irised open until it was an oval portal wide and tall enough to admit a person, and Elsa lunged in.

The insides of portals weren't, strictly speaking, existent places, and that was precisely how it felt to be there—as if one no longer existed. It was freezing cold and perfectly dark in a way that felt like the concepts of temperature and light were absent. Elsa knew to keep walking, even though there was nothing to walk on, and nothing to walk toward, and then it was over as suddenly as it had begun.

She stepped through into a room full of light and smoke, the portal automatically closing behind her. Elsa covered her face with her sleeve for the second time that day—Montaigne's shelves of worldbooks were burning. The thieves must have set fire to the study after they'd come through.

A surge of terror flooded her veins. The Veldana worldbook was hidden here, and if the book was destroyed, so was the world. Coughing, she ran to the blank wall where the worldbook's secret chamber lay hidden. Elsa pressed her palms against the wall the way she'd seen her mother do so many times, but the chamber refused to open for her. She screamed her frustration and slammed her palms against the wall again, but it was useless—the chamber was designed to open only for Jumi, and Jumi was gone.

Elsa struggled to rein in her racing thoughts. Other books—other worlds—were burning as she wasted time standing there. She should at least try to save what she could. Turning to run for the shelves, Elsa tripped over something on the floor and stumbled. It was a body: portly, middle-aged, lying facedown in a pool of blood. Charles Montaigne, Veldana's original creator. The abductors were also, apparently, murderers.

Elsa stared in shock. Jumi had found him infuriating, and had been careful to never leave Elsa alone with him, but murder still seemed an extreme solution.

A waft of smoke scraped at her lungs and sent her into a fit of coughing. Time was of the essence. The flames consuming the bookshelves had jumped to the curtains of the nearest window and were tentatively starting to crawl across the wooden floor. Elsa scanned the shelves for the familiar spine of the Veldana worldbook, in case it was outside the wall vault, but she didn't find it. So she went to the shelf with the lowest flames. Squinting against the heat, she pulled down the least scorched of the volumes—the ones that might not be damaged beyond repair. She rescued another mildly blackened volume from the floor near Montaigne's body and fled, her arms full, her lungs scoured with smoke, from the house.

Out on the street, Elsa was surprised to see that a small crowd of Montaigne's neighbors had gathered. Evening was falling over Paris, yellow gaslight from the streetlamps pooling along the cobblestones. The smoke from the fire cast a gray blot against the dark violet of the sky. Elsa stumbled down the front steps and dropped her armful of books in the street, then nearly went down with them as a coughing fit overtook her. Her lungs felt scorched dry, as if the fire had gotten inside her, and the damp evening air provided no relief.

She turned to run back in and rescue another armload of books, but someone grabbed her and held her back.

"You can't, miss! The house is lost," the man said.

She struggled and kicked. "You don't understand. The worlds are burning!"

Either the onlookers did not know the house belonged to a renowned scriptologist, or they understood but simply did not find her argument compelling. Another of Montaigne's neighbors came over to help drag her back. Frustration bloomed in her chest like a dark flower. She should not have wasted time on those other worldbooks, she should not have left without Veldana—if she couldn't get the wall safe to open, she should have beaten down the wall with her bare fists and dragged the whole thing out.

The fire was spreading too fast, flames already visible in the front of the house through the sitting room windows. Her world was still inside, but there was nothing she could do now.

Elsa sagged in their grip, despairing, and they let go, returning immediately to a distance dictated by propriety. "The fire brigade's been called for," the first one said, as if this would be a comfort. He reached down to retrieve his top hat, which had fallen in the struggle. "Are you well now, miss?"

"What a ridiculous question," she snapped, and turned away from him.

She knelt on the cobblestones beside what books she had managed to save. She opened the closest one and pressed her fingers to the pages, feeling for the familiar buzz of a live worldbook. There was a subtle vibration, like the rubbing together of a cricket's wings, but it swelled and receded in a disturbing fashion. A finished worldbook should feel confident and solid, but this one was weak with fluctuations.

Elsa could feel the eyes of the crowd, as hot against her back as the fire itself. She had neither time nor patience for considering what they made of the situation—an angry brown girl in peasant clothes emerging from the house of their respectable, well-to-do neighbor. But whatever they thought, a crowded avenue was not the place to assess the extent of the fire damage done to the books.

Elsa pushed her sweat-damp hair out of her face and looked around. On the far side of the street, a black coach clattered by, the horses rearing and rolling their wide eyes in fear, the coach-man shouting curses as he fought for control. When the carriage had passed, Elsa scooped up the books and stalked across the street, away from prying eyes.

She turned the first corner, putting a building between her and the curious gazes of the crowd, and stood in a patch of shadow between the streetlamps. Using her legs like bookends, she set the books down between her feet to free her hands, then took her pocket-sized book from its belt pouch. It wasn't a proper world-book so much as a directory of places—a means by which to target the portal device and open a door from one location on Earth to another. A heretical application of scriptology, by the standards of European science, but for Elsa it was an achievement worthy of pride.

She skipped past the core text in the front, where the book's properties and functions were defined, and flipped through the destinations described in the back. Her hands shook a little as she considered where to go. Her mind went immediately to the one person on Earth whom she knew could be counted upon for assis-tance: her mother's old mentor, Alek de Vries. So she found the page where she'd scribed a description of the canal outside de Vries's flat in Amsterdam.

Taking out the portal device, she read the coordinates from the little doorbook, then tuned the brass knobs to the proper set-tings. When she flipped the switch, the dark disk of the portal widened, slicing through the very air of the alleyway—it hung there, unattached to anything, and even though Elsa had done this before, the sight of a portal with no Edgemist still disquieted her a bit. The real world didn't work in sensible ways.

As she tucked the portal device back into its pouch, she heard the distant clatter of dozens of hooves and the creak of massive wheels behind her—the Parisian fire brigade, at last, arriving too late to do more than quell the spread of the blaze. Elsa let out a frustrated huff, hefted her stack of rescued books, and walked into the portal. She stepped through the infinite coldness and out onto a cobbled walkway tucked between a narrow canal and a row of looming four-story brick buildings all squeezed together like books on an overfull shelf. Amsterdam.

The portal winked closed of its own accord, and Elsa stepped up onto the stoop and shifted the books to rest on her hip, freeing one hand. She yanked down on the bell pull for de Vries's flat, counting the seconds until he opened the front door.

De Vries was tall and skinny, bald on top but with the thick, cultivated mustache of a Victorian gentleman. He was wearing a burgundy smoking jacket, the velvet a little worn around the cuffs. Elsa thought of him as tragically old, though there weren't any Veldanese older than about forty years, so she supposed she didn't have much basis for comparison. In any case, he had laugh wrinkles around the eyes and frown lines between his brows, and at the moment the latter were the more prominent.

"Elsa, dear, what are you doing here? Where's Jumi?" he said in Dutch, adjusting his wire-frame spectacles as if she might be some sort of illusion.

"A lot has happened. Let me in, it will take some time to explain," Elsa said, smoothly switching to Dutch.

One of the characteristics scribed into the Veldana world-book gave Veldanese the ability to speak a new language within minutes of hearing it—no fuss over grammar, no laboring to memorize vocabulary. Though Elsa had known de Vries since she was a baby, so Dutch felt almost as natural to her as Veldanese.

"Of course, of course," de Vries said, holding the door open wide and running his other hand over his hairless pate.

De Vries reached to unburden her, but Elsa held on to the books and pushed past him up the stairs to his second-floor flat. Out of politeness, she waited at the top for de Vries to let them both in.

"So?" de Vries said as he closed the door behind them. "Are you going to tell me why you're soot-stained and smelling of smoke?"

Briefly, Elsa wondered how de Vries could even tell, considering that both he and his sitting room smelled strongly of pipe tobacco. She dropped the stack of worldbooks on a credenza beside the door and said, "Montaigne was killed. The library was in flames when I came through from Veldana. I saved what I could."

De Vries swore a long chain of words he really oughtn't say in front of a lady. He had been close friends with Montaigne—how *that* had worked, given the uneasy truce between Montaigne and Jumi, Elsa couldn't guess—and the loss of Montaigne's library was a terrible waste by anyone's standards.

"De Vries!" she said, needing him to focus. "That isn't all. I don't have the Veldana worldbook. Jumi is the only one who can open the chamber where it's kept. Veldana was still in the house when it burned."

"Oh, Elsa. That doesn't mean . . . ," de Vries began, awkward in his gentleness. "I don't know much about the design of her wall safe, but the worldbook may very well have survived the fire precisely because it was locked inside."

"Perhaps. But if the worldbook's damaged, I can't risk going back there. Not ever." Elsa ground her teeth together, determined not to let him see the anxiety that burned like acid behind her breastbone. A damaged worldbook meant a damaged world, and without its core properties intact—properties like breathable air and solid ground—she'd be opening a portal to her own unpleasant demise. Not to mention that there'd be no one left alive to return to.

He put a comforting hand on her shoulder. "If Veldana is intact, your mother will realize you're missing and port here to look for you. Don't worry, you won't be stuck with me for long."

"No, I'm afraid she won't." The words caught in her smoke-roughened throat, and Elsa had to force them out. "She's gone, de Vries. There was a kind of smoke that makes you sleep, and when I woke up, she was missing. Taken."

"Gone," he repeated, and sat down suddenly on a footstool, the news landing like a blow. "Jumi is in the hands of God knows who?"

"Which means there's no one left in Veldana who knows how to operate a portal device. The link between our worlds is severed, if Veldana still exists at all."

"It means more than that," de Vries said, his lips pressed together in a grim line. "A talented scriptologist like Jumi being abducted . . . it could mean someone is making a play for power. But who? The French government?"

Elsa blinked, unfazed by his concerns. "I don't particularly care for your Earth politics. What I need is to find a way to ascertain the status of Veldana." Quietly, she added, "And a way to find my mother."

He nodded. "We can go to the house in the morning. If Veldana was destroyed, we may be able to establish it from the wreckage. And either way, we should look for clues while the scene is still fresh. Whoever took Jumi must have come through the portal from Veldana at Montaigne's house, and they may have left something behind in their haste."

A seed of shame planted itself in Elsa's chest. Montaigne's house was the only link she had to her mother's abductors, and she'd run away from it like a scared little girl, naively hoping de Vries could make everything all right. "We should go back now . . . ," she said, reaching for the doorbook.

He raised his eyebrows. "And do what, precisely? Stand in the street all night while the fire brigade stops the fire from spreading? Dig through the ashes in the dark? No, we'll get some sleep and go in the morning. Then, at least the ashes will be cold."

"The ashes may be cold, but the trail will be, too," Elsa said, folding her arms.

"I imagine that's why they killed Montaigne and set the house ablaze," he said quietly. "To make it impossible for anyone to learn who had been there."

"So you're saying it's hopeless?"

"I'm saying this isn't the sort of problem we're likely to solve before supper. Which I'd guess you could do with some of, after your ordeal."

Elsa wanted to snap a denial at him, but in truth she was famished. Since breakfast, she'd had nothing but a couple of wild plums found during her survey work. She sighed, relenting. "I'll go try to find something clean to change into."

In de Vries's guest room, Elsa unbuckled her belt and shed her soot-stained Veldanese apron and dress, then filled the washbasin and cleaned herself up as best she could. Only then did she discover that both of her knees were quite impressively bruised

21

from the spill she'd taken on the slate floor of the cottage. There hadn't been time to notice the pain.

Leaving in such a rush, she also hadn't spared a moment to let anyone know what was happening. Assuming Veldana still existed, did everyone back home think she and Jumi had abandoned them? Elsa couldn't claim to be friends with Revan anymore, but she found she didn't like the thought of him wondering why she'd vanished.

Of course, he might not be wondering anything anymore. He might never again have the chance to feel anger or hurt or any other emotion. Revan, and everyone else in Veldana, might be dead. The thought made Elsa's chest so tight she could barely breathe, and she had to splash water on her face again to dispel the panic. She did her best to push the idea out of her mind.

In the wardrobe hung a couple of her mother's spare dresses—French fashions with high collars and puffed sleeves, ridiculously impractical compared with simple Veldanese garb. She'd worn them whenever she came to visit. Elsa leaned close to take one of the dresses off its hanger, but froze when a familiar smell reached her nose: lemon verbena, Jumi's favorite scent, still lingering in the cloth. Suddenly, she wanted her mother with the fervency of a small child lost in the woods, her eyes stinging with the start of tears. The weight of everything that had happened, losing Jumi and Veldana in quick succession, felt like it was crushing her. She bit down on her lip hard, and swore to herself she *would not cry*.

In the morning, Elsa took de Vries with her through a portal to Paris. She knew he did not generally approve of the doorbook's method of travel, thought it was too dangerous for casual use, but this time he reluctantly agreed they shouldn't waste time taking the train. As they stepped out of the portal, de Vries brushed a hand down the front of his jacket as if surprised to discover all his body parts had made it through in their correct orientations.

From the street, Montaigne's house looked a sodden, ashy ruin. The second story was still standing, but only barely, the roof having collapsed into the bedrooms at the front of the house. What windowpanes remained unbroken were coated in black soot. Elsa didn't know much about fire control, but it seemed lucky the blaze hadn't spread up and down the street.

"Well. I suppose it could be worse," said de Vries, climbing the front steps. "Watch your footing."

The front door was off its hinges, so they walked right in through the empty doorframe. Sections of the interior walls had collapsed, leaving behind a skeleton of charred wooden structural beams, and avalanches of wood and plaster fragments cluttered the floor. The hem of Elsa's skirt collected soot as she waded deeper into the wreckage, making her glad she'd dressed in her already ruined Veldanese clothes.

In the back of the house, Montaigne's study was hardly recognizable. Elsa could see into the bedroom above through holes in the scorched ceiling, and she didn't feel entirely convinced the second floor wasn't going to collapse on top of them. The smell of burnt books lingered in the air, but it looked as if the authorities had removed Montaigne's body—or whatever remained of it after the fire—which came as a small relief.

"What are we looking for?" said Elsa.

De Vries lifted a burnt book, the pages crumbling in his hands. Paper ashes swirled in a shaft of morning light like motes of dust.

"I'm not sure. If the covers aren't too badly damaged, it would be worth doing an inventory of the titles. Or your mother might have left some small clue for you, assuming she was conscious by the time they brought her through the portal."

She took a moment to orient herself. That pile of charred wood on her left was all that remained of the desk where Jumi had so often sat, the desk she used when scribing changes into the Veldana worldbook. Elsa turned to her right, picked her way over to the place where the Veldana worldbook's chamber had been. The wall had collapsed, leaving nothing but empty air between the support beams. Elsa swallowed hard, feeling as if she might choke on her next words. "It's gone."

De Vries came over and crouched down, sorting through the pile of debris. She bent down to help him. After a few minutes of meticulous searching, he said, "No book remnants—not even a scrap of leather from the cover. That's odd."

"There's nothing here! Nothing that looks like a wall safe, intact or otherwise." Elsa pushed herself to her feet, frustrated. "Where could it be? Do you think someone might have removed it after the fire?"

He frowned thoughtfully at the place where the chamber should have fallen when the plaster and laths of the wall collapsed. "The police, maybe? If they thought the contents of a safe might prove important to their investigation. Assuming they know the fire was arson, and not an accident."

Either way, Veldana was beyond Elsa's reach. There was no going home. This was a reality she had to come to terms with. She drew a deep, rattling breath, determined to set aside the terror of having lost her home. "Then we focus on finding Jumi."

They spent the morning doing as thorough and systematic a

search as was possible, given the chaos left behind by the fire. It was nearly midday when Elsa spotted a large rectangular shape amidst the rubble. She knelt down and put a hand out to touch it. The charred leather casing disintegrated beneath her fingers, revealing the Pascaline mechanical calculator it held. The heat of the fire had warped the brass faceplate, but the row of input dials—each shaped like a tiny spoked wheel—looked intact.

"I used to play with it when I was little, while Jumi worked on the Veldana worldbook."

De Vries came over to see what she'd found.

"One time, I disassembled it to see how it worked," she said as she held it up. "Jumi just about had a fit when she saw it all in pieces. I suppose Montaigne would have been furious if he'd found out, but I put it back together just fine."

An odd silence stretched between them, and when she looked up from the Pascaline, de Vries was staring at her as if seeing her for the first time.

"What?" She frowned at him, confused. "Do you have a particular dislike for Pascalines?"

He suddenly declared, "We have to go."

"Right this second? Why?" Elsa said obstinately. She didn't understand his sudden change in mood, and that set her on edge.

De Vries made a frustrated noise in the back of his throat, but when he spoke, he chose his words carefully. "Did Jumi ever talk to you about . . . the madness?"

"Yes. When someone is brilliant at something, like scriptology, you Earth people say they have the madness."

"It's not quite so simple. The madness is brilliance, yes, but it's also a sort of single-minded drive. An obsession. No one could succeed at scriptology without being at least a little obsessive. Jumi has it, and you do, too."

Elsa shrugged, still not sure how this was relevant. "If you say so."

"We can't stay in France. Your mother was infamous. If the nationals get ahold of you, you'll spend the rest of your life in a very comfortable prison scribing worldbooks for the Third Republic. Amsterdam is hardly better than Paris. Lord, what a fool I've been."

"Is," Elsa corrected him. "My mother *is* infamous."

De Vries shot her a look of pity. "Of course. My apologies."

Elsa didn't particularly like the idea of being rushed off somewhere with little explanation, but if her mother trusted anyone on Earth, it was de Vries, and he seemed genuinely afraid for her. For now, that knowledge would have to be enough. "So, where do we go, then?"

He pursed his lips for a moment, thinking. "Do you speak Italian?"

"Not yet," said Elsa. "But I will."

"Abbiamo bisogno di pratica."

"It doesn't happen that fast," Elsa replied, still in Dutch. "I have to listen for a while before a new language clicks."

De Vries smiled, as if her response was funny. "I said, 'We have need of practice.'" He cleared his throat, and his tone turned serious. "I have friends in the Kingdom of Sardinia—we'll go there, to the city of Pisa. Of the four Italian states, Sardinia is the safest, and Pisa in particular has a long history as a refuge for persecuted scientists."

She nodded. "Very well."

Before they left, Elsa gently lifted the wounded Pascaline

into her arms, intent on taking it with her. She'd lost so much—she wasn't going to give up on this, too, without at least trying to repair it.

They took the doorbook back to Amsterdam, surprising a pair of old ladies with parasols half to death when they appeared out of nowhere on the sidewalk. They cast furtive glances at de Vries and Elsa before nervously scurrying away down the sidewalk.

Up in the flat, Elsa washed up and changed again into her mother's laborious European clothing—chemise, stiff-boned corset, long skirts, high-necked white blouse, fitted jacket. The clothes were uncomfortable and impractical, and it struck her that she'd never asked Jumi how she'd felt when she traveled in Europe. Elsa had thought she'd known everything about her mother, and this small detail suddenly seemed of desperate importance. Panic roiled in her stomach. What else didn't she know?

Elsa pulled herself together, finished with the jacket buttons, and gathered whatever else of Jumi's possessions she could find that might be of use. De Vries gave her a pair of carpetbags: a larger one for the stack of rescued books and a smaller one for the Pascaline and her mother's personal items. She looked at him curiously when he came out of his room with his own set of packed luggage—she'd assumed he would return immediately to Amsterdam after making the introductions—but he offered no explanation.

"Well, I think that's everything," said Elsa. "Have you been to Pisa before?"

"It has been some time," de Vries said, stretching out the words with a reluctance that made Elsa wonder if there was more to the story. He didn't seem to be in a forthcoming mood, though, so Elsa decided not to press him.

"Any time is good enough, so long as you've been there. Just describe a particular place to me. Something unique." She opened the doorbook to a fresh page. "Do they have any distinctive buildings in Pisa?"

He smiled. "Yes, you could say that."

De Vries gave her details and Elsa scribed them onto the page in the proper order, but her mind kept straying elsewhere, back to the events of the past day. Had the intruders taken Jumi because of her madness? It would've been easier to abduct someone here on Earth if they just needed a scriptologist. So they probably wanted Jumi specifically, but to what end? How could Elsa get Jumi back if she didn't even know who had taken her or why?

So many questions, and no answers in sight.

3

They stepped out of the portal's darkness into a bright, pale world. Elsa looked around: they were standing on a flat, featureless plain, everything around them obscured by white haze.

De Vries squinted, wiped the condensation off his glasses with a handkerchief, and looked around again. "This . . . I don't believe this is right."

"No," Elsa agreed primly. "We quite failed to get there."

He paled. "You mean to say failure was an option?"

"Oh, no need to worry. I scribed the doorbook to shunt you to a fabricated world if the description isn't accurate enough to connect to the destination. Minimal possibility of accidents with bad portals. It's proved thoroughly reliable so far."

"The fact that the doorbook hasn't brought you to an untimely demise *yet* is hardly a consolation. I've told you before, the very idea of connecting two locations on Earth to each other makes me nervous. It's unnatural."

"You have a talent for worrying. Has anyone ever told you that?"

"Yes," he said. "Your mother. Frequently."

Elsa set down her carpetbags and sat cross-legged beside them. The ground was smooth and flawless like polished stone, but not as hard. Actually, it felt almost supple. She pressed her fingertips into it, and five imprints remained when she pulled her hand away. They slowly disappeared as the material rebounded. "Fascinating, isn't it? How a world will spontaneously generate properties that weren't specified in the text."

"I'm afraid the study of emergent properties has been somewhat out of fashion in recent years," de Vries said.

"Right. Of course. Because of Jumi." People were a difficult thing to create—when they were directly scribed into the world-text, they turned out like puppets, capable of basic call-and-response communication but with no consciousness, no sense of self. The Veldanese were the first successful attempt at scribed people, created as subtext using emergent property theory. Veldana was scribed with cottages and agriculture and drinking water, but the people themselves were not specified in the text; they were merely implied by the existence of human infrastructure.

The Veldanese were considered a major breakthrough in the science of scriptology. But when Jumi had fought back, demanding autonomy for her people, the scientific community had banned the creation of more populated worlds like Veldana.

Elsa sorted through her belt pouches and brought out a fountain pen, a bottle of ink, and the doorbook.

"You're not going to do that here, while we're still inside, are you?" de Vries said, aghast. "What next—shall we modify an airship engine while we're in the air?"

"Relax. I'd have to do something monumentally careless to strand us here forever. How did you ever get to be one of Europe's preeminent scriptologists with such a cautious attitude?"

Grumpily, he replied, "By living longer than all of the really brilliant ones."

Bending over the doorbook intently, Elsa copied what she'd written onto a fresh page. She'd been distracted and gotten sloppy, so now she adjusted the syntax and asked de Vries for additional details to flesh out the description. After a few minutes of work, she said, "There. I think that should work now. Shall we give it a try?"

"How sure are you that it's not going to kill us?"

"Um . . . ninety-seven percent sure?" Elsa grinned. She handed the book up to him so he could hold it open while the ink dried, then put away her writing supplies and stood.

De Vries harrumphed. "Well, at least you're smiling about *something*. Not the thing I would have picked, though."

Elsa sobered. For a moment there, she'd been too swept up in their adventure to remember her mother was missing. Guilt blossomed in her chest, and she swore to herself: no more smiling until she got Jumi back.

She dialed the new coordinates into her portal device, activated a portal, and tucked the device away again. Then she picked up her luggage and stepped through without turning to see if de Vries would follow.

He did, of course, emerging from the darkness a few seconds behind her. They stood in a broad, grassy square near the right transept of an elaborate cathedral. The facade was an excess of columns and arches carved out of pale stone. To the left, near the front entrance of the cathedral, was a squat, round baptistery built in the same style. On their right, a multitiered bell tower tilted precariously away from the cathedral.

"That," Elsa observed, "is some poor architecture."

De Vries tilted his head back to look at it. "The Leaning Tower. It's famous in part because it's doomed."

"How morbid." She tried to make her tone light, even though there was something chilling about all these old monuments. Elsa told herself the buildings were intentionally designed to inspire awe, and so the feeling in her gut belonged to some long-dead architect's imagination, not to her. But in truth, there was a part of her that couldn't help wondering how many centuries the tower had seen, how many people had lived and died and turned to dust in the shadow it cast over the city. The weight and silence of all that history felt like too much for anyone to bear.

It came as a relief when de Vries led the way out of the square and onto a broad street paved with gray cobblestones. Elsa was also glad he seemed confident about which way to go. She could explore off-trail through unfamiliar woods and never get lost, but navigating city streets was not a skill she'd put much effort into developing. Now that she was stranded outside Veldana and Earth was the only inhabited world available, Elsa felt a bit foolish for neglecting to learn it.

"The Kingdom of Sardinia is just one of four independent states ruling different parts of Italy," de Vries explained as they walked. "We're lucky to have friends here—the Sardinian government is very forward-thinking and supportive of the sciences."

"Not so in the other three states, I take it?" said Elsa.

A pained expression crossed his face, as if he had some personal experience with the danger of other governments. He cleared his throat and said, "Not so elsewhere. They exploit mad people when it suits them."

Elsa was curious to hear more, but she could tell de Vries was reluctant to share the details. Instead, she asked, "So what exactly is our destination, now that we've made it to Pisa?"

He seemed relieved at the change of subject. "The place we're going to is a sort of haven for madboys and madgirls. No one will be able to get to you there. You'll be safe."

Something in his tone made Elsa suspicious that there was more at play than he was letting on. Why the sudden onset of concern for her safety, back in the ruins of Montaigne's house? But she decided to follow his lead anyway, as Jumi would have advised her to do, and trust that he would enlighten her at the proper time.

De Vries moved rather slowly on foot—the last time Elsa had visited him with her mother, Jumi had argued it was time for him to acquire a walking cane for his stiff left hip, but he was still walking without one. In Veldana, it would have driven Elsa mad to have to walk so slowly, but here she didn't mind. Their plodding pace gave her time to eavesdrop on the other people out walking the streets, so she could absorb their language properly.

Everyone—the men especially—gestured a great deal with their hands as they talked. She wondered if the gestures served some critical linguistic function, though she could detect no obvious grammatical structure in the motions.

As she watched the citizens of Pisa, Elsa caught their stares lingering on her in turn. These were a pale people not so different from the French, whereas the Veldanese all came in shades of brown. She could not guess what they thought of her, with her black hair and bronze skin and a pale elderly gentleman for an escort. Hot pinpricks of self-consciousness traveled down her spine.

"*Stai imparando?*" de Vries asked, interrupting her thoughts.

"I don't know what that means yet," Elsa snapped, feeling edgy and exposed. She wished the new language would hurry up and sink in so they could get off the streets and out of sight. They were both quiet for a minute or two, and she started regretting her curtness. "Thank you for your help, de Vries. I know I don't always make it easy for you."

He smiled down at her. "You can call me Alek, you know. After you've dug through a pile of burnt wreckage and run off to Toscana with someone, the need for formality has faded somewhat."

Elsa shrugged. "I'm accustomed to de Vries."

He chuckled to himself. "So like your mother. Sometimes I wonder if you aren't a window back in time."

"What do you mean?" she said sharply.

"Why, that she keeps everyone at a distance, of course. Everyone except you."

Elsa scowled at him, but she noticed his use of the present tense—*keeps*—and was silently grateful for it.

She calmed her anxious thoughts and turned her attention back to the most immediate problem: language. As Jumi would have said, *How can you hope to master your world if you cannot master your own mind?* So Elsa started with herself, and focused on listening to and absorbing the words of passersby.

The words began to churn in the back of her brain, mixing

and clarifying. Yes, Elsa realized, it was not so unlike French in its grammar or etymology—startlingly familiar, now that she could hear it properly. She felt dizzy with the swelling knowledge.

"Steady there," said de Vries, and caught her by the elbow as she swayed.

They had stopped walking. Elsa didn't recall exactly when. Come to think of it, she'd lost track of where they were, too— she looked around at the cobblestone plaza they stood near the edge of, wondering how far they'd come from the Leaning Tower.

"Not much farther," said de Vries as he led her toward a broad four-story stone building. He presented it with a wave of his arm. "Casa della Pazzia." *House of the Madness.*

The front doors were framed with an elaborate lintel and pilasters, which gave the building a sense of monumental authority. Elsa couldn't help but think "house" was a bit of an understatement; Fortress of the Madness might have been a better name.

De Vries stepped up to the doors and lifted the heavy brass knocker. After a minute, Elsa could make out the muffled sound of bolts sliding, and one side of the double doors opened.

The woman who answered was middle-aged, short and plump, with dark hair pulled back in a practical chignon. The stains on her smock looked like they'd come from an engine instead of a kitchen.

"Alek! What a surprise," she said in Italian, her eyes lighting up. She pulled him forward and, much to Elsa's surprise, planted a kiss on each of his cheeks. "Do come in."

De Vries stepped inside, Elsa following warily. The foyer was expansive. A giant gasolier hung from the cavernous fresco-painted ceiling, blue sky and sunset-tinted clouds of pink and orange. The inlaid-tile floor was polished so smooth it reflected and scattered the gaslight. Two curved staircases, one on either side of the room, led up to a balcony on the far wall. Elsa hadn't expected anything so lavish and formal from an acquaintance of de Vries.

De Vries, however, seemed perfectly at ease. "You look well, Gia. Is your husband home?"

"I'm afraid he's in Firenze for the week. Business with the Order."

"In that case, may I present Signorina Elsunani di Jumi da Veldana. Elsa, this is Signora Gioconda Pisano, headmistress of Casa della Pazzia." Elsa gave her a nod, and de Vries added, "I do wish Filippo were in town. I'm afraid it's a matter of some concern for the Order."

Signora Pisano folded her hands together. "Yes, I had supposed so, on account of your sudden arrival. Shall we go to my office?"

"One moment." De Vries turned to Elsa, switching back to Dutch. "How are you doing with the Italian?"

"Listening is easy. I imagine it will feel strange on my tongue for a while, though." She watched Signora Pisano's face, registering the incomprehension there. Good—they could speak privately then. "I have an odd feeling about this place. Are you certain we can trust these people?"

"I would trust them with my life," he said gravely.

"Well, that's good," Elsa sniped. "Since that's precisely what you're expecting me to do."

De Vries gave her a look of mild reproof. "Patience, my dear. I promise—"

"Watch out!" someone shouted in Italian from above, startling

36

everyone, including Signora Pisano. Elsa looked up to see a young man with a rapier in his hand leaning over the balcony railing. "It's coming this way!"

He vaulted over the railing and Elsa sucked in a breath, thinking he was falling to his death, but he landed light as a cat on his feet. The boy looked up, and for a second their gazes locked. He was a study in brass—tawny eyes and olive skin, blond hair grown long enough he had to shake it away to see her clearly. Elsa felt heat rise in her cheeks.

"Leo, really!" Signora Pisano scolded in a tone that implied shock at his manners more than fear for his safety.

He broke eye contact with Elsa and turned his head to respond, but a loud buzzing noise began to emanate from the wall beneath the balcony, and a cloud of plaster dust started billowing into the foyer. Leo spun around, lifting his rapier to a ready position. Elsa found herself yet again covering her nose and mouth with her sleeve. A large section of wall detached from the rest and collapsed into the foyer with a crash, and through the cloud of plaster dust a two-meter-tall shadow was visible.

The imposing shape stepped forward—*No*, Elsa thought, squinting through the dust, *not step so much as roll*. Though Leo held his rapier as if waiting for an opponent to advance, the thing he faced was machine, not man, and it had treads instead of feet.

Leo stepped forward to meet the metal monster, and as the plaster dust began to settle, Elsa's view of it improved. A round saw blade whirred at the end of one of its six limbs, and two more brandished rapiers. The other arms terminated with a flame-thrower, a mallet, and an enormous crablike pincer.

"Terribly sorry," said Leo, though his ear-to-ear grin did not give Elsa the impression of remorse. He whipped his rapier through the air, parrying and lunging. "I'm afraid I've improved the training bot rather too much."

Elsa didn't know much about swordplay, but the fact that the boy was still in one piece seemed a fair indication of his competence. Even so, flamethrowers and saws hardly made for a fair fight. Elsa drew the revolver from its holster and cocked back the hammer.

The bot had a head, but without a closer look it was impossible to know if anything important was located there besides the optics. Instead, she aimed for an exposed tube underneath one arm and fired. The tube burst open, spilling thick red-brown fluid down the side of the bot. The bot's movements became slow and jerky, and after a few seconds its limbs sagged and went still.

"You shredded the hydraulics!" Leo said. "That'll take hours to replace." He gave her an annoyed look, which did nothing to lessen the perfect angles of his features.

Instead of answering, Elsa busied herself with tucking the gun away in its holster. The whole situation was so strange, she was unsure whether she would actually be expected to apologize for stopping the rampaging machine. She leaned closer to de Vries and muttered in Dutch, "Yes, I feel very safe here already."

Signora Pisano was pinching the bridge of her nose between thumb and forefinger. "Why, pray tell, would you add a radial saw to a training bot?"

Leo shrugged and sheathed the rapier, then slipped his hand out of the intricate metalwork of the guard. "It seemed like the thing to do at the time."

Signora Pisano took a closer look at the training bot. "How many times do I have to tell you, Leo? No flamethrowers in the house!"

"It's only a small one," he protested.

"You," she said, pointing a finger close to his nose, "I will deal with later." Then she looked away from Leo. "Casa?"

A disembodied voice echoed through the foyer, making Elsa jump. "Yes, signora?" The voice was deep and resonant, but with a somewhat feminine softness around the edges.

"We're ready for repairs here."

"Very well, signora."

A small army of clockwork bots hurried in, ambling single file like ducklings. Elsa stood still, frozen by amazement. Some of them were tall and narrow with long brass limbs, some were barely knee-height, with a dozen different tools sticking out in all directions. One squat little bot cleaned the floor with round, rotating scrub brushes as it moved along. Elsa felt a sudden longing to grab it and take it apart to find out how it worked—her fingers itched for the feel of its delicate gears.

"Elsa . . . Elsa!" De Vries had his hand on her shoulder.

She shook her head to clear it and blinked up at him. "Yes?"

"There will be time to examine the bots later."

"Right . . . of course," she answered slowly.

"Come along," said Signora Pisano, "let's find somewhere we won't be disturbed again." At this she cast a scalding look at Leo, then led Elsa and de Vries out of the ruined foyer.

Signora Pisano's office was comfortably small compared to the grandiose vastness of the foyer, with wall-mounted gaslamps bringing out the warm tones of the wood paneling. Her shelves displayed mechanical baubles and trinkets instead of books. Signora Pisano sat behind her polished-wood desk while Elsa and de Vries took up the comfortable armchairs placed in front of it for guests.

When de Vries finished relating all that had happened,

Signora Pisano leaned back in her chair and said, "That's quite a story. You're right, Alek, the Order will need to hear of this at once."

"Naturally," said de Vries. "I felt it was essential to secure protection for Elsa first, though."

"Yes, yes." Signora Pisano nodded thoughtfully. "I must say, Elsa, given your parentage, I would have thought scriptology would be your calling, not mechanics."

"Well, I do scribe, of course," said Elsa politely. "My mother taught me when I was little. We're not exactly living in the steam age in Veldana, though, so I'm afraid I don't know much about mechanics."

Signora Pisano gave de Vries a significant look, complete with a raised eyebrow. "Both?"

He cleared his throat. "It appears so. Hence why I thought it best to bring her here immediately."

Signora Pisano let out a breath and sat back in her chair. "Jumi da Veldana's daughter, and a polymath besides." She used the Greek word—*polymathes*—and it stood out sharp and cold against the lilting Italian syllables. Elsa jerked as if the word were a slap, unprepared for another new language so soon.

"What does that mean?"

De Vries took her hand in both of his, as if to deliver bad news. "You must understand, Elsa: most madboys and madgirls have a very specific interest or set of interests. They won't—perhaps can't—turn their attention to any topic beyond their chosen obsession. A polymath, however, is someone who experiences the madness but has no particular focus, being able to apply his or her genius to any field of study—scriptology or mechanics or alchemy, or any combination of the three—and thus having unlimited potential."

"They're exceedingly rare," added Signora Pisano. "So rare some people claim they no longer exist. There are historical examples, of course, but no one alive today. If you are indeed a polymath . . ."

She frowned, as if sorting through the implications in her mind. Elsa felt unmoored. Last week she'd known exactly what her place was, but now she was in a different world, one she didn't fully understand. And Signora Pisano did not seem to think being "rare" was a good thing.

De Vries said, "It puts you in a precarious position. Most madboys and madgirls are of limited use on the international stage, because their range of talent is too narrow. A government cannot commission a weapon from a madboy who only builds trains. But you . . ." He trailed off, unwilling to put the conclusion into words.

Elsa nodded, slipping her hand out of his grasp to knot her fingers together in her lap. Now when she spoke, her voice was small. "Everyone who wants power will want me."

"Jumi hid your talents well. Even from me. What a fool I've been, thinking she was letting me keep up with her, when she was always two steps ahead."

"Well, *someone* caught up," Elsa said darkly.

Signora Pisano pursed her lips. "That they did. And we must assume they left you behind only because they didn't know—"

The door flew open and a girl burst in. She was about Elsa's age but dressed like a wealthy Parisian woman, her hourglass figure accentuated with a corset, the wine-dark velvet of the dress turning her light olive skin almost milky. The curves of her small mouth and round cheeks would have identified her as

Signora Pisano's daughter even if she didn't immediately say, "Mamma, you'll never guess—" Her smile vanished. "Oh, you have company."

"Yes, Porzia dear, that's why the door was closed," Signora Pisano said, but she sounded more amused than annoyed. "There will be plenty of time for you to become acquainted with Signorina Elsa after we've finished here."

Porzia paused in the doorway for a moment as if considering her options, but decided to take the hint. "Yes, Mamma." She did a brief curtsy in the general direction of Elsa and de Vries, then swept out of the room, pulling the door closed behind her.

Signora Pisano paused, momentarily distracted. "Well, as we were saying, I suspect it was your mother's ingenuity at hiding your talents that has kept you safe thus far. But since these unknown assailants now have Jumi in their possession, they may be . . . learning more."

Stony-faced, Elsa replied, "You mean they may be torturing her for information."

Beside her, de Vries inhaled sharply. "There's no point in speculating."

Signora Pisano leaned forward for emphasis. "Elsa, my husband and I—and Alek, as well—belong to a society of mad scientists called the Order of Archimedes. Its mission is to prevent the exploitation of mad people and to protect the integrity of our science. The Order will find your mother; this is precisely the sort of problem it exists to solve. Now, Casa, would you prepare a room for our guest?"

The house's voice seeped out of the walls. "Already done, signora."

"Excellent." To Elsa, she said, "Try not to worry, dear. We'll get your mother back soon."

Right, thought Elsa. Her whole world had fallen apart—perhaps literally—and she was supposed to simply not worry. Signora Pisano seemed kind enough, but not excessively realistic. Still, if she was going to argue against staying here, best not to do it in front of the lady of the house. Elsa decided to hold her tongue until she and de Vries could speak alone.

Casa sent a little brass bot to act as a guide, leading Elsa to her new accommodations. The bot led her and de Vries up two flights of stairs—what Elsa wouldn't give to disassemble the motile mechanism allowing it to do that!—and down a long, window-less hallway.

"Here you are, signorina," Casa said, the bot spinning around to face them and gesturing toward the door on their left with its metal claw.

De Vries gave a start, as if suddenly recognizing where they were. "*This* door, Casa?"

Casa hummed innocently, choosing not to answer.

Elsa glanced around sharply. She hated feeling like everyone else knew something she didn't. "What is it?" she asked de Vries.

"Nothing. It's only . . . I knew the previous occupant, that's all." He reached out to open the door for her, but his grip on the knob was hesitant, as if he expected it might burn him. Elsa followed him inside.

The entrance opened onto a richly furnished sitting room, with doorways on the left and right leading to a bedroom and a study. In the center of the room, a sofa and two armchairs were arranged together, all upholstered in green-and-beige damask with arms and legs of finely carved wood ending in animal claws.

Elsa set her carpetbags beside the door and carefully laid out the contents of her belt—the gun, portal device, stability glove, door-book, and scribing materials—on a marble-topped commode. Then she went to examine the bedroom, which also displayed an excess of polished wood and fine fabrics. How in the world was she supposed to live here when it all looked too old and too fancy to be touched, let alone used?

When she returned to the sitting room, she saw de Vries had taken Jumi's gun from the holster and was holding it gently, as if it were a fond memory.

Elsa said, "It was a good gift, you know. The sort of thing she would have gotten for herself. She'd never say it, but I think she likes that you understand her."

De Vries blinked heavily, as if to clear his eyes of moisture. "Thank you. She was never easy, but always worth the effort."

Elsa sank down onto the sofa. "Do you love her?" she said, trying to catch him off guard with the directness of the question.

"Like a daughter," he answered easily. He set the gun back down and came over to sit beside her. "Which is why my first priority is to protect you, in accordance with what she would want me to do."

"I'm not a child anymore. I could be useful."

"And that's precisely what I'm afraid other people might realize."

Elsa narrowed her eyes at him, remembering how Signora Pisano had asked Casa to prepare a room for *our guest*, singular. "How soon?" she said.

"What?"

"I know you aren't staying. You're going to leave me here with these people. So, how soon?"

De Vries rubbed the back of his neck, reluctant to admit it. "I'll catch the evening train to Firenze tonight. But you must know I wouldn't leave you with just anyone—I've known the Pisano family a long time, they're dear friends. You'll be safe here."

"Safe and useless," Elsa said sulkily.

"Yes, safe and useless," de Vries repeated, as if it were a triumph.

"You can't stop me from leaving." Elsa was the one who'd scribed the doorbook that could transport her anywhere in the real world—means of escape were hardly the problem.

"Please, Elsa—stay here. I couldn't bear to find Jumi, only to have to tell her that I'd lost her daughter." Then his tone brightened, as if to coax her toward enthusiasm. "Besides, this is a house of madness—it shouldn't be too difficult to keep yourself occupied. Make friends, learn from them. Jumi's an excellent scriptologist, but she couldn't teach you the other sciences. Think of this as an opportunity, not a prison sentence."

Elsa glowered. *An opportunity.* But could she afford to ignore de Vries's advice when she knew so little about what it meant to be a polymath in Europe? He seemed genuinely afraid that some government would snatch her off the street.

"Fine, I'll stay for now," she grudgingly agreed, "but I'm going to search Montaigne's books for clues. You know how he was, always hiding away inside his worlds—he may have left behind something relevant."

"That's a fine idea." De Vries gave her an indulgent smile, as if he saw this activity more as a distraction than a viable strategy for finding Jumi. "But don't worry overmuch—the Order of Archimedes will uncover what happened to your mother."

After he left, Elsa pulled open the top drawer of the commode and slipped the gun inside. Better not to leave it out for anyone else to find. She trusted de Vries, but his trust in these people was another step removed from that. Her mother would warn her to be cautious, to keep her guard up. On second thought, she tucked away the doorbook and portal device beside the gun. It was rather too obvious a hiding place, but if she hid them more thoroughly she would lose time retrieving them whenever a hasty departure became necessary.

It wasn't that she believed de Vries would betray her. It was just that it all seemed . . . too fortunate. If her luck the past two days served as any indication, she had better be prepared for the worst. Even if it meant turning away from de Vries's well-intentioned help.

Jumi had taught her that love was a weakness—that if you let someone in, you gave them the power to hurt you. But before today, Elsa had thought of this as an untried philosophy, a theoretical truth that she had never gotten the chance to test.

She loved her mother and she loved Veldana, and now they were both beyond her reach, possibly both destroyed. She had never felt pain like this before, so acute it made her breath catch in her lungs. Her mother had been right—it was those you loved who could hurt you the most.

At the same time, she had to wonder: Was it simply the losses that hurt? Or did it also hurt to have nothing at all left to love?

Leo needed the help of five of Casa's cleaning bots just to haul the damaged training bot back to his laboratory, and a trail of hydraulic fluid leaked along the floor in his wake. He hoped Casa could get that mopped up before Gia stepped out of her office again—there was only so much mess the poor woman could take. He didn't mean to be such a source of trouble, but things always seemed to spiral out of hand.

In Venezia, Aris had been the troublemaker, the ringleader whom the younger boys would follow anywhere. Rosalinda used to say that if Aris jumped in the Grand Canal, Leo would jump in two seconds after—she'd meant it as a criticism, though Leo had chosen to take it as a compliment.

Now, like it or not, Leo managed to make his own trouble. He wondered if his brother would be proud. He wondered what Aris's grin would look like now—still magnetic as ever, but in a grown man's face?

Leo shook his head to clear those futile musings. It was just the broken mask that had him thinking of his childhood, and all he'd lost. He perched himself on his favorite tall stool at the high worktable and resolved to focus on the repairs.

"I love what you've done with the place."

He glanced up; it was Porzia, stepping through the gaping hole in the wall where the door had been. When Leo had activated the training bot, it had plowed its way out of the laboratory, taking the door and part of the walls with it. Now there was nothing to deter visitors.

Porzia lifted her skirts to pick her way through the rubble and entered uninvited.

Leo frowned at her. "What do you want?"

"Why do you always think I want something? Isn't it enough that I came to say hello?" Porzia said, but she motioned with her eyes, casting a significant look at the worktable. With feigned casualness, Leo reached over and flipped a switch on the top of a device shaped like a cube.

"The scrambler's on," he said. "It's safe to talk."

Porzia glanced at the ceiling. "Casa? You're a dusty old junker with grinding gears. I wouldn't spit on you if you were on fire." She paused, waiting for a response. "I guess it works."

Leo tapped a finger on the top of the box. "Like I said— instant blind spot. Casa can't monitor us when it's on. So what's happening?"

Porzia settled herself primly atop a packing crate, as if it were a fine-upholstered settee. "Papa's friend Alek de Vries brought us a new girl today."

"I know, we met in the foyer," Leo said, omitting the part about battling the runaway bot.

"Yes, well. There's something odd about her. Do you know which rooms Casa prepared for her? Uncle Massimo's old rooms—with the scriptology study opposite the bedroom."

Leo frowned. "Perhaps Gia . . ."

Porzia tilted her chin down and gave him a scathing look. "Mamma would not instruct Casa to prepare *those* rooms for a guest. Really, her deceased brother-in-law's rooms?"

"Right." He leaned forward, planting his elbows on the work-bench. "That means Casa is taking initiative, and the house only makes independent decisions when something significant is going on. Do we know for certain the girl's a scriptologist?"

A lock of hair had come loose from Porzia's elaborate updo, and she wrapped it around her finger thoughtfully. "Mamma didn't give us much of an introduction, but why else would Casa choose those rooms? She's a scriptologist, I'll bet, and Casa thinks she's here to stay."

"Mm," Leo agreed noncommittally. He hadn't missed the way Elsa had stared—like a woman possessed—at the cleaner bots, or the way she'd neatly targeted the one system that would cripple the training bot.

Could she be a scriptologist . . . *and* a mechanist? A polymath in hiding? Better to keep what he'd seen to himself for now, at least until he knew what it meant.

The thought of polymaths called up the image of Aris's face as he leaned over Leo's shoulder to watch Leo struggling at a scriptological problem. *What's wrong, little brother? It's so simple I bet Pasca could do it, and he's hardly out of swaddling clothes.* The memory had edges as sharp as broken glass, and Leo shook his head to dispel it. What was the point in thinking about his brothers when they were dead?

4

IF YOU ARE ALONE YOU BELONG ENTIRELY TO YOURSELF.
IF YOU ARE ACCOMPANIED BY EVEN ONE COMPANION YOU BELONG
ONLY HALF TO YOURSELF OR EVEN LESS . . . ,
AND IF YOU HAVE MORE THAN ONE COMPANION YOU
WILL FALL MORE DEEPLY INTO THE SAME PLIGHT.
—*Leonardo da Vinci*

Elsa tried to keep herself busy for the rest of the afternoon. She took the singed books into the study attached to her sitting room and laid them out on the ample writing desk. She set the Pascaline on a side table beneath a window, where she'd have excellent light by which to examine it in the morning. But no matter how she tried to distract herself, it was impossible not to dwell on the unknown fate of her homeland.

Perhaps Jumi's abductors had taken the Veldana worldbook with them when they fled the house. But no—she was certain it had been inside Montaigne's study when she'd arrived. A portal returning to the real world from a scribed one would always open near the location of the worldbook. So had the Veldana worldbook been safely locked away in the wall chamber, or had it been somewhere else in the room?

Her own possessions unpacked, Elsa set about exploring every drawer and cabinet in the study to take inventory of what supplies the previous occupant had left behind that she might make use of. At the same time, she composed in her mind a gruesome narrative of Montaigne the collaborator.

The abductors would have needed someone who could open the wall chamber, or at least someone who knew the coordinates to Veldana by heart. Jumi hadn't given him access to the chamber, but he would've had ample opportunity to study its weaknesses, if so inclined. Or perhaps the abductors had forced him to open a portal, but then why did he die facedown with a book in his hand? It was as if he were at ease in their presence, and felled by a surprise attack from behind. No, they must have gained his confidence, betrayed him, set fire to his library . . . and the Veldana worldbook lay unprotected somewhere in the room as everything burned.

Veldana was gone—gone from her reach at the very least, and probably destroyed. The cottage where she'd lived her whole life, the lands she knew so well she could walk them with her eyes closed, the people. All the people. Oh, Revan—the last words she'd spoken to Revan were a cold rebuke. What if her admonishment was the last thing he heard before he ceased to exist? And now she must live with the knowledge that they would never heal the rift in their broken friendship.

Stop, she had to stop. The sense of panic tightening her chest was not helping anything. If Veldana was truly gone, there was nothing she could do for Revan now, but Jumi might yet be saved. Yes. She had to focus on finding and rescuing her mother.

They must have set fire to the library for a reason. Montaigne had known too much and for that he had to die, but why burn the library? Perhaps to destroy the evidence of Montaigne's collaboration, to destroy whatever clues he'd left in his worldbooks. As far back as Elsa could remember, he'd always been the secretive type, preferring to conduct his studies from inside scribed worlds instead of using his desk in Paris. Probably because he didn't want to leave any important papers out where Jumi could see them.

There was a good chance Montaigne had hidden something important inside one of the worldbooks she'd rescued. These remnants of the library were now her connection to Jumi's abductors. She needed to repair the books and search the worlds for clues; it was the only way she could think of to find her mother.

Elsa had just lit the gaslamp in her study to compensate for the dwindling daylight when a knock came at her door. Her heart leapt with hope—perhaps it was de Vries again, perhaps he'd reconsidered and decided to take her with him. She set down the matchbox and rushed to answer the door.

Porzia Pisano, still in her fine French dress, stood on the other side.

"Oh," Elsa said, crestfallen.

Porzia's eyebrow twitched, but she only said, "It's suppertime. I thought I'd come collect you. I'm told this place can seem a maze until you learn your way around."

Elsa wasn't sure precisely what she was expected to say to that, so she responded with "Very well" and followed Porzia down the stairs to the dining hall.

Porzia seemed welcoming enough. But something about her felt off—a penetrating edge of curiosity revealed in the arch of her dark eyebrows and the quirk of her small lips.

"Your Italian's quite excellent," Porzia said as they walked. A compliment, yes, but was she actually fishing for information?

Elsa smiled thinly. "De Vries taught me," she replied, which was not entirely untrue.

"Really," she replied. "I've always had the impression he felt a little uncomfortable outside his native tongue."

Elsa wanted to retort *And what business is that of yours?* but instead she said, "Perhaps. But I've a mind for languages."

The corridor opened up into a high-ceilinged dining hall with a row of tall, arching windows along the far wall. There were a startling number of rowdy children in the room. Elsa swept her gaze over them and counted nineteen, plus Porzia and herself. They ranged in age from sixteen or seventeen all the way down to toddlers.

"Where did they all come from?" Elsa said, taken aback. Signora Pisano was the only adult she'd seen since arriving, and they couldn't possibly all belong to one woman.

"Three of them are my siblings; the rest are mostly from Toscana, a few from farther away. Pazzerellones tend to die young—in laboratory accidents, or simply from neglecting their health—so there are always a fair number of orphaned children. Casa della Pazzia is one of the places the orphans end up." The whole explanation was accompanied by more of those superfluous Italian gestures.

"*Pazzerellones?*" Elsa asked, but worked out the etymology before Porzia could respond. "Ah, meaning 'mad people.' A slang term?" For whatever reason, her skills worked faster with formal language than with vernacular.

The other girl gave her a look. "Like I said: you do have a superior grasp of Italian."

Porzia steered her toward a couple of boys who were talking together. One of them was the brass-haired boy she'd met in the lobby, Leo. The other boy was brown-skinned and black-haired, and could almost pass for Veldanese if he weren't so very tall. Elsa was surprised at her own feeling of relief—there was something tiresome about being constantly surrounded by people who looked different—and she had to remind herself that, regardless of appearances, he was still one of them. Still from Earth.

"Elsa, this is Faraz Hannachi, and this is Leo Trovatelli."

Elsa was unsure of the local customs, so she did not offer either of them her hand, but she gave a polite nod to Faraz. "Pleased to meet you."

"Likewise," he replied.

Leo gave Porzia a look, some subtle communication flashing between them, but then he turned on a winning smile and swept right past the moment. "Actually, Elsa and I are old friends. We go way back—all of four hours or so."

Porzia rolled her eyes skyward. "Lord spare us from Venetians who aren't nearly as clever as they think they are."

"Did you hear that?" Leo said to Faraz in a mock whisper. "She thinks I'm clever."

"I think you have a problem with selective hearing," Porzia harrumphed.

Casa's voice interrupted, booming over the noise. "Sit, you mewling progeny! Sit, sit!"

The children all began to seat themselves. Elsa looked around anxiously, hoping to spot Signora Pisano, but she didn't appear to be attending supper, and Porzia was already dragging Elsa with her to one end of the long table. They sat opposite Faraz and Leo, the younger children arrayed down the rest of the table's length. There was no chair or place setting at the head, Elsa noticed, but perhaps that was simply the custom in Toscana. She glanced around, wondering how they were supposed to acquire food to fill their empty plates.

"No servants here, unless you count Casa. Everything's automated," Porzia explained.

"Automated . . . ?" Elsa started to ask, but she was interrupted by a ratcheting *click-click-click* noise. A set of metal rails like miniature train tracks swung down from the wall and attached to the head of the table, while a section of the wall slid open to reveal a dark compartment. Elsa craned her neck to see inside but couldn't make out anything.

Leo leaned across the table, his eyes alight. "You're going to like this part, I think."

A soft mechanical whirring began to emanate from the hole in the wall. The sound grew louder, and a tiny clockwork locomotive emerged from the wall as if from a tunnel, each flatbed train car behind it carrying a serving tray laden with food. The locomotive chugged down the length of the table, and when it reached the foot, it huffed to a halt, and the children descended on the serving plates like a pack of wolves.

"Manners!" Porzia shouted. "Sante, Olivia, and Burak are serving. Everyone else, I want to see hands off the table." Then she stood from her own seat and began serving their end of the table.

Elsa found it somewhat disconcerting to have someone else shoveling food onto her plate, but the wonderful train provided enough of a distraction that she didn't protest. Her fingers twitched against the corner of the table, wanting to disassemble the clockwork locomotive much more than her stomach wanted to eat the food it bore.

Once everyone was served and Porzia was seated again, Leo seemed eager to restart the conversation. "So . . . you're not from Pisa, I take it?" he asked Elsa.

Faraz leaned over to mutter to him, but Elsa still caught the words: "It's cheating if you ask her."

Leo elbowed him but kept his gaze on Elsa, inviting a response.

"No," she said slowly. "I'm not from Pisa. I was in Paris and Amsterdam, most recently." She hoped that would be enough of an answer to put his questions to rest.

"Oh!" Porzia exclaimed. "Terribly rude of me, I should have mentioned it with the introductions: Leo's a mechanist, Faraz is an alchemist, and I"—she pressed a hand to her chest—"am a scriptologist. So if you need help with anything, you know who to ask."

"Right." First de Vries and now Porzia—why did everyone think she wanted help?

Porzia blinked innocently at Elsa. "And which field is yours?"

Elsa stared back at her for a second, wishing for a way to smoothly escape such a direct question. She settled on saying, "Scriptology," which was more than she wanted to admit but significantly less than the whole truth.

After that, Elsa picked up her fork and tried to look intent on her food, which turned out not to be a difficult thing at all to fake since the food was curious indeed. The first course was white rice prepared with cream and some kind of meat that—believe it or not—looked as if it might have come from the inside of a mollusk. The bits of seafood tasted pungent and a little fishy, but not entirely unpleasant.

"Finish your risotto, Aldo. There are people starving in

Napoli," Porzia admonished one of the younger children. Elsa's cheeks warmed, and she stopped poking at her food and forked it into her mouth instead.

The idea of not having enough food was foreign to her; Jumi had never allowed the Veldanese to go hungry, not when new croplands could be scribed into the world to meet their needs. When Elsa finished chewing, she said, "Do people really starve in Napoli?"

Porzia raised her eyebrows in surprise at the question, but it was Leo who answered. "It's a French dynasty that rules the Two Sicilies. They haven't invested in industry and infrastructure the way we have here in the Kingdom of Sardinia. The common people are overtaxed, and with no industry in the cities there are no jobs, so yes—people starve."

Porzia shot him a warning look, but her tone was light when she said, "I think that's quite enough politics for the dinner table. Terribly dull business."

Elsa didn't understand why the other girl wanted the subject dropped, but she let it go anyway. She already felt like enough of an outsider, and the last thing she needed was to blunder into forbidden conversational territory.

When everyone had worked their way through the rice, Porzia lifted the next serving dish and doled out portions of fowl roasted with mushrooms and herbs, with salad on the side. This, at least, resembled something she might have eaten at home. Jumi had never shown much aptitude or interest in cooking beyond the strict necessities of nourishment, but Revan's mother, Baninu, could work wonders with the wild herbs and fungi Elsa collected on her forays around Veldana.

Baninu bending over the hearth fire . . . little Elsa and Revan kneeling on the bench because the table was too high for them otherwise, ripping the juicy green tubes of wild onions into pieces with their fingers. Baninu never wasted her one steel knife—an Earth import—on anything that could be cut another way.

Elsa felt her throat tighten with grief, and she pushed the memory aside. Best not linger on those thoughts, not while she was trapped at the table surrounded by strangers.

Dessert involved tangy yellow fruit and some kind of sweetened, white fluffy substance, and Elsa wondered if she would ever be allowed to leave. Finally, when all the food was gone, they were permitted to stack their plates on the train's empty serving trays. As the younger children rose from their seats, Porzia shouted orders. "Sante, take the little ones to the nursery, please. Aldo, bedtime in one hour, and I'll be up to check so you better not still be reading. . . ."

But even as Porzia orchestrated the children's bedtime, Leo and Faraz lingered in the dining hall, standing about and chatting some more. They acted familiar with each other in a way that made Elsa uneasy, but in light of de Vries's request for her to get along with them, she didn't want to be rude so she stayed as well. Mostly she watched them; the boys clearly shared a long-standing friendship, unconsciously matching their tones and gestures to each other. Leo had his pocket watch out, but he was fingering it idly instead of using it to check the time.

When the children were gone, Porzia circled back around to the sphere of their conversation.

"Done?" said Faraz, glancing up at her return.

"Time for my parlor trick," Leo boasted.

"Parlor trick?" Elsa asked, hoping her alarm didn't show in her voice.

"He observes and deduces," Faraz said with a slight shake of his head.

Leo clapped him on the shoulder, grinning. "Step back and give the deductive genius some space, will you?"

"You may not have noticed that Leo *must* be the center of attention at all times," Porzia said dryly. Then she leaned closer to Elsa. "It's something of an initiation around here, you see. And quite popular at parties."

For all their posturing, Porzia and Faraz seemed not just tolerant but eager to hear Leo's analysis. In the pause before Leo spoke, the empty dining hall fell disconcertingly silent.

"Let's see . . . ," Leo said, narrowing his eyes at Elsa. "The dress is well-made but the tailoring doesn't quite fit, so it's likely secondhand. Not exactly proletariat, but she doesn't come from money either. Speaks excellent Italian but pokes at the food as if it might bite back, so she was educated but cloistered—hasn't seen much of the world yet. Oh, and hesitant with her peers. Quite reserved. I suspect she's spent too much time around adults and not enough with those her own age."

Elsa felt hot with embarrassment at his scrutiny, at her own awkwardness, but she held her tongue. She broke eye contact and ducked her head, looking down at her feet. "What an impressive trick."

"Oh, look at that!" Leo crowed. "Falsely deferential. You think yourself superior, but you're accustomed to hiding it."

Elsa's patience was rapidly waning. She pulled herself up to her full height and quietly said, "Engine oil beneath your fingernails."

"What?"

"Engine oil. You spend enough time working that it's not

59

worth scrubbing it all the way out until the end of the day. The nails themselves are bitten down, a nervous habit, but you avoid letting other people catch you doing it. You put on a nice show of self-confidence, but secretly you worry about how other people see you." At this, he visibly paled, but Elsa kept going.

"That pocket watch you keep fiddling with, are you planning to tuck it away anytime this week? It's old, the silver backing a bit scratched up—a family heirloom perhaps, given to you by someone significant, someone who stays in your thoughts." She paused, wanting to take the watch all the way to its ultimate conclusion, but decided it would be unwise to say *your father is dead* purely for the sake of showing off. Instead, she let her gaze travel up to meet his own. "That is just your hands. Shall I go on?"

Tight-lipped, Leo said, "You've made your point."

"Excellent. I do *so* appreciate successful communication."

"Quite," he said, his tone putting worlds of meaning behind the word. He sounded embarrassed and furious and intrigued all at once.

"And no, I'm not from around here." With satisfaction, she added, "In fact, I'm not from Earth at all." She turned away from their shocked faces and paced unhurriedly from the room, a smile playing on her lips.

She might not be able to blend into their world as de Vries hoped she would, but when it came to verbal sparring, she could still hit the hardest. She was untouchable, the way Jumi taught her to be.

It was late by the time Alek de Vries arrived at the Order's headquarters in Firenze. His bad hip protested as he climbed the front steps, stiff from sitting still for too long on the train ride. He was getting too old for all this excitement and intrigue. But Jumi needed him.

He located the secret lever concealed within the intricate stone facade beside the entrance, and gave it a yank. The door unlocked and swung open for him with a ratcheting *click-click-click*. Inside, the main floor was eerily quiet—most of the Order members must have already gone home, or else up to their guest rooms on the third floor. Gia had sent a message ahead over the wireless, though, so her husband was waiting in one of the burgundy leather armchairs that decorated the broad, flagstoned lobby.

Filippo looked up at the sound of the door and stood. He was shorter than Alek, and he had more gray in his hair and more paunch around his middle than the last time they'd met.

"Alek," he said, "it's good to see you. I wish it were under better circumstances."

"It's been a long time," said Alek.

"Too long." Filippo pulled him into an embrace. In their youth, Filippo had been like family to Alek. But now every time Alek visited the living brother, all he could see was the ghost of the dead one. *Massimo.*

It was a little easier now. After all, Filippo aged, while the memory of Massimo in Alek's mind stayed always the same. Always in his prime, with ink on his fingers and that devil-may-care grin, achingly beautiful forever.

Alek cleared his throat. "So, what have I missed?"

"You know the Order," Filippo replied with a rueful grin. "We can't possibly arrive at a course of action after only a single afternoon of debate. But finding the people responsible for

Montaigne's murder is now a top priority. This matter will not go unresolved, I promise you."

"And Jumi," Alek corrected him. "Finding the people responsible, and rescuing Jumi."

Filippo blinked. "Yes. Yes, of course. Jumi, too."

Despite Filippo's reassurance, there was no denying the doubt that began to twist in Alek's gut. The Order had their own priorities, and in this matter, they might not be the stalwart allies Alek had expected. Perhaps Elsa was right not to rely on their assistance.

He had hoped the damaged worldbooks would simply serve to keep her occupied and safe; now he hoped she would prove him wrong. Jumi's life might depend on it.

The bed was too soft. After an hour or two of tossing around trying to get comfortable, Elsa yanked the heavy blankets off the bed and made a cocoon for herself on the floor instead.

The clear spring sunlight woke her early, and though the exhaustion of the past two days' events had not entirely left her, Elsa resisted the urge to roll over, cover her face with the blankets, and go back to sleep. There was work to be done.

She needed to figure out who had taken her mother. The salvaged books were her only lead, and they weren't going to repair themselves. While Jumi might very well rescue herself, or become a beneficiary of the Order's assistance, Elsa couldn't rely on either of those possibilities.

She untangled herself from the blankets and stood, stretching. "Um . . . Casa? Are you there?"

"Yes, signorina," Casa replied. "I am always here."

"Would it be possible to have some food brought here, to my rooms? I'm eager to get to work," she said, which was true, of course, though part of her was also eager to avoid Porzia's prying questions and Leo's overcompensating self-assurance.

By the time Elsa finished washing up at the washbasin and dressed herself, her breakfast had arrived at the door, carried by a waist-high brass bot with an arm that ended in a serving tray instead of a hand. It rolled quietly inside and used its other arm—the one with digits—to transfer the food onto the low table in front of the sofa. Then the bot turned around and made a silent, dignified exit. Elsa nibbled at the soft cheese and white bread—still warm from the oven—while considering the dilemma of the damaged worldbooks.

There was no way around it: she would have to repair the books by hand before she could look for clues about Montaigne's involvement. If he had hidden notes or plans or letters inside one of the worldbooks, she wouldn't be able to tell just from reading the text—she would have to go inside the worlds to retrieve his papers. And for that, the worldbooks needed to be fully functional. Elsa rinsed her breakfast from her fingertips and began straightaway.

First she opened the cover of each book in turn and pressed her fingertips to the paper, concentrating. None of them felt dead; they all had a bit of the tactile vibration that indicated a live worldbook, but the buzz swelled and receded as if the books were struggling for breath. It was not the steady, strong hum of a complete worldbook, a world that would be safe to enter.

Then Elsa flipped through the books page by page, noting the extent of the damage and trying not to despair. When possible, she wrote down her guesses about what the singed sections might have contained. Often, only the top line or two of a page were too badly blackened to read, sometimes only one word in the corner. Other pages were worse, and lost sentences would be difficult to reproduce with perfect accuracy.

Evaluating the condition of the books was slow work, and to patch up all the ruined sections would be even slower. She'd never tried to repair a burned worldbook before—the sheer number of pages that needed work was much greater than anything she'd attempted. To finish even one book would take her days.

Her mother could be dead in a week, for all she knew. There wasn't time for this, but what other option did she have? Montaigne had known the abductors, but with him dead, the only way to get that knowledge was to go through his papers, which were stuck inside the damaged worlds.

An unexpected knock at the door made Elsa jump and smear the ink where she was taking notes. She sighed, sheathed the pen in its holder beside the inkwell, and got up to see who had caused the disturbance.

Elsa opened the door. Porzia strode in past her, as if she'd been invited, and asked in a casual tone, "How are you finding your stay here on Earth? Have everything you need?"

Porzia regarded her with perfect innocence, lips forming a small, polite smile. But Elsa suspected the other girl was burning with curiosity. "I'm quite fine, thank you," she replied.

"Well, if there's anything . . . *particular* you require, as a non-Terran, please don't hesitate to ask." Porzia wandered through the sitting room into the study. "Settling in already, I see."

Elsa followed her, wary of having the other girl snooping around. She quickly closed the covers of all the books lying open on the writing desk.

"Can I help you with something?" Elsa asked, her tone a little stiff.

"You weren't at breakfast," Porzia said, as if this were sufficient explanation for her intrusion.

"No, I wasn't," Elsa agreed, watching as Porzia wandered over to the side table where Elsa had set down the Pascaline last night. She reached out to fiddle with the damaged dials, and Elsa snapped, "Don't touch that!"

Porzia turned, giving her a raised-eyebrow look. "I hardly think my touch could ruin it any further."

"It's not ruined. It can be fixed," Elsa said tightly. Her omission of who, exactly, would be doing the fixing was deliberate. No need for Porzia to know that.

Porzia sighed, turning away from the table to face Elsa. "About last night . . ."

Elsa raised an eyebrow of her own. "You're here to apologize for your friends being presumptuous cads?"

"Actually, I was going to say it wasn't entirely diplomatic of *you*, either. Everyone likes Leo—you won't win any friends by humiliating him."

Elsa pulled herself up to her full height and dropped her tone from chilly to downright arctic. "I don't need anyone to like me, I just need them to understand I'm not to be toyed with."

Porzia shrugged. "Just offering a bit of advice."

"I have work to do."

"I'll leave you to it, then." Porzia swept out of the room with the same unflappable grace as always, leaving Elsa to wonder what exactly the other girl was trying to accomplish.

Porzia's warning irked her, and even more irksome was the small twinge of worry she felt. No, she did not care to make friends with these people—they were at best a distraction, and at worst a danger to her and her mission to find Jumi. She pushed the worry aside and made herself focus.

Midday came and went, Elsa hardly noticing except to nibble at the rest of the bread and cheese when her stomach growled.

She'd started with the book she thought had the highest probability of containing relevant information—a small world scribed to serve as an office, the worldtext written in Montaigne's own hand. Perhaps Montaigne had corresponded with the abductors ahead of time, in which case there could be letters or telegrams with identifying details.

Her own study here in Pisa was well equipped for scriptological endeavors. Fishing through the drawers and cabinets, she quickly found a sheaf of loose paper, a bottle of paper glue, and a narrow-bladed shaping razor. She began with the first damaged page, gently brushing away the charred fragments and then cutting a small triangle of new paper to match the shape of the damaged section. She slid a gluing board under the page, lined up the burned page with the patch, and carefully brushed a thin layer of glue over the edges to fuse them.

Elsa sat back to admire her work. Page one of book one, nearly finished. This was a section of mild damage, so when the glue dried, all she would have left to do would be to get out her ink and scribe in the three words missing from the top line. They wouldn't all be so easy, but she was determined to do this. One page at a time.

Right now, though, she needed to stretch her legs, to focus her eyes and her attention on something else for a minute. Perhaps she'd take a break from the grueling work of book repairs to tinker with the Pascaline a bit.

"Casa?" she said, standing up from the chair. "Is there a place I could find a clockmaker's toolkit, or something of the kind?"

"Why yes, signorina. Mechanists often have need of fine-sized tools. I would be happy to direct you."

A knee-high brass bot arrived at her door as an escort, and Casa led Elsa around to a side stairwell much narrower than the main stairs in the foyer. The bot rolled to a stop at the head of the stairs, but when Elsa descended to the first floor, another bot met her there.

She followed the new bot—down a hallway and around a corner and down another hall—until it stopped in front of an empty doorway. The wood of the doorframe looked new, still raw instead of finished, and hinges had yet to be installed. A pair of bots were industriously repairing damage to the walls on either side. The first had three arms—two ending in hands and one in a hammer—and was installing wide wooden laths over a hole that went clean through the wall. The other bot had a palette knife for a hand and a can of plaster fastened to its side, and was smearing wet plaster over the recently installed lathing.

"Um," said Elsa. "What happened?"

"Oh, that?" said Casa bashfully, as if the house had been hoping no one would notice. "Some minor repairs. A hazard of hosting so many pazzerellones, you know."

Elsa declined to point out that she did not, in fact, know. Did they all really live in a constant state of destruction and reconstruction here? The idea sounded rather exhausting to her, but then she came from a world too small to afford destruction—every last leaf and pebble of Veldana was precious.

"So . . . there are tools in here?" Elsa asked, stepping through the new doorframe.

"Oh yes, signorina," Casa assured her. "Many kinds of tools."

The laboratory beyond had a sunken floor with half a flight of steps leading down to it from the entrance. Enormous machines hulked here and there, some of them twice as tall as a person. She stared in wonder. It took her a moment to remember to breathe, and another to remind herself that she wasn't here to go poking around inside someone else's inventions.

She quashed her curiosity and tried to focus on her original intent: repairing the Pascaline. Where would the tools be stored? There were some scattered across the nearest worktable, but the surface was a far cry from organized. Elsa wondered how anyone could expect to find anything in all this mess. A tall cabinet stood against one wall, but when she opened the doors, the contents of the shelves inside seemed to lack any sense of order.

She sighed. "Aren't you at least going to give me a hint, Casa?"

"Yes . . . ," Casa answered slowly. "Go back to the worktable and look under the pile of design sketches."

Elsa lifted a corner of the messy pile of papers and peered underneath. Yes, there was something small wrapped in brown suede. She dragged it out and flipped open the leather coverings, revealing a kit of fine clockmaker's tools.

"What are you doing in here?"

Elsa jumped. Leo stood just inside the doorway, his arms folded across his chest and his sleeves rolled up to the elbow, showing the cords of muscle in his forearms. Odd that she hadn't heard him approach.

Feeling guilty as a pickpocket, Elsa yanked her hands away from the worktable and knotted her fingers together. If she was to keep her mechanist tendencies a secret, Leo mustn't find out she'd come looking to borrow tools. "Sorry. I, uh . . . I'm afraid I must have gotten turned around. The corridors are a maze, you know."

Leo sauntered in until he was standing on the opposite side of the table, facing her. There was a spark of deviousness shining in his eyes. "Right. Well, this is my personal laboratory and machine shop. Now you know where it is."

Elsa's eyes flicked up angrily, wanting to snap at Casa, but she bit her tongue. Why ever would Casa send her here, of all places? Surely there were other ways to acquire tools.

When she failed to reply, Leo quirked an eyebrow at her. "Would you like a tour of the lab? It's mine, so naturally it's all fascinating."

"No, I . . . I didn't mean to disturb you. I should go." She slipped around the table and hurried past him, wanting nothing more than to be safely alone. Leo's presence disquieted her in a way she couldn't quite put her finger on.

Behind her, he said, "You're really going to walk out like that? Without the tools you came for?"

Elsa stopped but didn't turn, her cheeks suddenly flushing with hot dread. Did he *know*?

"Normally I wouldn't let anyone but Gia borrow my tools, though in your case I think I can make an exception."

Deciding the damage was done and there was no use in denial, Elsa walked back to the worktable. She took the toolkit, but kept her gaze locked on it instead of looking him in the eye. "Thanks," she muttered.

"Do you . . . need me to fix something?" he said, but the words sounded more like a cautious foray than a challenge.

Elsa's mind raced, searching for a response that wouldn't give her away as a polymath. "It'll be a simple repair, I think, but I'll let you know if I can't figure it out."

"I am at your disposal," he said, letting the subject of her talents go. His gaze left her and flitted about the room, as if searching for a different topic. "So . . . you're not from Earth."

"No, I'm not." She fidgeted with the toolkit. She shouldn't have told him that.

"Veldana?"

"You've heard of Veldana?"

He snorted. "Every pazzerellone with ears has heard of Veldana. The first populated worldbook—and unless some pazzerellone has defied the Order's ruling on the matter of scribed humans, still the only populated worldbook."

Unless Veldana was gone, Elsa thought bitterly, in which case she and Jumi would be the only scribed people left alive in all of existence. "I wonder," she said, "is that rule intended to protect people like us from people like you, or the other way around?"

Leo looked surprised. "I'm not sure, actually. When Montaigne scribed Veldana, I doubt he expected his creations to have the madness. You're more interesting than anyone could have predicted."

There it was again in his tone—the implied question. But he did not ask it outright, he did not say the word *polymath*. He suspected the truth, but apparently he also respected her right to share it in her own time.

"My mother's missing," she said as if the words had bubbled up in her throat and needed to come out.

"Missing? What happened?"

"I don't know, I don't know . . . anything, really!" Elsa took a deep breath; she wasn't explaining this well at all. She started over. "My mother was taken—abducted from our world."

He stepped closer. "I am sorry——"

Elsa hugged her arms against her stomach, suddenly regretting her openness and his proximity. "Anyway, that's why I'm here."

Leo stopped, rebuffed, and then looked around his lab in mock bewilderment. "Here? I'm fairly certain she isn't hiding under one of my tarpaulins."

Curtly, Elsa said, "By 'here' I meant Earth, which I'm certain you understood."

His eyes softened, a silent apology. "Of course. This tongue has a nasty habit of turning everything into a jest, I'm afraid."

"Why?" she said, morbidly curious. "Is it . . . some sort of experiment?"

"An experimental replacement tongue? Sadly, no—it's the one I was born with. Though perhaps it would be wise to pursue an alternative, since this one simply refuses to behave itself."

Elsa narrowed her eyes at him. "You're a bit strange, you know."

"Says the girl from a different world," he retorted, but there was a grin playing at the corners of his lips, which took the edge from the words. The curve of his mouth made her flush again for an entirely different reason, and she suddenly felt as if she didn't know where to look.

She frowned at her own silliness. No daughter of Jumi da Veldana would succumb to such hollow charms. "I . . . should get back to work."

"Naturally. I'm sure you must get back to whatever it is you're doing." He gave her a hopeful look, as if this were an invitation for her to explain more, but Elsa had exceeded her quota of sharing for one day. She just wanted to retreat back to the quiet of her rooms.

"Thanks again for the tools," she said, and made her way toward the door.

"Oh, and Elsa?" he called.

She turned on the steps to look at him. "Yes?"

"You know you don't have to do everything alone."

"Of course," she answered, thinking, *If only that were true.*

5

TO APPLY ONESELF TO GREAT INVENTIONS, STARTING FROM
THE SMALLEST BEGINNINGS, IS NO TASK FOR ORDINARY MINDS;
TO DIVINE THAT WONDERFUL ARTS LIE HID BEHIND TRIVIAL AND
CHILDISH THINGS IS A CONCEPTION FOR SUPERHUMAN TALENTS.

—*Galileo Galilei*

After seeing Leo's messy but nonetheless well-stocked laboratory, it occurred to Elsa that she could use one of those, too. Jumi's abductors had used metal canisters of knockout gas, which meant at the very least they had a mechanist and an alchemist in their employ. For a rescue operation to work, Elsa would need the ability to combat every kind of madness.

It wouldn't surprise her if there were a few extra mechanics labs stashed away in some unused wing of the giant house, but with Porzia already poking around, she doubted her secrets would last very long if she asked Casa for help. Elsa suspected Casa had deliberately arranged her encounter with Leo, for whatever inscrutable reason.

Elsa wasn't sure she liked Casa's ever-present watchfulness. It gave the back of her neck that hot, prickly feeling; it reminded her of when she was a child learning to scribe, of how Jumi would hover over her shoulder, judging and correcting her work. *Don't get sloppy with your syntax. Remember, you need specificity in your word choice. Not the most elegant solution, but it will do.* Then, at least, the scrutiny had come from a trusted source, whereas now Elsa couldn't begin to guess at Casa's motives.

So, that left only one option available to her: she would have to scribe a laboratory for herself. Repairing the Pascaline would have to wait. When she arrived back at her rooms, she set down the clockmaker's tools and turned to face the scriptology shelves.

Her study came with an ample supply of ready-made empty scriptology books, which made her wonder again who the previous occupant had been. He or she had either been rich enough to purchase such a stock or had made a hobby of bookbinding. Elsa herself didn't have much experience with bookbinding—they had the technology for crude papermaking in Veldana, but scriptology paper was another matter altogether. Her books had always come imported from Earth.

From the shelf of empty books, Elsa selected as small a volume as she could find, only a little larger than her doorbook. She would never understand why Earth scriptologists favored working with enormous tomes. For a whole world like Veldana, it was admittedly necessary, but a small book would almost always suffice to scribe a single room. There was no telling what obstacles she might face when rescuing her mother, but with a portable lab book, she'd be prepared for anything no matter where she went.

Elsa sat at the writing desk and began with the basics of any usable world: gravity, air, time. The reference library in her study was small compared to the one in Montaigne's house before it burned, but it had the basics, so Elsa didn't need to reinvent the entire field of scriptological physics. She merely opened a physics reference book and cited the properties she needed her lab worldbook to take on.

To be useful as a laboratory, she'd need not only work space but also materials to work with. She scribed supply rooms full of tools and chemicals and mechanical components, and then she designed a property such that whatever object she desired would automatically shift to the front of the room. Elsa hated looking for things and not being able to find them.

Focused on her work, she lost track of time until she looked up at the window and was startled to see the daylight dwindling. The little pendulum clock mounted atop the bookcase reported that the dinner hour was nearly upon her.

To her surprise, Elsa found she didn't dread the thought of seeing Leo again at supper, but she couldn't afford to form attachments here—these people could only serve to distract her from her goal. She needed to arm herself with a laboratory worldbook and then find her mother. So she looked back down at her work and let the dinner hour pass.

The next day, Elsa stayed sequestered in her rooms. She repaired six more pages of the first of Montaigne's damaged books, but she reached an impasse with her lab book. A normal scriptologist wouldn't have use for the technical manuals she'd need to reference in order to stock her laboratory with equipment. She would have to venture forth from her rooms to complete the lab book.

Reluctantly, Elsa broke the silence in her rooms. "Casa, do you have a larger collection of scriptological resources anywhere? Or technical manuals, perhaps?"

"Why yes, signorina. In the library, of course."

Elsa stood up from her chair. "Might you direct me there?"

Doubting the wisdom of it, she nonetheless consigned herself once more to Casa's guidance. Soon, Casa had led her down to the first floor and into the rear of the house.

Elsa rounded the corner and stopped dead in her tracks. A short stretch of hallway ended in a broad, arched doorframe—to the library—but between her and the doors stood Porzia, Leo, and Faraz, casually conversing. Casa had once again delivered her, probably quite deliberately, into the company of the other residents. Elsa's first instinct was to back around the corner before any of them noticed she was there. And she would have—except for the allure of the fascinating creature perched on Faraz's shoulder.

Elsa had never seen an alchemically fabricated life-form before, but she knew it instantly for what it was. Most of its mass appeared to be tentacles (of which there were at least ten, Elsa estimated) and large, hairless bat-wings (of which there were, sensibly, only two). One enormous eye shone wetly in the center of its body, and if it had a mouth, Elsa couldn't see where.

"What a curious creature!" The words were out of her mouth before she could stop herself.

They all turned to look at her—Porzia with a little jump of surprise, and Leo with a cool insouciance, as if he'd known she was there all along. "Elsa," he said, "I see our newest scriptologist has found her way to the library." There was something odd about the way he emphasized *scriptologist*, but Elsa couldn't focus on that with such a diverting specimen in front of her.

She stepped forward for a closer look, and the creature reached one tentacle out to her curiously. Faraz gently batted away the tentacle before it could touch her, admonishing, "Manners, now. No grabbing, you know that frightens the girls."

"Oh, that's fine," Elsa said. "I don't mind creatures. Whenever there's an expansion in Veldana, I try to sketch all the new species. Or I used to, anyway."

"Do you . . . want to hold it?" he asked, sounding abashed, as if he were bracing himself for her to respond with disgust.

Elsa held out her arm, but Leo said, "I wouldn't do that if I were you. Sometimes it strangles people for no reason. And it's got these little poisonous fangs—"

"Don't listen to him," Faraz said, unperturbed by his friend's unflattering descriptions. "He's a lying liar who lies."

To the creature, Elsa said, "Don't worry, little darling—I don't believe him for a second."

It crawled with a sort of undulating motion, its wings spread wide for balance as it moved down Faraz's arm and transferred itself to her shoulder. Slowly, Elsa lifted a hand to stroke it. She'd expected slime, but its skin was dry and slightly bumpy beneath her fingers. It snaked one tentacle down the back of her dress, the suckers clinging to her skin for stability, and though the suction force was surprisingly strong, Elsa didn't find the sensation disquieting. The tip of another tentacle brushed her cheek tentatively, as if saying hello.

"Hi," Elsa cooed. "What's your name?"

"Skandar," offered Faraz.

"Well. Pleased to meet you, Skandar. Aren't you a sweet little thing?"

Porzia made a gagging sound. "Is it really necessary to coddle Faraz's disgusting tentacle monster like a newborn babe?"

Faraz sniffed. "Just because you convinced Gia to ban Skandar from the dining table doesn't mean the rest of us have to share your squeamishness."

"And with an attitude like that, it's no wonder you have to fend off all your adoring female suitors with a stick," Porzia said sarcastically.

"Well, I think Skandar's wonderful," Elsa offered.

"And I think," said Leo, "that we should stop loitering in the hall when there are perfectly comfortable seats inside." He led the way, apparently confident the rest of them would follow.

The library was a cavernous eight-sided room three stories tall and topped with a domed roof. The books were shelved along the walls, with two floors of balcony running around the circumference for perusing the upper bookshelves. Four tall windows were spaced around the third story. On the main floor, clusters of couches and armchairs, tables and reading lamps occupied the center of the space.

Aside from the four of them and Skandar, the library had only one occupant, a boy of eight or nine years with a large book open on the table in front of him. He swung his legs against the rungs of the chair while he read, too short for his feet to touch the floor.

"Ah," said Porzia, following Elsa's gaze. "My youngest brother. Say hello, Aldo!"

"Don't bother me, I'm reading!" he shouted back.

Leo flopped down on a couch and sprawled over it as if it were a much-battled-over hill and he was planting a flag.

Porzia sighed, looking first at Aldo and then at Leo dominating the couch. "Sometimes I think Casa takes the right approach with the children, treating them like a pack of feral animals. No manners."

Porzia and Faraz found armchairs, and Elsa took a chair beside Faraz. She tried to hand the creature back to him, but it held on rather firmly.

"Looks as if someone's made a new friend," Faraz said, surprised. "Skandar doesn't usually like other people."

Leo said, "Yes, that *is* curious. I've never seen Skandar take to someone who wasn't an alchemist before."

Was he trying to goad her into revealing her secret? Elsa struggled to keep her expression neutral. She never should have trusted him.

Elsa had little experience with alchemy, and she wasn't sure how much affinity she might have for it. Except she had felt an instant fascination with Faraz's alchemical creation, hadn't she? And she'd always loved the creatures of Veldana, even if they were prickly or slimy or had too many legs, even when no one else appreciated them.

Stroking her fingers down one of Skandar's leathery wings, she replied, "Well, if I were Skandar, I certainly wouldn't take to anyone who thought I was a hideous tentacle monster, either. It's hardly Skandar's fault."

Aldo stomped over, holding the large volume tight against his chest, and gave them all a severe look. "Libraries," he pronounced, "are supposed to be quiet." Then he turned on his heel and left the room in a huff.

Porzia watched him go. "With the way he clutches at books, he's going to break Mamma's heart."

"What do you mean?" said Elsa, thankful for any distraction from the topic of alchemy.

"He's sure to turn out another scriptologist," Porzia explained.

"Yes, I understood that part," she said. "But is that a bad thing?"

"To keep the house in the Pisano family, there must be a mechanist in every generation—someone capable of maintaining

79

Casa's exceedingly complex systems. That's why Papa married Mamma, you know. Poor grandmamma had six children and none of them a mechanist. It was apparently quite the scandal, and now here we are again, with two scriptologists and two children who haven't settled on a field yet. If Sante and Olivia don't settle soon, I'll have to start courting mechanists."

"What a terrible thing to say," Faraz said. "That your father married your mother only for her talent, and for producing an heir."

Porzia shrugged. "There are worse reasons to take a wife." There was a note of pride in her voice that Elsa didn't quite understand.

"The truth is always preferable, even if it is an ugly truth," Elsa said, aware she was parroting her mother only after the words had left her mouth.

Leo, who'd been fidgeting throughout the conversation, vacated the couch, ran up to the second-floor balcony, and climbed up on the narrow wrought-iron railing. He proceeded to walk along it, placing one foot carefully in front of the other, arms out for balance.

"Show-off," Faraz harrumphed.

Porzia rolled her eyes. "If you fall and break your neck, I'm not cleaning it up. Casa? You have permission to dispose of Leo's corpse in the nearest furnace."

"Very good, signorina," Casa serenely replied.

"And if you're going to die anyway, I'm taking your seat," Faraz said as he shifted over to the couch.

From his precarious perch atop the railing, Leo declared, "Have no fear! I'm a trained professional, raised in the finest circus in Vienna."

Elsa looked at Faraz, who said, "That one's definitely not true."

"I don't know what a circus is, in any case," she replied.

This seemed to deflate Leo somewhat. "Well, that's no fun. What is the point of inventing an outlandish background if it doesn't even make sense?" He crouched down to grab the railing and swung off, then dropped the rest of the distance to the floor. He landed gracefully, as if he were quite accustomed to jumping off things. Given how they'd first met, Elsa supposed this impression must be accurate.

"Did you have something in mind you needed from the library?" Faraz said to her rather suddenly, as if the thought had only just occurred to him.

"Oh, yes." Elsa felt the heat rise in her cheeks, embarrassed that she'd let herself get so thoroughly diverted from her task. "Well, nothing in particular, but I did fancy a look through the scriptology section."

"I suppose that's my area to assist with," Porzia said, and rose from her chair as if she were performing a reluctant favor.

"No need for that," Elsa said hastily. "If you could simply point me in the right direction . . ."

Too hastily, it seemed, since a spark of curiosity lit in Porzia's eye. "It's no trouble at all. I'd be happy to help you with . . . whatever it is you need."

This time, Elsa succeeded in transferring the still-reluctant Skandar back to its perch on Faraz's shoulder. She could feel Leo watching her as she followed Porzia up to the second-floor balcony and around to where the scriptological texts were shelved. She carefully ignored his gaze. Then it was Porzia prodding her for information while Elsa browsed through the titles, trying to think of a way to get the other girl to leave her alone with the books.

"Ooh!" Elsa exclaimed, taking a familiar volume from the shelf. "Wolker's treatise on fundamental physical principles. And in the original German—perfect." In truth, the book was dreadfully tedious, but she hoped it might discourage Porzia's interest.

Porzia's face fell. "Right, well, now you know where the books are. If you're sure there's nothing else you need help finding, I should get back to my own studies."

Elsa took the unwanted volume down to a reading table and feigned interest in it for the next half hour, until Porzia finished with her own research and left the library. Then she could finally go back to the shelves and find the technical manuals she needed to finish scribing her lab book. She pulled down several volumes and hauled them all back to her room, intent upon completing her laboratory before the day was out.

Leo was trying hard not to think about Elsa. Even working on his amphibious walker—a difficult, ongoing project that should be sufficiently diverting—his mind kept wandering back to her. He couldn't help but wonder what Elsa would think of these gear ratios, or wish there was a smaller pair of hands to help him tighten that bolt.

Of the twenty children in residence, most were too young to have settled on a discipline. Burak was the only other mechanist, and while he sometimes provided assistance, Leo wasn't in the mood for the company of a thirteen-year-old. Not now that ward number twenty-one had arrived, and she was Leo's age, and brilliant, and quite possibly loved machines. . . .

"She's a secretive one, isn't she?"

Leo banged his head on the chassis, surprised at the sound of Porzia's voice. He crawled out from inside the enormous machine and rubbed the back of his skull. "What do you want?"

"Aha," Porzia said, hopping up on a stool next to the work-bench. "You didn't say, 'She? She, who?' from which I infer you know I'm speaking of Elsa. And you agree she's secretive."

He grunted and squeezed past her to switch on the signal scrambler so Casa couldn't overhear. "I'm not in the mood for games, Porzia."

"You? Not in the mood for games? Someone find me a stone tablet, so we may engrave it to memorialize the day Leo didn't fancy a game."

"Maybe it's just your presence I don't fancy," Leo retorted.

Porzia ignored the jibe. "She's up to something—hiding in her rooms all day, scriptology books scattered everywhere, leaving only to visit the library. We've seen enough recent orphans walk through our doors to know this is not the usual behavior. Aren't you the least bit suspicious?"

He shrugged. "Perhaps she simply enjoys her work."

"She's trouble, that one. I don't know what kind of trouble yet, but I intend to find out."

"Porzia . . . this is an orphanage for mad kids. We're *all* trouble."

She narrowed her eyes at him. "You know something, don't you? I can't believe you found something out and you're keeping it from me, you traitor!" She slapped him on the arm.

Leo gave her a withering look. "Why don't you worry less about how she spends her time and more about fulfilling your duties as a hostess."

83

Porzia arched an eyebrow. "And I suppose you've made a list of my failings in that regard?"

"You could at least see to it that she doesn't starve herself. She hasn't had a proper meal since her first night here." Leo watched Porzia's expression harden and knew he'd gone too far. She took pride in Casa, in the role she would inherit from her father. He should not have criticized her hosting, but the words had already left his mouth and it was too late to swallow them now.

Porzia pinned him with a frosty stare. "Very well, I'll see to it that she's at dinner," she said, climbing off the stool. "And if you won't assist, I'll have to uncover the truth for myself. This is *my* family's house, and I certainly don't need your help protecting it."

Elsa was adding the finishing touches to her lab book when Porzia arrived to drag her off to dinner. Inconvenient timing, but the other girl proved too insistent for Elsa to politely refuse.

In the dining hall, Porzia ushered her to a seat beside Faraz and then sat across the table with Leo. Though Elsa sensed there was some significance to the seating arrangement, she hadn't the faintest idea what it meant. Was there something possessive in the way Porzia positioned herself beside Leo? Not that it mattered, of course; Elsa had no interest in trying to insinuate herself into their social circle.

The dinner train arrived, laden with another grand meal: white bean and tomato soup, pale fillets of fish served atop ribbons of pasta, and a custard pie decked with chestnuts. Elsa had thought she was hungry only moments before, but looking upon all the rich food she'd be expected to consume, she wondered if she wouldn't soon explode.

She leaned close to Faraz, lowering her voice. "Do they eat like this every night? I thought perhaps it was for show the first night, on account of my having just arrived."

"This is Italy. Food counts as an art form." Faraz shared a knowing smile. "Don't worry, you'll get used to it. I did."

Elsa looked at him with surprise. She'd known Faraz wasn't Italian, but somehow it had never occurred to her that he might also have once felt out of place here—the foreigner who did not comprehend the customs everyone else performed as a matter of course. Perhaps they were alike after all. "Where did you live before?" she asked.

"When I was younger, I apprenticed with an alchemist in the city of Tunis. But when the French invaded Tunisia he sent me away." Faraz sounded wistful, and he addressed this information more to his place setting than to Elsa.

She wondered if it had been a mistake to ask. "I'm sorry."

"It was for my own good. As a Turkish citizen, my mentor could not be conscripted into French service, but I was a Tunisian and had no such protections." The words had an undertone of doubt, as if he were trying to convince himself more than her of the necessity of his mentor's actions. Then he looked up at her with a sad smile and added, "We've all lost things. That's how we end up here."

"I am sorry," she said again, and meant it.

Porzia ladled soup into Elsa's bowl, and the scent of garlic and rosemary made her mouth water. *Revan would love it here*, Elsa thought. He was always eating—he'd happily join any culture that spent hours at the dinner table. Watching Leo, Porzia, and Faraz made her ache for the childhood friend she might never see again. It no longer mattered that they'd hardly exchanged a civil word in years. He was the only friend she'd ever had, and he might be dead, along with the rest of Veldana. Her throat felt suddenly tight, and she was grateful for the custom dictating that no one should eat until all were served, because at the moment she could barely swallow.

Get a grip, she chastised herself. *Don't think about it.*

Once the soup was served all around and everyone settled down to consume it, Porzia got that prying glint in her eye. "So, Elsa, tell us about your family. It must be very strange to be apart from them, in a foreign world."

Overhearing this, the children sitting closest to their end of the table perked up, and Elsa could feel their curious glances burning into her, even though she did not look at them.

She shrugged, self-conscious and trying to dodge the topic. "There's not much to tell."

"Oh, come now." Porzia leaned closer and adopted a confidential tone. "I've told you all about my family's fears and scandals."

"Very well," said Elsa. She wasn't especially eager to share anything, but perhaps Jumi's history could distract Porzia from inquiring about her present situation. "In the early days of Veldana, Jumi—my mother—was involved with a man. He died. Some time later, Charles Montaigne scribed children into the world, and Jumi became retroactively pregnant without her consent. Hence why she fought so hard for Veldanese independence."

When she stopped speaking, everyone was staring at her. Leo had frozen with his wineglass halfway to his lips, and Porzia had covered her mouth with one hand. Most of the younger children had ceased their racket and were sitting with uncharacteristic stillness, eyes wide as saucers. Someone dropped a fork, and the clatter of it landing on the floor was the only sound at their end of the table. Elsa wasn't sure what she'd said wrong. Now she was starting to feel flushed under the weight of everyone's stares.

"What?" she snapped.

Porzia arched an eyebrow. "It's funny how on some matters you know next to nothing, and on others you are shockingly well informed."

Faraz swallowed, as if there were something stuck in his throat. Elsa didn't like the look of pity in his eyes. "So, you were born because—"

She cut him off, relieving him of having to finish the question out loud. "Yes. In the days before Veldana's independence, Montaigne forced a number of unsavory changes upon our world. Including creating pregnancy, whether the Veldanese women liked it or not."

Porzia looked away and busied herself adjusting the lay of her cloth napkin in her lap. "Well, that's men for you."

"Hey," Leo said indignantly. "Us menfolk are still sitting here, you know. It's not as if we're all evil masterminds looking to forcefully impregnate a bunch of innocent natives."

In the seat next to Elsa, Faraz tensed at *innocent natives* as if he did not like those words, but he held his tongue.

Porzia glanced down the length of the table at the ranks of eavesdropping children, then gave Leo a pointed look. "And that, I think, is quite enough discussion of issues inappropriate for the dining hall. We're all lucky Mamma took her meal in her office."

Not a minute later, Signora Pisano appeared in the dining hall doorway as if Porzia's words had somehow summoned her. Everyone—except Elsa—jumped guiltily at the sound of her voice, and then made themselves busy with their meals. Elsa still wasn't sure exactly what the problem had been. For a supposedly civilized world, Earthfolk could be such prudes about certain matters.

For her part, Signora Pisano looked too flustered to notice anyone behaving oddly. "Porzia, dear—a word?" she said.

Porzia cast a wide-eyed look at Leo, who raised his eyebrows in response. Elsa guessed the silent conversation meant something like, *What's going on?* and *It wasn't me, I swear.* Then Porzia was out of her seat in one smooth motion.

Signora Pisano lowered her voice, but Elsa could still overhear. "I'm afraid matters with the Order have become . . . complicated. Your father's requested my presence in Firenze. You'll have to take charge while I'm away."

Elsa, who expected Porzia's reaction to involve some self-important blustering, was surprised to hear the other girl softly say, "Of course, Mamma. What needs to be done in your absence?"

"I'll write you a list." Then Signora Pisano raised her voice to ensure all the children heard the instruction to obey Porzia's authority in her absence. The Pisanos, mother and daughter, left together to settle the details, while the dining hall erupted with curiosity and supposition about the mysterious goings-on of the Order of Archimedes.

Elsa found her appetite had vanished as she worried over what, exactly, *complicated* was supposed to mean. De Vries was in Firenze, meeting with the Order. He'd seemed so confident they would help, but what if he'd been wrong?

In all the commotion, Elsa slid off her chair and crept out of the dining hall, freeing herself of the obligation to sit through the entirety of the too-long meal. She thought she'd managed to make a clean escape, but the sound of footsteps in the hall behind her told her otherwise. She looked back to see Leo jogging to catch up, and with a sigh of defeat she stopped walking.

Even as he rushed up to her, he managed to preserve an unhurried air about himself, as if he hadn't a care in the world. "You left early," he said. "If I were the easily offended type, I might come to the conclusion that our presence repels you."

Elsa shrugged. "I like being alone."

"Nobody likes being alone," Leo insisted, his voice suddenly too sharp. "You adapt to being alone if you must, but no one *enjoys* it."

She blinked at him, surprised by the sentiment. His mood changed like a sea breeze that couldn't decide from which direction it should blow. "Who elected you Speaker for Everyone Everywhere? I, for one, enjoy a bit of solitude." To Elsa it was a foreign concept that anyone might abhor being alone.

"Sure, just keep telling yourself that," Leo said with a slight grin, his sharp edge vanishing as quickly as it had come.

Elsa huffed out a breath, uncertain how to deal with him. "I have work to do."

Leo tucked his hands into his pockets and leaned against the wall of the corridor. "The Order's urgent business—first Signor de Vries and now Gia rushing off to Firenze—this is all about your mother, isn't it?"

Elsa knotted her fingers together to keep her hands from clenching into fists. "I have every confidence in de Vries."

"De Vries and two dozen other pazzerellones you've never met before?" Leo said skeptically. "You're not seriously going to sit by while some strangers in another city may or may not be looking for your mother, are you?"

"Well . . . yes," Elsa lied.

"No, you're not! And do you know how I know?" He pushed away from the wall, his breath rapid with agitation. "Because if there were even the slightest chance that I could be reunited with my family, no power on Earth could stop me. That's how I know." He turned abruptly as if he meant to stride off, but he stopped short. His shoulders hitched as he took a deep breath, mastering his temper.

Reluctantly, Elsa admitted, "I am . . . investigating my own line of inquiry, but it's slow going."

He turned back a little, not quite facing her, but at least she could see him in profile. He had the pocket watch out again and began slowly walking it across his knuckles like a very large coin, staring down at his hands as if it required his full concentration. "I can help you save your mother, if you'll let me."

His pain was too raw to bear, etched like shadows around his eyes. Quietly, Elsa said, "It won't bring you comfort, to watch me get back that which you cannot."

"I know."

"Then why?"

Still without looking at her, he said, "Because no one should lose everything. It isn't just, and I was raised to believe in a just world."

She stared at him, searching for any sign of false intentions. How much harm could it cause to explain what had happened?

Elsa pursed her lips for a moment, then related the details of the abduction, Montaigne's murder, the fire, and the damaged worldbooks. She left out the part about being a polymath; she did not have to tell him all her secrets.

Leo defied her expectations and proved to be a patient listener. When she finished the story, he frowned thoughtfully and said, "That's not much to go on."

"I don't know who took my mother." Saying the words aloud made her chest ache with renewed fear, as if she were reopening a partly healed wound. "I don't know if the Veldana worldbook survived the fire, and even if it did, I don't know where it is now. All I have is the hope that they burned Montaigne's library for a reason—that somewhere in his worldbooks there's a clue they didn't want anyone to find."

"So you've been trying to repair the books by hand? That's insane, it could take you months to get through all of them," Leo said. "Whoever abducted your mother, whatever their intentions . . . even if she refuses to help them at first, there are ways of persuading a person. Unpleasant ways."

Elsa's voice rose, a note of desperation creeping in. "You think I don't know that? I've been prioritizing as best I can. What else can I do?"

His expression brightened with the light of a dawning scheme, his amber eyes seeming to glint. "What if there was a faster way to repair the books?"

"'What if,'" Elsa muttered, impatient with his ambiguity. "Are you saying there's a faster way? Tell me what it is!"

Leo simply offered a sly smile. "Get the worldbooks packed. I know where we have to go."

6

Nestled along the rugged coastline north of Pisa, Leo said, were five little villages collectively referred to as Cinque Terre, and near one of those villages hid the ruins of the Pisano ancestral castle. Once a refuge for pazzerellones, the ruins still contained a collection of old inventions. When Leo was twelve, the Pisanos took him there for the first time, and he felt like a knight running amok in a dragon's hoard while the dragon was away, with room after room of old treasures to be discovered.

And he still remembered, in one large laboratory, the book restoration machine.

Leo took the corridors at a jog. He burst through the cracked-open door of Gia's office to find Porzia on the other side.

She looked up from her seat at her mother's desk. "Mamma's already left for the train station. You just missed her."

"Actually, I was hoping to find you," he said, a manic edge to his voice making the words spill out too fast.

"Really . . ." Porzia stretched the word out like caramel. She got up from the chair and came around to the front side of the desk. "Have you finally come to your senses? Going to tell me what it is Elsa's hiding?"

"No time for that," he said impatiently. "Grab the keys! We have to get into the Corniglia ruins." Ruined or not, the castle was still presided over by the Pisano family.

Porzia cast him a skeptical stare and planted her hands on her hips. "First off, there are only two trains a day to Cinque Terre, so no one's going anywhere tonight. And second, you've gone insane if you think I'm going to take a trip out to the ruins now, of all times. I can't leave Casa unattended for a whole day with Mamma out of town."

"No need to stay on my account," Casa said placidly.

Porzia rolled her eyes, exasperated. "I didn't mean to imply *you* needed supervising, Casa—but your occupants do."

"Hmph," replied the house. "I am perfectly capable of herding those squalling human progeny in your absence."

Leo raised an eyebrow. "Right. Because referring to the children as 'squalling human progeny' really instills confidence in your caretaking abilities."

"See? I simply can't get away," said Porzia.

He shrugged. "That's fine. I know how to find the place, so if you lend me the keys—"

"Absolutely not!"

"Hmm," Leo said, pursing his lips as if Porzia were a troublesome engine. "Think of it this way: Would Gia be angrier with you if you lent me the keys, or if you abandoned the children?"

"I'm not going to do either," Porzia said through gritted teeth.

"Please. It's important."

She folded her arms cattily. "Important enough you'll tell me what Elsa's hiding, and why you're going to such lengths to help her?"

"Her life is not a story written for your amusement! There are larger forces at work here than our ridiculous games. I keep quiet for her protection," he said, though this was not entirely true. Actually, he thought it might be better to have Porzia and Faraz informed and ready to assist, but he knew he had to respect Elsa's wish for secrecy if he wanted her to accept his help.

"You think this amuses me?" Porzia said indignantly. "Casa belongs to my family—I am responsible for everything that goes on under this roof. If I am overinquisitive, it is with good reason. Leo, she has you in her thrall. What if you are the one who needs to be protected from her?"

Was that jealousy he read in the tightness of her lips? Was that what it all came down to—Porzia and her carefully calculated plans to acquire a mechanist husband? He said, "You have no claim on me. We're not betrothed. My life is mine to spend as I will."

Porzia jerked as if the word *betrothed* had been a slap. Her eyes went wide, then she stalked across the room, fished a ring of keys out of a drawer, and threw it—hard—at Leo's chest. He was caught off guard, and the key ring hit him and fell to the carpet. He knelt to retrieve it.

"There," Porzia spat. "Go get yourself killed for all I care."

Leo stared at the keys. He shouldn't have said what he did. Whatever else Porzia intended, she'd been a good friend to him, and even now she did not withhold from him what he needed. "I hope it doesn't come to that—anyone dying—but it might." He paused. "I'm sorry."

She made a frustrated noise in the back of her throat. "You're impossible. Why can't you simply explain what's going on?"

"Because it's not mine to explain," he said, and left with the keys.

Elsa gently placed the burnt books one at a time into the carpetbag, which still held a lingering smell of smoke from the last time she'd transported them. She tried not to think too much about what she was doing. A grain of hope was necessary, but too much hope could easily transmute into crushing disappointment. She tried to think of Leo's plan not as the miraculous solution to rescuing her mother that she so desperately wanted it to be, but simply as one more avenue of inquiry to pursue.

Elsa jumped when Leo burst through her door without knocking, and she nearly upended the inkwell on her writing desk. "By all means, let yourself in," she called into the sitting room.

He came to stand in the doorway of her study. Instead of replying to her quip, he said, "I think we should tell Porzia and Faraz what's happening."

Elsa looked up from straightening her scriptology supplies. "What! Why?"

"We need Porzia, and not just for the keys," he said, holding up the key ring. "The Pisanos are not a bridge we want to burn."

"Have you told them all *your* secrets?" she asked bitingly.

"I've told them . . . enough. I know it's a risk telling anyone, but I vouch for them both."

Elsa scowled at him. How was it someone so proficient at lying could, at other times, manage such raw sincerity? His unguarded expression unnerved her. Jumi had raised her to be self-sufficient and taught her that depending on others was a kind of weakness. But here was this strange boy practically begging her to share her confidence.

Still resistant, Elsa said, "It's not necessary for them to know."

"You can't know what's necessary when you keep yourself sequestered away from anyone who might help you. If you hadn't kept the books a secret, we could have gone to repair them two days ago. How much more time are you willing to lose because you refuse to trust people?"

"Says the boy who lies about everything to everyone," she retorted.

Leo gave her a steady, serious look, his eyes catching the lamplight like twin pools of molten bronze. "My lies don't matter—my family isn't coming back."

Elsa rubbed her face with her hands, wondering if all her meticulous hours of book repair had indeed been needless. "Fine. Fine! I'll do it."

Leo instructed Casa to ask the others to meet them in the library. Elsa dragged her heels on the way downstairs, still unsure this was a wise idea. When all four of them were settled in the plush library armchairs, Elsa told them about Jumi's abduction as succinctly as she could, in a flat tone, without looking them straight in the eyes.

"Wait," Porzia interrupted, "so you don't know what became of the Veldana worldbook?"

"No," Elsa said, her throat tightening.

Porzia covered her mouth with one hand, her eyes wide as saucers at the horror of losing such a world.

Faraz leaned forward in his seat. "And you think this Montaigne fellow may have left a clue behind in one of his worldbooks."

"They—whoever 'they' are—could not have gotten into Veldana without Montaigne's help, and he always kept his notes and papers inside scribed worlds." Elsa turned to Leo. "We should get to sleep. It'll be an early morning."

She stood and left the library without giving Porzia and Faraz a chance to formulate any more questions. She'd done what Leo asked of her, but she didn't relish the idea of hanging around to satisfy their curiosity with more sordid details. She'd made it halfway down the hallway before Porzia followed her out, running to catch up with her.

"Wait," the other girl called.

Elsa stopped and turned. "I have nothing else to say on the matter."

"But I do," she said. "Elsa, I'm . . . I'm so sorry. You're more than a guest in my home, you are a refugee in a sanctuary, and I fear I've treated you rather poorly."

Elsa, taken aback, said, "I was not fishing for apologies."

Porzia rested her hands on Elsa's shoulders in a distinctly maternal gesture, and though Elsa had never thought of Porzia as much of a caretaker, she supposed being the eldest of four children might have something to do with it. "We will find your mother," she said. "I swear it."

Alek was beginning to wonder if the council meeting would continue all night. Perhaps some archaeologist of the future would unearth the Order's headquarters in Firenze and find their bones still seated in their chairs.

97

A movement out of the corner of his eye caught his attention. The door stood ajar, with Gia Pisano's face framed in the opening. Alek glanced across the table at Filippo, whose focus was so strongly locked upon the discussion that he had not noticed the arrival of his own wife. Alek hid a smile—paying attention to more than one thing at once had never been Filippo's strength. So Alek levered himself out of his seat and slipped from the room as quietly as he could into the grand entrance hall.

The latch clicked behind him, and he bent to accept the kisses Gia placed upon his cheeks.

"How goes it?" she said, her voice lowered so as not to disturb the people inside.

Together they drew away from the closed council room door, with Alek saying, "About as well as you might expect. One pazzerellone murdered and another missing . . . it's, well, it's a madhouse in there."

For that pun Gia cast him an arch look. "Too many hypotheses, too few data, zero plans of action?"

Alek nodded. "That about sums it up."

"All right, then," she said, ever the voice of practicality. "Let's find ourselves a room with a blackboard and work through the problem, see if we can't make some progress—something Filippo can bring to the table tomorrow."

Alek let her lead the way, keeping the protests of his tired bones to himself. He really was getting too old for this.

Elsa lay in the too-soft bed that night, not sleeping, all the details of the day and concerns for tomorrow churning around in her brain. She considered offering the doorbook to shorten the journey, but eventually decided against it. The trip would only be a matter of hours by train, and she'd rather keep the doorbook a secret. Especially from Porzia. The doorbook was practically heretical by the standards of European scriptology, and Elsa already felt like enough of an outsider without having to weather the storm of Porzia's shock and disapproval. Would they still accept her, still want to help her, if they knew about the doorbook? Perhaps; perhaps not.

Best not to mention the doorbook for now.

When that issue was settled in her mind, she moved on to worrying about de Vries. Not that she'd expected him to work a miracle in just two days, but the way Signora Pisano had been suddenly called away concerned her. What did the Order know? Would they fear Elsa more than they feared *for* Jumi?

Useless speculation. Elsa pressed her face into the pillow, trying to squeeze out the thoughts. She gave up on the bed and tried the floor again instead, and finally managed some sleep.

Elsa rose early and dressed in some clothes sent to her, via house-bot, by Porzia. She tried to decline, of course, but Casa insisted the clothes would make her less conspicuous for traveling in public. They were excessively complicated, and Elsa struggled into the chemise, the corset, and the dress only with some assistance from one of Casa's bots.

Finally dressed, she lifted her carpetbag of books and met Leo in the foyer to depart for the train station. Porzia and Faraz were staying behind to watch the children and maintain the appearance of normalcy.

Instead of exiting through the front doors, Leo led the way out a side entrance and along a covered walkway to the carriage house. Elsa followed but cast him a puzzled look.

"I thought we were taking a train."

"Certainly, but we're not going to *walk* all the way to the train station." He said the word *walk* as if it were blasphemy. With a flourish, he pulled open the carriage house doors. "Not when we have this. May I present: the spider hansom."

Elsa peered into the semidarkness within. The spider hansom was an eight-legged walking machine with a small, open-topped passenger compartment in front of a moderate steam engine. Aside from a narrow smokestack sticking straight up in the air toward the back—to direct the furnace smoke away from the passengers' lungs, Elsa presumed—it did rather resemble a spider's anatomy. Despite herself, she was impressed with the uniqueness of the design.

"My invention, of course," said Leo without a hint of modesty.

At rest, the passenger compartment touched the ground, making it a relatively simple matter to climb onto the seat. Leo's European manners dictated that he should, nonetheless, help Elsa in, which she suffered with no small amount of irritation. When they were both settled, Leo set his hands and feet to the levers and pedals, and he fired up the engine. The cab rose in the air so they hung suspended between the eight legs and stepped out into the street with a jerk.

The motion startled a horse pulling a hansom of the more traditional kind, and the driver gestured angrily at them from his perch behind the cab. Leo hardly seemed to notice. Apparently the residents of Casa della Pazzia were so accustomed to enraging the regular citizenry of Pisa that a single irate driver did not merit Leo's attention.

As Leo drove, Elsa watched the reactions of the pedestrians they passed. Some looked curiously at the spider hansom, while others didn't give it a second glance. But she saw no fear or suspicion, no nervous ladies with parasols like on the streets of Amsterdam; Pisa was a city that accepted its pazzerellone residents as a customary feature of everyday life.

They drove through a broad piazza surrounded by impressive old buildings. Off to one side was a marble statue of a man standing on some sort of fantastic creature; Elsa squinted, trying to get a better look as the hansom clattered by, and wondered what in the world that was about. Then they took a bridge over the river to cross into the southern half of the city.

With Leo at the helm of a shiny brass walking machine, a manic grin on his face and the wind lifting his hair, Elsa felt like a character in one of the adventure novels she used to pilfer off de Vries's bookshelves when she was small. The spring air seemed potent with possibility, and she could almost forget the sense of panic that had clawed at her ever since the moment she realized her mother had been taken.

While they rode, Leo talked at length about the walker and about engine theory in general. "There's a German pazzerellone doing glorious things with thermal efficiency," Leo was saying. "He had something of a setback last year, nearly blew himself up, but—"

"You call that a *setback*?" she interrupted.

"Well, you can hardly hold that against him." He waved a hand, dismissing her concern. "If things aren't exploding now and again, it means you're not trying hard enough." He flashed a roguish grin.

Elsa folded her hands in her lap and gave her carpetbag a worried glance. "If the spider hansom explodes while we're in it, I hope you know I shall be very put out. It would cost me a substantial delay."

"The mechanical theory's all sound, so there really isn't any cause for concern." He schooled his expression, as if his invention could be held together with confidence alone.

The spider hansom let them down before the wide portico of Pisa Centrale station, and Elsa watched with interest as the machine proceeded to walk off on its own with no driver at the controls.

"Autopilot," Leo explained. "It's programmed to follow a homing beacon back to the carriage house at Casa della Pazzia."

No longer safely sequestered in the high perch of the spider hansom, Elsa felt exposed. Her spine crawled with the sense that people were noticing her. Because she was dark and foreign? Because she did not act sufficiently urbane? She and Leo walked under an arch of the portico and through the front doors, and Elsa felt secretly relieved to have someone with her to handle the purchasing of tickets and the navigating to the correct platform. The station was crowded with people walking in all directions and with strange noises and smells, and she hadn't expected the whole experience to feel so overwhelming.

Leo, on the other hand, seemed quite at ease counting change at the ticket counter and navigating the station, all while keeping one eye on everything else around them. They passed by a man hand-cranking a mechanical organ, and Leo handed a coin to the organ grinder's monkey, which was dressed in a fancier coat than the organ grinder himself.

Turning back to Elsa, Leo said, "That's the worst rendition of 'La donna è mobile' I can imagine."

Elsa gave him a confused look. She had no idea what he was talking about. For that matter, she wasn't sure why there was a man playing music in the station, or why Leo had given the monkey a coin.

" 'La donna è mobile,' " Leo repeated, as if this were an explanation. "From *Rigoletto*. You should listen to it sometime."

Elsa resisted the urge to ask what a rigoletto was. At least she wasn't trying to navigate this utterly foreign country alone. She didn't like to admit it, but perhaps there was some merit to the idea of accepting help. Leo was proving himself to be an impressively competent escort.

When they boarded the train, Leo selected a box on the left, and he hefted her carpetbag onto the luggage rack. Elsa settled herself on the plush bench seat across from him, uncomfortable in her borrowed clothes. The corset boning held her spine straight, making it impossible to slouch. But at least she attracted fewer stares dressed as she was.

"Have you ridden a train before?" Leo asked, perhaps mistaking the source of her discomfort.

"When I was younger, to visit de Vries in Amsterdam." Before she'd scribed the doorbook, but she left that part out.

"We're lucky the Kingdom of Sardinia has an excellent rail system. The modern infrastructure is rather spottier in the other Italian states, but I suppose that's what happens when you conscript and imprison pazzerellones. Progress requires intellectual freedom."

"Huh." Elsa didn't know much about the role of pazzerellones in European society, how they might be subject to the whims of their government. For that matter, she had never considered the process of how inventions went from prototype to common use on Earth; Veldana was too young a world to have seen much of anything invented.

The train rumbled and lurched forward out of the station, gaining speed as it headed down the track. Elsa watched out the window as the train crossed over the river again, heading north, and sped away from the city into the hilly Tuscan countryside. Every now and again, they would pass a field so overtaken by some kind of scarlet flower that the earth would seem like a frozen red sea. The flowers were quite striking, but Elsa caught herself wondering why anyone would scribe such a persistent agricultural weed—until she remembered that no one had.

What a strange world, built of random chance and long, difficult refining.

Elsa shifted her gaze to Leo. Now that he was settled in the confined space of the train with nothing pressing to do, he was acting oddly subdued. It seemed as if his nearness were an illusion, and if she stretched out her hand, she would find he was actually beyond her reach.

She didn't like him retreating into the realm of his private thoughts after just last night cajoling her to share so freely of herself. It was hardly fair turnaround.

Elsa folded her hands in her lap and said, "So, now that you and all your closest friends know my secrets, are you going to tell me what your story is?"

Leo leaned forward, resting his elbows on his knees, and looked at her with serious eyes. "My father was chief cryptographer to the king of Sardinia, and my mother an Austrian spy, so you see their love affair was doomed from the start, and her inevitable betrayal—"

Elsa held up a hand, begging him to stop. He was really quite good when he committed himself to a story—so sincere with those mesmerizing tawny eyes and the smooth cadence of his voice. Revan had been a terrible liar. When they were children and got in trouble, he would always try to talk their way out of it, and

Baninu would always see through her son's improvised excuses. Revan hesitated when he lied, needing time to sort the details in his mind before saying them, but with Leo the words flowed as if he were reciting real memories.

Silence hung in the air between them for a minute before Elsa said, "Are you ever going to tell me the truth, or just keep making up ridiculous stories we both know are lies?"

"Oh, definitely the second option, I'd say." He grinned and turned to look out the window, as if to deflect her question as neatly as he might parry a rapier thrust.

"Look, I know they're all dead, all the people you cared about." His head snapped back to stare straight at her, making her suddenly doubt the wisdom of saying it. She continued uncertainly, "So, you . . . ah . . . don't have to keep up the pretense on my account, is all."

He stayed silent so long she wasn't sure he would ever answer. Then he quietly said, "Sometimes pretense is the only armor we have against the world."

"But you still wear that every day," she said, casting a significant glance down at the pocket watch chain hooked through a buttonhole on his waistcoat.

Leo looked down. "I saw the bodies. My father had this on him when he died." He slid the watch out of his waistcoat pocket. "Forgetting was never the goal."

"If you're so convinced of the worthiness of your friends, why do you never speak of your own history, even with the people you claim to trust?"

He cleared his throat uncomfortably. "They know enough."

Elsa cast him a skeptical look. "I have to wonder whether you're trying to convince me or yourself."

This time, Leo didn't answer. His gaze shifted to the window, the beginnings of a scowl furrowing his brow.

Elsa bit her tongue, fearing she'd pushed him too far. She should not have been so forward, not here and now, not with Leo, whose help she needed.

Her mother had raised her to be forthright, to speak her mind. *Never forget that words have power*, Jumi would say, pacing the slate floor of the cottage while Elsa sat diligently at the writing desk. *We use them to remake the world. Our best weapons are words.* Jumi had taught her how to make war with words, but not how to make peace with them. And even a sword made of words has two edges.

7

POURING FORTH ITS SEAS EVERYWHERE, THEN, THE OCEAN
ENVELOPS THE EARTH AND FILLS ITS DEEPER CHASMS.
—*Nicolaus Copernicus*

Leo found he couldn't look Elsa in the eye for long—there was something disconcerting about her gaze. Maybe it was the chiaroscuro effect of her dark skin turning those green eyes startlingly clear and bright, like spotlights in an opera house. Or maybe it was the way she seemed to look right through him, as if she could read his thoughts as easily as she could the words on a page. Certainly, she had demonstrated an uncomfortable tendency to skewer the truth no matter how carefully he concealed it beneath layers of lies.

Leo did not want to examine why he felt the need to hide it in the first place. He did not want to admit to the disservice he did his friends, even if it was out of self-preservation. To share the truth would be to make it more real, and it already felt too real to bear.

It seemed safest to stare out the window, only acknowledging Elsa with the occasional sideways glance. She had a sharp beauty, and he fancied it might cut him if he gazed upon it too long. *Exotic* was the word he wanted to use, though Faraz abhorred it (*Exotic, meaning "from the outside,"* Faraz would say, *someone who can never, no matter what they do, count as "one of us."*). But in truth, Elsa was exotic, she was as exotic as it was possible for any human to be: she was not from Earth. And if he read her properly, she intended to return from whence she had come as soon as physically possible. Yet another reason to keep her at arm's length.

In the end everyone left, one way or another. Aris, who had seemed an unstoppable force of nature right up until the moment he was stopped. Little Pasca, brilliant and sensitive. Father, who had never fully been there in the first place, his mind always on matters larger than his sons. All of them gone.

Even Rosalinda—who had dragged Leo kicking and screaming from the house fire in Venezia, who for weeks afterward had sat up with him when the nightmares made sleep impossible. Even she let him go when the Order demanded custody, as they did for all mad orphans. Not that Casa della Pazzia turned out so bad for him, but as a frightened, traumatized ten-year-old, the last thing he'd wanted was to be dragged away from a familiar face and thrust in amongst strangers.

In any case, Elsa was not here to stay. So Leo knew very well he ought to keep his distance.

They changed trains at the station in La Spezia, and by the time they were pulling out to follow the Cinque Terre line, it seemed to Elsa that Leo had regained some of his usual spirit.

The terrain outside the window had transitioned from rolling hills to sharp little mountains. They passed through a series of tunnels and emerged quite suddenly into the glare of sunlight scattering off waves. The enormity of the ocean made Elsa's breath catch. Her mind struggled to accept that any world could contain such a vastness of water; Veldana's little sea seemed nothing but a puddle by comparison. The distant horizon filled her with an awe bordering on dread.

They pulled up at a train stop, and while other passengers were busy disembarking, Leo grabbed her hand and led her across the train to an empty compartment on the other side. Elsa was too shocked at the sudden physical contact to protest; his touch felt almost electric against her palm, like the buzz of a finished worldbook.

"We don't have time for sightseeing, but you should at least get a glimpse of Riomaggiore," he said.

Bright-painted buildings rose up on two sides of a narrow valley, blocks of red and orange, salmon-pink and white. The train tracks bridged over a narrow, sea-green inlet lined with colorful rowboats. The surrounding landscape was a jumble of exposed gray cliffs and greenery, with a mountain rising up behind the town as if to shield it from the rest of the world.

The whistle blew, and Leo and Elsa returned to their compartment. The train followed the coast from there—sometimes passing through tunnels, sometimes clinging precariously to the cliffside, the blue-green ocean lapping at the rocks below.

Soon the train was pulling into Corniglia station, and Leo was standing to retrieve the carpetbag from the luggage rack. They stepped out onto the open-air platform. It was the lone construct down near the sea, at the foot of the steep slope leading up to the town. Unlike the first two fishing towns they'd passed through, Corniglia was built atop a towering cliff.

"I'm afraid we have to proceed on foot," Leo said. "The locals don't have much use for hansoms in a village this size. Will you be all right?"

Elsa looked up. A broad set of brick stairs switchbacked up the cliff side. It was, admittedly, a climb of perhaps a hundred meters, but it wasn't as if he were asking her to scale the bare rock. "It's not a problem."

"Are you sure?" He gave her a worried look.

His skepticism irked her; she was Veldanese, not some soft highborn lady. "There are stairs. I doubt they were built for their aesthetic appeal."

So they climbed. Despite her confidence, the corset was more of a hindrance than she'd expected, and Elsa felt quite winded by the time they reached the village at the top. The brightly painted houses clung together in tight, precarious clusters on either side of a main road that ran the length of the town. It took them only a minute or two to cross the width of the narrow village.

Terraced vineyards dominated the valley on the other side, and so they descended into a landscape of stone walls, rough-hewn steps, and verdant grapevines displaying clusters of tiny young grapes. It all looked startlingly overengineered to Elsa's eye. Corniglia itself couldn't have held more than two or three hundred people—close to the population of her own village in Veldana—but they had practically rebuilt the entire landscape by hand in order to grow sufficient crops.

"Why would anyone put a town here? Seems unaccountably foolish, to build on such unforgiving terrain."

"This isn't Veldana, we can't just create more arable land

when we run out of space. We have to work with what we have," Leo said. "Besides, most of these families have probably lived here for centuries. A thousand years ago, somebody decided the remote location would be a good defense against, I don't know, Ostrogoth raiding parties or something, and ever since then, they've kept living here because this is their home."

Elsa tried to digest this idea, tried to think of cities like Paris and Amsterdam and Pisa as accumulations of their history, the strata of historical events layering atop one another over the long years. Pivotal moments with lasting consequences that no one could predict. It made her head hurt.

"Earth is weird," she concluded.

As they crested the ridge on the far side of the valley and passed into the shade of trees, Elsa snuck a sidelong glance at Leo. He looked fresh and bright-eyed, as if their journey on foot hadn't taxed him in the slightest. A trickle of sweat down the back of his neck was his only concession to the midday heat, his brown-and-gold-brocade waistcoat still buttoned. The climb hadn't been too much of a challenge for her either, despite the corset, but Elsa often spent her days surveying Veldana and was well accustomed to getting places under her own steam.

They walked until Elsa could see the blue sea sparkling with sunlight between the tree trunks. Leo stopped at a small outcrop of sedimentary rock, its layers of deposition still obvious when viewed from the side, and set down the carpetbag. He hooked his fingers beneath the top layer of stone, and after a moment of flexing his biceps, it hinged up like the top of a storage chest.

"What—" Elsa said, coming over to look under the layer. There was a brass control panel with a keyhole fitted horizontally inside the hollowed-out rock. "Hidden controls?"

"Ah, yes . . ." There was a note of strain in Leo's voice. "And I'd forgotten how heavy this thing is. Would you mind getting the key? In my left side pocket."

Elsa reached into the pocket of his waistcoat; the key ring was stuffed in there beside his father's pocket watch, and there was hardly room for her fingers. Through the fabric, she could feel the tense washboard muscles and the heat of his skin. She pulled her hand away quickly and felt her face flush as she fumbled with the key ring, looking for one that seemed a likely fit for the keyhole in the control panel.

"This one?" she said, holding up a key for Leo to see. Her voice came out a little unsteady.

"That looks right." A bead of sweat was crawling down the side of his face. "Turn the key, then flip all the switches in order, top to bottom."

The key fitted snugly and turned with a satisfying *ka-chunk*. The brass switches were stiff beneath her fingers, but she managed them all, then quickly removed the key.

"Done," she said, and stepped away to give Leo space to close it. He let the lid down heavily and shook out his arms to release the tension.

Elsa looked up. Where before she'd seen nothing but a rocky outcrop dropping away into a seaward cliff face, now she saw a castle built into the steep slope above the cliffs. It looked ancient, the dark stone weathered and speckled with lichens. One of its towers had collapsed into debris that spilled over the sidewall and across the ground.

"An illusion?" she guessed.

"Yes," he said, "the best cloaking projection I've ever seen. Designed by Fresnel himself, or so Gia likes to boast."

Elsa had no idea who Fresnel was, but she was still impressed with the optical finesse it would take to hide an entire building in plain sight. The castle itself was impressive, too. Leo strode off toward the doors, but Elsa followed more slowly, craning her neck up to look at it.

"It's so *old*," she said in a hushed voice, too awed to want to break the silence.

"Nine hundred years or so. And the Roman ruins it was built on top of easily double that figure."

Elsa gently placed her hand upon the weathered stone. "We don't have anything old in Veldana. Our whole world is new."

"Well, in this world, we've had to endure plenty of history. The castle's believed to be the origin of the Order of Archimedes. The Pisano family made it the first official sanctuary for pazzerellones in Europe, dating back to the Dark Ages, when the Church liked to behead pazzerellones for heresy. It's been more or less unoccupied since the Renaissance, when the Pisanos deemed it safe to relocate to Pisa and built Casa della Pazzia."

"So, being old—does that make them important?" Elsa said, thinking of Porzia's father in Firenze. "The Pisano family, I mean."

Leo shrugged. "It certainly doesn't hurt, but political influence is a complex matter."

Elsa rubbed her forehead, frustrated at how much she didn't understand about the real world. With Veldana, she'd walked every square meter of land, knew every person by name, and read every word of the worldtext—she was the master of her world. But the real world was impossibly large and complex. No matter how hard she studied and how much she learned, she would never fully understand Earth, because no one ever could.

And that thought filled her with a sort of existential terror she worried might never go away.

She felt a sudden, intense longing to go home to her finite, comprehensible world, or even simply to be sure Veldana still existed. What would she do if the fire had destroyed everything she knew?

Leo used another key on the key ring to unlock the bronze front doors. They stepped into a broad entry hall with a cavernous ceiling and a wide, once-majestic stairway that ended in midair, a pile of rubble scattered on the floor below. The air inside was cool and musty. Sunlight filtered in through the distorted glass of four tall windows, and each footstep Elsa took called up swirls of dust to dance in the light. Leo shut the doors behind them with a clang that echoed, and then an eerie silence followed.

Several archways led away from the entry hall, dark and sinister as gaping maws. Through one of them came the sound of uneven footfalls, loud against the stifling silence, and Elsa tensed. A pool of lantern light bobbed and jounced into view, followed by the man holding the lantern.

The man paused in the archway and declared, "Simo!" then hung the kerosene lantern from a wall peg and came toward them. He looked to be in his fifties or sixties, with graying hair and veiny hands clasped together in front of him like an overeager servant. His once-fine clothes were worn to rags. His face seemed stuck in a wide caricature of a smile, and there was something odd about his gait, too, as he loped over to them.

Elsa leaned toward Leo and said in a low voice, "I thought you said it was unoccupied."

"I said 'more or less.' Simo is the castle's caretaker. He's simple, and more than a bit insane, but mostly harmless."

"Now you have me worried about your qualifiers. Define 'mostly harmless.'"

"He used to be a scriptologist, but he accidentally rendered himself textual, and now it's hard to guess whether there's anybody left at home in the old noggin. Isn't that right, Simo?"

"Simo!" said Simo.

Elsa had never before met anyone whose mind had been damaged by scriptology, and the sight of Simo made her a bit queasy. Of course Jumi had warned her of the dangers of scribing names into the worldtext—putting someone in the text would irrevocably link them to the worldbook in a way that eliminated their free will. The worldbook would control them. Jumi's explanation, so technical and logical, had not frightened young Elsa, but it was a different matter entirely to view the results herself.

"He lives here all alone? It seems . . . I don't know, irresponsible to leave him on his own like this."

Leo shrugged. "I assume he manages well enough. The Pisanos saw fit to give him the caretaker job, anyway."

She looked askance at Leo. "My confidence in the efficacy of this plan is not feeling especially bolstered at the moment."

"We'll see what we can do about that," he replied.

Leo led her down a corridor, Simo walking ahead of them to light the kerosene wall sconces.

"Ah, here we are," Leo said, and unlatched a wooden door on his right. Elsa followed him in.

They were in a very old, very dusty mechanist's laboratory. The narrow windows were smudged with soot, as if the former occupant or occupants had been in the habit of lighting things on fire, but not so much in the habit of cleaning up afterward.

"Which is the book restorer?" Elsa asked.

"All of that," Leo said with a sweeping gesture.

The giant machine covered the back wall of the laboratory, taking up the entire width of the room. Several sheets of canvas were draped over it to keep off the dust, and they obscured its true shape in a way that turned it vaguely sinister to Elsa's eye.

Leo said, "So, I suppose you understand now why no one ever tried to move the restoration machine."

"Yes," said Elsa. "Quite."

He began removing the canvas covers, each one pulling free with a visible puff of dust. "It works as a sort of assembly-line process—scanning, trimming, scribing. You set the book in here," he said, giving the leftmost hub of the machine a pat, "where it removes the pages from the binding—"

"Removes the pages!" Elsa said, aghast.

"Yes." Leo shot her an apologetic look. "I'm afraid the machine will have to disassemble the book and rebind it when the restoration is complete."

Elsa did not look upon this development with great enthusiasm. "It's bad enough the poor books were lit on fire. We're trying to preserve whatever subtextual content they still contain, not erase it. Won't taking them apart effectively make them new books when they're reassembled?"

"Mm, right. I'd wondered about that, too. According to Porzia, 'theoretically, no.'"

Elsa pursed her lips. "You and your qualifications again."

"Hey! This time it's Porzia's qualification. I wash my hands of responsibility."

Elsa was not amused. "I do hope you understand that the books will be useless without the subtext." If the worldbooks were effectively reset back to the condition they were in when they were brand-new, any content Montaigne had added—such as objects he'd carried in from Paris, or notes he'd written down while inside—would be lost.

"Only one way to find out for certain if it'll work," Leo said, folding up the last of the canvas and stacking it in a pile. "Shall we fire it up?"

She reluctantly set down the carpetbag near the first machine hub. "Very well."

"Simo!" Leo called, and when the man appeared in the door-way, he asked, "Is there coal in the power room?"

"Simo!" said Simo enthusiastically.

"Get the boilers going, then," said Leo, and Simo hurried off.

A few minutes later there came a rumbling from beneath their feet, the sound pitched so low it neared the boundary of human hearing and was felt more as a vibration behind the sternum. Leo, who had been fiddling with the controls impatiently, grinned and immediately reached for a large electrical switch on the far side.

"We've got power. Here we go." He gripped the wooden handle of the switch in one hand and gave it a firm yank, then snapped it into place in the opposite position. The switch cast a rain of yellow sparks, forcing Leo to jump out of the way, and the res-toration machine hummed to life.

He said, "Ready to start?"

Elsa reached into the carpetbag and selected the worldbook she thought least likely to be important—an older volume she hoped Montaigne wouldn't have used recently. Unimportant as this first worldbook was, if it came through with the subtext intact, that meant they could repair all the others. She took a deep breath, let it out, and handed the book to Leo. "Let's do this."

Leo set the book inside the first machine hub, which neatly

unstitched the binding and spat out a stack of loose sheets. He carefully carried the stack to the next hub. Elsa stood right beside him, their shoulders almost touching, so she could watch as he carefully fed the pages in one at a time.

She was suddenly aware of just how close he was standing, close enough that she could feel the heat of his skin warming the cool air. He turned to face her. There was nothing guarded about the way he looked at her now.

"Elsa, I . . ."

He's going to kiss me, she thought.

But before she could decide how she felt about that, he mumbled, "Never mind," and turned back to the work at hand.

Now Elsa felt as if the last ripe plum of the season had been dangled in front of her and then snatched away. Had she misread his intention? Was she merely projecting her own desires onto him?

Her mother had warned her how denial could enhance desire. *Notice your desire, acknowledge it, then let it go*, Jumi had instructed her that day when they sat together by the creek and watched the water, long before there was a sea to watch instead. *If you want something from someone, that gives them power over you*, her mother had said.

She had never really believed she would need her mother's lessons on the subject of men. Elsa, who loved solitude and independence. How could it be that such feelings had taken seed in her heart? It must be the loss of her mother, the chaos of her abrupt departure from Veldana, leaving her unmoored and defenseless. She would have to be more careful, and squash this weakness.

After that, Leo kept his attention focused on the machine. When all the pages had been fed through, he took the stack of repaired paper to the final hub for rebinding. Elsa hovered anxiously, her confusion over Leo forgotten in the face of more pressing concerns.

The machine finished with a soft hum, and Leo lifted the newly bound worldbook. He held it out to her, his amber eyes alight with hope. "Moment of truth."

Elsa sucked in a nervous breath. The activity of the machine had warmed the book, so it felt almost like a living creature in her arms. She lifted the cover and handled the paper to test for that distinctive new-book feeling, but the pages hummed low and dull with age beneath her fingertips—steady, but not eager and frenetic like the buzz of a new book. Relief flooded through her, and despite herself, Elsa broke into a smile.

"It worked! The subtext should be intact."

Leo returned her smile, his expression like the clouds parting to unveil the full brightness of the sun. "The machine's hungry. Shall we feed it another?"

Elsa pressed the warm leather cover to her cheek, allowing herself a luxurious moment of hope. "Yes," she said. "We shall."

8

WHAT A CHIMAERA THEN IS MAN, WHAT A NOVELTY, WHAT A
MONSTER, WHAT CHAOS, WHAT A SUBJECT OF CONTRADICTION,
WHAT A PRODIGY! JUDGE OF ALL THINGS, YET AN IMBECILE
EARTHWORM; DEPOSITORY OF TRUTH, YET A SEWER OF
UNCERTAINTY AND ERROR; PRIDE AND REFUSE OF THE UNIVERSE.

—*Blaise Pascal*

They made it back across the valley to Corniglia and down the steps to the station in time to catch the afternoon train to La Spezia. By then, the sun hung low over the Ligurian Sea, capping the waves with liquid gold, and a few wisps of cloud glowed unreal shades of pink and orange. Elsa thought she couldn't have scribed a more appealing view if she tried.

Leo hefted the carpetbag of worldbooks, all now restored, into the luggage rack. There had been no time for a thorough check of each book—not if they were going to catch the train—and now Elsa couldn't help fidgeting nervously in her seat, her mind cycling with fresh urgency through the questions that had haunted her for days. Who had taken Jumi? How was Montaigne involved? She felt certain the answers were waiting in the repaired books.

With a puff of smoke, they pulled out of the station. The two towns they passed through, Manarola and Riomaggiore, were even more strange and beautiful when bathed in the slanted afternoon sunlight. Then the train entered the final bend to turn inland, wheels screeching against the tracks and passenger compartments rattling. Elsa put out a hand to steady herself against the shaking. In a moment it was over, but Leo leapt out of his seat, his expression tense.

Elsa stood up to follow him a second later, confused. "What's happening?"

"I don't know," he said, "but something's wrong. We took that corner too fast. Didn't you feel it?"

"It's not as if I have an abundance of experience to compare this ride against," said Elsa defensively, annoyed with herself for missing the significance of the shaky cornering.

"I'm going to check with the engineers," Leo said.

"Then I'm coming with you."

He raised his eyebrows, but didn't argue.

They had been seated in the second passenger car. Leo yanked open the door at the front end and stepped over the gap to the adjacent car, Elsa at his heels. Some part of her yearned to linger there in the gap, the wind whipping at her skirts and the tracks racing by beneath her feet, but Leo was already striding purposefully through the front-most passenger car.

Opening another door, they found themselves face-to-face with the metal wall of the coal car. A narrow ledge wrapped around its side, leading to the locomotive car. Looking at it, Elsa had to wonder if the designer had really intended anyone to traverse the distance while the train was moving. They had to sidestep the whole way, hugging close to the wall of the car, coal dust smearing their clothes as they went.

When they rounded the front corner, the locomotive finally in view, Elsa considered if that hadn't been a spectacularly bad idea. What if one of them had fallen to their death? What if some-one stole the carpetbag while they left it unattended? But a quick survey of the cab's interior revealed that the risk had probably been a necessary one.

One of the engineers was on the floor, struggling to sit, a hand pressed to the back of his profusely bleeding skull. The other engineer was frantically examining the controls, which had all been reduced to melted nubs of metal protruding from the backhead of the engine. The floor was littered with a collection of brass wheels and lever handles that had, presumably, once been attached to the controls.

Leo stepped across the threshold into the cab, and the poor engineer—the one still on his feet—nearly had a heart attack at their sudden, unexpected arrival.

"You can't be in here!" he croaked, clutching at his ribs in a manner suggesting he'd also taken an injury.

"We're here to help," Leo said authoritatively. "What happened?"

"Sabotage. They destroyed the controls!"

The engineer with the head wound added, "Men in black . . . Didn't see their faces. . . ." He attempted to haul himself to his feet but fell back into a sitting position.

"Keep still, my good man. Don't worry, we're pazzerellones." To the better-off one he said, "See to your friend."

The engineers ceded control of the situation, the one without the head wound watching Leo with an expression of unveiled awe. Elsa hadn't realized the mere mention of madness carried with it such gravity and expectation. How odd Earthfolk could be.

"We've got to slow down, or we'll be off the tracks at the next sharp corner. If you're a mechanist too, as I suspect, now would be the time to confess it," Leo said, brisk and matter-of-fact, making Elsa flinch with surprise. He didn't see, though, as he'd already turned his attention to examining the ruined controls. "Looks like there's not much we can do from here, unless we want to try disassembling a steam engine while it's running."

"That sounds like an excellent way to get boiled alive." Elsa hesitated to say more, but now was not the time to play coy with him about her abilities. "What's our alternative? Can we access the running gear while we're in motion?"

"I suppose that depends on your definition of 'access,'" Leo qualified.

She snorted. "Well, let's at least have a look at what we've got to work with."

Elsa turned back to the entryway of the cab, lay down on her stomach, and inched forward until her torso hung down in the narrow space between the rail cars. The corset stays cut into her painfully and made the already awkward position nearly impossible. Leo joined her, his blond hair sticking up as if from an electric shock as he hung upside down.

Trying to ignore the awful corset, Elsa watched the complicated interplay of rods and levers that spun the wheels. After a moment, a picture resolved in her mind of how the pair of pistons must work together. "What a lovely valve gear!"

"Yes, I'm rather fond of this design. Quite clever. Invented by a Belgian pazzerellone, I believe," Leo said with fresh enthusiasm. "Are you ready to admit you have mechanist tendencies?"

Elsa deflected his question with one of her own. "Could we

find one of those valve gears to disassemble later? I'd fancy a closer look."

"I don't see why not. Of course, there is still a runaway train to deal with," he said mildly. "Hurtling toward our untimely demise, and whatnot."

"Oh. Quite right. We should probably do something about that." The adrenaline was making her almost giddy. She thought for a moment. "Release the coupling that connects the locomotive to the passenger cars?"

"It's under too much pressure. The couplings aren't designed to be detached while the train's in motion."

"What do you suggest?"

"Well," Leo said, still hanging upside down beside her, "I can see good news and bad news. The good news is it's an older model and doesn't have air brakes."

"Air brakes?"

"A centralized braking system for the passenger cars that runs on compressed air, powered by the boiler. So the good news is we can disable the boiler without compromising the brakes."

"Ah." From this description, Elsa could foresee the bad news. "No centralized braking means we might need to repair the brakes in each passenger car individually, if they've all been tampered with."

"Precisely."

Elsa shimmied back inside the cab and stood, then waited for Leo to follow. "You get started on the brakes, and I'll shut down the engine," she told him.

Leo's brows drew together, and instead of rushing to get to work, he stood his ground. "First, I want to hear you say it."

"Ugh, we don't have time for this!"

His serious gaze fell on her with all the heat of a spotlight. "You're right—and we don't have time for amateur mistakes, either. Elsa, I need to know if you're up to this."

She huffed her frustration, but she was cornered and she knew it. "Fine, fine! I'm a polymath, all right?"

He nodded, the tense stillness of his body melting into motion. "Very well, then. I'll see if I can pry the flooring up so we can manually engage the locomotive brakes."

"Excellent."

Elsa took her lab book out of her belt pouch, handed it to the uninjured engineer, and instructed him to guard it with his life. That done, she dialed the necessary coordinates and opened a portal to her laboratory.

"Elsa! Where are you going?" Leo, who was kneeling by the place where the brake lever used to be attached, called over his shoulder.

"Well, I'm certainly not going to find the right tools by standing here and wishing hard enough," she said, and stepped through the cold blankness of the portal.

Her laboratory seemed especially solid after the shivering, jouncing motion of the too-fast train. In the main room, the wooden floor panels did not even creak beneath her shoes. Empty worktables stood at the ready beneath a broad, blank window.

She walked through a doorway to her raw materials room, where she kept supplies of every element found on Earth and a few that weren't. Vats of molten metal lined one wall, and chambers of chilled gases lined the other. She had powders and crystals and fluids, all meticulously organized. Whatever item she was looking for would always be positioned closest to the entrance for ease of access.

She pressed her eyelids closed and envisioned the element she needed. When she opened her eyes, there it was, right in front of her: the vat of liquid nitrogen.

Leo pried up the floor panels and scowled at the damage done to the brake controls. Heat radiated off the steel wall of the firebox, where the fuel burned, and the pulse hammering fast in his veins only flushed him further. No tools, no time, and he had to jury-rig a way to force the brakes to engage. Sure, fine, but it wouldn't be enough if they couldn't also cut the drive power. The muffled roar of coal combustion served as a constant, terrible reminder that the train was gaining speed instead of losing it.

Leo heard the soft *whoosh* of a portal reopening. "Finally," he said, without turning away from the brake mechanism. "Where have you been?"

"Get the fire doors open," Elsa's voice said behind him.

Leo looked up. Elsa had a large brass canister strapped to her back, a tube snaking over her shoulder attaching it to the long contraption in her arms, which she held two-handed like a rifle. She was wearing thick leather elbow-length gloves and goggles atop her traveling attire. She looked magnificent—every inch the pazzerellona she was.

"What are you waiting for?" she yelled at him. "Open the firebox!"

Leo shot to his feet. The lever that should have controlled the firebox's small metal doors was broken. He grabbed a detached lever off the floor and jammed it in the crack between the fire doors, prying them apart. Heat blasted out, singeing the fine hairs on the backs of his hands, and he darted aside.

Elsa aimed the contraption into the firebox and sprayed some kind of liquid at the glowing coals. The liquid hissed and boiled, filling the air with a cool, odorless steam. Leo found himself feeling short of breath.

"Crack that window!" Elsa shouted, and as soon as she'd emptied her canister into the firebox, she ran to the opposite side of the cabin to open the other window, too.

Relief washed over Leo, as rejuvenating as the fresh air breezing in through the narrow window frames. "We're not gaining speed anymore, but we still need the brakes," he said, turning away from the window to discover Elsa already kneeling beside the opening in the floor, evaluating how far along he'd gotten.

He moved to help her, but she waved him off. "I've got this one. See if you can get the passenger car brakes working again."

Leo felt an unexpected flash of anger at her perfunctory dismissal, but now wasn't the time to bicker about who was in charge. He made his way back to the passenger cars, checked the pulse of the unconscious porter who was supposed to be operating the brake, and then got down to work. This mechanism wasn't as badly damaged as the locomotive's brake system, which should have been a relief.

Instead, a sort of nauseous shame settled in Leo's gut. The crisis was drawing to a close without him having done much of anything to resolve it.

Elsa's rush of excitement was beginning to drain away, leaving her tired and irritable. The muscles in her shoulder were knotted up from carrying the weight of the nitrogen tank. She was filthy with coal dust and sweat, and wanted more than anything to sink into the cool, clear water of the bathing pool downstream from her village in Veldana. There was no end to the things she'd taken for granted about her home.

It was several minutes more before the train finally ground to a halt and Leo reappeared, sidestepping around the coal car. "Well, that ride was rather more diverting than I'd expected. What was in there, anyway?" he said, gesturing at the now-empty tank.

"Liquid nitrogen." She sighed. "I'm afraid it's probably fractured the casing of the firebox, but—"

"Only an alchemist should have thought of that," Leo interrupted. He ran a hand through his already mussed hair, making it stick out in all directions. "You built a freeze ray. In *two minutes*, using a fake laboratory you carry around in your pocket."

She blinked at him, wondering what the problem was. "Essentially, yes."

"Just because you're a polymath doesn't mean you have to be brilliant at everything," he said crossly. "For heaven's sake, couldn't you stick to just two disciplines?"

Men really were unbelievable—he had no logical cause to be annoyed with her. What did he want her to do, pretend to be dumb? "Next crisis, I'll be sure to invent a creative, lifesaving solution in two minutes while simultaneously stroking your ego so you don't feel overly threatened by a woman doing your job for you."

Leo flushed bright red. "I see we've come full circle, back around to flinging daggers. Perhaps you could send a calling card ahead, so I know to come to the conversation fully armed?"

A small flower of guilt unfurled in Elsa's chest, but she kept the feeling hidden. Impassively, she said, "You should know this by now: I always come to the conversation armed."

The trip back to Pisa was full of stony silences. It bothered

128

Elsa more than she cared to admit. Why should she worry over a petty argument with Leo when she had a pile of repaired books from Montaigne's library to contend with when she got back? She could finally begin the search for her mother in earnest. The wounded pride of some young man of her acquaintance hardly mattered when held up against a sabotaged train and Jumi's abduction.

It was just the awkwardness of being stuck in such close quarters with him that made Leo seem like the most important thing in the world. He had a frown line between his brows, and Elsa wanted desperately to ask him about his theories on who had sabotaged the train. Were they connected to Jumi's abductors? Were they trying to stop her from finding her mother? But it didn't make sense to try to kill her now, when they'd had ample opportunity in the cottage after the knockout gas put her to sleep.

Elsa kept her questions inside, and so they went unanswered.

The Italian transportation system's procedures for dealing with broken-down trains left something to be desired, so they were lucky to get a cab ride back to La Spezia in time to catch the last train departing for Pisa. More than once, Elsa weighed the merits of using the doorbook to port directly back to Casa della Pazzia, but she decided not to antagonize Leo with yet another invention. By the time they rolled into the Pisa station, it was well past dark.

Leo silently helped her with the carpetbag full of books, and they stepped out onto the dimly lit platform. The night had turned cool, and aside from the other passengers departing from the train from La Spezia, the station looked deserted.

Elsa opened her mouth to apologize, but all that came out was, "Do you think we'll be able to catch a hansom cab at this hour?"

Leo snorted. "Maybe in Paris. I hope your feet aren't tired yet, because it's a long walk."

He still held the carpetbag, so as a courtesy she declined to point out that she was accustomed to walking all day through the wild terrain of Veldana.

"You ought to be able to summon the spider hansom to you," Elsa mused.

"Well, I can't," Leo snapped.

She sighed. She hadn't meant it as a criticism. "I know. I simply meant it was theoretically possible, if it can navigate back to Casa della Pazzia on its own. An idle thought, that's all."

"Oh, yes—I'll get right on it," he said sarcastically. "Perfecting the hansom is, clearly, a top priority."

Elsa held her tongue and walked ahead.

Leo pushed out a noisy breath of frustration. "It's just that we don't even know what happened back there on the train. We have bigger concerns at the moment."

They arrived at Casa della Pazzia long minutes later, both of them exhausted. Porzia appeared in the entry hall as soon as they were through the front doors; she took one look at them and clicked her tongue against her teeth disapprovingly.

"You're late. And filthy. What did you do, walk all the way back from La Spezia? Casa, please prepare baths for the both of them."

"That won't be necessary," Elsa said, grabbing the carpetbag out of Leo's hand. "I need to check the worldbooks."

"You look exhausted," Porzia replied, hands on hips, a pose that made her look every inch the daughter of Signora Pisano. "We'll all need our wits about us to explore the worldbooks. It isn't the sort of thing one should do in the middle of the night after a full day of traveling."

Elsa frowned. "I'm fine. It's not your concern."

Porzia put an arm around her shoulders and guided her up the stairs. "You won't do your mother any good if you get trapped in a broken world, or disintegrated in a patch of Edgemist, or eaten by a scribed creature."

Without saying a single word, Leo stalked past them, taking the stairs two at a time.

As soon as Leo was out of earshot, Porzia leaned toward Elsa confidentially. "He's in quite a state. What's wrong with him?"

Dryly, Elsa replied, "I've been compiling a list. Would you care to see?"

Porzia rolled her eyes. "I meant what happened? Did he have some trouble getting the restoration machine working?"

"No, that part went smoothly. But the train back from Cinque Terre was sabotaged, and that *was* troublesome."

"Sabotaged!" Porzia stopped dead in her tracks and grabbed Elsa by the shoulders. "This is important, Elsa: Did Leo think it was a coincidence, or was the saboteur targeting you specifically?"

Elsa shrugged off the other girl's grip. "I don't know, he didn't mention any theories either way."

"Hmm." Porzia went quiet, seemingly lost in thought as they went down the hall. But when they reached Elsa's rooms, she bent down and deftly pulled the carpetbag out of Elsa's grasp.

"Hey!" Elsa protested, too surprised to keep ahold of the worldbooks. "What are you doing?"

"Confiscating these until you're well rested. Reckless mistakes get people killed, and I have a house full of orphans to prove it."

"I *need* those books—there could be a clue to my mother's whereabouts in one of them."

Porzia tilted her chin down and gave Elsa a maternal glare. "Sleep first."

"I can't believe you!" Elsa protested, but Porzia was already striding down the corridor toward her own rooms, taking the stolen carpetbag of books with her.

"Good night, Elsa," she called over her shoulder.

Elsa heaved a frustrated sigh, planted her hands on her hips, and stood there in the hallway debating the merits of chasing after Porzia for a confrontation. Porzia had acted out of concern, and whether or not Elsa liked to admit it, investigating the contents of the worldbooks in her current state of exhaustion *could* be dangerous.

Porzia was certainly right about one thing: her clothes were filthy—coated in a layer of coal dust, and speckled with solder and lubricant from the process of constructing the freeze ray. Elsa went down the hall to the bathroom, struggled out of the dress, and grudgingly accepted the bath Casa had prepared for her. Back in her rooms, she had to pull all the covers off the bed again (one of the house-bots kept sneaking in to make the bed) so she could curl up on the floor.

She would investigate the worldbooks tomorrow, she promised herself. The very first thing tomorrow, but for now, she had no choice but to rest.

By the time Leo found himself alone in his room, the fire of jealousy in his chest had dwindled somewhat but not yet been extinguished. His elder brother, Aris, had been a polymath, and his younger brother, Pasca, had given every indication that he would follow in Aris's footsteps; everyone had expected Leo to display the same breadth of skill, but he never developed a feel for anything but mechanics.

Only Rosalinda made him feel talented instead of stupid. She was the boys' fencing instructor, and fencing was the one thing Leo did well that his brothers did not. She pushed his training harder than she did with Aris or Pasca, and despite her dour demeanor she would sometimes smile a little just for Leo. But even Rosalinda's hard-earned praise could not erase that deep-seated sense of his father's disappointment.

Leo had spent so much of his childhood wishing desperately for a polymath's talents, and here Elsa was, wielding those talents as if they were as easy as breathing.

Shame followed quickly on the heels of his jealousy. In all other respects, Elsa's position was hardly enviable. He knew it was not especially mature of him to resent her for her competence—competence that had saved his life. But that was part of the problem, wasn't it? He wanted very much to be the one doing the saving.

Leo let himself out onto his balcony; he should have already had his fill of night air after the long walk from the train station, but the confines of his bedroom made him feel restless. Sleep, he suspected, would be a hopeless cause. Instead, he leaned against the wrought-iron railing and threw his head back to watch the stars.

The door unlatched behind him, and he knew it must be Faraz, because anyone else would have knocked first. They'd been friends a long time and knew which liberties were safe to take with each other. Footsteps crossed the bedroom, and Faraz appeared at the balcony railing beside him.

"Porzia said you were back."

"Did she." It was a clear night, and with the lights extinguished in the cloister garden below, the stars were piercingly bright.

Faraz draped one arm over the railing. "She also mentioned you had some . . . ah, *problems* with the train."

Leo grunted a reluctant confirmation.

"Coincidental," he pressed, "or do you think the sabotage was meant for you and Elsa?"

Leo finally looked down from the sky and met his friend's eyes. "You know I don't believe in coincidences."

"Which means either Casa della Pazzia, or the train stations, or the Pisano castle is being watched. Or any combination of the three." Faraz paused. "We should report this to the Order."

"I hardly think they'd allow us to pursue the search for Elsa's mother if they found out we're in danger. No, we have to keep this to ourselves."

Faraz sighed. "Well, at least Porzia can't blame me for not trying to knock some sense into you."

"Porzia should learn to mind her own business, and so should you," Leo snapped.

Faraz blinked at him, unfazed by his moods. "Are you entirely well?"

"No, but I'll feel a lot better when we get Elsa's mother back. I don't know whose political game we're playing in, but I am so very tired of the collateral."

"You think it's political?"

Leo snorted. "Everything's political." If his father had taught him anything, it was this.

Somehow, even though he thought he didn't want to talk about it, Leo found himself giving in to Faraz's questions and relating the details of what had happened. When he set his mind to it, Faraz could be as gently unopposable as the tides wearing away at a rocky coastline—there was nothing to resist, just water sliding out of reach. Leo described the sabotage and told him about Elsa's ingenious solution, admitting his own failure in the process.

When the story was done, Faraz frowned thoughtfully. "Elsa's no pawn in the political game, Leo. She's the goddamned queen. Whoever took her mother may have seen her as nothing more than a loose end, but leaving her behind in Veldana was a serious miscalculation on their part. These people are going to figure out who stopped the train—there were witnesses, after all—and when they do, they'll come after her. Whatever advantage we might have had in being young and unworthy of notice, we've lost it now."

Leo rubbed his eyes with the heels of his palms, frustrated. "I *know*. You think I don't know that?"

If only he'd come up with a solution first, her identity as a brilliant polymath would be safe. Why hadn't he just told her to wait in the passenger car, like he should have? Or at least sent the engineers away so there would be no witnesses. Stupid, stupid.

Faraz put a hand on his shoulder and gave him a reassuring squeeze. "Try to get some rest. I suspect we won't have much chance for it after tonight."

9

Elsa woke to the sensation of butterflies in her stomach. With the worldbooks practically calling to her from across the house, she couldn't even consider trying to eat anything. She hastily got herself ready, grabbed the stability glove from the commode in her sitting room, and ran down the stairs.

Porzia was waiting in the library, seated at one of the reading tables and sipping a cappuccino out of a broad-rimmed china cup. The carpetbag rested on the table at her elbow, looking to Elsa's eyes rather like an inanimate hostage. Elsa rushed over, opened the bag, and started laying out all the worldbooks on the table.

Porzia regarded her with raised-eyebrow amusement. "Rested then, are we?"

Elsa spared a moment to glower, then finished unpacking the books.

Faraz and Leo arrived with one of the younger children in tow. He was a scrawny lad with wide, dark eyes and a quick smile; Elsa was fairly sure this was the one named Burak.

Leo paused in the doorway and said to the boy, "This is very important: don't let anyone inside. We have secret business to do for the Order, and we're not to be disturbed."

"Right," Burak said. He glanced curiously inside, but did not press Leo for details. A grin flashed across his face. "If all of you die in there and leave me out here guarding your corpses indefinitely, I'll be rather put out."

Leo grinned back and clapped him on the shoulder. "If that happens, I'm afraid I'll be past the point of feeling your ire."

When the doors were shut, Burak on the far side of them, Porzia gave Leo a dry look. "I didn't realize you required a private guard, Mr. Trovatelli."

Leo sauntered over to their table, back to his usual insouciant self. If he was still mad about yesterday, Elsa could see no outward hint of it. He said, "If all four of us are going to be inside the books, don't you think it's wise to keep curious children from wandering in and playing with them?"

Porzia sniffed, granting him nothing. "In any case, shall we get started with the least damaged world?"

She reached out a hand for the book, but Elsa snatched it up, irked by the other girl's bossiness. Flipping through the pages, she tested the feel of the paper beneath her fingertips. The gentle hum felt the same as yesterday: old and comfortable, settled, well-developed. A finished worldtext satisfied with its contents.

"They feel successfully repaired to me. But," she grudgingly admitted, "we do have to start somewhere."

The least-damaged world would also be the least risky to

enter. This world didn't seem a likely candidate for containing Montaigne's private notes, but Elsa could evaluate its structural integrity. If the book repair process had left no residual damage here, it would probably be safe to proceed with searching the other worlds.

It cost her an ounce of pride, but Elsa made herself hand the book to Porzia, letting the other girl set the coordinates into a portal device. Porzia's device was much newer and fancier than Elsa's, with decorative silverwork set into the brass backing.

"Ready, everyone?" Porzia paused to glance up at them, nervous determination in her eyes. Then she flipped the final switch. "Here we go."

The portal yawned open in the air before them. Elsa slid her hand into the stability glove, activated it, and stuck her arm into the portal up to the shoulder. She wasn't entirely certain the glove would be able to detect an unstable world through the portal, but it seemed like a reasonable precaution. She drew her arm back out again and checked the indicator light, which had turned neither red nor green but remained dark instead. Inconclusive.

Porzia, one eyebrow raised, leaned over to view the results for herself. "Well, your arm didn't fall off. That's a good sign."

"I suppose," Elsa said. "Shall we risk it?"

Porzia surprised Elsa by linking arms with her. She'd expected Porzia to be the voice of caution and didn't know where the other girl's brash confidence came from. Together they stepped through into the frigid black nothingness, the boys right behind them, and out the other side.

Elsa craned her neck to take in their new surroundings. They stood on a ledge overlooking a dark, mist-shrouded abyss. A cliff face rose above them, decorated with a network of ledges, wooden ladders, and dark cave openings. Artificial terraces supported beds of tilled earth, but nothing grew in them. The wind whistled low and eerie, playing the cave-pocked cliffside like a flute.

Elsa held her arm out and splayed her gloved fingers, hoping to detect any potential instabilities. After a moment, the light turned green. For whatever that was worth. "It should be safe to move around a bit," she said.

Leo leaned out to look over the edge and whistled. "Long way down."

"It's Edgemist," said Elsa, grabbing the back of his waistcoat to pull him away from the edge. "Concealed behind a bit of scribed fog for the aesthetics. If you fell, you'd never hit the ground—you'd simply cease to exist. So try not to fall, will you?"

"You make a gentle death sound so ominous," Faraz said lightly, while Leo tugged at his waistcoat to straighten it. He turned his tawny eyes on her with an inscrutable look, and Elsa turned away, feeling heat rise in her cheeks.

"It's all nicely done," said Porzia appreciatively, "but I can't say I understand what it's for."

Relieved to have something else to focus her attention on, Elsa said, "Montaigne was obsessed with the idea of scribing subtextual humans as an emergent property of a worldbook. This must be one of his early attempts."

Faraz looked around, interested. "So why didn't it work?"

"Not enough arable land, and nothing to hunt. It was obviously designed by someone who'd never needed to grow his own food," she said, not trying to hide her scorn.

Leo shook the nearest ladder to check for structural stability and then started climbing. "We should take a look around anyway."

Up the ladder, they spread out, each taking a different cave to examine. Elsa's was a single room outfitted as if a person might call it home. A fire pit just inside the entrance, where the smoke would be carried away by the breeze instead of pooling inside the cave. A rough woven blanket laid out along one wall. A neatly arranged collection of clay bowls and pots in a variety of sizes. A broad, flat stone for grinding grain into meal.

The emptiness of the world began to seep into Elsa's bones, and she shivered. It felt far worse than any abandoned place— this was not simply a place where people used to be and no longer were. This was a place where people never had been and never would be, and that pervasive absence of life seemed to emanate from the very walls.

"We should go," she called to the others.

Leo clattered down a ladder to her ledge, a manic glint in his eye. "So soon? What fun is that?"

Elsa folded her arms. "This world is a failed attempt. Montaigne wouldn't have left anything important here."

Faraz edged slowly over a narrow strip of ledge to join them in front of Elsa's cave just as Porzia made her way there as well. She held up her portal device and said, "Anyone care for a ride? I'm stepping back. This is lovely and everything, but we need to stay on task."

Against the rock wall of the cliffside, a portal irised open, as if an especially dark cave entrance were suddenly appearing before them. Watching it widen, Elsa felt a pang of regret that her mother had never altered the Veldanese portal dynamics. The way Montaigne had written her world, portals could only be opened at the Edgemist; perhaps if Veldana had been as flexible as this world, with portals opening any old place, Elsa could have caught up with Jumi's abductors that first day.

Elsa shook off the feeling. Self-pity and what-ifs would not save her mother. She had to stay focused, objective, unsentimental— this was the only way to help Jumi.

They all stepped through the nothing-moment of the portal back into the comfortable warmth of the library. Gathering around the table, they looked at the array of worldbook candidates.

Porzia chewed her lip. "Which one next, do you think?"

Elsa fished around in the pile. "Montaigne had an office scribed somewhere . . . that's probably our best chance. Now which one was that?"

She picked up an older book to check it, but as soon as she cracked the cover open, she remembered it was the world scribed in an alphabet she didn't recognize. This was the book she'd found lying on the floor beside Montaigne's lifeless hand. Without the restoration machine, she never would have been able to repair this one, at least not until she'd mastered the language.

"Where did you get this?" Faraz suddenly exclaimed, grabbing the volume out of Elsa's hands. "Montaigne had this in his library?"

Elsa blinked. "Yes. Actually, he was holding it when he died. What's wrong?"

He opened the book, intent on examining it. "The cover's newer—it's been rebound—but look at this paper, this ink. Don't you understand? This is an original Jabir ibn Hayyan scribed world!"

"Who?" said Elsa, baffled.

Faraz, at a loss for words, cast a disbelieving look at Leo.

"A famous eighth-century polymath from Persia," Leo explained. "He revolutionized the science of alchemy. He also redesigned all the materials used in scriptology, which, I understand, provided the basis for modern scriptological technique."

Porzia stepped closer to take a look. "If it was important to this Montaigne fellow, I'd say it's worth taking a look inside."

"We must be careful," Faraz said. "Jabir was notorious for his use of steganography in all his treatises. There's no telling what we might be walking into." Somehow, though, the excitement in his tone failed to convey a sense of warning.

Elsa had heard of steganography, the practice of hiding coded messages in written works, but she had never seen it in a world-text before.

"I'm afraid we'll have to go in blind or not at all," said Porzia. Then she raised her eyebrows at Elsa. "Unless you can read classical Arabic text?"

Elsa shook her head. "It would take me a while to learn, especially if the scriptologist was prone to using idiosyncratic syntax."

"Blind it is, then!" Leo declared, grinning. He rubbed his palms together as if he were expecting to receive a treat.

Porzia rolled her eyes. "You could at least pretend to be concerned for our collective safety."

"What's the worst that could happen?"

"Anything really," said Elsa. "The walls might eat us. Or perhaps the atmosphere's pure sulfur tetrafluoride and the acid dissolves our lungs. Or it's a world where fluids can't exist, so our blood instantly freezes in our veins."

Everyone stared at her. Leo's mouth hung slightly open.

"What? I'm not saying we shouldn't go. I can't imagine why

anyone would *want* to scribe a world like that—it's just possible, is all."

Very delicately, Faraz set the book back on the table. "Um, maybe this isn't such a brilliant idea. . . ."

Leo narrowed his eyes at Elsa. "Melting lungs, you say?"

"I really think it's very unlikely," she said, flipping open the book cover to look for the coordinates in the front. "Faraz, can you tell me which of these symbols are numbers?"

Faraz folded his arms. "I'm becoming increasingly certain this is one of those ideas normal people would know not to follow through on. You know, the kind that gets pazzerellones killed before their time."

Elsa was beginning to regret she'd said anything; caution could only impede the search for her mother. "Well I'm going. We'll never get through this stack of worldbooks if we stand around wringing our hands all day. So read off the coordinates for me, will you?"

With a sigh, Faraz reluctantly found the settings for the portal device and read them aloud. In the end, when the black oval irised open, they all decided to go through.

Elsa stepped through nothing and emerged into a world with light, air, time, and solid ground beneath her feet. So far so good. She took a deep breath, just to be sure, and looked around.

They were in a large square room with a domed ceiling. An arched doorway was set into the center of each wall, all of them leading to darkened alcoves. Everything was constructed of seamless stone, as if it had been hollowed out from a single piece of rock.

The place felt *old*. It wasn't just the spare lines of the cut-stone architecture—such a contrast with the intricate, fine detail of classical Italian design—or the thick swirls of dust settled on the floor. No, Jabir had imbued his creation with that indefinable something else: essence, or atmosphere, Elsa didn't know what to call it. Whatever the effect was, it took her breath away.

"The Lost Oracle," Faraz said. "I can't believe it's real. I can't believe *we have it*."

Elsa gave Faraz a look, wondering if he was going to start jumping up and down with joy. What was it with Earth people and their history? The obsession with the past held no appeal for her—the present was all that mattered. She hardly needed historical context to appreciate the talent required to create such a fine world as this.

It was Porzia who asked, "Lost Oracle?"

"It's said Jabir had a fascination with the oracles of ancient Greece, so he scribed a world with the property of divination," Faraz explained. "In his treatises, he describes it as a temple with four alcoves representing the four directions, but the book itself has been missing for a couple centuries."

Elsa tapped a finger against her lips thoughtfully. "Well, that explains why Montaigne would have acquired it. The Oracle isn't a person, but if it's intelligent and aware, it would be something of a precursor to scribed humans. He must have studied it when he was working on Veldana."

"But is it?" mused Porzia. "Intelligent and aware, I mean. It seems a bit . . . like an empty room."

Leo waved his arms in the air and shouted, "Hello?" The sound echoed. He turned to Faraz. "So how do we turn it on, or wake it up, or whatever you want to call it?"

"I can't say for sure. I'd guess you have to step into one of the alcoves to receive a prophecy."

"There's one way to find out," Elsa said with a shrug, then stepped toward one of the alcoves.

"Wait," Faraz hissed, his hand darting out to grab her arm. "You shouldn't. What if the Oracle's functional?"

Elsa paused, taken aback. "You think it can actually tell the future?"

"It's a Jabir ibn Hayyan—anything's possible," said Faraz. "What if the Oracle has the ability to dole out perfectly accurate self-fulfilling prophecies? What if accessing the Oracle changes the real world to fit its predictions?"

"That *would* be dangerous," Elsa conceded as she gently pulled away from Faraz's grasp.

"Sounds impossible to me," said Porzia. "How could a scribed book affect the real world?"

Elsa said, "There is one obvious solution—I'll simply avoid asking about the future. Facts about the present only, no predictions. Just in case."

She walked toward one of the doorways, and as she moved closer, the dark alcove began to brighten. She stepped inside, expecting the light to have a source, but there were no sconces or lamps, only a directionless ambient glow. The effect was surreal, and she couldn't help but wonder how Jabir had succeeded in so elegantly twisting the laws of physics. He'd been a master of his craft, no doubt about that.

On the wall there was a single raised carving of a stylized hand, fingers pointing down, with a large eye in the center of the palm. The hand seemed to be shaped from the same stone as the wall, though the eye looked like colored glass, with a black pupil and deep-blue iris surrounded by white.

Elsa leaned in to get a closer look. The eye *moved*, focusing on her as if it were alive, and she jerked away from it.

"You have questions, young mortal," said a deep, resonant voice. The voice, like the light, seemed to come from everywhere and nowhere at once.

Elsa hesitated and glanced back at everyone else behind her, several meters outside the alcove. They wouldn't be able to hear. She cleared her throat. "Where is my mother?"

"She is with her abductor."

"Okay . . ." Elsa rested her hands on her hips, trying to think of a way to elicit a more helpful response. "So then who is this abductor?"

"A brilliant man—a man intent on accomplishing great and terrible deeds. A man who crushes hindrances like cockroaches beneath his boot heel. If you pursue him, you will lose something precious to you."

"No predictions!" Elsa snapped. "I only want to know about events that have already come to pass. Why did he take my mother?"

"Because she can scribe the book," said the Oracle.

"The book? A specific worldbook?" Elsa thought of the one that had gone missing from the cottage along with Jumi.

The Oracle said, "The book that resides with the man who betrayed her."

"Betrayed her—you mean to say my mother knew one of the men responsible?"

The Oracle paused. "I said precisely what I meant to say."

"Yes, of course," said Elsa impatiently. "But did she know one of them?"

146

"Certain events would not have been possible were it not for the betrayal committed by a man she knew."

Elsa glowered at the Oracle's eye. "You aren't overly fond of specifics, are you?"

"The details are as grains of sand. One cannot perceive the desert if each grain must first be weighed and measured. . . ."

The voice trailed off and the glass eye's focus shifted to something behind her. Elsa turned to see Faraz standing uncertainly in the doorway to the alcove.

"How goes it?" he said, torn between caution and reverence.

Faraz had aimed the question at Elsa, but the Oracle answered for her. "The world has entered a time of flux. Much depends on the choices you make."

Faraz stepped closer, drawn in by a fascination that seemed to Elsa almost magnetic in nature. " 'Much'? What does that mean?"

"I wouldn't—" Elsa warned, but the Oracle cut her off.

"I will tell you what I see, son of Allah," said the Oracle. "The waters writhe with eldritch horrors. A plume of ash ten thousand meters high blocks out the sun."

Elsa shivered. The Oracle's voice gave her a sensation like insects crawling down her spine. She had no idea what *son of Allah* meant, but Faraz's eyes went wide and the color seemed to drain from his face as he listened to the prediction.

She grabbed his arm. "Don't say another word."

He nodded mutely. They both stood, transfixed.

You will lose something precious. She'd already lost Jumi and Veldana; what else could she possibly lose? Alek, perhaps, who was the closest thing she and Jumi had to family, or maybe something more abstract, like her freedom. Or it meant those precious things—her mother, her world—weren't truly lost yet, but could be.

"Elsa?" Faraz prompted.

She shook herself. "Yes, we should go. But . . . let's not mention this to Leo and Porzia, all right?"

He nodded, half-reluctant and half-relieved. "No use making them worry."

They stepped away from the Oracle's eye, moving back toward the others. "We can't even be sure the Oracle truly has prophetic abilities," Elsa said, trying to convince herself as much as Faraz.

"Right," he agreed. "Nothing to be done about it now, in any case."

In truth he seemed as shaken as she herself felt, and sharing the prophecies would solidify her fears into something too real to be ignored. Better to pretend it had never happened and forge onward.

She couldn't afford to hesitate when Jumi's life depended on her.

10

They returned once again to the library in Casa della Pazzia, and this time Elsa forbade them any distractions. They would go to the office worldbook next, where Montaigne presumably had kept his notes and journals and correspondence. It seemed an awfully obvious place to hide something as important as evidence of his connection with Jumi's abductors, but for the sake of thoroughness, they would need to eliminate it.

Elsa found the book for the office and dialed the coordinates on her portal device, and they all stepped through. But instead of an office, they landed in an empty foyer facing three closed doors.

Porzia rested a hand on her hip and said, "Huh."

Faraz said, "So are we supposed to pick a door?"

"Montaigne did love puzzles," Elsa said. "Couldn't resist the opportunity to show off how clever he was." This much she remembered from her limited interactions with him as a child. It seemed a good sign that he'd protected the entrance to his office with a puzzle; they might find something important in there, after all.

She stepped closer to give the three doors a proper examination. The door on the left was flanked by columns, and the stone cornice above had leaves carved into it. The middle door's frame had a rounded arch with a prominent keystone. The door on the right bore a circular stained-glass window and was set into a pointed-arch frame.

"Greek, Roman, Gothic," Porzia declared, pointing at them from left to right.

The names didn't mean much to Elsa. "So?"

Porzia grinned. "France is known for its Gothic architecture."

Leo strode past them, declaring, "Door on the right it is, then." He pushed it open and crossed the threshold.

Elsa felt a flash of irritation at his impulsiveness. She would have preferred to go first with her stability glove at the ready, but she followed Leo through without mishap, Porzia and Faraz right behind her.

For once Leo's impulse to action didn't lead them all into danger. On the other side of the door was a replica of Montaigne's real-world study, so accurate that Elsa might have thought she was back in Paris if she hadn't seen the original burned to ashes. A large writing desk sat in a position of prominence in front of two tall windows. To her left stood a pair of bookcases, and to her right was a standing case displaying an assortment of gadgets and trinkets behind glass doors. A grandfather clock ticked quietly in the corner, and Montaigne had even scribed a copy of the Pascaline mechanical calculator—this one flawless, unlike the original version Elsa had rescued from the wreckage.

Disappointed, Elsa said, "For a genius, Montaigne wasn't exactly overflowing with imagination. This is exactly like his study in Paris. What sort of person duplicates a room they already own in another world without any improvements?"

She'd meant the question rhetorically, but Faraz answered, "Someone who likes routine and familiarity when he works. Someone who doesn't trust that his real-life study is safe from prying eyes."

Elsa sighed. "At least there are plenty of papers to look through—I wasn't sure he was the type to save his correspondence. I'll start with the desk." Leo had already begun opening cupboards and drawers to investigate, so she just said, "Porzia, do you want to take the bookcase?"

It felt strange to sit in the familiar plushness of Montaigne's leather-upholstered desk chair when she knew the original one was, in fact, reduced to ashes. She sorted through the loose papers scribbled with notes, then checked all the books on the desk. A few were scriptological references, but two of them appeared to be journals. One was older and filled to the very last page, the other more recent with a fair number of blank pages left in the back. Elsa opened the more recent journal and began to read.

Some time later, Porzia threw a book down on the floor, startling everyone. "Ugh! This is pointless. I've done two shelves, and all I've learned is Montaigne had a fondness for the trees and shrubs of southern Europe."

"Not much here, either," said Elsa, flipping to the next page as she scanned the journal. "He goes on at length about someone named Garibaldi, who's obsessed with uniting the four states of Italy. Does that mean anything to anyone?" Anxiety roiled in her gut, and the longer she sat there, the more poignantly she felt the need to jump up and do something, *anything*, to find her mother.

"Garibaldi?" Porzia came around to read over her shoulder. "He must mean Giuseppe Garibaldi, the general. But he died in 1860." To Elsa, she explained, "Garibaldi was a highly respected general for our king—the Sardinian king—and a proponent of Italian unification. He sailed to Sicilia to support a popular uprising against the Kingdom of Two Sicilies, but his ships were set afire by Archimedes mirrors before they could land in Marsala."

"Archimedes mirrors?" Elsa asked.

"Giant convex mirrors designed to reflect and focus sunlight. They were first conceived of by Archimedes—the same man for whom the Order is named—though they weren't actually built until this century."

"So . . . a pazzerellone built them. For the Sicilian government. To use as a weapon." Elsa was beginning to understand why the Order worked so hard to keep pazzerellones out of politics. She had never considered using her talents for destruction instead of creation, and the thought chilled her.

"I think we can rule out Garibaldi as a suspect," Faraz said dryly, "on account of immolation at sea."

Elsa scowled. "So we have nothing?"

Porzia reached over her to flip the page. "What if this isn't so much about the man as the ideology? Maybe Montaigne got involved with the unification movement somehow, and those people were the ones who killed him and abducted Jumi. The Carbonari, perhaps?"

Leo, who was crouched in front of the bottom shelf of the display case, stood suddenly. "The Carbonari aren't terrorists. They don't kidnap and murder pazzerellones."

Porzia cast him a skeptical look. "Whatever you may like to believe, violence is a tool in their kit."

"The Carbonari have an understanding with the Order of Archimedes," he insisted. "Each group stays out of the other's way. They can't have been involved—it would violate their agreement."

Elsa tilted her head back, exasperated. "Would anyone care to explain who the Carbonari are?"

"A secret society of revolutionaries." At this Porzia snorted, but Leo persistently added, "They're dedicated to achieving Italian unification and promoting the interests of the people."

Elsa looked at him sharply, suspicious of the ease with which he rattled off the explanation. She knew that was how she sounded when she was parroting some shred of wisdom taught to her by Jumi. Did Leo have some personal connection to these Carbonari? But all she said was "I see."

Porzia said, "The Kingdom of the Two Sicilies would call the Carbonari terrorists."

"A king's 'terrorist' is the common man's freedom fighter," Leo argued. "The Carbonari fight to give Italians the power to rule themselves—not the French or the Austrians or the Church."

Elsa spoke up. "I thought the Order eschews politics. Why would they have any kind of agreement with a bunch of political radicals?"

In unison, Porzia and Leo said, "Nobody likes the Papal States."

Elsa blinked, still confused, so Faraz explained, "The Catholic Church runs the government of Roma and the surrounding regions, called the Papal States. They have a nasty history of beheading pazzerellones for so-called heresy. To them our madness is unnatural."

Leo folded his arms. "And if the Order would fight *with* the Carbonari, instead of merely stepping out of their way, we could put an end to the rule of anti-intellectual tyrants once and for all and rule *ourselves*."

Porzia rolled her eyes in a fashion that suggested this was a well-worn argument. "And then we can spend the rest of our lives fighting wars instead of actually doing science."

Faraz held up his hands in a conciliatory gesture before Leo could respond. "We don't even know yet if the Carbonari are involved."

"Hold on," said Elsa. She had flipped ahead to a later journal entry. "Listen to this: 'I am unsure it is wise to give Garibaldi what he wants.'"

Leo leaned in. "Does it say what he wants?"

Elsa read on for a bit, then reported, "No, Montaigne keeps it fairly vague. But the entry is dated March 3, 1891—that's not even two months past!"

Porzia said, "The timing is suspicious." She thought for a moment, then planted her hands on her hips and took on a commanding tone eerily similar to Signora Pisano's. "Faraz, could you send a wireless to the Order's archives department, asking if there are any living Garibaldis registered with the Order? It's a risk contacting them, but we need their information, so make up an excuse—tell them we've found a lost book or something inscribed with the name Garibaldi."

"Right," said Faraz.

"I'll work through Casa's library and see what I can dig up on

Montaigne, the Carbonari, and anyone named Garibaldi. Elsa, why don't you bring Montaigne's journals back with us and see if we've missed any important details."

Elsa's first instinct was to snap at Porzia's bossiness, but she clamped down on that urge. She didn't understand this world, or its politics, or how best to acquire information on a potential abductor. So if letting Porzia take charge was the price she had to pay to find her mother, she would pay it and be grateful.

"What, no task for me?" said Leo dryly.

Porzia raised her eyebrows at him. "When we need something skewered with a rapier, I'll let you know."

Porzia picked up the portal device and opened the way back to the library. Elsa quickly stacked up the journals and loose papers, her heart hammering against her ribs. At last she had a direction in which to investigate. That infuriatingly ambiguous Oracle may have refused to provide her with any specifics, but now she had a concrete detail to sink her claws into. Now she had a name: Garibaldi. She hoped that would be enough.

Leo leaned in the doorway of the tiny room at the top of the house where the wireless transmitter lived. It was more of a closet, really, with a single wooden chair and a desk holding the teleprinter input—two rows of little piano keys with the alphabet written across them. Behind that was the large cylinder of the induction coil attached to the spark-gap transmitter, with wires snaking up the wall and through the ceiling to the antenna on the roof.

Faraz sat at the desk typing the message, each depressed key triggering a staccato electrical *bzzz bz-bzzz*. Music to Leo's ears.

Jokingly he said, "Hold on, shouldn't the mechanist be the one operating the wireless?"

"It's not as if Porzia asked me to *build* a Hertzian machine," Faraz said, pausing as he tapped out the message. "Besides, I'm faster at typing and you know it."

"Hmph. I admit nothing." Leo folded his arms but failed to muster even a little annoyance at Faraz, knowing from experience how impossible it was to stay vexed at him for any length of time. And anyway, Faraz actually was the faster typist.

"Done," Faraz said, pressing the last key and leaning back to wait dutifully for a reply. "I told them we found a book marked 'property of Garibaldi' and wondered who to return it to."

Leo said, "You know, you needn't do everything Porzia tells you to."

"This is her house, Leo, or it will be soon enough." Faraz threw him an arch look. "At least one of us ought to be a courteous guest, don't you think?"

Leo suppressed a grin. "I think no such thing."

"Obviously not." Faraz raised his eyes to the heavens in a long-suffering expression, but a smile pulled at the corners of his lips. "Frankly, it's baffling Gia considers you a candidate for inheriting Casa, given how much damage you cause on a regular basis."

Leo made a face. "Porzia's not going to marry me—I'm practically her brother."

"A fact universally understood by everyone except Gia." Faraz flashed a teasing grin. "She must really be desperate."

"Thanks a lot." Leo gave Faraz's shoulder a good-natured shove.

Together they waited. Anxiety started to set in, and Leo

struggled not to fidget. Faraz stared at the roll of ticker tape on which the reply would be printed, but no reply came.

"Huh," said Leo, trying to hide his unease. "I guess the Order's too busy to bother checking their receiver."

"They're probably waiting for some poor, hapless apprentice to run up the stairs and fetch the message for them," Faraz replied, but there was a crease between his brows that belied the joking ease of his tone.

"Well, if they're not in a sharing mood, I suppose we'll just have to get the information some other way," Leo said. "How are your robbery skills? Do you think we could break into the archives without getting shot?"

Faraz regarded him with a healthy dose of side-eye. "Proving your worth to Elsa won't mean much if you get yourself killed in the attempt."

Leo felt his best friend's words landing in him like an arrow to the chest. Leo did not care to acknowledge the part of himself that craved approval.

He composed his features and feigned ignorance. "I'm sure I don't know what you mean."

"I'm saying you're running a bit low on self-preservation instinct, and it's likely to get you killed," said Faraz.

"As is the custom of our people," Leo joked. "Really, Faraz— with all your caution, are you sure you're a pazzerellone?"

Faraz opened his mouth to reply but was interrupted by the Hertzian receiver whirring to life, the metal typeface characters tap-tap-tapping against the ticker tape. Faraz held out a hand to catch the message as the tape unspooled from its roll, and bent his head to read from it.

"'All materials pertaining to Garibaldi are to be viewed exclusively by the Order.'" He paused, staring at the message. "You're not going to like the next part: 'Sending courier to acquire.'"

"What!" Leo said, indignant at the Order's presumption. "They can't just steal all our clues! We worked hard to find Montaigne's journals."

Faraz raised his eyebrows, mild as ever despite the news. "Apparently we're not talking about a dead general, after all. They must consider this Garibaldi fellow a serious threat."

"Thank God for the Order of Archimedes," Leo grumbled. "Interfering in everyone's business since 1276 AD." His well of patience had run dry. He pushed away from the doorframe and strode down the hall.

Faraz called after him, "Where are you going?"

"To my lab, of course. Where else?" Leo's hands were itching to hold some tools. Perhaps he would repair the training bot Elsa had shot with her revolver when she'd first arrived. Even if he was powerless to solve Elsa's crisis, he felt an urgent need to fix *something*.

Alek de Vries entered the office of Augusto Righi, the current elected head of the Order, and found Filippo already seated across the desk from the man himself. Righi was a portly gentleman with a prominent nose and a dramatic oxbow mustache. He looked close in age to Filippo, making Alek his senior by a decade or more, though Alek did not expect much deference from him; Righi carried with him the full authority of the Order and all the pomposity that went with it.

Filippo looked up, and Alek detected worry in his gaze.

"What's happened?" he said, even before easing himself down into the last empty seat.

Righi leaned forward in his fine leather desk chair. "Tell me, Signor de Vries: when Signorina Elsa arrived at Casa della Pazzia, did she bring anything with her?"

Alek flicked his gaze over to Filippo, wondering where Righi was going with this, but his old friend held his tongue. Reluctantly, Alek said, "Yes, she had a stack of Charles's books. And a Pascaline mechanical calculator, which is how I learned about her other abilities."

Righi raised one thick eyebrow. "And you didn't mention this to the Order why?"

"The house was on fire, she grabbed some books at random . . . I didn't expect any of them to have relevance for the Order's investigation." This was the reasoning he'd told himself when he left Pisa without the books, but now Alek recognized it for the excuse it was. Even before arriving in Firenze, some part of him was already hedging his bets—leaving Elsa the chance to investigate, in case the Order proved unhelpful. Which, apparently, was exactly what she was doing with the help of Casa's other wards. He didn't know whether to rue the day he'd urged her to befriend them, or to be grateful that at least she wasn't chasing this danger all alone. Really, he had no one to blame but himself.

Righi did not look pleased with his answer. "Well, apparently one of those 'random' books contains recent correspondence from Garibaldi."

Alek felt as if a shard of ice were piercing his heart. He hadn't heard that name in twenty years, and could have happily gone to his grave without ever hearing it again.

Beside him, Filippo said, "Ricciotti Garibaldi? I'd assumed

he'd gotten himself shot in the head by a Papal executioner, or something of the sort."

Righi pressed his lips together in an expression of grim humor. "Oh come now, Filippo—when have we ever been that lucky?"

Alek swallowed the lump in his throat so he could speak. "You think he's been in hiding this whole time? Why resurface now? If that is indeed what's going on."

"How much do you know of him?" said Righi. "If I recall, you were hiding in Holland the last time Garibaldi confronted the Order."

Alek did not appreciate Righi's insinuation of cowardice. He'd run from the acute agony of Massimo's death, not from his responsibilities to the Order. Still, that was ancient history, so he let it go and said simply, "I was not much involved at the time, no."

"They say the worst threats always come from within." Righi's eyes turned hard with disapproval. "Garibaldi was one of those—a pazzerellone who believed, *devoutly*, that we're meant to use our abilities to plot the course of history. Who could not see the dangers of applying science to warcraft—either the dangers to the world, or the dangers to the scientists themselves."

"Italian unification at any cost," Filippo added quietly. He shared a weighted glance with Alek.

Alek knew all this already—knew it intimately—but he let Righi speak his piece.

"If Garibaldi makes a play for power and fails, it could be catastrophic for us," Righi continued. "Widespread loss of intellectual freedom, as governments the world over slap chains on their pazzerellones. It could even cost us the Order."

Privately, Alek thought *the world over* was a bit of an exaggeration. The Order served pazzerellones throughout Europe and the Near East, as far south as India even, but it was far from all-powerful. Alek held up his hands. "Hold on, let's not jump to conclusions. It could be a mere coincidence."

"Or it could mean Garibaldi's back," said Righi. "We can't take that chance, not with evidence of direct communication between him and Charles."

Alek sat back in his chair. "What exactly are you saying?"

Righi broke eye contact, as if he knew Alek would not like what he had to say next. "I've decided to put a hold on the investigation into Jumi's abduction until we know if and how it relates to Garibaldi. We need to focus the entirety of our resources and efforts on him."

Alek felt the news land like a punch to the gut. He did not know Righi well—they were barely acquainted—but still it felt as if the Order itself had betrayed him. Filippo was already protesting Righi's decision in the typical argumentative fashion of the Italians, but Alek himself could find no words. His mouth had gone as dry as a desert.

It was true, Alek had not been here for the final schism, but he remembered the first time Ricciotti Garibaldi pleaded his case to the Order. It must have been 1862, or '63? (And Alek was usually so good with dates.) In either case, Ricciotti was hardly out of boyhood, no older than Elsa, and full of the hot righteous indignation of youth. He'd lost his father and eldest brother to war, and he sought vengeance against the Kingdom of Two Sicilies—not only for their deaths, but for using pazzerellones to build the weapons that had killed them.

Young Ricciotti wanted to fight fire with fire, mad science with mad science. The Order, of course, said no.

But Massimo's eyes had lit up at the idea, and later he confessed his interest to Alek in private. Alek still remembered Massimo's exact words: *The kid's right, you know. If we put our heads together, we could be the ones running this continent instead of living in fear of those who do.*

The world-weary old Alek who sat in Righi's office wanted to shout at the memory, *You have to be careful!* But there was no way to change the past, and the younger Alek of 1863 had not dissuaded Massimo from that path. He had, in fact, supported Massimo's pursuit of such ideals.

Massimo met with young Garibaldi in secret. The two of them went to Napoli to change the world, but only one of them ever returned. By the time Garibaldi made his final plea to the Order, Alek had already fled his grief.

Alek could have blamed Garibaldi for planting the seed of the idea that would kill Massimo. He didn't. He blamed himself for encouraging it to grow. Had blamed himself every day since.

Later, when Alek and Filippo were freed from Righi's presence, they retreated to the Pisano apartment on the third floor to strategize. While Filippo told Gia about the meeting, Alek poured three glasses of grappa from the decanter on the sideboard. They were all going to need a stiff drink.

"There's still a chance," Filippo was saying. He stood with one hand resting on the mantel above the lit fireplace and accepted a grappa glass from Alek with the other. "Perhaps we can convince the other members of the council to oppose Righi's plan."

Alek cast him a look mixed with equal parts skepticism and weariness, though it was Gia who said, "I wouldn't lay money on those odds, dear."

Filippo sighed. "I have never wanted to throttle Augusto as much as I did today."

Alek gave his old friend a wry grin and eased himself down into an armchair, careful of his stiff hip. "If I were thirty years younger, I'd offer to hold him down for you."

"No you wouldn't, you insufferable pacifist," Filippo said, amusement crinkling the corners of his eyes.

"He has you there," Gia added.

Holding it by the stem, Alek tilted the tulip-shaped glass, watching the play of firelight through the pale liquor within. "It's a terrible mistake," he said. "I don't know how we're going to convince Righi, but convince him we must. I'll admit Jumi never was much of an ally to the Order, but I can promise you this: Elsa will make a worse enemy."

Gia picked up her own glass, fingering it thoughtfully. "How strong is she?"

He immediately thought of the doorbook, with all its heretical implications. Alek had half a century of experience on Elsa, and she'd still managed to create a book of which the inner workings stymied him. And that moment in Paris . . . Elsa in her soot-stained dress, kneeling in the rubble, holding the charred wooden box of a Pascaline with its heat-warped gears and saying, *I used to play with it when I was little* . . . how Alek's heart had stopped when he understood what that meant.

"She's a polymath," he replied. "I wouldn't know how to begin answering that question. Is there even a limit to what she's capable of, to how powerful she can become?"

Lord help him. Alek tipped the glass and let the sweet burn of grappa slide over his tongue.

11

Leo sat on the floor of his lab, ripping out the section of hydraulic tubing with the bullet hole in it. He couldn't help but think about how neatly Elsa had aimed and pulled the trigger when they'd first met, and the corner of his mouth quirked up at the memory. He hadn't known whether to be annoyed or intrigued. When he thought of Elsa now, he still felt a little of both.

Leo wiped the hydraulic fluid off his hands with an old rag. He'd worked all afternoon, and he still hadn't decided whether he should patch the bot into Casa's network so the house could control it, or keep it autonomous and simply modify its programming to only attack strangers. Of the two machines, Casa had the best deductive abilities by far, and it therefore would be much less likely to falsely identify a delivery boy as a hostile assailant. However, there were arguments in favor of autonomy. . . .

Leo's concentration frayed under the assault of an annoying sound—*thunk, thunk thunk, thunk*—until he was forced to look up. The source quickly became evident: the cleaning bots had ceased to clean and were twirling in circles across the floor, bumping against one another.

"Uh, Casa?" he said. "What in the world are you doing? Or perhaps I should say, *not* doing. The cleaning bots have gone insane."

Casa answered slowly, the words stretching like molasses. "I am . . . otherwise occupied . . . at the moment."

"What do you mean? Occupied with what?" He glowered at the malfunctioning cleaning bots.

"No need to . . . worry. You children . . . should not concern yourselves . . ."

"Concern ourselves with *what*?" Leo demanded. "Casa!"

The house finally relented. "Power surge. Several sectors . . . knocked out."

Leo frowned. "But Gia just ran maintenance on the power distribution system last year."

"The . . . origin of the surge was . . . not internal."

Leo got that cold feeling in his chest—the one that meant he could stop anxiously waiting for the next catastrophe, because it had arrived. "Are you saying someone took down your security systems so they could get inside?"

With effort Casa managed whole sentences. "I can't see enough to be certain we've been infiltrated. I am fighting, but my control of the rear sector is still patchy. The library remains entirely dark."

Leo inhaled sharply. "Elsa's in the library."

He yanked open the laboratory door and sprinted down the hallway, praying he could find Elsa before the intruder did.

Elsa was reshelving the history book Porzia had given her to read when she heard the door creak open behind her. It must be Porzia returning from her study. She turned, saying, "Did you bring any—" but the words died on her lips. It wasn't Porzia.

The figure in the doorway was swathed in black clothing, nothing left uncovered except his eyes. Something about the man's posture made Elsa's pulse jump, even before the gasoliers hanging from the ceiling flickered and went out, plunging her into darkness.

Elsa's eyes struggled to adjust to the dim twilight filtering through the windows as the intruder stalked toward her. He had something in his hand, something that flashed with reflected moonlight from the windows above. *A knife*, she thought, only a fraction of a second before he lunged at her. Elsa yanked the history book off the shelf again and swung the heavy volume up to block his attack. The knife blade slid off the hard leather cover and grazed her forearm, but shallowly. She barely registered the sting of steel on skin.

She swung the book again, trying to knock the weapon from her attacker's hand, but he moved too fast, darting out of range for only a second before closing in on her once more. This time, the book connected with his elbow, making a satisfying *thwack*, but the strike hardly seemed to faze him.

Behind the assassin, a shape appeared in the open doorway, silhouetted against the light that spilled in from the hall. With the library still dark, it took Elsa a second before she recognized Leo. He seemed to move as silent as a snake winding through grass, or perhaps it was only that her pulse was pounding in her ears. Leo reached down to pull something from the top of his boot. When it caught the light, Elsa saw polished metal—a small, narrow-bladed dagger.

"Hey!" Leo shouted, and when the man turned, he threw the dagger through the air. It tumbled end over end and landed in the assassin's chest with an audible *thud*. The assassin looked down at the protruding hilt in confusion, touched his chest where his own lifeblood was leaking out. Then his knees went weak and he collapsed. Dead.

Elsa's lungs kept heaving like bellows, her body refusing to acknowledge the danger was past. Leo had killed the assassin. It seemed surreal, even with the gruesome proof lying at her feet.

"Well," she said, trying to compose herself. Her frantic heart rate refused to calm, and her hands shook. Afraid she might drop the already-abused book, she set it down carefully on the nearest table. "I suppose if they're sending agents to kill us, that means we must be looking in the right direction."

She glanced over at Leo, expecting a witty reply, but his chin was tucked and his shadowed expression unreadable. When he finally spoke, he did not sound amused. "That was close."

She didn't want to think about just how close. When the Oracle said she'd lose something precious, she hadn't considered that it might mean *her life*. The Oracle's words seemed to settle over her like a death shroud. Elsa shook herself, trying to dislodge the sensation. "What happened with the gaslights? Casa?"

The house didn't answer, but Leo said, "Never mind that.

Are you hurt?" He stepped toward her, hands out as if he wanted to look her over for injuries.

She waved him off. "I'm fine. Really."

To keep herself from dwelling on what had almost happened, Elsa knelt down beside the body. She meant to search it for clues, but she hesitated, not wanting to touch it. *Don't be silly, it's just organic matter, there's nothing to be afraid of.* When she laid her shaky hands upon it, the body was still warm, but limp in a way that was not at all like the limpness of a sleeping child. Elsa cringed, but she made herself rifle through the assassin's pockets anyway. There was nothing to find. She peeled off his mask. His neatly trimmed beard spoke of someone who took care with his appearance, but there was nothing particularly distinctive about his facial structure—he could have been Italian or French or Austrian.

Elsa sat back on her heels and sighed. "Of course he doesn't have a calling card or anything else to hint at who hired him. Because that would be too easy."

Leo didn't answer, and when she looked up, he was staring at her with a stricken expression.

She said, "It's over, Leo. I'm alive, he's dead, so let's just . . . leave it at that." Her hands still shaky, Elsa brushed loose strands of hair out of her face—his stare was making her self-conscious of how disheveled she'd gotten in those few seconds of fighting for her life. She had to fight down the note of hysteria that tried to edge its way into her voice. "Would you like to help me figure out what to do, or would you like to stand there like a statue?"

Leo snorted and shook his head, keeping his thoughts to himself, but at least he started to move. He went over to the nearest of the eight walls and pulled on a section of bookcase. The bookcase creaked as it swung inward, heavy on its hinges, and revealed a triangular closet behind. The space had plenty of dust and cob-webs, but was otherwise empty.

"This will have to do for now," Leo said, and he proceeded to grab the assassin beneath the arms. Then he looked up at her expectantly.

"What?" said Elsa.

"Give me a hand, grab the ankles," he said as if it were obvious.

"Sorry, I'm a bit lacking in experience when it comes to mov-ing corpses," she grumbled, but she bent down to help.

Lifting the corpse made her feel flushed and queasy. Once Leo had the body positioned inside the closet, Elsa let go with no small sense of relief.

She watched him swing the bookcase back in place. "We can't keep the body in there forever. It'll start to smell."

"I know, but this is better than leaving it out in the open. If one of the kids sees it, Gia will skin me alive." His tone had returned to his usual level of nonchalance.

"What do you do with your dead?" she asked, desperate to keep him talking—anything to distract herself from the reality of what had almost happened.

Leo gave her a strange look. "I'm afraid I don't have much experience with clandestine body disposals."

"No, I mean in general. Earth has been around for a long time, and there are so many of you. It seems like you'd be up to your necks in skeletons by now."

He scratched his head. "Well, we bury them mostly. Some cul-tures burn them. We certainly don't leave them lying in the streets, if that's what you're envisioning. Why, what do the Veldanese do with them?"

"We haven't had much death so far . . . Veldana's too new for it," Elsa said. Yes, this was good, this was something to focus on besides the nauseous panic coiling in her gut. "We don't have any old people yet. A baby died once—stopped breathing in his sleep—and we sent him into the Edgemist. But that's hardly an option here. So the furnace, then?"

"We can't burn this, it's evidence! We . . ." His face flushed, and he finished lamely, "Might . . . need it."

"Need it for what, precisely?" There was something he was skirting around, trying to keep from her, but Elsa was finding it hard to focus. The cut along her arm throbbed, the pain distracting her.

Leo said, "Oh, you know. Identification purposes."

"I don't know who he is. You don't know who he is. It's not as if we can send a wireless to Firenze for help. 'Sorry to disturb you—stop. Dead assassin in library—stop. Please advise—stop.' You think Signora Pisano would still let me stay here—let you and Porzia and Faraz keep helping me—if she knew I'd brought *this* into her home?"

"It's hardly your fault. And anyway, I . . . wasn't thinking of Gia," he said cagily.

"What." Feeling light-headed, she paused to take a deep breath. "What is that supposed to mean?"

"There's . . . someone else who might know him."

Elsa was about to reply when a wave of dizziness washed over her, and she had to grab the closest bookshelf to keep herself on her feet. She pressed her other hand to her face, willing the sensation to pass.

"Are you well?" Leo said, frowning with concern.

"Dizzy, that's all. I'm sure it's nothing," she said, right before her vision tunneled and the world slipped from her grasp.

Leo saw Elsa's knees buckle and lunged forward to catch her before she hit the floor. He had not expected her to faint—he'd thought she was made of stronger stuff than that, even if this was her first dead body. After all, wasn't she the one discussing immolation so casually? He patted her cheek, annoyed, trying to rouse her. This was hardly what he'd pictured when he'd thought about finally getting his arms around her. Limp and unconscious did not factor into that particular fantasy at all.

She wasn't responding. That was when he noticed her sleeve was torn and stained. He'd assumed it was blood from the assassin's body, but when he pulled the fabric away, it revealed a long, shallow scratch running down her forearm, where the tip of the assassin's dagger must have grazed her. Poison on the dagger? Icy fear filled the pit of his stomach.

Leo put his fingers to her neck to check her pulse: it felt weak and thready, the rhythm uneven. Oh, God, there wasn't much time. Think, *think*. He couldn't afford to panic just now. Faraz would be his best chance for an antidote, so he had to get Elsa to the alchemy lab.

Leo yanked a handkerchief from his pocket, grabbed the assassin's dagger, and wrapped the blade, hoping to preserve some of the poison. Then he tucked the dagger through his belt and heaved Elsa into his arms. She was small, but apparently even small people were difficult to carry when entirely limp. Adjusting his grip, he staggered out into the hall.

When he burst through the alchemy lab door and saw Faraz inside, a wave of relief flooded through him. Faraz, unlike Leo, actually kept his work space neat, so there was an empty table upon which to lay Elsa. Leo set her down gently, careful not to crack her head against the wood.

"What in the name of God is going on? Casa reported an intruder." Faraz rushed over to look at Elsa. "Did she faint?"

"She's been poisoned. With this." Leo handed the dagger over to Faraz, then pulled back Elsa's sleeve to show the cut. "We have to synthesize an antidote."

"I'm—I'm not qualified," Faraz stammered. "I don't work on humans."

"Seeing as how the only other person with alchemical talent in this house is twelve and enjoys mixing *perfumes*, I really do think you're the most qualified candidate."

Faraz gave him a wide-eyed look of horror. "I wasn't suggesting we consult Olivia. Maybe someone at the university . . ."

"I hardly think a carriage ride across the campus will do her good. She hasn't much time. Now, I can assist with whatever you need," he said, rolling up his sleeves. "We know it's an alchemical poison used by the Carbonari, which narrows down the possibilities somewhat, and we know it attacks the heart. So what do we do?"

Faraz unwrapped the blade, handling it with precision and care. He lifted it close to his face to give the poison an evaluative sniff, then looked at Leo. "We get to work."

Even with Leo's passing knowledge of Carbonari poisons, it took Faraz several minutes to narrow down the possibilities and definitively determine which agent was, even now, killing Elsa. Faraz did not waste a moment on interrogating Leo about his familiarity with the Carbonari, though Leo could see the question lingering in his friend's eyes.

Leo took a damp cloth to Elsa's flushed face while Faraz rummaged furiously through his supply cabinets, glass vials clinking together.

"We'll need a chelating agent to bind the toxin," he said. A vial fell from the shelf and crashed on the floor, spreading yellow fluid and sparkling glass shards everywhere, but Faraz ignored it. "And a cardiac stimulant to counteract the symptoms, and maybe . . ." His voice trailed off into mutterings Leo couldn't quite hear.

Precious minutes ticked by while crystals were dissolved and liquids were boiled and distilled and mixed together. Leo didn't quite follow every step, but he decided not to ask Faraz to waste time explaining anything to him.

"Come on, come on," Leo muttered, checking Elsa's pulse again. "Can't you work any faster?"

"Of course," Faraz snapped with uncharacteristic sarcasm. "There's a much faster way to do it, but I decided to take the leisurely route just to drive you insane."

Leo winced.

Faraz's hands were steady as he grabbed the neck of a glass flask with metal tongs and moved it away from the burner flame, but tension pulled at the corners of his mouth and his gaze turned intense. Even Skandar seemed to pick up on his stress and crawled into the narrow space underneath a cabinet to hide.

The seconds passed like hours. At long last, Faraz held up a glass test tube and met Leo's gaze.

"Is that it?" Leo said, heart in his throat.

"Only one way to find out," said Faraz, bringing the vial

over to the table where Elsa lay. "It's the best I can do. Whether it will prove to be an antidote or not . . ."

Leo grabbed the vial out of his hands. "Stop stalling and hold her mouth open, will you?"

"Wait!" said Faraz, grabbing a hypodermic syringe. "Unconscious people don't have a swallow reflex—it'll end up down her lungs. We have to inject it intravenously."

Faraz insisted on injecting the antidote very slowly, and in several different arteries. Leo thought he might indeed go insane from waiting. When Faraz finally set aside the empty syringe and pressed his fingers to Elsa's throat to check her pulse, Leo let out a breath he hadn't known he'd been holding.

"How is she?"

After a pause, Faraz said, "I think it's working. Her pulse is stabilizing."

"Thank God." Leo scrubbed his face with his hands, relief flooding through him. But a little stream of anxiety followed quickly behind, because Elsa would not truly be safe until they knew for certain who had ordered the attempt on her life. He wrapped the dagger again, tucked it into his belt, and said, "I have to go."

"You're leaving *now*?" Faraz said, gaping at him.

Leo tapped his fingers nervously against the side of his leg. "Is she going to live?"

"I . . . I think so. Yes."

He reached for the door. "Then there's something I have to do."

Elsa awoke to the feeling of a tickle against her cheek. She cracked open an eyelid to see Skandar's huge eye staring at her from a few centimeters away, one tentacle anxiously poking her face.

174

With her eyes open, she grew increasingly aware of the pounding headache at the base of her skull, and the room spun around her. It took a minute to confirm that she really didn't recognize the brown leather couch she was lying on, or the neatly organized shelves of jars and vials that lined the walls. In the center of the room, Faraz was standing at a worktable, cleaning up the detritus left over from some recent experiment.

"Hi, Skandar," Elsa said hoarsely. And then, "Faraz?"

"You're awake," he said, looking up from what he was doing. "Good. Porzia will be relieved to hear it—she's been a nervous wreck."

"What happened?"

"Do you remember the attack? The assassin's dagger was dipped in poison. I've administered an antidote, but you're not out of the woods yet."

Elsa picked her head up, trying to get a better look at her surroundings, and the motion caused a wave of nausea to wash through her. "Where's Leo?"

"He . . . He'll be back soon, I'm sure." Faraz busied himself organizing a shelf of little glass vials, as if the question made him uncomfortable.

"How long was I out for?"

"A couple hours."

Elsa dragged herself into a sitting position, her head still swimming. She pressed the heels of her hands against her eyes, willing the dizziness to recede, but she still felt disoriented. When she opened her eyes again, the room seemed to tilt to the left.

Faraz turned, saw what she was doing, and rushed over. "Lie back," he admonished. "You shouldn't try to get up yet. You nearly died, Elsa."

She gave in and let Faraz guide her back into a more relaxed position. He gave her a stern look before going back to the worktable to finish tidying up. Skandar, now content that she wasn't dead, crawled up onto her stomach and settled there. She idly scritched the creature with one hand.

Staring at the ceiling, Elsa wondered where Leo could have run off to while she was busy surviving a poisoning. To go talk to this mysterious *someone else* who might be able to identify the assassin? Why go alone instead of waiting for her to recover first? She was aware in a distant, academic way that she ought to be furious with him for leaving, but in the haze of her recovery, anger would have required too much effort.

Elsa turned her head to look at Faraz. "Can I ask you . . . what happened to Leo's family?"

"What, now?" he said, surprised. "You should be resting."

"Yes, because *listening* is so very taxing," she said, and then realized it was the sort of thing Porzia might say. The other girl's sarcasm must be rubbing off on her. "Besides, if I fall asleep, Skandar will go back to poking me in the face."

Faraz kept his hands busy with rolling up a long strip of medical gauze. "They all died. In the Venetian rebellion seven years ago. His father was an advocate for Italian unification, and they were attacked in their home during the riots. The way it haunts him, I'm fairly certain he . . . you know, saw it happen."

"That's awful," Elsa said, trying to imagine the trauma of seeing one's family slaughtered at such a young age. Even now, the thought of Jumi being hurt was almost too much to bear. "How did he escape?"

"A servant, I think, managed to sneak Leo out and get him to safety. I don't know the details—he hardly ever speaks about his family."

"So he hides things from you, too."

Faraz shrugged it off. "Find me a person who has never hidden anything from anyone." But the way he avoided her gaze made Elsa think it bothered him more than he was letting on.

There was a swift knock at the door, and Burak stuck his head into the lab. "Everyone alive in here?"

Faraz waved him in, but Elsa found she couldn't reply—her throat went suddenly tight with rage. Someone had gone to great lengths to see her dead. What exactly had she done to deserve this? Elsa was simply trying to rescue her mother. Who did these people think they were?

"What did you find?" Faraz was saying to Burak.

The younger boy scooted around the worktable and took something out of his pocket to show Faraz. "We've definitely been bugged. I found one in the library and a few in Casa's control room. We'll have to sweep the whole house."

"What is it?" Elsa said from her place on the couch. Faraz handed her the device—a fat brass beetle the size of her palm, complete with legs for scurrying and sensors for spying. It tried to climb off her hand and escape, but she flipped it upside down so its legs waved uselessly in the air. Skandar lifted a tentacle curiously, but Elsa clicked her tongue to tell the little beastie it wasn't for him.

Faraz asked Burak, "Do you recognize the design?"

"No, but it's genius. I've never seen anything so small and sophisticated. No off switch that I can see—we'll have to get creative to disable them. Leo should really take a look inside." Burak glanced around, noticing Leo's absence.

"I'm sure he will," Faraz said ambiguously, declining to explain Leo's whereabouts. "You should deliver an update to Porzia—you can tell her Elsa's awake, as well—and then find Sante and Olivia and anyone else Porzia assigns to you, and start sweeping the house. All right?"

Grinning, Burak snapped a mock salute, took the bug back from Elsa and ran out of the room. Silence stretched between Elsa and Faraz for a minute after the boy had gone.

"It's not unusual. Leo disappearing for a while, I mean," Faraz eventually offered, though Elsa had not pressed the issue. "He goes off on his own sometimes. He always comes back, though."

Off on his own to meet with this mysterious other person who might be able to identify the body. Elsa snorted. "Well this time, Leo better come back with some answers."

Faraz did not disagree.

12

IF AN OFFENSE COME OUT OF THE TRUTH, BETTER IS IT THAT
THE OFFENSE COME THAN THE TRUTH BE CONCEALED.
—*Saint Jerome*

Leo should've taken the spider hansom, stealth be damned. It was a mistake to walk—walking gave him time to think, and the more he thought about it, the angrier he became. There was no escaping the fact that the assassin had been Carbonari-trained and had carried a dagger forged by the Carbonari's own bladesmith. Both of which inevitably led Leo to conclude that the Carbonari had ordered Elsa's death. By the time he was crossing the bridge over the river, he felt convinced Rosalinda must have known about the hit—his dear Auntie Rosalinda—being as she was the only Carbonara currently residing in Pisa, and high up within the rebel organization.

Leo paused halfway across the Middle Bridge and leaned against the stone sidewall, staring out over the calm waters of the river Arno. The bridge was the oldest in the city, a Roman construction, wide and low with three arches supporting it. It was one of Rosalinda's favorite places in Pisa—she liked to pause in this very spot whenever she went out for a stroll.

Rosalinda had never been an especially warm or maternal sort of person. She only visited the Trovatelli household to give fighting lessons, but despite her gruff manner, young Leo had always felt he was her favorite. He would call her Auntie, though there was no blood relation between them, and she would pretend to be vexed by the name. When his father and brothers were killed, it was Rosalinda who got him safely out of Venezia. And when the Order claimed guardianship of Leo, she followed him to Pisa, just to stay close.

Now, to have Rosalinda violate not only the Order's agreement with the Carbonari but his bond of trust with her—it was unthinkable. But what other conclusion could he draw?

Leo pushed away from the wall and made his feet move again, disgusted with himself for wanting to delay the moment of truth.

South of the river, there were fewer grand plazas and more red-tiled houses packed snugly together along narrow streets. Leo found his way to Rosalinda's door, the route so familiar he could have walked it in his sleep. He knocked, and the seconds before the door opened seemed to stretch to infinity, his stomach roiling with a mixture of anxiety and betrayal.

And then, suddenly, they were face-to-face. Rosalinda looked the same as always: dressed in men's breeches, with her silver-shot brown hair pulled back in a no-nonsense bun. Leo pushed past her into the house, and though she could have stopped him if she wanted, she allowed it.

Rosalinda followed him down the short entry hall to the sitting room. "Leo, what's happened?"

"You are very, very lucky," he said, his voice cold with fury, "that no one died."

She gave him a curious look. "My dear boy, I haven't the faintest idea what you're referring to. Why don't you have a seat and start at the beginning."

Leo did not sit. Instead, he paced an angry line across the floor. "Oh, spare me. Did you really think a Carbonari assassin could roam the halls in Casa della Pazzia without my knowing it?"

Rosalinda took her own advice and settled on the brocade sofa, but there was a stiffness to her posture that belied her calm demeanor. "You know as well as I that we don't interfere with the affairs of the Order."

"Well, the body I hid in the library closet says otherwise." Leo stopped pacing and planted his feet in a wide, angry stance. He took the dagger from his belt, unwrapped it, and tossed it on the table before her. "As does this."

She picked up the dagger delicately, pinched between two fingers, and gave it a thorough examination. She kept her expression impassive, and only someone who knew her as well as Leo did would have noticed the almost imperceptible rise of her eyebrows. Genuine surprise. His anger cooled a bit upon recognizing her emotion.

Leo cleared his throat. "He died easily. Not one of your best, I take it."

"No. The truly excellent ones never betray me." She gave him a steady look, as if daring him to be a counterexample. "It's the mediocre ones you have to worry about. Always looking for a quick way to improve their standing in the world."

Leo ran a hand through his hair, uncertain what to think. "So he didn't get his orders from the Carbonari?"

"If someone within the Carbonari ordered this, they were wise enough to keep me in the dark," Rosalinda hedged. "I would not have permitted violence to cross your threshold."

Leo forced himself to think past his confused emotions—was Rosalinda deceiving him? Or had the Carbonari betrayed them both?—and dredged up the name Elsa had found in Montaigne's journal. "Could this have been the work of someone named Garibaldi?"

The color drained from Rosalinda's face, and she leaned back in her seat, as if afraid his words might burn her like heat from an engine furnace. "Garibaldi? Where did you hear that name?"

Leo frowned, wondering at her reaction. "It's . . . a bit complicated. Abductions and thefts and murders, a sabotaged train and now this Carbonari assassin, and the only substantive clue we've found is 'Garibaldi.'"

She touched her face with her hand, an uncharacteristically vulnerable gesture, and when she spoke the words seemed more for herself than for him. "So he's come back, after all. Perhaps I should have hidden you."

"*Who?*" he demanded. "What are you talking about?"

"Leo . . ." She took a deep breath and let it out, as if steeling herself. "The Venetian rebellion . . . not everything happened the way you think. Your father and Aris are still alive."

"Why would you say something like that?" Leo's hand went to the chain of his father's pocket watch and clutched it like a lifeline. "I saw the bodies with my own eyes."

"What you saw were homunculi—alchemical copies that looked like your family."

"That's not possible!"

"The fire was supposed to destroy the evidence," she explained,

"but the Carbonari recovered enough pieces to determine they weren't genuine human remains. Whatever else I might say about him, your father was always a talented alchemist."

Leo felt like his legs might fail him. It couldn't be true—it was simply too much to believe. This whole time he'd been alone in the world, they were out there somewhere, alive and still together. Still a family. "Why didn't you tell me? I *grieved* for them."

Rosalinda gave him a pitying look. "You think it would have been easier, knowing they were alive but—" She cut herself off then.

"Had abandoned me?" he asked. This time his words barely came out in a whisper.

"I made a decision to spare you that knowledge. Try to understand, I did it to protect you."

"I'm not a child anymore! I don't need you or anyone else to shield me."

"But you were—you *were* a child," she insisted. "When should I have told you about their plan to leave you behind, so carefully thought through, days or perhaps weeks before the riots began? Explain to me how it would have been a kindness to tell a child this."

His jaw worked, tense with fury. "It may not have been kind, but it would have been the truth."

"I only did what I thought was best for you."

Leo tried his best to swallow his anger. There was a question he must ask. "And what of my younger brother? You said Father and Aris, but not . . ."

"I don't know if Pasca lives. We searched what remained of the house, but found no evidence either way." She paused for a moment. "Leo, your father wasn't born Rico Trovatelli—he was living under an alias to protect you and your brothers, and to continue his work in secret. His real name is Ricciotti. Ricciotti Garibaldi."

Leo stared at her, eyes wide. "I think I need to sit down."

"You already sat down."

"Oh. How nice for me." He glanced down at the wooden arms of his chair. When had that happened?

"Your grandfather was the late general Giuseppe Garibaldi, famed champion of the people. I know this must come as a shock."

Leo snorted at the vastness of her understatement. "But what does Father want? Why all this subterfuge?"

"His goal is the same as ours, the same as your grandfather's: to unify Italy into a single state. He used to be an ally of the Carbonari, but there were some . . . philosophical differences about how to achieve unification." She covered her lips with her fingers for a moment, thinking. "We lost a number of Carbonari during the riots, and they were all assumed dead. But now I think perhaps some of them stayed loyal to your father and left with him."

Leo dropped his head into his hands. Through the web of his fingers, he mumbled the most important question. "Why did they leave me behind?"

"I can't tell you, my dear boy. I don't know why."

In his heart he knew the answer, though. They'd left him behind because he wasn't good enough, had never been good enough— he was no polymath.

Gradually, Elsa managed to once again master the fine arts of sitting and standing. She even successfully downed a cup of chamomile tea brought to her not by a house-bot, but by a girl named Olivia. The girl looked like a younger version of Porzia, pretty with her dark hair and round cheeks, but unlike her sister, Olivia was painfully shy and disappeared as soon as she delivered the tea.

Porzia, on the other hand, strode in like she owned the place. "Where's Faraz?"

Elsa, seated on the couch, replied, "He went to help sweep for bugs, now that I'm stable enough to be left alone."

"Mm-hmm." She leaned in close, squinting at Elsa. "You don't look nearly as almost-dead as I was led to believe."

"It seems Faraz does good work. Otherwise, I believe I'd be looking all-the-way dead." Elsa felt oddly comforted by Porzia's brisk, unworried manner. It made her brush with death seem not so frightening after all.

"Well, I'm glad you didn't expire, because there's simply so much happening and I really need you alive and conscious. While you were resting, a courier arrived from the Order to confiscate anything having to do with Garibaldi."

"What!" Elsa sat up straighter. "All of Montaigne's books?"

"No, no—the worldbooks are safe. I gave the courier just the one journal with Garibaldi's name in it, the one we've already read. Everything else I hid before he got here." Porzia's mouth curled up into a sly little smile.

"Oh, that's good." Relief cooled her veins, though a moment later she had to wonder if Porzia was feigning all that apparent confidence. "But . . . your parents are in the Order. Won't you get in trouble?"

"Only if I get caught," Porzia said, though the lightness of her tone seemed forced. There was tension across her cheeks, as if she was not entirely happy with herself for what she'd done. "Besides, the worldbooks weren't mine to give. I just did what I thought you would if you weren't busy being poisoned."

Elsa gave the other girl a scrutinizing look; a hint of fear and insecurity hid in her eyes. "Well, I know it was a risk, so thank you."

"Everything in life is a risk. Now," Porzia declared, changing the subject. She clasped her palms together eagerly. "If you're feeling well enough for a short walk, I've a surprise for you."

"Sounds ominous," Elsa grumbled, half joking. She accepted the support of Porzia's arm when she unsteadily stood.

Porzia led her out of Faraz's workshop into an unfamiliar hallway, reminding her once again how massive the house was. Elsa almost gave up when she saw the "short walk" was to include climbing a flight of stairs, but she leaned heavily on Porzia and huffed her way up one stair at a time. Each breath was something of a struggle, and the effort made her light-headed.

Finally they arrived at a wide room that looked like a seamstress's parlor. Heavy bolts of cloth hung from the far wall, and half-finished projects were strewn about on the worktables. Half a dozen mannequins were clustered in one corner, like a grove of pale trees. To Elsa's right, a pair of open doorways led to two cavernous walk-in closets.

"Here we are," said Porzia. "I had a few items altered to suit you. I think the tailor bot finished only one outfit before all the bots went haywire, but one's enough for now."

Tired from even so short a walk, Elsa let herself down on a low settee beside a stand of full-length mirrors. "An assassin infiltrated your mother's stronghold, and your response is . . . clothes?"

Porzia busied herself while she talked, clearing off a table and laying out the items for Elsa to see. "Whether you like it or not, the train incident was your debut into mad society. Someone was watching, and we need to be ready to show that particular some-one you're not to be trifled with."

Elsa gave her a skeptical look. "And new clothes will accomplish this?"

"You already are a powerful madgirl, a polymath with danger in every pocket. Now if only you would consent to dress like one—"

"Wait, what? How do you know that?" Elsa interrupted.

"Oh, please." Porzia gave her a frank look. "If Leo had been the one who stopped the train, he would've been crowing from the rooftops instead of stalking around in a foul mood. Process of deduction, darling. I may have never met a polymath before, but I can still put two and two together."

"Oh."

"Now, as I was saying, if you'd dress like a polymath, perhaps you'd project more confidence in your powers. In my experience, your sartorial choices can have as much effect on how you feel about yourself as they do on how others perceive you."

Elsa shook her head. "The clothes do not make the monk, Porzia."

At that Porzia fumbled in surprise, dropping a boot on the floor and then quickly retrieving it. "Why did you choose those exact words?"

"What?"

"That phrase is an idiom. Not one you're likely to have heard in the short time since you learned Italian. So how did you know to say it?"

Elsa shrugged, uncomfortable with the intensity of Porzia's gaze. "I must have overheard . . . ," she started to say, realizing even as the words left her mouth that she didn't know how that phrase had popped into her head.

"You know things you shouldn't know. You can do things you shouldn't be able to do. You don't play by the rules the rest of us follow here in reality," Porzia quietly said. "*They* should fear *you*, not the other way around."

Elsa remained doubtful that the way she dressed would change anything, but she didn't want to seem dismissive of Porzia's efforts. She abandoned the comfort of the settee to stand and let Porzia help her into the new outfit.

First came a cream-colored linen work shirt, loose and comfortable. Over this went a leather bustier, which laced up the back like a corset but lacked the too-rigid boning that Elsa had found so constrictive. The bustier was decked out with brass loops and chains, compartments and pouches, all the attachments she would need to comfortably carry an arsenal of gadgets with her. A gun holster to hang at her right side, with a strap to anchor it to her thigh so it wouldn't bang about. Molded leather cases for her portal device and her books.

There were yet more pockets in the thick, heather-gray trousers. Trousers! Veldanese women never wore trousers. And even the tall leather boots had secret compartments for stashing tools— or knives, as Leo kept in his, Elsa supposed.

Porzia steered her over to the mirrors, and Elsa inhaled sharply at the sight of her own reflection. She did look different— and *feel* different—as if she were a distilled version of herself. Her reflection looked like someone who was born for the laboratory.

"We'll have to decide what to do with your hair," Porzia said, brushing a few black strands over Elsa's shoulder. "Something practical, of course, if you're going to be crawling around inside machines."

"Why are you being so kind to me?" Elsa asked.

Porzia fussed with Elsa's sleeves, straightening them. "You don't have much experience with friends, do you?"

"No, I suppose not." There had only ever been Revan. Even if he wasn't dead, he probably thought she'd abandoned Veldana and him with it. Revan alive and hating her was the best scenario Elsa could imagine. She swallowed, her throat tight. "Not much experience."

"Well," Porzia said primly, "you ought to get used to it."

Elsa felt a sudden desire to embrace the other girl. Would Porzia think it improper? She wasn't well versed in the ways of affection. *Just do it*, she told herself—she threw her arms around Porzia's neck, squeezed, and then immediately retreated to a safe distance.

"Thank you," Elsa said, feeling heat rise in her cheeks, but Porzia didn't look embarrassed at all.

"I don't mean to interrupt," said Casa, "but a hansom's pulling up outside. I believe Signor Trovatelli has returned."

By the time they reached the foyer, Leo was already inside and closing the front doors. He had with him an older woman, tall, thin, and dour-looking in dark-gray men's clothes.

Porzia tried to intercept him. "Where did you run off to? And who's this, may I ask?"

"She's here to identify the body" was all Leo said, and then he strode quickly past Porzia, the older woman at his side.

Elsa couldn't believe it. After all his prying into her affairs, all the secrets she'd shared, now he wanted to leave her and Porzia in the dark. "I'm alive, by the way!" she called after him, thoroughly annoyed. "Thought you might care to know."

Leo stopped, the mystery woman already a few steps down the hall that would lead to the library. He turned to look at Elsa, his expression inscrutable, and then hurried to catch up with his guest.

Porzia said, "What in the world has gotten into him?"

Elsa frowned. "And if everyone from his past is supposed to be dead, who's that?"

Porzia tugged her skirts straight, as if she were mustering her courage. "Come on, then. We'll not get any answers out of him if we keep standing around here."

When they reached the library, the closet was open, and the older woman was crouched over the body. "Yes, I recognize him," she was saying. "He's one of the Carbonari who went missing during the Venetian rebellion. Presumed dead—wrongly, it seems, until now of course."

Leo was standing with his back to the door and did not turn at the sound of their footsteps, seemingly unaware they had followed. He ran a hand through his hair, mussing it. "At least there's no room left for doubt."

The assassin's body drew Elsa's gaze like a magnet, and she abruptly forgot about being vexed at Leo. The attack flashed through her memory, making her pulse jump and her palms dampen. This man had come perilously close to killing her.

Porzia planted her hands on her hips and cleared her throat. "Leo, what is going on? Who is this woman you've brought into my house?"

Leo finally turned to look at them. His throat worked and his lips parted, but the words didn't come. The older woman stood, stepped around the corpse, and filled the silence for him. "Rosalinda

Scarpa," she said to Porzia. "I looked after Leo when he left Venezia, before your people laid their claim."

Porzia arched an eyebrow. "You sound as if you'd like to stick a flag in him."

While Elsa was curious how this woman from Leo's murky past had suddenly appeared, she was more anxious to know the identity of her would-be assassin. "So the invaders who abducted my mother do have some connection with these Carbonari people?"

Leo sucked in a breath, as if her words had edges like broken glass. "You could say that. Some connection, all right."

"Would you . . . care to elaborate?"

"Leo, you don't have to—" Rosalinda started to say, but he interrupted her.

"The man named Garibaldi from Montaigne's journals . . . he's my father," Leo said, his voice cracking. "My father's alive."

Rosalinda brushed his shoulder as if to remove a fleck of dust from his waistcoat, and she leaned in close. They shared a brief, muttered conversation, Leo's expression somewhat glassy-eyed. Then he left the library without another word to anyone else. Elsa exchanged a look of disbelief with Porzia, who also seemed to be wondering exactly who this woman thought she was.

When Leo was gone, Rosalinda turned to them. "The boy has had quite a shock. You should let him rest. There will be time enough for hunting down Garibaldi once Leo has adjusted to the idea."

Elsa herself could hardly believe it—Leo's father was alive, and connected to her mother's abduction. She narrowed her eyes at Rosalinda. "You've had the information we needed this whole time? How long have you been keeping this from him?"

Rosalinda pursed her lips. "Don't judge what you don't understand, child."

Beside Elsa, Porzia folded her arms angrily. "I think *you* can judge how you like the feel of the night air after you walk yourself back out of my house. I'll even show you the door."

Elsa—who was so accustomed to standing alone in every conflict—grappled with the surreal feeling of having someone else defend her. How strange, to find herself shielded behind Porzia's words when only a few days ago those same words had had their sharp points aimed at her. Was this what friendship meant, standing unified against common foes?

After Porzia bid Rosalinda a rather perfunctory good night, she and Elsa went looking for Faraz. They found him in a long, windowless room deep in the bowels of the house. A large engine chugged and huffed at the far end, and the walls on either side were lined with small alcoves, some occupied by house-bots and some standing empty.

Faraz looked up as they came in. He had a thick black rubber glove over his right hand, and a brass bug struggled in his grip. "What are you doing up and about? You should be resting."

"Leo's back," Elsa explained.

He zapped the bug with an electrical prod and tossed it, still smoking, into a bucket of deactivated bugs. "Ah," he said. "And?"

Elsa told him about Rosalinda's visit and related what Leo had said about Garibaldi.

Faraz pulled the glove off and tossed it in the bucket. "Just to be clear, we now believe Leo's father—who's supposed to be dead—is somehow connected to, or perhaps even responsible for, abducting your mother? Doesn't anyone else find this situation troubling?"

"This was always the situation," Elsa said. "The only part that's changed is now we know."

Faraz pressed his lips together. "I barely remember my own parents. . . . To think I used to feel jealous of how close Leo had been with his family, how well he'd known them."

Porzia shuffled her feet, her usual confidence drowning in doubt. "Perhaps we should let the Order handle this, after all."

"Because they've done such an outstanding job so far," Elsa said. "What precisely have they accomplished? Had a bunch of meetings?"

"Garibaldi has already made two attempts on your life!" Her voice rose an octave, shrill with distress. "What if he succeeds the third time?"

Faraz shook his head. "We can't tell the Order about Leo's relation to Garibaldi—it would call his loyalty into question." He set his hands on his hips, exhaustion showing in the slope of his shoulders. "On the other hand, the house is effectively defenseless now, thanks to these damned bugs infiltrating Casa's systems. Burak is still evaluating the extent of the damage, but I'd guess we're in rather sore need of Gia's assistance."

Casa's disembodied voice harrumphed. "I am not defenseless. This is merely a . . . a setback."

"I meant no offense," Faraz said soothingly. "You've been through an ordeal, and we simply wish to see you restored to your full glory as soon as possible."

Porzia rolled her eyes at the word *glory*, but the house seemed mollified. "Oh, my dear humanlings, flattery will get you everywhere," Casa said.

Elsa had a thought. "Porzia, could we get a message just to

Alek or your mother in Firenze, without the rest of the Order finding out?"

Porzia bit her lip, considering. "We'd have to send a telegram instead of using the Order's Hertzian machines. And it would be best if the contents were vague. Something only one of them would be able to correctly interpret."

"Then that's what we'll do first. Come on, I need paper and pen."

Elsa quickly settled on the contents of the message for de Vries: *Ran the experiment you told me not to. Complicated results. How should we proceed?* Porzia wrote a message for her mother as well, saying Casa needed maintenance, though of course not mentioning why. It was late, but Faraz agreed to take the notes to the telegraph office first thing in the morning.

What they would do after that, Elsa didn't know.

Leo sprawled on the roof of the veranda below his balcony, staring up at the stars, the terra-cotta roof tiles cool against his back. He ought to try sleeping—oblivion would be a welcome change from the roiling of his emotions—but his thoughts refused to settle.

Soft footsteps shuffled across the floorboards inside the bedroom, and then Faraz's silhouette appeared over the balcony railing, upside down from Leo's perspective.

"I thought I might find you here," said Faraz.

"Why don't you join me?" Leo joked halfheartedly.

Faraz, who wasn't fond of heights, said, "I think not."

"Oh, fine." Leo picked himself up off the roof tiles and vaulted over the railing to join Faraz on the balcony. "Look at all those stars. They make our problems seem insignificant in the grand scheme of the universe, don't you think?"

Faraz shrugged. "Our problems don't have to be significant to the universe—it's enough that they're significant to us." He casually shifted the subject. "I told Elsa about Venezia, by the way."

"You *what?*"

Faraz gave him a steady look. "She wanted to know. You expect her to trust us not only with her secrets but with her mother's life, yet you withhold your own history—your own secrets—from her?"

"Lies can carry as much truth as facts, sometimes." The words left his mouth, and Leo immediately thought of Rosalinda's deception. He laughed harshly. "I never thought I'd be on the receiving end of that particular lesson."

Faraz pursed his lips and chose his words carefully. "I'm glad you know because we need that knowledge right now, but . . . it's a terrible thing, to be unwanted. This is one commonality I wish we didn't share." Faraz's own father had sold him into an apprenticeship in Tunis when he was six years old, and Leo knew he had not seen his birth family since.

"Mm," Leo grunted, not yet ready to voice how he was feeling.

Faraz, patient as ever, allowed a companionable silence to settle over them. Leo was grateful his friend knew him well enough not to pry, and not to ask him if he was all right when he clearly was not. Above, the stars wavered, light bending through atmosphere.

Eventually Leo offered, "I think I hate him."

"If you're hoping to be dissuaded from adopting that particular view, I'm afraid I'm not the man for the job." A rueful smile pulled at the corners of Faraz's mouth.

"I don't know what I'm hoping for," said Leo. "An explanation that will somehow make all of this okay? Doesn't seem likely I'll get one."

"No, it doesn't," Faraz said.

What his father had done still didn't quite seem real in Leo's mind, as if the cognitive dissonance threatened to erase his memories. "He kidnapped Elsa's mother. He put an entire passenger train in mortal danger just to, what—test my skills as a mechanic? He sabotaged Casa and sent an assassin into a house full of children!"

"None of that is your fault."

"Of course it's not my fault!" Leo snapped.

Faraz raised his eyebrows at Leo's reaction, and Leo let out a frustrated huff. The truth was, he *did* feel guilty—he felt guilty because it was *his father* who'd done all these horrible things. And he felt guilty because there was still a part of himself who loved his father and yearned for his approval, and wanted nothing more than to be reunited.

"You're a good friend," he said, by way of apology.

Faraz snorted, then gave Leo's shoulder a sympathetic squeeze. "Somebody's got to keep you out of trouble. Now, get some sleep."

"I'll try," Leo agreed. Faraz was right—he would need to be rested, to rally his strength. The knowledge of his abandonment felt like a barb beneath his ribs, a sharp pain making it difficult to breathe.

Now, the anger brewing inside him was about more than Elsa's mother. Leo needed to face the man who had thrown him away, the man who had shattered his childhood like porcelain hitting the floor. His father.

13

Elsa jerked out of a deep sleep, heart hammering against her ribs, unsure what had awoken her. She fumbled for the matches on the bedside table and lit a candle, then slipped out of bed and pulled a dressing gown on over her chemise.

She paused, ears straining against the silence. The sound came again, muffled and indistinct. A person? Or some function of the house? Elsa couldn't be sure. Fumbling in the near dark, she retrieved her revolver from the top drawer of the commode and stashed it in the pocket of the dressing gown. After the assassin in the library, she wasn't about to get caught without a weapon. Then she lifted the candlestick and padded barefoot into the hall.

The flame guttered when she quickened her pace, and the pocket of the dressing gown, weighed down with the gun, bumped against her leg with each step. She moved down the hall, pressing her ear against each closed door and listening for the source. A minute passed with nothing save the sound of her own breathing, and Elsa was beginning to feel quite foolish. There was no danger, no need for her to be up wandering the empty halls in the dead of night.

Just as she turned to go back to her own rooms, someone screamed—a bloodcurdling wail that Elsa could only imagine must be the product of having one's innards torn out or some equally gruesome fate. Her heart leapt into her throat, and she quickly passed the candlestick to her left hand, freeing her right one so she could reach for the gun if she needed it. The scream was fading even as she found the right room and jerked the doorknob open.

Elsa burst through the doorway to find, of all things, Leo asleep in his bed. He was thrashing in his sleep, the sheets tangled about his legs, his hair damp with sweat. The fear and vigilance drained from Elsa, leaving behind a giddy relief. She'd expected blood and death and assassins, where there were only nightmares.

Leo was shirtless, his clothing below the waist—or lack thereof?—concealed by the bedcovers. For a moment Elsa stared at the sight of his smooth, golden skin seeming to glow in the candlelight, the ridges of his muscles accentuated by the play of light and shadow. She shook her head, feeling foolish, and set the candle on the table beside the bed.

"Leo?" she said softly, and then a little bolder, "Leo!" but her voice didn't rouse him.

"Aris . . . ," he moaned in his sleep. "Lemme go, we have to go back. . . ."

Elsa perched on the bed beside him, reached forward, hesitated, then grabbed his shoulder and shook him. "It's only a dream, Leo. Wake up."

He jerked at her touch, and his eyelids peeled open. "Elsa?" he said blearily, as if unsure whether he was awake or still dreaming. "What's happened?"

"You were crying out in your sleep."

He looked at her again, and his eyes went wide as saucers, as if the fact of her presence had finally sunk in. "What are you . . ." He tugged at the blankets, but it was a poor show of modesty—since Elsa was sitting on the bed, the blankets pinned beneath her, he would have had to dump her on the floor to cover himself thoroughly.

"Oh, for heaven's sake," she said, exasperated. "It isn't as if I've never seen a boy without his shirt before."

If she'd thought it wasn't possible for him to look more shocked and horrified, he now proved her wrong. *"It isn't?"*

"You're as prudish as an Englishman." She crossed her arms. "I promise not to take advantage of you in your current immodest state."

Even by candlelight, she could see him flush. He sat up and scooted away from her, hands still knotted in the sheets. "No—I'm not—Y-you shouldn't be here . . . ," he stuttered. "What would people think?"

"Let me worry about my own virtue," she said. "Now, are you going to tell me?"

He rubbed his face with one hand, as if trying to scrub away the memory. "As you said: only a dream."

Elsa abandoned any remaining mockery in her tone in favor of seriousness. "Do you always have nightmares that set you to screaming?"

"Not for a while now," he answered quietly. "It's just this business with . . . Never mind. It's not important, I'm fine. Are *you* okay? I'm so sorry about my father and the assassin and—"

"Stop," Elsa interrupted. "You have nothing to apologize for. You are in no way responsible for Garibaldi's actions."

Leo's jaw clenched, but he said nothing.

Elsa decided to try another cautious foray into the subject of nightmares. "You said a name in your sleep. Who's Aris?"

He didn't respond for so long she thought he was ignoring her, but eventually he arrived at some sort of decision and said, "He was my older brother. Or is? I don't know."

Outside, the clouds parted from the low-hung moon, and pale silvery light spilled into the room through a pair of glass doors— balcony doors, Elsa realized when she looked up. The moonlight softened the shadows of his face and turned his olive skin wan as a ghost.

"Do you want to talk about it?" she said softly.

He looked away toward the windows, avoiding her eyes. "I used to think, What's the use? Talking never brought back the dead. But now they're alive after all—my father and Aris and maybe even Pasca—and the man I knew as Father never really existed in the first place." His throat worked, as if the words threatened to choke him.

How awful, Elsa realized, to be abandoned by one's own family. They'd fled from Venezia and left him behind like an obsolete machine.

"I'm not sure this isn't worse." His voice fell almost to a whisper as he stared, unseeing, past her. "Before, when I thought they were dead, it wasn't their fault they were gone. But to be discarded like this . . ."

He was like a fine piece of clockwork that had been carelessly dropped too many times, the delicate gears jarred apart so they spun and spun but never connected. Broken. She brushed a strand of his brass-blond hair out of his eyes. He gave a very slight twitch at the feel of her fingertips on his face, but did not pull away. Oh, how she itched to open his chest and set the gears straight again. The thought surprised her; she'd often felt the urge to fix objects, but this sudden desire to fix a person . . . where did it come from?

Elsa shook her head. "You mustn't leap to conclusions with so little evidence. Perhaps they believed *you* had died, or hoped you'd lived but didn't know how to find you."

Darkly, Leo said, "They sent that assassin to kill you. They probably arranged the train hijacking, too. I'd guess they knew exactly where I was ever since Venezia."

Elsa swallowed, her throat tight. How many people would have died if they hadn't been able to stop the train? And the assassin *was* dead, not to mention Montaigne. Apparently, Garibaldi did not hesitate to gamble with the lives of his own compatriots, let alone with the lives of innocent bystanders.

No one was safe. Least of all herself and Leo. But that wasn't what he needed to hear just now, so Elsa simply shrugged and said, "Family is complicated."

Leo snorted, the corners of his lips curling up into an unwilling smile. "You have a way with words, signorina."

"I know this seems like an impossible mess, but we'll figure it out together. I promise."

"I don't see how. My father is the sort of man who has no qualms about abducting or killing people. I wonder if I ever knew him at all. Even his name was a lie." Pain was etched along his brow and under his eyes.

Elsa couldn't remember ever hating anything as much as she hated Garibaldi in that moment—not just for stealing her mother, but for how he'd hurt this beautiful, brilliant boy. Her hatred felt cold and pure as ice, but at the same time she knew Leo could never feel that clarity of hate for someone he'd once loved. She would have to carry the hatred for both of them, to hate Garibaldi on his behalf.

So she tucked the hatred away in a hidden corner of herself for safekeeping, and she gave Leo's hand a quick, reassuring squeeze. "Try to sleep, if you can. There's nothing to be done now. We'll start afresh tomorrow."

He sighed. "You're right, of course."

"I should probably . . . ," she said, shifting her weight to stand, but his hand flashed forward and caught her by the wrist.

"Don't go," he whispered.

Elsa knew she should resist that magnetic pull she felt behind her sternum, but there was something strange and desperate in his expression, and she found she could not deny him. "I'm no talisman against nightmares, but I suppose I could stay if you—"

Leo suddenly leaned forward, and his lips brushed tentatively against hers, sending unexpected sparks of desire through her. She gasped, and when her lips parted he reached for her and deepened the kiss. His fingers tangled in her hair, holding her close. Her hands explored the shape of his collarbones, the arch of his neck, the rope-cord muscles up and down his back.

She had kissed a boy before—Revan, of course—in the experimental way of children playing at being adults, but never had she been kissed like this. Like a spark held to a gaslight mantle, once lit it would keep burning and burning, ever brighter.

Leo leaned back, pulling her along until she lay over him, and she could feel his heart measuring a rapid rhythm in his chest. She swept her curtain of hair out of the way and kissed his throat beneath the line of his jaw, eliciting a soft moan. One of his hands traversed the curves of her waist and hip, down to her thigh, and then—

Leo froze. Elsa, sensing something was wrong, pulled away and propped herself up on her elbows to look at him. "What?"

He fumbled in the pocket of her dressing gown, drew out the revolver, and squinted at it in the dim light. "That *is* what I think it is."

Elsa rolled off him, snatched the gun from his hand, and tucked it away again. "I heard a noise in the middle of the night," she said. "And the house isn't exactly the impenetrable fortress I was led to believe it would be."

He quirked one perfect brass eyebrow at her. "Were you planning to shoot me if I grew too bold?"

Elsa snorted. "You're the one who's excessively concerned with our respective virtues."

"Someone has to be," Leo said defensively. "This isn't proper, this isn't how it's done. . . ."

"Your idea of 'how it's done' is completely absurd." She knew Porzia saw marriage as a matter of power and position rather than love, but now Elsa began to wonder if that was truly how Porzia felt, or if she was simply bending to the rules of her society.

Leo's hands fisted in the bedsheets. "You're not in the wilds of Veldana anymore, we can't just—"

"The *wilds*?!" Elsa snapped. "Where we Veldanese savages rut in the bushes, I suppose?"

"That's not what I meant—"

She stood. "I am sick of your world's rules, and doubly sick of your superior attitudes!" Face hot with humiliation, she yanked her dressing gown tighter around her and stormed out of the room.

"Elsa . . . ," he called. "Elsa!" But she was already slamming the door closed behind her.

Having forgotten the candlestick in Leo's room, Elsa stumbled down the hallway blind, one hand held out to the wall to guide her. How could she have been so stupid?

It is always the woman's fault, Jumi recited in her mind. *That's the way men are. If you wanted it, you seduced him; if you didn't want it, you denied him.*

She should have known better than to let anyone worm their way into her heart.

Leo thought about chasing after Elsa to apologize, and then he considered smothering his stupid mouth with a pillow. But instead he elected to lie awake and stare up at the ceiling for a long while after Elsa left. If only telling the truth wasn't so exhausting, if only it hadn't come as such a shock to find himself with Elsa on his bed in a compromising position, if only the whole encounter hadn't felt too strange and wonderful to be true—maybe then he could have managed to go one night without destroying something precious.

"Casa," he said into the darkness, "Elsa's room is awfully far away for her to have heard me."

"Signor?" said Casa innocently.

"Did you wake her up?"

Casa paused. "It is important for you children to look after one another."

Leo scowled. "You manipulative psychopath. Now everything's ruined."

"One must be a human to be a psychopath," Casa replied, sounding perfectly self-satisfied. "And I would say things are progressing quite nicely."

"She hates me now."

"Hmph. We'll see. She is a magnificent specimen, is she not?"

"You're unbelievable!" Leo tossed his hands in the air and let them fall back onto the bed. "She's not a specimen, and I've had enough of your interference."

Smugly, Casa said, "I'm not the one who kissed her."

In the morning Elsa skipped breakfast. Between the poison and Faraz's cure, all those chemicals had left her stomach feeling unsteady, and the last thing she wanted was to face Leo while also fighting nausea. Would things be awkward between them now? Would he avoid her, or pretend nothing had happened? Her absence left her to envision Leo performing his usual brash confidence over cappuccinos and pastries, serenely unruffled, as if nothing ever touched him. She couldn't stand that idea, and she needed desperately to find some diversion upon which to focus her attention. She had to get out of her rooms.

The library seemed the most logical destination. But when she pushed open the door, the library was not empty—there was a figure slumped over one of the reading tables amidst chaotic piles of open books.

"Porzia . . . ?" Elsa said, disbelieving. "Are you well?"

The girl lifted her head off her arm with a groan and scrubbed her hands over her face. Elsa had never seen her looking so disheveled. Porzia let down her sleep-mussed dark hair and ran her fingers through it, working out the tangles. "I must have dozed off."

Elsa narrowed her eyes in mock scrutiny. "Aren't you the one always cajoling us to sleep and eat and whatnot?"

She shrugged off the question. "I thought I'd go over my research again, now that we know exactly who Garibaldi is. I've been trying to identify places that might be significant to him." She shuffled through a pile of hastily discarded books at the far end of the table and pulled out a large atlas. Laying it open before Elsa, she said, "Here, have a look."

The page was a map of southern Europe, showing the Italian peninsula carved up into four independent political units. The north, including Pisa and Firenze, belonged to the Kingdom of Sardinia. A chunk in the middle around Roma was labeled *The Papal States*. Below that, the southern end of the peninsula was part of the Kingdom of Two Sicilies, along with the island of Sicilia itself. The far northeast was labeled VENETO, including the city of Venezia, where Leo had grown up. Opposite the map was a loose sheet of paper Porzia must have tucked between the pages, cities and dates listed on it in her elegant cursive. *Marsala— 1860—father Giuseppe and brother Menotti killed. Venezia— 1867(?)—establishes himself under assumed name.* And so on.

"The atlas is in German, sorry," said Porzia.

"That's fine," Elsa replied. "I read German."

Porzia blinked in surprise. "How many languages do you know?"

"Veldanese, Dutch, French, and now Italian," she said, ticking them off on her fingers. "I can also read English, German, and Latin, but haven't had the chance to hear them spoken yet. Oh, and I've just started Greek, but I'm not very far along. That's more your fault than mine, though, since none of you seem inclined to speak more than a word or two of Greek at a time."

Porzia shook her head, a wry grin pulling at the corners of her mouth. "I can see why you've awoken in Leo such a sense of inferiority."

Elsa felt heat rise in her cheeks. Porzia's eyebrow twitched at her too-transparent reaction to Leo's name, but she let it pass unremarked upon. Quickly, Elsa said, "So where did you get with the Garibaldi research?"

"Well, as I see it, we have three problems: locating your mother, reaching her as soon as possible, and escaping with her."

Porzia's hand rested on the open page of the atlas, her gaze focused on her notes as if determined to rake through them for undiscovered information. Elsa felt a pang in her chest as she watched the other girl. She'd stayed up all night doing research alone so Elsa could sleep and recover; she'd agreed to conceal Leo's parentage from the Order, whatever the consequences might be for her own family. It was past time to trust Porzia.

Elsa took a deep breath and said, "Well, I don't know how we're going to locate Jumi, but getting to her won't be a problem once we have." Before she could change her mind, she pulled out the doorbook. "We'll use a portal."

Porzia shook her head. "That's not possible. A portal device by itself, without a worldbook nearby, is useless here on Earth. Without a worldbook, there's no way to specify a destination."

"The book assigns numerical coordinates to a particular place, and the device opens a portal to that location, right? So all you need is a book that can assign coordinates." She held out the doorbook, offering it to Porzia. "This is how I make portals on Earth. I keep it with me, so I always have access."

Porzia gingerly accepted the doorbook and lifted the cover to look inside. The core text was scribed in Veldanese, taking up the first dozen pages, so Elsa had to walk her through the structure and syntax. "This is the trickiest part, here: since Earth isn't a scribed world, you can't simply reference its worldbook. It took me quite some time to figure out the necessary parameters to link the book to Earth."

Porzia flipped through to the most recent page—the description of Pisa, scribed in Dutch for de Vries's benefit. She frowned thoughtfully. "I don't know whether to call this brilliant, or heretical, or both."

Elsa let the corner of her mouth quirk with amusement. "There's nothing sacred about your so-called 'real' world."

"It *is* the original world, you know. The only natural one," Porzia argued.

There was a time when those words would have filled her with resentment. Now Elsa was beginning to understand that this belief served to hinder Porzia's scriptological ambitions. Porzia was brilliant, but she still thought of her world as the One True World, and her own perceptions were hobbling her.

"The fundamental architecture of all scribed worlds is rooted in the architecture of this universe, which renders the real and the artificial functionally indistinguishable from each other. If an alchemist were to take my blood and yours and compare them side by side under a microscope, he would detect no differences. What is scribed *is* real."

Porzia nodded, frowning, struggling to absorb this idea.

"Finding Jumi will be another matter, though." Elsa tucked the book away again. "In a world the size of Veldana, we could design some kind of device to detect her proximity, but Europe is much too large for that."

A grin slowly formed on Porzia's lips, brightening her expression like a rising sun. "We've got a pair of excellent scriptologists here. Isn't the solution obvious? We write a world designed to locate your mother."

Elsa grinned back at her—Porzia was really starting to get it now, starting to think like a Veldanese. "That's the best idea you've had all day."

"It's only, what, nine in the morning?" Porzia pointed out.

"We've got time, then," said Elsa. "Let's see what else we can come up with."

Leo holed up in his laboratory with his tools and a live bug that Burak had saved for him to examine. He flipped it upside down, clamped its legs to hold it stationary, and adjusted his magnifying glass stand. Then he carefully unscrewed the brass casing on the bug's underside, grateful he owned a spare set of clockmaker's tools—he couldn't bear facing Elsa to ask for the kit she had borrowed. It was so much easier to hide in the familiar mess of his lab than to face the impossible mess his life had become.

Machines were pure and objective. He could poke around in the gears and learn what they were made to do, and why, and even by whom. Machines could be fully, completely understood. People were a different story. After the depth of his father's deception, how could he ever trust himself to know another person? Mere days ago, he'd possessed such confidence in his ability to read a person the way Porzia might read a book, handpicking all the little revealing details of their behavior and appearance, and now that version of himself seemed like a stranger. In light of his utter failure to comprehend his own family, the life of a hermit had begun to sound awfully appealing.

With this clockwork device, at least, he was equal to the task. Observe, disassemble, analyze. He selected a pair of fine-tipped pliers and yanked out the half-wound mainspring with a metallic twang. With the power source removed, the still flailing tips of the legs slowed down, as if stuck in molasses, and then stopped altogether. Leo carefully pulled out the tiny gears one by one, lining them up in order on his worktable.

As he explored what should have been familiar territory, a hollow feeling settled in his gut. The electromagnetic inductor was much too small, and over here—were those miniature components designed for wireless transmission? The Order's network of Hertzian machines had been designed by a master of wireless telegraphy out of Bologna, but no one could make such a function fit inside this tiny compartment. It simply wasn't possible—not with mechanics alone.

Leo's first thought was that this looked like something Elsa would build, like how her freeze ray combined mechanics and alchemy. But no, that wasn't precisely correct. Every pazzerellone developed unique quirks in their designs, and these quirks did not remind him of Elsa's. Yes, the bug had been designed by a polymath, but this signature belonged to a different one— an uncomfortably familiar signature, though Leo had not seen its like in years. The closer he looked, the more certain he became.

His brother Aris had designed the bugs.

With the exception of her very first projects, for which Jumi would edit her syntax, Elsa had always scribed alone. Having help with the conception and design of a worldbook was an entirely new experience. What unique properties would this world need? How could they leverage existing physical principles to produce the effects they wanted? It surprised Elsa how much faster she and Porzia arrived at an optimal design by working together.

By midafternoon, they'd finished mapping out the theoretical framework and were ready to start committing the worldtext to the page, so they moved the whole operation up to Porzia's study. Her rooms were set up much like Elsa's, though her study was a little larger and much neater, since Elsa hadn't yet taken the time to clean up the supplies she'd been using for worldbook repair.

Elsa sat at Porzia's writing desk with a new worldbook open before her, scribing in the bare necessities—air, gravity, Euclidean geometry. Porzia stood in front of her shelves, considering and discarding possible reference books.

Elsa finished a sentence about temperature and paused, tapping the end of the fountain pen against her chin thoughtfully. "We need a reference map." She fished around in a drawer, found a wooden-handled stitch cutter, and held it out to Porzia. "You'll have to take a page from the atlas."

Porzia stared wide-eyed at the stitch cutter as if the little implement might bite her. "You can't be serious. You want me to destroy the binding on Mamma's good atlas? She'll be furious!"

"It's just a regular book—it's not as if I'm asking you to tear apart a worldbook."

"Atlases are very expensive to print," Porzia said.

Elsa pressed the tool into the other girl's reluctant hand. "If you insane Europeans weren't constantly invading one another and moving the boundaries all around, we could use an older map. But as things are, I need the most current version."

Porzia sighed. "Oh, fine, you're right. Copying the map would take too long. We'll have to paste it into the worldbook." She went for the door, grumbling, "Mamma *is* going to kill me for this."

While Porzia was in the library extracting the map, Elsa finished scribing the fundamentals into the worldbook and looked through Porzia's notes. They had yet to decide upon the exact methodology for scribing the locator machine that would complete the world. Linking the scribed representation of southern Europe to the real-world geography would be reasonably simple—it required a tweaked version of the same principle she'd used for the doorbook. And locating a particular person was not so different from locating a particular place. Elsa scowled down at the loose sheets of paper scribbled all over with ideas. The real problem was how to identify the person she wanted the locator to target.

Porzia returned with a loose page from the atlas, and she peered over Elsa's shoulder to see what part she was stuck on. "We should break for the night. Get some food and sleep, and look at it with fresh eyes tomorrow."

Elsa let out a heavy sigh. "But we're so close!"

"If by 'so close' you mean 'almost halfway done,'" said Porzia.

"You may be indefatigable, but I was up doing research most of last night. And anyway, we should wait on a response from Firenze before we go charging off after Garibaldi. For all we know, the Order's already hatching their own plan to rescue your mother."

Elsa pressed her fingers against her eyes. She *was* tired, and Porzia was right to worry. A mistake now could prove catastrophic later—such was the nature of scriptology. But there was no way to know if her telegram had gotten through to Alek, or to be sure he would correctly interpret her message. And every hour that passed might be the hour that ended her mother's life. There was no time.

Porzia went to bed, but she left the gaslight in the study burning so Elsa could continue to work long into the night.

14

The moon glowed faintly from behind a veil of clouds, barely visible, but the mirror-smooth surface of the river Arno shone like liquid gold in the light from the gaslamps. Leo spotted Rosalinda as soon as he got close to the old bridge. She leaned against the sidewall, looking stiff and severe, as if she might merge with the stone and become a gargoyle.

As Leo walked up beside her, she said, "Thank you for coming." As if there were any doubt that he would.

"After yesterday, I'm not entirely sure Porzia hasn't banned you from the house. I thought I'd better come to you, and not the other way around."

Rosalinda nodded solemnly, no trace of amusement crossing her features. "How are you?"

Leo bit the inside of his cheek. "Fine."

She exhaled through her nose, almost a snort, but she let the lie go unchallenged. "I made some inquiries. There's a rumor circulating through the Carbonari network that your father has acquired a very dangerous weapon, and that the weapon is . . . *scriptological* in nature."

"A weapon made with a worldbook?"

"If the rumors are to be believed. But this could explain why Ricciotti needed to forcefully conscript your friend's mother—assuming it is Ricciotti who took her."

"Maybe," Leo said. "Except . . . you were right."

"About?"

"Aris. He's definitely alive, and he's with our father. Helping him attack my home." His throat felt raw and tight, as if he'd swallowed an entire lemon slice by slice.

Aris the polymath, who could compose worldtext in three languages by the age of twelve. What did Ricciotti need Jumi for, when he already had Aris on his side?

"Well," Rosalinda said, "the only part of which I'm certain is that we don't have all the information yet."

Leo's mouth twisted into a rueful grin—it was such a very *Rosalinda* sort of thing to say. An axiom of spycraft for every occasion. As if uncertainty could be a comfort now. Oh good, his father and brother were only *probably* in possession of a scribed weapon—a dangerous perversion of pure science, and the embodiment of everything the Order stood against.

Lord, how could he tell Porzia about this? Concealing the assassination attempt from the Order was already putting enough strain on Porzia's loyalties. Leo honestly couldn't guess whether or not she'd agree to withhold this news as well.

"Is there anything you can do?" Leo asked tentatively. "You have connections. . . ."

Rosalinda huffed, frustrated. "The Carbonari can't get involved in pazzerellone affairs without an express invitation from the Order. You know that, Leo. I've already bent the rules dangerously far just providing you with information."

"Of course. I know." The Carbonari were already in open rebellion against two governments—the Papal States and the Two Sicilies—and they could not afford to make enemies here in Sardinia. Especially not powerful pazzerellone enemies.

Rosalinda said, "Ricciotti is not as clever as he thinks he is. You *will* find him—but I can't help you with whatever you're planning to do then." Her hands, pressed against the stone, were tense.

"This is why you kept training me, even after the fire. It was all to prepare me for this." Leo ducked his head, avoiding her gaze. "Wasn't it?"

Rosalinda took his chin in her hand, lifting it up; Leo wouldn't have let anyone else touch him like that, but this was Rosalinda. She appraised him with those stern eyes of hers. "I could have made a fine agent out of you, Leo, perhaps the finest I ever trained for the Carbonari. But you're right—it wasn't them I've been training you for."

"I would have, you know." His voice came thin and hoarse. "I would have fought for you."

"You have your own battles to fight now." She moved her hand to the back of his neck and drew him into a fierce embrace.

Leo froze, bewildered by her sudden tenderness. Rosalinda had never been prone to fits of maternal nurturing the way Gia was, and though he knew she cared about him as a teacher cares

216

for a pupil, he'd never imagined she felt a parental sort of affection.

Rosalinda pulled back to look him in the eye, holding his face in her calloused hands. "You can defeat them. You're stronger and faster than your father and Aris both."

Leo stared at her. Her eyes were hard as a hawk's, and what wrinkles she had spoke more of determination than worry or joy. Could it be that this unsentimental woman loved him, when his own father had not found him worthy of love?

"Stronger and faster, but not smarter," he whispered.

Rosalinda harrumphed. "Smart enough, dear boy," she said. "Smart enough."

Alek lowered himself stiffly onto the stone bench in the gardens behind the Order's headquarters, and he waited. The sky was turning pale, but the sun had yet to crest the horizon. From within a nearby shrub, a songbird whistled a melancholy tune.

He pulled the folded telegram out of the pocket of his waist-coat, smoothed the creases as best he could, and read the words again. No, he had not mistaken Elsa's meaning—she was asking permission to proceed with Jumi's rescue.

"This isn't like you," Gia said, settling onto the bench beside him. "Clandestine meetings at dawn."

"I need a favor."

Gia looked at him steadily. "You want me to go back to Casa della Pazzia."

"I have no obligations waiting for me in Pisa—it would look suspicious if I leave."

"So instead of running off to collude with Jumi's daughter,

you want me to go in your place," she said. "The Order is divided on the matter of how to deal with Garibaldi's return. Filippo needs my support here."

"Please, Gia. I know this is a lot to ask, but Jumi is like a daughter to me," he said. "What would you do if Porzia were in her place?"

Gia pursed her lips at him. "That's a low blow, old friend. And what am I to do with the girl? I thought you wanted her safe."

He dropped his chin to his chest. "Elsa was never going to leave this alone, I should have known that. And I never thought . . ." He paused, the unbelievable situation momentarily robbing him of words. "These pazzerellones don't care about rescuing Jumi. Some of them actually believe she's working *with* Garibaldi."

"I received a telegram, too—from Porzia, asking for help. Not in so many words of course, but . . ." Her voice trailed off and she frowned thoughtfully for a minute. "Do you think it's wise to encourage them? They're hardly more than children. What would you have me do?"

"Tell them the truth," said Alek. "Tell them not to wait for help from the Order, because there is none coming. Tell them to save Jumi."

"This is madness. They're too young to face such dangers."

"You'll be there to guide them, at least. We were just as reckless in our youth, and for lesser reasons."

"And how well did that work out for the Pisano brothers?" she said sharply. "Have you forgotten?"

"Of course not." *Speaking of low blows*, Alek thought. A muscle in his jaw tightened at the memory of what they'd had, and all they'd lost. "We can't lock our children away from the world forever, Gia. Better they act with our support than behind our backs."

"God forgive me," she said with a sigh. "I'd better go if I'm to catch the morning train."

Leo paced Porzia's too-small sitting room from one side to the other and back again. How Faraz could stay seated—the very picture of patience and calm—he could not fathom. Midday had come and gone with Elsa and Porzia remaining closed up in the study. "Why is this taking so long? What do you imagine the girls are doing in there?"

"Scriptological feats of genius never before conceived of, I'd assume." Dryly, Faraz added, "It might be another minute or two. I hear it takes time to bend the laws of reality."

"Not as much as you'd think, when Elsa's involved," Leo muttered.

"Will you sit down? You're making Skandar nervous." Clinging to Faraz's shoulder, the little beast fanned its wings and batted uncertainly at the air.

"Oh, well, if the tentacle monster's nervous . . . ," Leo said sarcastically, but he tried taking a seat anyway. He quickly found that sitting still only worsened the anxious tension in his chest, so he hopped back up and resumed pacing.

Finally, Elsa and Porzia emerged from their scriptological sanctum. Elsa cradled a book in one arm, and Porzia was holding a portal device.

Leo stopped midpace. "Is it done?"

"We've designed a tracker," said Porzia. "Now we just need to input a target."

"And how long is that going to take? What does that even mean?" He threw his hands in the air, his already frayed patience giving way.

"Leo," Elsa said quietly, putting a calming hand on his arm. "It means we can use the tracker to locate anyone. Including your father."

He looked at where she was touching him—delicate brown fingers against the white cloth of his sleeve. Strange, how such a small gesture could evaporate all that pent-up frustration.

When he didn't reply, she pulled her hand away, embarrassed. "Are you well?"

Leo cleared his throat. "There's something I need to tell you all: Rosalinda heard a rumor that my father has acquired a very powerful weapon. Something made using scriptology."

He could see Elsa's mind racing. "Do you think Garibaldi's compelling Jumi to create scriptological weapons?"

Porzia said, "All the more reason to confirm whether or not Garibaldi took Jumi, and to get her away from him."

"Yes." Leo took a deep breath and let it out. "Yes, right. Let's do this."

Elsa shook her head as if to clear it. "I'm going to need an object that belonged to your father to target the tracking device."

"I have his pocket watch," Leo said, unfastening the chain from the buttonhole on his waistcoat.

"But you've been carrying that thing around for years," Faraz protested. "If the tracker relies on some intangible sense of possession, won't the watch's ownership have switched by now?"

Elsa frowned. "Potentially. Leo, do you ever think of it as yours?"

"No . . . it's my father's, always my father's. That's the point

220

of wearing it, after all." Leo swallowed, his throat tight. The pocket watch felt odd in the palm of his hand—a suddenly foreign object, the old meaning stripped away. How could he keep carrying around a remembrance of the dead when no one had died?

"Then we've got what we need to test this world," Elsa said. She held the book open to the first page for Porzia to input the coordinates. As the portal irised open, she added, "Oh, and . . . I suggest everyone remove their shoes."

They stepped through into cool, ankle-deep water that let off the salty scent of the ocean. A few meters away, a narrow strip of land stretched to their left and right, more blue water visible beyond. Elsa stepped closer for a better look, eager to make sure it had manifested properly, and there it was: a scale model of the Italian peninsula, fifty meters long and ten meters wide, with the rest of Europe laid out beyond.

"Oh dear Lord," Porzia swore behind her. "I'm standing in *the middle of the Adriatic.*"

Skandar had one tentacle wrapped around Faraz's neck and was leaning precariously off his shoulder to get a look at the miniature ocean below. Faraz put a hand up and steadied the overcurious beast.

"You can move around," Elsa told everyone. "Just be careful not to wander off the edge of the map."

The hem of Porzia's skirts was drenched, and she struggled to hold it up above her ankles without dropping the portal device. Elsa had tucked her own skirts over her arm before crossing through the portal, and was secretly amused at how uncomfortable the sight of her bare brown calves made the boys. That thought recalled the memory of Leo's bedroom, though, and the mirth drained out of her. There seemed to be an unspoken agreement between them to pretend nothing had happened, so she squared her shoulders and stepped up onto land.

The topographical contours felt rough on the soles of her bare feet—she'd scribed the model to withstand the weight of giants like herself tramping all over Europe, but hadn't considered that the extra-firm structural integrity might be rather uncomfortable from the giants' perspective. Elsa picked her way cautiously through the jagged peaks of the Alps, which were just tall enough to bang her shins against if she wasn't careful. She crossed through Switzerland and over Paris, and waded out through the English Channel to the Atlantic.

Rising from the water was a shiny brass podium with a glass front like a grandfather clock, displaying a complex interplay of gears within. At the moment, the inner workings were still and silent. Elsa slid open a small drawer on the side, checking the contents: a silver-backed pocket compass with not one but two needles, nestled in a bed of red velveteen cloth.

Satisfied, she closed the drawer and held out her empty palm to Leo. "I do believe we're ready to begin."

His amber gaze locked on her. There was tension around his eyes, but otherwise his features were schooled to appear calm. Resolute. He dropped the watch into her outstretched hand.

Elsa placed the watch atop the podium, pressed a series of buttons, and yanked down on a lever. The innards whirred to life, gears singing against one another. Soon, she could hear the *ka-chunk, ka-chunk, ka-chunk* of the target settling into place. Then the mainspring let out a soft twang, and the machine fell silent again.

She picked up the watch and handed it back to Leo while Porzia waded to shore, staring down at the map. Elsa followed, calling, "Do we have a location?"

A beacon of light pulsed in southeast France along the coast. "The city of Nizza," Porzia said. "That makes sense, I suppose."

Faraz said, "How so?"

"Leo's grandfather, Giuseppe Garibaldi, was a native Nizzardo. Ricciotti has returned to his family roots."

With sudden savagery, Leo declared, "That man cares nothing for family."

"Still," Faraz said in a soothing tone, "perhaps he inherited property there. French-occupied Nizza is as close as you can get to Italian soil without actually crossing into Sardinia. It's an ideal location for a man in hiding—just outside the reach of anyone who might be looking."

For a moment Leo seemed to wrestle with his temper before tamping it down, and even then, his words came out clipped. "Yes. Well. Let's go, then." His fist, tense around his father's watch, loosened one finger at a time, and he tucked it away in the pocket of his waistcoat.

"Not so fast—we still need to confirm our destination," Elsa said, her palm resting on the carved-wood grip of her mother's revolver, holstered at her right hip. She took a deep breath, drew the gun, and gently laid it upon the pedestal. "Moment of truth."

The whole tracking world seemed to hold its breath as the machine chugged away. Or perhaps that impression simply came from the way the molecules of air rang in her ears. Elsa waited for the finishing twang of the mainspring, but it did not come— instead the machine fell prematurely silent, as if too tired to complete its task.

Porzia glowered at the revolver. "It's not working."

"What does that mean?" said Faraz.

She's dead, thought Elsa, and pressed the back of her hand against her lips to hold in the cry of grief that threatened to erupt from her lungs. But then she remembered Jumi's old lecture: *We are stewards and caretakers—do you understand, darling? None of this is ours, it belongs to all Veldanese.* She'd thought her mother meant Veldana—the trees and stones and water—but what if Jumi did not believe in the individual ownership of possessions in a general sense? Their world had so many shared resources that private property was not a terribly Veldanese concept. Even young Elsa had needed the idea of *not yours* explained to her when she'd disassembled Montaigne's Pascaline.

She said, "I don't think we Veldanese have a very strong sense of ownership. Even a few days of carrying around Jumi's revolver is enough to confuse the targeting machine about who owns it." She didn't say, *Either that or Jumi's dead.*

Porzia said, "Do you have anything else of your mother's?"

"Nothing I haven't been carrying or wearing or otherwise using." Elsa jammed the revolver back into its holster, frustrated. There was no way to confirm that Garibaldi had Jumi with him, or even that she still lived.

Leo held out the pocket watch again. "Then we rely on what we do have."

Elsa took the watch and retargeted Garibaldi, then grabbed the two-needled compass from the drawer on the side of the machine as Porzia turned the dials on her portal device. Porzia went first into the portal to return to her sitting room. Elsa stepped through next and collided with Porzia on the other side.

"What are you—oh."

On the settee sat Gia Pisano, arms crossed, aiming a none-too-pleased glare at her daughter.

Porzia swallowed, and then said with forced brightness, "Mamma, you're back. How was Firenze?"

"When you wrote that Casa needed maintenance," Signora Pisano said, "I didn't imagine you meant the house had been *sabotaged*."

Leo and Faraz piled into the room behind them. Leo looked at Gia, looked at Porzia, muttered that he'd be right back, and fled the room.

Porzia watched him leave with a withering look, as if she considered him a coward for his sudden retreat in the face of an angry Gia. Then she squared her shoulders and said to her mother, "Casa's upkeep is a family matter. I thought it prudent to keep the details private."

"Mm-hmm," Gia said skeptically. "And all of this?"

Porzia blinked, the very picture of innocence. "All of what?"

"Whatever it is you've been cooking up on the other side of that portal," her mother said. "You children are going after Jumi's abductor by yourselves—I suppose that's also a family matter?"

"That's my fault," Elsa offered, though she had some difficulty mustering anything like contrition.

Dryly, Gia said, "Oh, well, in that case, my daughter is absolved of all responsibility."

"We were only going to do a little reconnaissance," Porzia insisted. "Confirm where Elsa's mother is being kept and by whom. Then we were going to bring the information to the Order, I swear—we wanted hard evidence first, is all."

225

Just then, Leo rushed back in, his rapier now hanging from his belt. Gia took one look at him and raised an eyebrow at her daughter. "Reconnaissance only, you say?"

Porzia flushed an impressive shade of pink. "Best to be prepared, just in case?"

Leo stopped short and looked annoyed at no one in particular. "I thought this would be sorted by the time I came back. We don't have time to stand around debating the finer points of—"

Gia stood from the settee and gave Leo a quelling look that made his jaw snap shut midsentence. Then she turned to her daughter. "I expect rash behavior from Leo. But you—I left you in charge because I thought you were mature enough to shoulder the responsibility. You were supposed to be watching the children, running the house, not hunting a dangerous pazzerellone!"

Elsa's chest twinged with a knot of sympathetic guilt. She knew exactly what it was like to have a mother with high expectations and a legacy that required massive responsibility. She could all too easily imagine how Porzia felt facing Gia's disappointment.

Porzia's eyes glistened with moisture, but her voice rose to match her mother's volume. "Responsibility! What of my responsibility to my friends? Am I supposed to refuse them help?"

Gia pointed her finger angrily at the floor. "You are supposed to prioritize the good of the house above all individual concerns."

"And you were supposed to convince the Order to rescue Jumi!" Porzia retorted. "How exactly is that going?"

"Augusto Righi is a coward. But your father and Alek are still working to convince—"

"Leo's right, time is of the essence," Porzia interrupted. "We're going, Mamma, whether you like it or not."

Tightly, Gia said, "You're right, I can't stop you. I can't leave the children here alone with Casa in such need of repair. But you must promise me not to engage with these people. Observe only. When you have more information, we will decide—together— what is to be done. Am I clear?"

"Understood," said Porzia. Elsa got the sense she was only barely resisting the urge to snap a sarcastic salute.

Gia took one last, long look at her daughter's face, as if trying to commit every detail to memory. Then she turned toward the door. "Casa—is Burak still working in the generator room? Tell him I'll be there shortly."

Her mother gone, Porzia took a deep breath, straightened her skirts, and said, "Well. Are we all set, then? We should go before the compass loses its charge."

A little flower of guilt bloomed inside Elsa. Porzia was fighting with Gia because of *her*, and she didn't know what to say to make that better.

Faraz stroked Skandar soothingly. The tension with Gia had made the poor beast anxious. "Ready as we'll ever be," he said.

Porzia threw him a blistering look. "You are not bringing *that thing* with us. We're trying to be inconspicuous, remember?"

Faraz harrumphed, but he pried Skandar off his shoulder and set the beast down on the armrest of a chair. "One of these days we're going to need him," he grumbled.

"I can't imagine for what," Porzia replied. "Now let's go."

After a short trip through the doorbook, Elsa, Leo, Porzia, and Faraz emerged onto the narrow, curving cobbled streets of Nizza. It was a maze of a city, not so overwhelmingly large as Paris but easily the equal of Pisa, Elsa guessed.

"Here," she said, handing the compass to Leo. "The black needle points toward magnetic north. The silver one points toward the tracking target. Garibaldi, in this case."

Leo frowned down at the compass and swiveled left and right, testing it. "It's a part of the targeting machine?"

Elsa nodded. "Yes—I figured we'd need an object from the tracking world to keep us on course."

Leo led the way as they began the uncertain task of finding one woman in a city of ninety thousand. Elsa felt hyperaware of his proximity, the angle of his shoulders, the small crease of concentration between his brows. *Just nerves*, she told herself, and tried her best to ignore the feeling.

It was late afternoon, and the city bustled with carriages and foot traffic. Here and there, Elsa caught snatches of English and French alongside the native Nizzardo dialect. The foreigners, though numerous, were overwhelmingly white, and self-consciousness burned down her spine—even without Skandar, she and Faraz were far from inconspicuous.

Elsa couldn't puzzle out why there were so many northern Europeans until they had to squeeze past a particularly obstructive cluster of Englishmen, and Porzia muttered, "Bloody English vacationers."

They followed the compass needle east and left the vacationers behind in favor of sailors and dockworkers. They circled around a ship-choked port that cut inland, the air heavy with the scent of brine and rotten fish. Leo slowed to a stop and tapped at the glass face of the compass.

"This can't be right. My father was a man of means, not a"— he waved his hand in the vague direction of a raggedly dressed man stumbling out of a tavern—"an unemployed deckhand."

Elsa took the compass from him, ignoring the way he looked at her when their hands touched. She pivoted back and forth on one heel, watching the compass needle hold steady, pointing to a run-down tenement house across the street. "It seems to be working fine. That's the place."

They ducked into a narrow alleyway to strategize. The sun hung low in the west, lighting up the wisps of cloud in shades of pink and orange, and the shadows between buildings had grown comfortingly dark.

Leo stared in disbelief at the ramshackle building. "This has got to be a malfunction."

"No, it's perfect," Porzia said thoughtfully. "Unsavory characters can go in and out all day without anyone batting an eye. And who would think to look for upstanding citizen Rico Trovatelli here? Not even his own son."

Leo's lips tightened angrily. "My father—"

"Your father was a fiction," Porzia interrupted. "We know little and less of the real Ricciotti Garibaldi, except for this: we know he can deceive."

For a moment, Leo looked as if he might like to slap her. Then his gaze shifted back to the tenement house, and Elsa could practically hear the gears of his thoughts shifting. "All right," he finally said. "I'm going in alone."

Porzia lifted her gaze to the heavens, as if begging a higher power for patience. "You're not leaving us behind now, Leo."

"Look," he said, exasperated. "We can't all go in together. If this doesn't go well for us, someone has to return to Toscana and report to Gia what happened. And, obviously, that would be accomplished most expediently if the return party had a scriptologist to open a portal."

Elsa stepped closer to Leo. "I'm sorry, but he's right."

"*What?*" Porzia screeched, clearly surprised to have Elsa side against her.

"Leo and I go in. Garibaldi knows about us already, so even if we're spotted, he gains nothing. But he doesn't yet know we have help, and we might need that element of surprise later."

"This is just ridiculous—" Porzia huffed, but Faraz put a gentling hand on her shoulder. She frowned but said, "Fine."

"Here," Elsa said, handing over the doorbook to Porzia. "In case you need it."

Porzia accepted it gingerly, the scowl vanishing from her features. "Are you sure?"

"I'm quite sure I don't want something this useful falling into the hands of our enemies." She shrugged a shoulder, hesitant, then added shyly, "Besides, I trust you with it."

Porzia nodded, her eyes wide, as if genuinely touched by the gesture. "I'll take good care of it."

Leo was fiddling with the grip of his rapier, anxious to get moving and oblivious to the weight of the moment Elsa and Porzia had just shared. He said, "Wait for us at the east end of the promenade. If we haven't met up with you by midnight, get yourselves back to Pisa and tell Gia what happened."

As Porzia and Faraz turned back the way they'd come, Elsa and Leo crossed the street, keeping to the shadows. The lamplighters had yet to grace this part of the city with their presence, so the growing dark was on their side. With whispers and hand gestures, they agreed to approach the building from behind. They snuck through the cramped, filthy alleyways, the walls of the tenement buildings muffling the sounds of the city. There was the splash of Elsa's shoes in the alley's damp muck and the steady hiss of her breath, but that was all. Leo moved as quiet as a cat—she knew he was still with her only by the dark shape of his silhouette.

They crouched low as they drew closer. The first-floor windowpanes were grime-smudged and warped, but they glowed with lamplight from inside, which would ease the task of spying somewhat. Leo crept up to the nearest window, and Elsa pressed herself close to the bricks beside him. The light drew a sharp line across his cheekbones as he peered inside. After a moment he withdrew, shook his head at her—*nothing*—and slunk over to the next. Pulse pounding in her ears, she followed. If the compass had led them true, one of these rooms might have her mother in it.

Elsa heard a *click* behind her. Before she could register what it meant, Leo spun around, his hand flying to the hilt of his rapier. Turning, she reached for her revolver, at the same time placing the sound: the click of a cocked-back hammer.

Black-clad Carbonari assassins emerged from the shadows, weapons out and aimed.

15

Relieved of her pistol, Elsa was half dragged inside by two burly Carbonari. Her instinct was to fight back however she could—with feet and fists and teeth—but Leo caught her eye and, with a subtle jerk of his head, warned against it. They were badly outnumbered and should wait for a better opportunity to effect their escape.

They were led up a narrow, dim-lit stairway. The smell of pine tar clung to one of Elsa's captors, and it burned in her nostrils. With a Carbonaro attached to each arm, she couldn't lift her skirts and stumbled on the stairs, but they just hauled her up and kept going.

On the third floor, they passed through a door into a room that was much larger than a single tenement, with rough patches where interior walls had been knocked down. A long, sturdy table that dominated the center of the room held an assortment of papers—maps, blueprints, shipping manifests, and others Elsa couldn't identify at a distance.

Leaning over that table was a man. All but two of the Carbonari retreated from the room, and when the door slammed, the man behind the table looked up. Elsa knew instantly who he was.

Ricciotti Garibaldi had the same high forehead, straight nose, and expressive mouth as Leo, but he was brown-haired, and—Elsa noted with a spark of surprise—he had a bit of a weak chin. The paternal resemblance was there, but far from complete. She found the differences oddly comforting, as if they were an outward sign of the differences within.

Ricciotti looked at each of them for a moment, his expression unreadable. Then he moved around the table and walked over to Leo.

"Ah, my son. I've been expecting you." He reached his hands forward as if to grab Leo's head and kiss his cheeks. Leo's eyes went wide and he shoved him away.

"Don't touch me," Leo said hoarsely.

"I see." Ricciotti straightened, rubbing the place on his chest where Leo's hand must have connected. "I knew it would be a difficult adjustment for you, returning to the fold, but we hardly have time for your childish antics."

"*My* antics? I'm not the one who sabotaged a train full of innocent bystanders as some sort of ridiculous test!"

Ricciotti shrugged it off as if Leo's accusation were of little consequence either way. "It has been hard to know the proper time to reintegrate you—you were much too immature when we fled Venezia. I wanted to observe a show of your abilities. But, to my dismay, you weren't the polymath who solved the problem."

Elsa's eyes widened at the brazenness of his admittance. What kind of parent subjects his own son to a life-or-death test?

But Leo did not seem horrified at this; instead he let out a bitter laugh. "Oh, poor Father. What a disappointment it must have been, to think I'd finally followed in Aris's footsteps only to discover the honor belonged to someone else. I suppose that's why you tried to have her killed?"

"Sending the Carbonari man was an error. My intelligence was incomplete—if I'd realized who your lovely companion was, I would not have targeted her." He inclined his head toward Elsa in a brief acknowledgment of her presence.

"Of course," said Leo. "Why destroy a person you already have means of controlling?"

Ricciotti continued as if Leo hadn't spoken. "In any case, my agent was under strict instructions to only deliver the poison. The train to test your mechanics, the poison to test your alchemy. And of course the problem of finding me, which would have tested your scriptology if you hadn't yet again allowed others to do your work for you." He gestured toward Elsa. "I never intended Jumi's daughter to die, and as she appears quite well, I hardly see what you're making a fuss over."

Elsa felt as if her mother's name were a punch to the gut, robbing her lungs of air.

"What is wrong with you?" Leo demanded. He looked about ready to pop a gasket. "I have to figure out you're alive by deduction and conjecture? You couldn't have—I don't know—sent a telegram *like a normal person?*"

But Elsa was still focused with the intensity of a microscope on those two small syllables: *Jumi*. "So you admit it," she snapped, the words like acid in her mouth. "You are the one who took Jumi da Veldana."

"She speaks," Ricciotti said, amused and unabashed. "Indeed, I have her."

Leo looked stricken at the shamelessness of the confession. He bent his head toward Elsa and spoke hushed words for her ears only. "There is nothing I can say in his defense. . . ."

She squeezed his arm. "You are not responsible for this."

"I told you," said a voice behind them, "we should have brought him back sooner."

Elsa jumped and whirled around, but Leo turned slowly, as if he already knew who it would be. A young man, perhaps a few years older than she, leaned casually in the doorway. His hair was dark, but he had the same wide-set tawny eyes she'd grown accustomed to seeing in Leo's face. He had Leo's beauty, too, but he wore it like a mask over whatever lay beneath. *Aris.*

He pushed away from the doorframe and sauntered over to Leo, and with the two brothers standing close to each other, she could see Aris was somewhat taller but also slimmer. "You should know it was for your own good," he said to Leo. "One doesn't bring children to war. I wanted to send you a message, at least, but Father insisted you would never be content to stay away if you knew we lived."

Leo shifted his weight, as if he wanted to step away but couldn't, held in place by the magnetic pull of brotherhood. "Well you're right on one point: there's nothing you could have done to content me after Venezia."

The corner of Aris's mouth quirked. "Haven't lost your flair for the dramatic, I see." His gaze flicked past Leo to land on

Ricciotti, and his voice took on layers of meaning that Elsa found difficult to parse. "Same old Leo, isn't he?"

Leo's hand flashed out and snatched ahold of Aris's sleeve, demanding his brother's full attention. "Aris—" His voice came out hoarse and urgent. "Where's Pasca?"

Ricciotti started to say, "Now is hardly the time to—"

"He's dead," Aris interrupted, staring intently back into Leo's eyes. Leo seemed pinned beneath his gaze. "Pasca was supposed to be at fencing lessons with you. Signora Rosalinda was supposed to get both of you out. By the time we knew he was unaccounted for, it was much too late."

Leo's eyes went wide, and all the color drained from his face. He looked as if he might be sick. Elsa couldn't begin to guess what he was thinking in that moment—but, apparently, his brother could.

Aris cupped Leo's face in his hands. Unlike with Ricciotti, Leo made no move to stop him, and this more than anything else chilled Elsa. "Oh, little brother," Aris said, "you couldn't have known. Pasca was always sneaking off, skipping lessons. It isn't your fault."

"Of course it's not *his* fault," Elsa said, her temper finally snapping like a brittle twig. "He's not the one who *set fire to the house!*"

The brothers both looked at her, Aris with a trace of annoyance, Leo as if he were trying to focus on her through a thick fog.

Elsa turned her wrath on Garibaldi. "We're not here for a reunion," she said through gritted teeth. "Why did you take Jumi? Where is she?"

Garibaldi clasped his hands behind his back. "As to the second matter, Jumi is alive, she is under my care, and I will remand her to you in exchange for a favor."

Fury flashed through her veins, but Elsa lifted her chin and tried to channel the brazen calm with which Porzia might have this same conversation, were their positions reversed. "And as to the first matter?"

"Therein lies the rub," he replied, the corner of his mouth lifting ruefully. "My men had instructions to gain access to Veldana with Montaigne's assistance, then acquire your mother along with a scriptology book she created."

Elsa felt an absurd sense of triumph at hearing Montaigne's betrayal confirmed. And the scriptological weapon they'd heard rumors of—it must be inside the worldbook that had gone missing from the cottage along with Jumi.

"Unfortunately," Garibaldi continued, "the mission went awry. A third party killed Montaigne, set fire to the house, and in the ensuing confusion made off with the book."

Elsa said, "So where is this book now? Who has it?"

"I know not. A double agent for the true Carbonari, some vindictive Veldanese, a spy for Sicilia or Veneto or the Papal States . . ." He took a breath, and for a second he almost seemed rattled before regaining his smug superiority. "I've had agents searching for it, unsuccessfully so far. But now I think this is no longer *my* problem to solve."

"You're proposing a trade. You want me to find it for you."

"Who better to find the book than the daughter of its creator?"

Elsa kept silent for a moment, watching him. The creator herself would surely be better than the creator's daughter, and this thought sent a spike of fear through Elsa. "I'll see my mother now. I want proof she's alive before agreeing to anything."

Garibaldi gestured to another door at the far end of the room. "Signorina, if you'll accompany me, I'll take you to her."

This seemed to sober Leo enough for him to regain control. "She's not going anywhere with you—"

Elsa rested a hand on his arm to quiet him. "It's all right. I'll be all right."

She followed Garibaldi despite Leo's protestations and found herself traversing a narrow, windowless hall, and doubting whether it was wise to be alone with him in a confined space. If anything, Garibaldi seemed amused by her stiff reluctance.

"Think what you will of me, but everything I do is for the good of the people. To put an end to foreign rule and crushing taxation, an end to religious laws strangling the progress of science. To unite my countrymen for a better future."

Elsa glared at him. "You have a funny way of showing it, abducting an innocent woman from her home."

"Innocent!" Garibaldi let out a surprised laugh. "Your mother is hardly innocent. She scribed the single most dangerous book in the history of mankind."

"But has she ever actually used it?" Elsa countered with a show of confidence. In truth she felt queasy at the thought of her mother using a worldbook to manufacture weapons—corrupting the beautiful, pure scientific discipline of scriptology. She did not want to believe her mother capable of such perversion, but at the same time she knew Jumi would do anything to protect Veldana.

Garibaldi led her into a smaller room, and what she saw there drove those thoughts from her mind. Her mother lay prone, unmoving, inside a glass coffin nested within a large machine. Elsa's breath caught in her throat.

"What have you done?"

"Everything I could."

"What is that supposed to—" She stopped midsentence as she got a better look at the machine. A mask with a thick tube trailing from it covered her mother's nose and mouth. A sound almost like hydraulics—hiss and suck, in rhythm with the rise and fall of Jumi's chest. A needle oscillated across a ribbon of paper, drawing a peak for each slow beat of Jumi's heart. It was medical equipment.

Softly, Elsa said, "What's wrong with her?"

"She is ill," said Garibaldi, "and not of my doing. I believe she has been ill for some time. Consumption, you see."

"You are mistaken. She has been quite well."

Garibaldi said, "A scriptologist of your mother's talent would have no difficulty scribing restorative properties into Veldana, so her symptoms would not trouble her while at home."

"No." Elsa's mind raced. His version of events sounded plausible, but perhaps Garibaldi had made her sick, or perhaps she was not sick at all. How could she know the truth when she couldn't trust a word he said?

"I did not cause her illness, and indeed it has been a matter of some inconvenience for me. Yet"—he spread his hands philosophically—"here we are."

"You claim to be faultless, and yet your Carbonari minions abducted her, and now you force her to stay in this toxic world."

Elsa pressed her palms to the curved glass lid of the chamber. She wanted to take her mother's hand, but even with her so close, she was still out of reach. It was too much. Elsa ran her hand along the bottom edge of the glass, desperate to find a release mechanism to open the lid.

Garibaldi grabbed her wrist. "I wouldn't do that. If you attempt to open the casket without entering the correct code, the machine will asphyxiate her."

Then Elsa saw the latch for the lid, and just below the latch a row of six metal switches. Six binary switches meant sixty-four possible combinations, of which sixty-three would kill her mother. She yanked her hand out of Garibaldi's grip. "You're a monster." A brilliant monster, perhaps, but she wasn't about to admit that aloud.

"Every great leader gets demonized by someone. It is the price we pay for pursuing our vision of the future. But I am just a man, and though my actions may seem abhorrent, I can assure you they are all in service of my country."

"If you are not a monster, then prove it: release her into my care immediately."

Garibaldi gave her a sad look, as if he pitied the simplicity with which she saw the world. "Alas, that is not an option. I require Jumi's book. If you can find and retrieve it before my men do, I will consider her a fair trade."

Elsa bit her cheek to force away the sting of angry tears. "Very well. But I warn you: if she dies for the sake of your ridiculous political games, I will rain destruction upon everything you hold dear."

Oddly, Garibaldi responded with a well-pleased smile. "I have every confidence it will not come to that. I do not think even you understand the depths of your power when you are . . . properly motivated. I expect our transaction will be completed quite soon."

Leo felt as if he'd been thrown from the seat of the spider hansom, the breath knocked out of him. He had steeled himself against the possibility of confronting his father, but somehow he had not prepared for this new version of Aris. Even the boy-Aris of his childhood memories held a certain sway over him. He'd always had that effect on people, drawing them in like moths to a flame. But this older Aris, more shrewd and subtle, had unfamiliar depths.

Who was this new Aris, grown son of Ricciotti Garibaldi? How could Leo and Aris be *Leo and Aris*, without the youngest brother to complete them?

His mind reeled, and Aris's sharp gaze seemed the only lifeline within reach. Aris said, "Everything is going to be all right now that you're with us again, brother."

Leo's lips parted, but he couldn't find the strength to contradict him. Instead, he said, "What are you planning?"

Aris cocked his head, as if he thought this an amusing question. "To finish our grandfather's work, of course: bring an end to the tyranny of foreign kings and unite our people. With Jumi's book, we can realize Grandfather's vision for Italian unification."

Leo thought back to the day before Elsa had arrived, to the earthquake that wasn't an earthquake, which had corresponded with chilling accuracy to the moment when the Carbonari abductors brought Jumi and her mysterious worldbook into the real world. He had no proof, but could it be that one was the direct result of the other—that the tremor had been the world's straining protest against the sudden introduction of such a powerful object? And, too, he remembered the shattered carnevale mask, the mask that had always reminded him of Aris.

"Listen to me, you can't use that book. If Elsa's mother has truly invented a way to make scribed weapons, no one can know about it. Can't you see that using it would endanger all scriptologists?"

Aris cracked a grin. "I know you've missed the benefit of my mentoring these past years, but really, Leo—have you forgotten that *anything* worth doing is going to be dangerous?"

"Don't mock me," Leo said hotly.

"You're angry, and I don't blame you for it," Aris answered, dropping the smile. "But we're not enemies, you and I."

Leo watched his brother through narrowed eyes. "I don't know what we are now."

The greater part of his concern was reserved, however, for Elsa. Surely Father wouldn't hurt her, not now that he knew how valuable she was. No, not hurt . . . but ensnare? He'd wanted all along for Leo to find him, and Leo had led Elsa right into his trap. *Rosalinda was wrong*, he thought. He was never smart enough. He couldn't see how to get himself—or Elsa—out of this mess. He cast a worried look in the direction she had gone.

Aris rested a hand on Leo's shoulder. "He won't make a play for her now. Not until he has that book in his possession."

"What?" Leo said, alarmed. Strange, how even after their long years apart, he could not seem to hide his thoughts from Aris.

"You're right to worry, though," Aris continued. "We both know how Father is about polymaths—he must realize what a powerful asset she could be."

Was Aris offering allegiance? Or attempting to goad, to

manipulate? Leo searched his brother's expression. "What are you saying?"

"Nothing, brother." Aris shrugged, a careful show of disinterest. "But I'd keep an eye on the Veldanese girl, if I were you. Wouldn't want to lose that one."

Leaving the tenement building—and with it her mother—Elsa felt as if she'd ripped out a vital organ and left it behind. The image of her mother, lying so very still within Garibaldi's stasis chamber, seemed emblazoned on the insides of her eyelids. She had to think about something else, anything else. If she dwelled on that image for one second longer, she would burst into tears right there in the street.

The worldbook, she would think about the worldbook. The most dangerous book ever created, which Jumi had kept hidden from her. The betrayal stung—they had always shared everything, or so Elsa had thought. What sort of weapons did it contain? Why would Jumi have created such a thing? No, the worldbook was no better, so she pushed the thought from her mind.

Instead, she focused on Garibaldi—his mocking smile, his casual dismissal of Leo's talents. She fanned the flames of her hatred until it outshone everything else.

"Your father is horrible," she told Leo as they hurried across a shadowy plaza. "Testing you like that, and then having the nerve to call you a failure."

"It's not horrible to speak the truth," Leo said listlessly. All the fight seemed to have drained out of him, his store of righteous anger depleted after the confrontation with his family.

Elsa, on the other hand, still had plenty to spare. "First, he set

243

preposterous standards for success. Second, he doesn't understand that the smartest way to tackle a problem is to use the people at your disposal—something you taught me, by the way. And third, is he even a polymath himself?" The medical chamber Garibaldi had shown her was an impressive combination of alchemy and mechanics, but he'd never actually claimed credit for its construction.

"No . . . ," Leo said. "He has some mechanist tendencies, but he's primarily an alchemist. His talents are unusually broad, but he's not a full polymath like you and Aris."

"So he expects more from you than he himself can deliver. Who the hell does he think he is, to suddenly come back into your life and judge you?"

Leo shrugged. "My father?"

She snorted. "He forfeited his claim to that title seven years ago when he abandoned his own children in a burning house."

Leo declined to answer, and Elsa clenched her jaw and forced herself to let the subject drop. He must be processing the encounter in his own way, trying to sort through deeply conflicted emotions, Elsa knew, and she should respect that—even if her own rage and terror were threatening to overwhelm her.

It was late by the time their footfalls landed with hollow *thunk, thunk*s on the wooden boards of the promenade. A fat gibbous moon rose in the east, and each wave crest caught and scattered the light. Elsa found she was grateful for what darkness the night could offer, obscuring just how endless the ocean was. How distant the horizon. She felt like some tiny tide-pool creature, swept away from her cloistered home into the impossible depths of the open sea. This was a vast world—a vast responsibility. *Much depends on the choices you make*, the Oracle had told Elsa and

Faraz. Could Jumi's worldbook truly lead to freedom for the Italian people, or enslavement for pazzerellones, or both? For the briefest of moments, she hated Jumi for laying such a weight upon her shoulders.

Leo's gaze swept left and right, picking out two darker silhouettes amidst the gloom, and he strode straight for his friends. Elsa couldn't recognize them in the dark, but she followed without questioning.

The moonlight glinted in Faraz's eyes as he turned. "Ah, you see? I told you they're still alive."

"Oh, thank the Lord!" Porzia exclaimed, throwing an arm around each of them and pulling them into a messy embrace. "Don't scare me like that. And you," she said to Faraz, "don't gloat—you were just as worried as I."

Faraz managed a casual poise, as if he had no idea what she was talking about. "I tried to tell her you'd be fine."

Porzia looked from one of them to the other, taking in Leo's dazed expression and Elsa's grim determination. Her jubilant relief settled into concern. "What went wrong? Didn't you find anything?"

"We found something, all right," Elsa said. "In a way, we found too much."

Together they all ported back to Casa della Pazzia, and Elsa and Leo related the events of their confrontation with Garibaldi.

Everyone agreed to reconvene in the morning to plan this new search for the book. As she trudged up the stairs, Elsa wondered if they were all thinking along the same lines as she. They would retrieve this dangerous worldbook . . . and then what? Trade it for her mother's life, and in so doing give Garibaldi exactly what he wanted? When she'd first fled to Amsterdam, all she cared about was rescuing Jumi and salvaging Veldana, but now the thought of helping Garibaldi left a bitter taste in her mouth.

Sleep refused to come. Elsa played through her encounter with Garibaldi, sifting through each memory as if to glean some overlooked grains of insight. Jumi lying so still inside the chamber that both sustained her and held her prisoner. Garibaldi's confidence that he would get what he wanted, one way or another. But Elsa's mind kept catching on one thought in particular, like a linen shirtsleeve snagging and tearing on a rough metal edge: there existed a worldbook that Jumi had deliberately hidden from her own daughter.

After a while she gave up the attempt to sleep, threw on her dressing gown, and wandered out of her room. She had no particular goal, other than to clear her head.

A little bot appeared at her heels, holding up a candlestick. In a hushed voice, Casa said, "Some light, signorina?"

"Thank you, Casa," Elsa replied. "How are you feeling?"

"Better, signorina. It is kind of you to ask."

Elsa tugged her robe tighter. "At least one thing is going well. We are overdue for some good luck."

"If you will excuse my forwardness, signorina: you are a pazzerellona. You make your own luck."

In her wanderings, Elsa came upon the door to the cloister garden, and on a whim she let herself outside. She left the little candlebot waiting on the veranda and stepped out under the stars. There was a stone bench toward the middle, which seemed a reasonable place to sit and think.

The garden was lovely at night. Crickets chirped, and the

pale glow of the moon transformed the fruit trees into a surreal landscape of light and shadow.

Movement in the corner of her eye caught her attention, and Elsa looked up to see Leo leaning against his balcony railing, one hand wrapped around the neck of a wine bottle. His hair was mussed, his shirt rumpled, the unbuttoned cuffs hanging loose about his wrists. Though his face was shadowed and his posture gave away nothing, Elsa could feel the precise moment when his gaze fixed upon her.

If he'd meant to be alone with his wine, he didn't seem at all put out to discover he had company—instead, quite the opposite. He vaulted over the balcony railing, picked his way down the sloped tiles of the veranda roof, and swung off the edge. Some of the wine splashed from the bottle when he landed, staining his white shirtsleeve. "Damn," he said absently, switching the bottle to his left hand and shaking wine droplets from his right.

"Can't sleep?" she called.

He strolled over to her, more or less in a straight line, and sat beside her on the bench. "How ever did you guess?"

Her instinct was to bristle at his sarcasm, but she managed to let it go instead. By now she could recognize his bravado for the defense mechanism it was. "Neither can I. I can't seem to switch off all the unsolved questions."

"Mm," he said, then held the bottle out to her. "Would you care for some liquid off-switch?"

Elsa raised an eyebrow and declined to take the bottle. "And how's that working for *you*?"

"Ask me again when it's empty," he said, and took a generous gulp.

Elsa stayed quiet, waiting for him to work his way around to what he really wanted to say. After a minute of silence, he spoke again.

"Don't you agree the nightmares ought to go away, now that I know my father's alive? But they're still up here"—he tapped his temple—"worming away at my brain. Everyone else makes it look so easy. Such a simple matter, sleep. But not for me, never for me."

"I'm so sorry, Leo," Elsa said awkwardly. She found herself wishing she'd spent less of her childhood sketching sea creatures and more time learning how to be a good friend. She didn't know what to do with this raw, exposed version of Leo. She didn't know what to do *for* him.

Leo took another swig straight from the bottle. "And you? What are you doing wandering the garden at this hour?"

"Can't get my own parent out of my head," Elsa confessed. "I thought I was the one person Jumi trusted completely. I thought she shared everything with me, but she was hiding things from me, too. If Alek is a fool for believing he knew her, then how much more foolish am I, who lived with her every day of my life and still didn't know?"

"Not sure it's possible to ever really know someone else. Know their mind." Leo was watching her with an oddly intense expression, as if the wine made it difficult to focus. Then he added, "Your hair is like shadows."

Elsa blinked at him. "Uh . . . what?"

"Shadows," he said again, as if repetition would make his point clear. He reached out for a strand of her hair and ran his fingers down its length. Elsa stiffened, but he didn't seem to notice, too intent on the strand. "Is like you could melt into darkness, dissipate like smoke. Poof. You're a phantom, Elsa."

"And you're a drunken idiot," she said, batting away his hand.

"You're not going to disappear on me, are you? Oh, Elsa, I don't think I could stand losing you too. . . ."

Elsa flushed with a sudden awareness of how close he was, how he leaned in toward her like a plant reaching for the sun. She could smell the wine on his breath; she wondered if she would taste of it too, tannic and sweet at once, if she pressed her lips to his. For a weak moment she wanted nothing more than to kiss him, to be drowning in him the way he was drowning in the wine bottle.

Leo's eyes narrowed at her and he leaned away, as if he somehow sensed what she was thinking. Apparently even drunk Leo had a firm sense of propriety.

Elsa could not help but smile at him. "I'm not going anywhere."

"I thought all you wanted was to get your mother and go home to Veldana," he said, the edges of his words worn ragged with pain. Even in the dark, she could see the deep-rooted fear of abandonment etched around his eyes.

Elsa whispered, "That's not all I want. Not anymore."

Leo focused his bleary stare upon her, as if he were trying to will himself to sober up enough to comprehend her meaning. Subtlety was wasted on the intoxicated.

Taking pity on him, Elsa stood and said, "Come along. I think you've had quite enough wine, and it's time to try your bed again."

"That's what all the ladies say to me," he said with a lopsided grin.

Elsa snorted. "I'm going to assume that's the wine talking."

"It was a joke!" Leo threw his head back dramatically, as if to plead his case to the stars. "Why must you always assume the worst of me?"

"If you always assume the worst, you can never be disappointed," Elsa quipped. Then she reached for his hand to drag him to his feet.

Leo did not resist her, but neither was he especially cooperative as they made their way inside and up the stairs. She tried to take the wine bottle but he fought to keep it, and since there wasn't much left at the bottom anyway, she relented.

In his bedroom, he managed to kick off his shoes with only a little difficulty, then flopped onto the bed fully dressed, wine-spotted shirt and all. He curled on his side, facing away from her, but kept ahold of her hand.

As his grip relaxed, she tried gingerly to ease her hand away, but he mumbled, "Don't go."

"You're drunk," she countered.

"Yes," he said, with surprising lucidity, "but I am not too drunk to know I want you to stay. That I always want you to stay. . . ."

Elsa huffed, but she gave in and stayed. It was pointless trying not to care for him—if she was honest with herself, she'd long since lost that particular battle. As his breathing slowed and deepened into the rhythms of sleep, she brushed his soft golden hair away from his face with her other hand.

People, like clockwork, needed care and maintenance. Leo's gears slipped and ground against one another, and his brass casing rattled, and his mainspring was always, always wound too tight. The thought filled Elsa with such righteous anger, knowing Garibaldi had broken the one thing she couldn't fix.

Before that moment, all she'd wanted from Garibaldi was Jumi's safe return. She'd known he was awful and she'd hated him, but not like this. Now she wanted to see Garibaldi pay for what he'd done—not just to her family, but also to his own kin. Now she craved vengeance on behalf of them both.

"For this," Elsa whispered to the sleeping boy, "for this I will destroy him."

16

Elsa spent the morning with Porzia, arguing over the possibility of modifying the map world to detect an object—namely, the missing worldbook—instead of a person. When their discussion devolved into a shouting match, Elsa decided that perhaps a different approach was called for.

Some time later, Faraz wandered into the library and set a plate of bread and cheese on the table beside Elsa's elbow. "You missed lunch again. How goes the hunt?"

Elsa was flipping through Montaigne's journals for the fifth or sixth time. "It doesn't make any sense. There's no mention of any political connections except Garibaldi. So if Montaigne wasn't the leak, how did this mysterious third party even know the theft was occurring?"

Faraz pulled out the chair opposite hers and sat. "Perhaps we're approaching this from the wrong direction. Could we make a list of everyone who knows the worldbook exists and might want to take it off Garibaldi's hands?"

"Montaigne would be at the top of that list, except for the part where he's dea— Oh!" she said, interrupting herself as a thought occurred.

"Oh?"

"Porzia!" she called.

Porzia leaned over the railing of the third-floor balcony. "What?"

Elsa waved a hand impatiently. "Get down here, I've had an idea."

Porzia, clattering down the stairs, said, "Casa? I believe it's past time you roused Leo."

"Leo is . . . somewhat indisposed," the house said delicately.

"I don't care, Casa. Drag him from his bed if you have to." She came over and leaned one hip against the table beside Elsa. "What is it?"

Elsa looked from Faraz to Porzia and back again. "Why kill Montaigne and burn the house? There are other ways it could have been accomplished. Killing Garibaldi's men, or using their own knockout gas against them. Why the fire?"

Faraz shrugged. "To cause panic or to destroy evidence."

"Evidence," Elsa said, latching onto the word. "When Leo was a child he saw his father's body, but it wasn't his real body, it was an inanimate homunculus. A copy. What if Garibaldi, in the process of befriending Montaigne, told him that story?"

Faraz's eyes went wide. "You mean Montaigne created a homunculus of his own? That just might be possible. He'd need an excellent alchemist, though—faces are a challenge."

Elsa sat back in her chair and shook her head, disappointed in herself. "The body was positioned facedown, and the house being on fire was rather a distraction. A shoddy likeness wouldn't have fooled Garibaldi himself, but his ex-Carbonari followers wouldn't have thought to look for the signs. I certainly didn't, and I'm a pazzerellone."

Porzia frowned thoughtfully. "Is that the sort of thing Montaigne would do? He was a scriptologist, after all, not an alchemist."

"Tricking someone using their own brand of subterfuge?" Elsa said. "Absolutely. He always loved proving how much smarter he was than everyone else."

Faraz tapped the table. "We need to establish whether he's truly dead."

"Who's dead?" Leo said groggily from the doorway. His hair was a mess, he squinted as if the sunlight through the window pained him, and he was still dressed in yesterday's clothes, now wrinkled in addition to wine-stained. At the sight of him, Elsa felt as if there were a hand around her heart, squeezing.

With some effort Leo pushed away from the doorframe and joined them, flopping down in the chair beside Faraz. "Or who's potentially not dead, rather?"

Porzia explained, "Montaigne may have faked his death."

The more Elsa considered this possibility, the angrier she became. If Montaigne was alive, was he also complicit in the burning of his library? Had he set the fire himself, knowing full well that it might mean the destruction of Veldana? Her home, her legacy, her people—all potentially destroyed. "That bastard! If he's alive, he's going to wish he wasn't."

Leo folded his arms on the tabletop and rested his head on them. "I don't suppose you could all whisper? My skull's about to explode."

Elsa clenched her teeth. "I need to know. I need to know for certain who's responsible for that fire."

"Fantastic," Porzia said, heavy on the sarcasm. "What are we supposed to do? Go to Paris and dig up his corpse?"

Faraz brightened. "Actually, I don't think that will be much of a problem. I've got this machine—"

"You have a *grave-robbing machine*?" Porzia screeched. Leo winced.

Faraz held up his hands. "It's not mine! I don't work on people, remember? It's something the previous occupant left behind in my lab—looks like it's been under a tarpaulin for forty years. I'm not even sure it still works."

"Oh, it works," said Leo.

Everyone turned to stare at him.

"What?" he said defensively. "There was a mysterious machine cluttering up Faraz's lab. I'm naturally curious."

After an awkward pause, Faraz cleared his throat. "The larger problem is how to find Montaigne's grave. It's not as if we can show up in Paris advertising our intent to exhume a corpse. There are laws about such things."

Porzia said, "If only one of us knew a revolutionary with a network of spies all across southern Europe. Do you think the Carbonari might have someone in Paris who could help?"

"Wonderful plan. After a little nap, I think," said Leo.

"Now." Porzia grabbed his arm and dragged him from the chair. "You need to call on a friend."

Rosalinda met him at the door with a penetrating scowl. "Are you hungover?"

Leo squinted against the afternoon sunlight, which seemed to be stabbing right through his eyes into his pounding skull. "We need a favor. Do you have an agent in Paris?"

Rosalinda let him inside but commanded him to sit while she prepared a pot of calendula tea. Cradling the warm cup in both hands, Leo realized this was her way of caring for him. She was a warrior—she understood the needs of the body. Her ministrations might be brusque, but this was how she expressed affection. How she always had.

By the time he was done explaining everything that had happened—even the conversation with Aris, which he'd kept to himself so far—the tea had eased his headache and settled his stomach.

Rosalinda tapped her long, dexterous fingers against the arm of her chair and watched him speculatively. "So do you believe Aris would side with you against your father, or do you only *wish* to believe it?"

"Ugh, I don't know." Leo set down his empty cup and rubbed at his eyes. "He could just as easily have been manipulating me at Father's request."

Her lips pressed into a thin line, Rosalinda seemed to arrive at a decision. "Very well, I'll reach out to my contacts in Paris regarding the gravesite. But you must do something for me: think carefully about how you'll proceed. Aris may prove unworthy of your trust, but that doesn't necessarily mean he's wrong about Ricciotti's interest in Elsa."

Leo gave her a rueful smile. "As Gia would say, even a broken clock tells the time twice a day."

She nodded. "Just so."

As much as he blamed his father, Leo desperately wanted to trust in Aris. Aris, who had teased his brothers mercilessly, but would not suffer a single word spoken against them by anyone else. He'd once broken the stable boy's arm in three places for making fun of Pasca. Leo remembered that day with perfect clarity, because it was the day when he thought, *Nothing can ever hurt me, because Aris will protect us.*

But he also remembered little Pasca, in tears, begging Aris to stop hurting the bloodied stable boy. And Aris, who'd taken a long time to stop.

"So this is where you put dead people, huh?" Elsa said, looking around. "It's not what I'd imagined."

They'd timed their arrival for after nightfall, and there were no gaslamps to illuminate the cemetery. By the light of the kerosene lantern Faraz held, she could make out a brick-paved walkway lined with skinny trees. Little stone buildings and statues cast a starburst pattern of long shadows away from where he stood. The cemetery stretched into absolute dark in all directions, so massive it was hard to believe they were inside the city. Somewhere in the darkness, an owl hooted.

"The grave's just over here," Porzia said, taking the lead.

They'd taken a portal directly to the gravesite to avoid attracting attention. Apparently, as Porzia had explained to Elsa, a group of foreigners entering a cemetery with a large machine in tow might be viewed with suspicion.

Leo said, "Hold on a minute." He flipped a switch on the digger bot's control box, but nothing happened.

Standing idle, the machine looked a bit like a giant ant. It had a narrow body almost two meters long, and three sets of multijointed legs. Leo gave the control box a good whack and tried the switch again, and the machine lurched into motion. It wasn't especially skilled at walking, so now it looked like a giant drunken ant.

As they all followed Porzia, Elsa watched Leo out of the corner of her eye. His scowl suggested he'd like to disassemble the bot for proper repairs right here in the graveyard, the very sight of a poorly functioning machine offending his sensibilities. Elsa hid a smile.

"It's this one," Porzia said, checking the name engraved on the stone to be certain.

The machine positioned itself above the fresh-turned earth and planted its feet wide. With a high-pitched whine, its belly split in half, revealing a column of smaller scoop-shaped appendages. As the machine warmed up, the methodical scoop-and-dump motions sped faster and faster until the digging arms blurred together and the dirt was flying. The machine lowered its body into the rectangular hole as it progressed downward.

"I don't get it," Elsa declared.

Leo looked up from the control box. "Get what?"

Elsa waved a hand vaguely, indicating the graveyard as a general concept. "Take the grave markers, for instance. If you're not supposed to dig them up again, why do they all need to be labeled so precisely? It'd be much harder to steal the right corpse if they weren't all marked."

Faraz gave her a look that suggested she was missing something. "The headstones are for the families. So they can visit their loved ones."

Elsa frowned, perplexed. "Their *dead* loved ones . . . ?"

Briskly, Porzia interjected, "Let's save the theological discussion for another time, shall we? The machine's almost finished."

Elsa still had no idea why anyone would want to visit a corpse disposal site, but she agreed with Porzia's assessment: this gap in her knowledge simply wasn't high on their list of priorities at the moment.

Metal scraped harshly against wood, the digging arms slowed to a halt, and the dirt stopped flying. With a chuff of hydraulics, the body of the machine slowly rose out of the hole in the ground, a casket held firmly in its clutches. The bot scuttled to one side, deposited the casket on the grass, and backed away, settling into idle mode.

"Let's see what we've got," Leo said, setting aside the control box and hefting a crowbar. He wedged the crowbar beneath the pine lid and worked it up and down, the fabric of his shirt taut over flexing muscles. Elsa caught herself staring and flushed, embarrassed, but in the dark nobody seemed to notice.

The nails of the coffin lid squealed against the wood as they pulled loose. Once fully open, an unpleasant stench rose from the casket. It wasn't the foul odor of putrefaction that Elsa had expected, though—it was something unfamiliar.

"Whew," Leo declared, holding his sleeve to his nose and backing up a step. "Smells like burnt rubber, only worse."

Faraz, on the other hand, stepped closer and crouched over the contents, holding the lantern close. His nose wrinkled, but otherwise he gave no indication of discomfort.

"I can't believe they buried this stuff in a graveyard," he scoffed. "No one could tell this isn't human? It's not even organic—looks like some kind of wax-based composite. Consider my faith in the intelligence of normal folk to be shattered."

Porzia raised her brows. "Don't rush to judgment. I certainly wouldn't volunteer to perform an autopsy on that. It's disgusting."

"And charred human bits wouldn't be disgusting?" Faraz countered. "Anyway, we have our answer. Montaigne is alive."

Elsa leaned over the casket, breathing shallowly. A sticky black tar-like substance coated what remained of a fake skeletal structure. The corpse she'd tripped over in Paris had never been real; it was all a misdirection. Even though she'd known Montaigne had little respect for the Veldanese, she still felt a sharp stab of betrayal that he would risk destroying Veldana to serve his own ends.

Leo scrunched his face. "You're not going to touch that mess, are you?"

"Oh dear Lord," Porzia groaned, as if she might be ill. "I can't look."

"No, no," Elsa reassured them, backing away. "Seeing it is proof enough. Faraz is right: Charles Montaigne lives."

Stepping away from the stench of the burnt homunculus, Elsa took a deep breath and let it out. So far, everything the Oracle had told her was true: Jumi's captor was a brilliant megalomaniac, and Montaigne—the man who had betrayed her—had the worldbook Garibaldi wanted. And what if the last piece of the Oracle's prediction proved correct as well?

You will lose something precious to you.

Everyone seemed subdued as they opened a portal back to Casa della Pazzia.

Leo cleared his throat. "Casa, would you give the digger bot a good cleaning and return it to Faraz's lab? Better not to track dirt all over Gia's floors." They were standing in the foyer, which meant the bot would scatter dirt through half the house to get back to the alchemy lab if it wasn't cleaned first.

"How atypically considerate of you, Signor Trovatelli," Casa mocked.

"Not really," said Porzia. "He just doesn't want to put Mamma in a mood before we talk to her."

Leo shrugged. "Guilty."

To Elsa and Faraz, Porzia said, "You two should go ahead to the library and see if you can track Montaigne's location. I have to go convince Mamma not to lock us all in the wine cellar until this whole business is over with."

Difficult as it was for her, she would have to trust in Porzia's persuasive abilities, so Elsa simply nodded. "Of course." She felt Leo's gaze lingering on her for a moment, as if he were trying to extract some hidden meaning, but she had no idea what he was looking for.

After Porzia and Leo left to find Gia, Faraz said, "I'll meet you in the library in a minute. I've got to pick up Skandar from the alchemy lab."

"Skandar?" She gave him a confused look.

"Let's just say the creature has its uses." Faraz flashed her a grin and went.

Elsa just stood there on the inlaid tile floor for a moment, exhausted. She watched as a tiny brass bot rolled into the room and began scrubbing down the much larger gravedigger. Then she made herself move, heading for the library. Time to track down Montaigne, and with him find the leverage she needed to rescue her mother.

Leo tugged on Porzia's elbow as they passed near his laboratory. She raised an eyebrow, but let him lead her down the half flight of steps and over to the workbench where the scrambler sat. He flipped the switch so they could talk in private.

"What are you doing?" she said, fists planted on hips.

He held up a hand. "Let's just think about this for a moment. This worldbook we're going after . . . if it really contains some sort of apocalyptic-level weapon, we can't let my father get his hands on it."

"Obviously," she said, her voice clipped with impatience.

"But we also can't tell the Order about it, which means we can't risk telling Gia."

Her eyebrows shot up and she took a moment to reply, taken aback. "Don't be ridiculous, of course I have to tell Mamma. Especially after . . . how we left things." Despite their Tuscan tempers, Porzia and Gia had always been close, and Leo knew it pained her to be at odds with her mother for any length of time.

He rubbed a hand across his forehead. "If the Order gets ahold of a dangerous worldbook, they're going to lock it away, all other concerns be damned. They'll write off Elsa's mother as an acceptable loss without a second thought."

262

"And what if your father is manipulating us? What if he has no intention of releasing Jumi, no matter what we do in exchange?"

"We won't let that happen. We'll have leverage!"

Porzia's face twisted in a pained expression. "I can't not tell my mother where we're going, Leo. I'm sorry, but that's asking too much."

Her hand darted out and deftly turned off the scrambler, and then in a swirl of skirts she was up the steps and out the door.

"Hold on! Porzia!" Leo called, but she did not stop.

Leo exhaled in frustration and chased after her, following her through the halls and down the basement stairs.

"Wait a minute!" he said, an urgency bordering on panic growing in his gut. "The last time we so much as mentioned my father's name to the Order, they sent a courier to divest us of everything we'd collected that even *might* have to do with Ricciotti Garibaldi."

"I know that," Porzia snapped. "I was the one who deceived the courier and sent him on his way with just a single journal from Montaigne's library. But you can only stretch my loyalties so far."

"What of your loyalty to Elsa?"

She stopped just inside the doorway of the generator room. Her eyelids squeezed shut and her hands curled into fists. "Can't you see you're tearing me in half?" she hissed.

"Please, Porzia. *Think*."

The room was so warm the air felt too thick in Leo's lungs, and pinpricks of sweat immediately began to tickle the back of his neck. The great hulking generators chuffed noisily, indicator needles vibrating just shy of the redline. Gia must have spooled them up to full power in order to test their functionality.

"There's nothing wrong with my thinking," Porzia squeezed out from between clenched teeth. "She's my mother, and the Order will hold her responsible for all of us. For whatever we do."

Burak's skinny, grease-smeared form appeared from around the side of a generator. He ran over, oblivious to the tension between them. "Leo! Where have you been? We worked all day and it's going to be a long night, too, and you're missing all the fun."

Leo managed a strained smile, feeling a little jealous that Burak was still young enough to think everything was fun. "Well, you're getting so good at this stuff, I figured you didn't need my help."

Apparently his smile was not convincing enough, though, since Burak's cheerful expression faded into uncertainty. "Signora Pisano went over to the charging room. Do you want me to fetch her?"

Leo turned to Porzia again, his tone imploring. "If she doesn't know, she can't be blamed. We'd actually be protecting her."

Porzia made a frustrated noise in the back of her throat, grappling with indecision. "Promise me," she said, and though she couldn't elaborate on the specifics with Burak listening, Leo knew her well enough to guess: *Promise me we'll rescue Jumi and stop Garibaldi; promise me this is the right choice.*

Leo flashed her a conspiratorial grin. "We can do this; I know we can."

She gave him a solemn nod—her official acquiescence.

Leo, still smiling, turned to Burak and said, "Never mind. No need to disturb Gia, after all."

Inside the tracking world, Elsa sloshed barefoot across the miniature sea and picked her way over the miniature mountains to the brass podium. She slid open the side drawer and returned the tracking compass to its proper place so the machine could retarget. Then she placed one of Montaigne's worldbooks atop the podium, pushed all the right buttons in the right order, and pulled the lever to start it up.

The gears whirred, warming up. The tracking machine went *ka-chunk, ka-chunk*—just twice—then the gears wound down to a slow idle, sounding to Elsa's ears as if the machine were too depressed to perform its duties. Elsa shut it all the way off. Maybe she'd made a mistake. She lifted the book off the top of the podium, wiped the surface down with her sleeve, replaced the book, entered the start-up sequence again, and yanked the lever.

Again, the machine refused to take the target.

Scowling, Elsa opened the return portal. The floor of the library was cold against her still-damp feet, but that was the least of her problems.

Faraz and Skandar were already waiting in the library, but before he could ask her how it went, Porzia and Leo arrived. At least Elsa wouldn't be required to relate the bad news twice.

"Well?" Porzia said, flushed with nervous energy. "Where's the bastard hiding?"

"Couldn't tell you," Elsa replied. "It didn't work."

That drew Leo and Porzia up short. Leo gave her a dumbstruck look. "What?"

Elsa pulled out a chair and flopped down, dismayed at the sight of Montaigne's worldbooks stacked on the table. She said, "All the worldbooks went through the restoration machine—they've not only been handled by other people, they've been completely disassembled, repaired, and reassembled by someone else's invention. The ownership must not have survived."

"Damn," said Porzia, hands on hips. "I hadn't thought of that."

Faraz said, "But ownership is a property you just invented. Can't you rewrite the map world so one of Montaigne's books will work?"

"Oh, of course," Porzia said. "If we had time to go to university and complete a doctoral dissertation on ownership properties!"

Elsa explained, "There's an element of stochasticity involved whenever you scribe a complex property. Porzia and I could spend weeks creating a dozen different variations on the map world and still fail to produce one that would accomplish precisely what we require."

Leo's eyes widened in horror as the realization sank in. "So now we have nothing of Montaigne's." He ran a hand through his hair, frustrated. "Damn it, we had exactly what we needed and we ruined it."

Had that been Montaigne's true intention when he set fire to his house? To leave no trace of himself behind, no fragment to be exploited, to sever all connections that might lead to the world-book's true thief? Unwittingly, Elsa had salvaged precisely the objects she would need to locate him; and just as unwittingly, she had completed the fire's work and destroyed those selfsame objects.

Porzia's eyes narrowed, her lips pursed. "Wait a moment, Elsa. Did you ever fix that Pascaline?"

Elsa's heart skipped a beat. "No, I didn't! I borrowed some tools, but I never started the repairs. And Montaigne owned it for years—it might have a strong enough ownership bond even with the fire damage." With a sudden burst of renewed hope, she shot out of the chair. "Porzia, you're brilliant!"

"Well I hardly think *that* was ever in question," Porzia said primly.

Elsa ran all the way to her study and back, returning breathless with the charred and warped Pascaline. The fire alone might have done it in. Or what about that time she'd disassembled it as a child? Still, it was their best hope—she could only pray the ownership was still intact.

All four of them went through to the map world together, as if Elsa needed help to be even more nervous than she already was. Her hand was shaking when she reached for the controls, and she had to squeeze it into a fist and then shake out her fingers to steady the muscles. Porzia pulled the lever for her.

Elsa held her breath through the first iterations—*ka-chunk, ka-chunk*—and did not relax until the twang of the mainspring signaled completion.

"Whew. I think it worked this time."

Porzia fished the compass out of its drawer and scrutinized it. "Seems to be pointing at *something*, at least."

Elsa sloshed through the ankle-deep ocean back to the continent, intent on discovering where their search would take them next. The sound of splashing water told her Porzia and the boys followed close behind.

"Unbelievable," she said, staring down at the pulsing red dot on the map. "He has a lot of nerve going there, after what he did."

Faraz stepped up beside her, curious to see. "Whatever do you mean?"

"I know exactly where he's hiding," Elsa explained.

The dot glowed over Amsterdam: the home city of one Alek de Vries.

17

THE MOVING FINGER WRITES, AND HAVING WRITTEN
MOVES ON. NOR ALL THY PIETY NOR ALL THY
WIT, CAN CANCEL HALF A LINE OF IT.
—*Omar Khayyam*

The doorbook took them to a too-familiar street. The quiet canal on one side, the narrow, squashed-together brick buildings looming up on the other, the warm pools of gaslight on the cobblestones. Elsa hardly needed to check the compass for confirmation, but Porzia held it out for her to see, so she glanced at it anyway. Her hunch had been right—the needle pointed straight at Alek's front door.

"We'll have to pick the locks," Elsa said. "I don't have a key."

"That won't be a problem," Leo said. He produced a set of lockpicks and crouched by the door.

Porzia kept an eye on the street, looking out for anyone who might notice their illicit behavior, though passersby were unlikely—the hour was so late it might better be called early. "Isn't this the part where you tell us all about how you grew up with a band of professional thieves, or some such?"

"It hardly seems fun anymore," Leo said, "if you're going to make up the lies for me before I get a chance to tell them."

He gave the torsion wrench a quick twist and the front door swung inward.

Elsa stepped inside. "Quietly now. He's on the second floor."

They climbed the stairs single file, hugging close to the railing to keep the steps from creaking beneath their weight. Elsa pointed at Alek's door, and Leo slid a pick into the lock. This time everyone stayed silent while he worked, hardly breathing.

When the lock popped open, Leo grabbed the door handle to hold it mostly closed. He raised his eyebrows at Elsa. The hinges were going to creak, she knew, but she gave him a quick nod anyway.

Leo tucked the lockpicks away and let the hinges creak. They were inside.

A sleep-blurred voice from the other room said, "Listen, Alek, I can explain—"

Then he rounded the corner and came face-to-face with them. Charles Montaigne was of de Vries's generation, grayed hair and tired skin, though he was shorter and more portly. "You're not Alek." He stared for a moment, dumbstruck, and then let out a short bark of laughter. "The daughter, of course! I should have guessed you'd come for it."

Elsa drew herself up to her full height and spoke with as much authority as she could muster. "Monsieur Montaigne, I need my mother's worldbook."

Montaigne considered her, his expression both sad and superior

269

at once. "I'm sorry about Jumi, I am, but you can't have the book. No one can—it's too dangerous."

Leo took a step forward, fingering the grip of his rapier. Elsa could practically feel the tension in his body vibrating through the air. He said, "Don't mistake this for a request. We're prepared to take it by force if we have to."

Montaigne let himself down into Alek's armchair, as if Leo's threat simply wearied him. "When Garibaldi approached me about acquiring it, I knew this was my chance to hide the book where no one can ever use it." He picked up Alek's pipe and began packing it with tobacco.

Elsa ground her teeth. "So you don't deny it's your fault she was taken."

He struck a match and sucked on the pipe, pulling the flame into the bowl for a nice, even light. "You know . . . I spent years afraid of her, hating her, but the truth is I brought it on myself. The arrogance, to think I knew what was best for the Veldanese simply because I'd created them. So you see, when it comes to that book, I'm just as culpable as Jumi. Though to be fair, none of this would have happened if Alek hadn't taught her to scribe."

Elsa was stunned at the man's talent for shifting blame, and it was Faraz who replied, "You tried to burn the Oracle worldbook— an original Jabir ibn Hayyan. And you call yourself a scriptologist." His voice shook with cold fury. "You are no scriptologist!"

Montaigne turned a sick shade of green at this accusation. His hand dropped to the armrest, as if the pipe were suddenly an unbearable weight. "The men I hired were supposed to take the ibn Hayyan along with Jumi's worldbook—I thought it would throw Garibaldi off my scent if they were seen stealing from my library. But some idiot dropped the ibn Hayyan in the struggle."

Privately, Elsa thought it was rather telling that the part Montaigne felt ashamed of was burning the books, when he had no shame over encouraging and facilitating Jumi's abduction. Even now, the Veldanese had little value to him beyond the scriptological accomplishment they symbolized—they were never going to be fully human in his eyes.

Which meant no argument about Jumi's welfare would sway him. Elsa's throat felt tight with desperation. "You cannot right one wrong by committing another. I need the book!"

Faraz stepped forward. "This is getting us nowhere." He tossed a small glass vial at Montaigne, which broke on impact, spreading a bluish ooze all over his shirt and up his neck.

Montaigne said, "Ugh, what is this foul—" And then he went, quite suddenly, as limp as a sleeping babe.

"Excellent," Faraz said, satisfied with the results. Perched on his shoulder, Skandar raised a few tentacles in glee, as if this were all a show Faraz had performed for the creature's enjoyment.

Leo stared down at Montaigne, curious but unperturbed. "What did you do to him?"

"When I heard about the sleeping gas from Elsa, I figured we could use some of our own. Don't touch it—the active ingredient absorbs through the skin. Not such a widespread effect as gas, of course, but better for close-contact situations, I thought. He'll be out cold for a few hours at least."

"Huh." Leo looked from Montaigne's motionless form to Faraz's attempt at an innocent expression. "Then I suppose I won't need this for anything," he said, resting a hand on the hilt of his rapier.

"I wish you hadn't done that," Elsa said to Faraz. "I still have questions."

"He wasn't going to tell us anything useful," said Faraz, though he looked abashed. Faraz was the last one she'd expected to act hastily out of anger instead of cool logic. He slipped out of the room to check the rest of the flat.

Elsa stared at Montaigne's slack expression. Did he know whether or not the Veldana worldbook had survived the fire? Did he even care?

She sighed. "What are we supposed to do with him now? If he were Veldanese, we'd send him into the Edgemist for this betrayal." But she could not even guess whether or not Veldana still existed.

"We can turn him over to the Order," said Porzia. "But only after we find the book."

Elsa knelt, careful to avoid Faraz's sleeping ooze, and examined Montaigne's right hand. "There's ink on his fingers. Still damp. He's been scribing."

Porzia folded her arms. "If I were trying to hide something important, I'd hide it inside a worldbook."

Elsa looked up at her. "A worldbook full of puzzles only you know how to solve?"

"Or perils only I know how to survive," she said.

Leo drummed his fingers against the rapier's pommel. "I might get to stab something, after all."

"Here it is," Faraz said, returning from the other room with a tome held open in his arms. "But wouldn't he scribe it to be inaccessible to anyone but him?"

Elsa shook her head. "Too risky—that's a great way to render yourself textual."

Leo said, "Shame he didn't do it, then."

"Leo!" Porzia scolded, as if she took deep offense at the idea of wishing someone textualized.

"Anyway, there's no such thing as an impenetrable security system," said Leo. "So are we going in, or what?"

Porzia took the book from Faraz and flipped to the beginning. Elsa stood to look over her shoulder. After a few minutes of inspection, Porzia said, "My French isn't perfect, but as far as I can tell, it doesn't look as if it'll kill us just to step inside. What do you think?"

Elsa took out her portal device. "Read me the coordinates."

Leo didn't know what he'd been expecting, but it certainly wasn't this.

They stood in front of a fieldstone wall seven meters high that stretched to their left and right, curving gently away in both directions. Behind them was Edgemist, and directly before them was a gap in the wall, like a doorway absent the door. The dimness inside seemed somehow foreboding, as if it had been a long time since light trespassed in its territory.

The silence stretched long while Elsa waved that glove of hers around. Leo watched her working for a moment, but he felt acutely aware that they were not alone. He tried looking away, but that felt obvious, too—was it more telling to stare or to avoid staring?

Apparently satisfied with the stability of the world, Elsa removed the glove and cleared her throat. "This doesn't seem so difficult. Obviously he must have hidden the book through there."

Leo rested his hands on his hips as he eyed the wall, forcing his brain to focus. "You see how the wall's curved, as if it might be one enormous circular structure? It's a labyrinth. Full of dead ends and nasty surprises, no doubt."

"Blind exploration and booby traps?" said Faraz lightly. "I thought you'd be thrilled."

"Normally, I would be, but time is of the essence. We can't afford to spend a week wandering lost in a maze."

"No, we really can't," Elsa said tightly. Was she thinking of her mother? Leo felt a sudden urge to reach out, make contact, but when Elsa's defenses were up it seemed as if *she* were the one behind protective glass, not her mother. Leo wasn't sure he could touch her even if he tried.

Porzia said, "We needn't explore the entire structure. If it is a labyrinth, everyone knows anything of importance will be located at the center."

Leo took a deep breath and let it out, steadying his resolve. The best comfort he could give Elsa would be the safe return of her mother. He looked to Faraz. "Into the wolf's mouth?"

Faraz grinned and replied, "May the wolf choke on us."

And with that, Leo led the way.

At first the darkness made it difficult for Elsa to see much of anything in the center of her visual field, and she had to rely on peripheral vision just to place her feet without tripping. But after a minute within the labyrinth's corridors, her eyesight adjusted to the diffuse lighting, and it became a relatively simple task to determine the difference between a shadow and a fallen fieldstone when one or the other crossed her path. She considered fetching a lantern from her laboratory worldbook, but if the light suddenly blew out, they'd all be left blind again.

Porzia was squinting at something she held in the palm of her hand. "Well, thank goodness for small blessings," she said. "This world has a magnetic north."

Elsa stepped closer. Porzia was holding the tracking machine's compass. The tracking needle swung listlessly, aiming at nothing in particular, but the magnetic needle pointed straight ahead. So the entrance where they came in must be on the southernmost edge of the maze. "Interesting. I never thought we'd need it just as a regular old compass."

Porzia said, "Between this and the curvature of the walls, we should be able to keep track of our progress relative to the center."

"That's good," Leo called. He and Faraz had gone ahead and were now standing at a wall where their current corridor terminated. "Does that mean you're going to decide: left or right?"

"Both," Elsa called back. "Let's evaluate our options."

Leo and Faraz disappeared from view in opposite directions. Elsa and Porzia caught up just as Faraz came back around a bend. "The eastward corridor looks like it doubles back and heads south again."

Porzia nodded and tucked the compass away. "So we'll try the southwest quadrant. See where it takes us."

They proceeded from there in much the same fashion, splitting up for a brief time at each intersection so as to make an informed decision about which path to follow. Though Elsa recognized this was probably the fastest way to find the center, it still made for slow going, and impatience burned in her gut. Damn Montaigne for this.

They wasted time pursuing two separate dead ends. Once, a slight tremor reverberated through the floor for a few seconds and they all froze until it passed, but whatever had caused it failed to make an appearance. At the third dead end, Porzia huffed, "Labyrinths are not supposed to have dead ends!" But otherwise, their exploration was proving uneventful. Elsa couldn't help but feel it was suspiciously uneventful.

They were walking a long stretch of corridor with no turn-offs when, up ahead, something caught her attention—a flicker of darkness, like a shadow in motion. She held up a hand, drawing the group to a halt. "Did anyone else . . . ?"

Her questioning frown elicited nothing but blank looks from her companions. She looked down the corridor, took a few cautious steps forward, scrutinizing every nook and cranny. Nothing but stones with the occasional weed pushing up through the cracks. "Strange. I thought I saw something move."

"We're all on edge," Porzia assured her. "And it's easy for your eyes to play tricks in this light."

"Right." That must have been it, though she could have sworn she'd seen something. An insect, maybe, she told herself.

They all began to walk again, Elsa slightly in the lead. She stepped forward, the stones of the floor looking entirely normal, and her foot landed on . . . nothing. Her stomach lurched as she tipped forward and began to fall. Faraz lunged, making a desperate grab for her arm, but even as his hands closed, her forward momentum slid her other foot over the edge. She dug her fingers into his forearm, clinging as her weight wrenched her shoulder joint, and the sharp-angled edge of the invisible chasm hit her hard in the ribs. She slid down as Faraz fought for purchase.

When her head dipped below floor level, the illusion vanished, and she could see the blackness gaping beneath her. The chasm yawned wide and deep, and the only wall visible through the gloom was the one pressed against her cheek.

"Give me your other hand!" Leo was screaming at her, crouched at the edge above. From the panicked, searching look on his face, it seemed they still could not see below the illusion, so all they had of her was an arm sticking up out of the floor.

Elsa flailed, trying to reach for Leo without compromising Faraz's already tenuous hold. After three failed attempts, Leo finally caught her wrist, and the boys hauled her back up.

Elsa sat on the floor for a minute, catching her breath, before she even tried to stand. Skandar, who had taken wing during the commotion, resettled on Faraz's shoulder and gave Elsa an accusatory glare, as if it were all her fault for displacing him.

Porzia appeared at Elsa's elbow to help her up. "Are you all right?"

"Lucky I didn't crack a rib on the edge," she said, holding her hand against her sore side. For once she felt a flash of gratitude for the corset stays that had spread out the impact, though tomorrow she imagined she'd have some lovely bruises.

Leo was cautiously shuffling across the width of the corridor, dipping his toe over the edge to map the extent of the hidden chasm. "No way around—it's as wide as the corridor. Do you think we could jump it?"

Elsa shook her head. "It seemed cavernous down there."

Faraz picked up a pebble and tossed it a few meters ahead. Instead of clattering against stone, it disappeared into the floor without a sound. "Definitely too far to jump."

Leo ran a hand through his hair. "Okay. So, in addition to dead ends, we have impassable gaping holes in the floor. Fantastic."

Elsa rolled her shoulder, testing for torn muscles, while she considered the problem. "Listen, when I was down there, I couldn't see the other four walls. The space looked much wider than this corridor. If we move one corridor to the left or right, I think we're likely to encounter the same chasm."

Porzia said, "So we retrace our steps. Go back to the entrance and try our luck in the southeast quadrant, instead."

Faraz stroked one of Skandar's tentacles. "Don't know if you've noticed, but our 'luck' hasn't been of much assistance so far."

Porzia rolled her eyes. "The southeast quadrant can't be *worse* than falling to our deaths in a bottomless pit."

"Now you've done it," Leo said with a wry grin. "Now we're definitely going to find something worse than a bottomless pit."

But in the end they all agreed that Porzia's plan seemed best. They followed the curve of the corridor, retracing their steps. Left, left, past two turnoffs, right, left again.

"Wait," Elsa said. Up ahead, the corridor ended at an unfamiliar wall. "Does this look right? Did we take a wrong turn somewhere?"

Porzia scowled. "We were all counting the turns. We should be able to see the entrance from here."

Faraz spun in a slow circle, looking around. "Where in hell are we?"

Leo planted his fists on his hips and exhaled sharply. This was getting ridiculous.

At this rate, they would need to go back for provisions, except that they probably couldn't. They'd lost the entrance, and he'd bet his favorite screwdriver that Montaigne had scribed the world such that portals could only be opened at the Edgemist. Which meant they were not only failing to find the book, they were also getting themselves increasingly entrapped.

It was time to try a more radical approach. He unbuckled his sword belt and handed it to Faraz.

"What are you doing?" Faraz said, accepting the rapier.

"We're lost." Leo flashed him a grin. "I think it's time we cheat."

With that, he wedged the toe of his boot in the crack between two fieldstones, and he began to climb.

"Oh good Lord," Porzia swore. "Be careful!"

"Fortune favors the bold!" he called down to her. Best to sound confident. The strain of clinging to the wall with only his fingertips was already making the muscles in his forearms burn, and a bead of sweat trickled down his spine.

"If you fall and split your skull open, I am not cleaning it up," Porzia huffed.

Leo had to smile at that. It was just so . . . so *Porzia*. An oddly comforting familiarity.

Finally he got his hands over the top edge and—through a combination of pulling and scrabbling that probably did not look especially suave to the watchers below—heaved himself onto the top of the labyrinth wall.

He stood, surveying the domain that stretched away from him in all directions. He'd known the labyrinth must be large, but it was a different matter to see the expanse with his own two eyes. The air was also eerily still. In the real world, if he climbed up on top of a structure there would be a breeze, or at least the feel of warm air convecting off the sun-heated stones. Here, nothing. There wasn't even a sun—the sky was the swirling bruise-purple of Edgemist, made luminous enough to cast a meager quantity of light down upon the labyrinth. No wonder it seemed like perpetual dusk down below.

Up here, with the world laid out at his feet, he could see that the group's current position was close to one side—presumably the south side—though the walls blocked them from the gap he guessed had been their original entry point. From the curvature, he could be reasonably sure of where the center was, though both the distance and the shallow angle of his line of sight made it difficult to discern. As he looked out across the vast expanse of curving corridors, he once again felt that slight tremor through the soles of his shoes. And as he watched, a section of wall sank into the ground, disappearing from view.

"We have a problem," he called down to his companions. "The labyrinth is changing."

Elsa frowned as she, Faraz, and Porzia followed Leo's directions. Leo walked along the top of the wall, keeping pace with them and occasionally instructing them on which turns to take. His apparent disregard for his own safety only served to irritate her more.

"I still don't like it," Elsa muttered to Porzia. "It's *too* easy."

"Perhaps Montaigne didn't expect to be pursued by an acrobatic Venetian swashbuckler," Porzia said. "The walls are plenty tall. I certainly wouldn't have made it up there." She gestured at her dress, which was admittedly not suitable for wall climbing.

Despite her suspicions, Elsa grudgingly had to admit to herself that Leo's plan was expediting their progress. From atop the wall, he could pick the shortest route to the center and watch out for changes in the labyrinth. They still had to retrace their steps a few times when the labyrinth grew a new wall to thwart their passage. But Elsa could tell they were getting close by the tighter curvature of the corridors.

"There's definitely a large space in the center, like a round courtyard," Leo called from above. "Hold on a minute."

He sat down on the top of the wall, rolled onto his stomach, then lowered himself off the edge, reaching for footholds in the stone. He scuttled down the wall deft as a mountain goat and rejoined them on the floor of the corridor.

"We're close. I've got the last few turns memorized," he said, as Faraz handed back the rapier.

They walked in silence for a minute or two, following Leo's lead. There was something eerie about the absence of sound inside the labyrinth. Veldana was a scribed world, but it had birdsong and wind through the trees, waves rolling over rocks and small animals burrowing in leaf litter. Here, nothing. It was quiet as death.

"Skandar's nervous," Faraz observed.

Porzia said, "The tentacle monster isn't the only one."

Elsa was watching for the flicker of shadow that would give away another camouflaged pit in the floor. "Just keep your eyes open, everyone." She half expected Leo to offer a snappy reply, but when she stole a glance at him, he seemed too focused on the path ahead.

They turned right into a corridor so sharply curved that Elsa could only see a few meters in front of them before the inner wall obstructed her view. Leo led them halfway around the circle to a place where the inner wall opened up onto a larger space beyond.

"Hah, this is it!" Leo crowed, but the mirth died on his lips as he stopped dead in his tracks.

Elsa peered around his shoulder, hoping to catch a glimpse of her mother's book—she imagined it on a stone pedestal, like some sort of religious icon—but instead the round inner courtyard of the labyrinth hosted a sharp-toothed monster. It bore some resemblance to a wolf but was much too large, with a row of spines protruding from its grotesquely arched back, taloned eagle's feet, and too many eyes, like a spider.

It peeled its lips back, and even the labyrinth's dim light was enough to glint off those rows and rows of dagger-shaped teeth.

18

I KNOW NOW THAT SHE IS DESTINED TO SURPASS
ME, IF SHE HAS NOT DONE SO ALREADY.

—*personal notes of Jumi da Veldana, 1891*

E veryone keep quiet and hold still," Faraz said under his breath. "It's not sure where we are."

Elsa wondered how that could be true, since the monster's head had swung around to face them. But then she noticed its nostrils flaring and its head cocking from one side to the other hesitantly. Montaigne might have spent his time liberally when scribing its slavering maw, but some corners had been cut on the matter of keen senses.

Leo swallowed visibly and muttered, "Unless I'm horribly mistaken, that's not a prize waiting for us in the center of the labyrinth."

Very slowly, he began to ease his rapier out of its sheath. The wolf-monster twitched an ear at him halfway through the task, generating a collective gasp from the humans and forcing Leo to freeze in place, but as soon as its attention shifted again, the blade came free with a soft *shnick*.

Faraz gave a barely noticeable shake of his head. "Don't. This is a scribed monster—you have a weapon of precision and no promise the vital targets will be in the right places."

"You give Montaigne too much credit for creativity. It will have a heart and a throat, at least, which is good enough for me. What do you want to do, stand here forever?"

Faraz gave him a warning look, but Leo ignored it. Icy fear threaded through Elsa's veins as Leo lunged forward, rapier at the ready.

He feinted left and right, testing the beast's reflexes. It could move fast for its size, but Leo was smaller and more agile. He darted forward and sank the rapier deep into the wolf-monster's throat. For a second, Elsa believed he'd done the beast in, but then it twisted to the side, wrenching the hilt from Leo's hand.

Seeing him disarmed, Elsa drew her revolver. At the same time, Faraz quietly said, "Skandar, attack."

Skandar's wings snapped open and it launched itself from Faraz's shoulder, tentacles flaring. Despite its apparent lack of a mouth, Skandar emitted a high-pitched "Shreeee!" so loud Elsa nearly dropped the revolver in her attempt to cover her ears against the piercing sound. If there had been any glass nearby, she imagined it would have shattered.

The wolf-monster shook its head as if addled by the cry and stumbled backward a couple of steps. As soon as the cry ended, though, it seemed doubly incensed. The beast lunged at Leo, the rapier still grotesquely skewered through its neck. Elsa took aim and squeezed off two rounds into its chest. The bullets slowed the monster, but it stumbled forward to take another swipe at Leo, who scrambled out of range of the beast's claws.

"Yes, well," he panted. "I'm willing to admit this isn't going as well as I'd hoped."

"Leo admitting he's wrong?" said Faraz. "If we weren't fighting for our lives, I'd take a moment to mark the occasion on my calendar."

Skandar, circling the beast's head just out of reach, let out another earsplitting "Shreeeeee!" Elsa winced, but at least the noise seemed to pain the wolf-monster much more than it did the humans.

Faraz folded his arms. "Skandar, stop playing around and finish it."

Skandar's one enormous eye seemed to regard them for a moment, and then the creature dropped from the air like a stone, landing on the wolf-monster's head with tentacles splayed. There was a *bzzzt* sound, and arcs of blue-white electricity and the monster's whole body twitched and jerked. Then Skandar released its tentacles' grip, and there was only the sound of limp flesh hitting flagstone and the reek of burnt hair.

Faraz calmly welcomed Skandar back to its usual shoulder perch while everyone else stared openmouthed at the dead wolf-monster.

Leo picked himself up off the ground and straightened his waistcoat, but his attention was on Faraz. "You told me that thing was harmless!"

Faraz regarded him mildly. "Because you have never lied about something important before."

"But . . . but it can electrocute things," he sputtered. "*To death.* And you carry it around on your shoulder."

"Well, Skandar wouldn't do that to a person. At least not unless I told it to, and probably not even then."

Porzia gave him a scathing look. "You don't *know* whether your tentacle monster would kill a human?"

"It's not as if I've had an opportunity to test the theory."

"Personally," said Elsa, "I think Skandar did a lovely job of vanquishing our foe. Thank you, darling." She reached out with her free hand to scratch the hollow under its wing, and Skandar's eyelid drooped with contentment at her touch.

Leo crouched beside the felled beast and tentatively tapped the pommel of his rapier to check that it wasn't too hot to touch. He must have found it acceptable, because he took hold and yanked it loose from the beast's throat. The rapier made an unpleasant wet noise as he pulled it free, and it came out dripping viscous yellow-ish fluid. Leo took a rag from his pocket and scrubbed the blade clean before returning it to its sheath.

Elsa decocked the revolver and holstered it. "So what now?" she said.

Porzia, hands on hips, walked a slow circle around the clearing. "I don't understand. The important things are always supposed to be located at the center of the labyrinth. Everyone knows that!"

Faraz stroked Skandar's wing, only half paying attention to Porzia's ongoing inspection of their surroundings. "Perhaps Montaigne needs to read up on his Minoan mythology."

"Very helpful, thank you," Porzia snapped.

Elsa started walking the perimeter, running one hand lightly over the curved wall that bounded the courtyard. There must be something they were missing—a secret passage, a hidden compartment. He was a man of ample ego—he would place the important object in the center of everything else.

Porzia stood in the middle of the courtyard, examining how the paving stones had been set in a spiral pattern. "Look at this," she insisted. "There should be something right here!"

Elsa's fingertips ran across a washboard of indentations in the stone, and she stopped to examine it more closely. An inscription.

"There's something carved into the wall here." She brushed the dust from the stones. "It looks like . . . French. '*Si c'est ici le meilleur des mondes possibles, que sont donc les autres?*'" *If this is the best of all possible worlds, what are the others?*

Porzia came over to see. "That's strange. It's a quote from Voltaire."

At the word *Voltaire*, the carved stone made a grinding noise and shifted, sliding backward ever so slightly relative to the rest of the wall.

Porzia and Elsa exchanged a look. Then Elsa leaned close to the stone and clearly enunciated, "Voltaire."

The stone slid farther away, as if it were a button pressed by an invisible hand, and when it stopped there was an audible *clank* from inside the wall. It was a test, Elsa realized—a kind of locking mechanism where the name was the key. But the unlocking process was not yet complete.

"Find the quotes," Porzia said, turning to the boys. "Find the quotes!"

They spread out around the periphery of the courtyard, scouring the walls for more inscriptions. The stones had a weather-worn feel to them, caked with dirt in some places and hidden behind ivy in others.

"Found one," said Faraz. "'*Un sot savant est sot plus qu'un sot ignorant.*'"

"Molière!" Porzia called from across the courtyard. Faraz

repeated the name into the stone, which slid into place and clanked audibly, just like the first one.

Elsa's fingertips detected a pattern on the stone, and she pulled the vines aside to get a clear look at the carving.

Frowning, she read, "*'Le grand architecte de l'univers l'a construite on bons matériaux.'*"

"Ooh! I know that one," Leo said. He jogged over and announced to the stone, "Jules Verne!"

The stone slid inward. Everyone looked at Leo.

"What? I read," he said defensively. "What's with all the French literature, anyway?"

Quietly, Elsa said, "It's meant to keep out Veldanese. My mother would borrow books from Alek sometimes, but it's not as if we have a library in Veldana. So I don't recognize the quotes."

"Oh," he said.

Typical Montaigne—making a show of his superiority as a real person and as a Frenchman. Elsa knew she shouldn't let it bother her, but the slight stung. She shook off the insult and said brightly, "Smart of him. It might have worked, if I'd come alone."

Leo grinned. "Good thing you didn't, then."

In all, they found eight quote-puzzles. Porzia solved most of them, with occasional help from Leo and Faraz. Elsa tried not to despair at her own uselessness. With all her talents for creation, she could not make herself recognize words she'd never read.

"Here we are. Last one," said Porzia. "*'Vous avez des ennemis? Mais c'est l'histoire de tout homme qui a fait une action grande ou crée une idée neuve.'*"

"No idea," said Faraz.

Porzia scrunched up her face, trying to dredge up the memory. "Ugh, it's so familiar! I can't quite put my finger on it."

Leo chewed his lip. "What if we came at it from a different approach? Which famous French writers are we missing?"

"Zola? No, it doesn't sound like Zola," Porzia said, immediately rejecting her own suggestion.

Porzia's gaze locked with Leo's and they said at the same time, "Hugo!"

She leaned close and spoke the name. "Victor Hugo."

The stone slid away and clicked into place. For a minute, nothing happened. They all exchanged questioning looks—had they missed an inscription somewhere? What exactly should they expect? Elsa feared that Porzia might have gotten one of the quotes wrong, or perhaps they needed to be triggered in a particular order. Year of publication, perhaps?

Then the ground shuddered, stone grating against stone, the courtyard echoing with the noise of it. Slowly, the inner portion of the courtyard sank into the ground, each paving stone lowering to a different height so that the spiral pattern became a spiral staircase.

As soon as the shaking stilled, Leo stepped close to the edge and peered into the dark hole. "Now there's an ominous sort of invitation if ever I saw one."

Elsa joined him at the top of the spiral stairs. Grabbing his arm for support, she tested the first step to make sure it would take her weight. "Not an illusion, at least."

Somewhere in the depths below, lights came on, as if the labyrinth knew they were there. With the bottom of the stairs bathed in gaslight, Elsa could guess the depth of the hole to be five or six meters—close to two stories. Letting go of Leo's arm, she stepped down to the second stair. The stones were thick, making the steps uncomfortably far apart, as if they were designed for a giant.

"Nope, not creepy at all," Leo muttered before following her.

There was no handrail on the inside of the spiral, and enough empty space in the middle to allow for a very quick trip to the bottom, so Elsa hugged closely to the outside wall as she descended. The cold of the stone seeped through her sleeve like icewater.

A few steps above, Porzia said, "By all means, let's walk into the trap." Her voice echoed weirdly in the stairway column.

Halfway down, the column opened up into an underground cavern. Elsa hurried to the bottom of the stairs, feeling precarious and exposed without the wall beside her, but she saw no slavering monsters lying in wait to attack them. Curious. She paused at the bottom and held up a hand to stall the others. There was something off about the air down here. Not the smell—though it *was* unpleasantly musty—but the way it felt when it filled her lungs. The density, maybe, or the temperature, as if she were breathing soup. Elsa took another deep breath, trying to analyze it better, and spots began to swim in her vision.

She spun around. "Get back outside. Quick!"

Ushering the others before her, she rushed back up the stairs, thighs burning with the effort. Above in the courtyard, she went to her knees on the flagstones, expelling the bad air from her lungs. Her vision tunneled, and she heaved a few deep breaths to compensate, her corset stays digging into her bruised side with each attempt.

Leo crouched beside her. "What's wrong? What happened?"

Elsa shook her head, focused on breathing. When her vision finally cleared, she said, "There's no oxygen down there. Porzia's right—it's a death trap."

"That's fantastic news," Faraz said in earnest. "It means the book is almost definitely down there."

Porzia gave him a look. "Death trap, Faraz. *Death*. *Trap*."

Leo said, "We need a breathing apparatus, like Fleuss designed for those construction divers on the Severn Tunnel project."

The names Fleuss and Severn meant nothing to Elsa, but she was already thinking of oxygen tanks. "It shouldn't take long to build a few. Here, hold this," she said, handing the laboratory book to Porzia.

She raised her eyebrows. "Seriously? You want me to just stand here holding the worldbook?"

"I need Leo and Faraz for this."

Porzia shook her head, exasperated. "Fine. But if I get eaten by another wolf-monster while you're all off playing in the lab, I shall be very put out."

Elsa set the coordinates and ported into her laboratory world with the boys in tow. Faraz and Leo looked around curiously, as if they'd never seen a laboratory before. Clearly, since it was her work space, she'd have to take charge.

"All right. Leo, we'll need gas canisters, tubing, something to work as a face shield. Go through that door for mechanical supplies," she said, pointing. He nodded and went, and she turned to Faraz. "If we're constructing it as a closed system—inhaling from and exhaling into the apparatus—we'll need a chemical to scrub carbon dioxide from the air we breathe out. What do you think, limewater? Caustic potash?"

He nodded. "We'll need something porous to suspend it in. Make a sort of air filter."

With three brains and three sets of hands, the construction process flew by. This project wasn't nearly as difficult as the tracking map she'd designed with Porzia, but the same principle applied: with the right help, everything went faster. Soon they were shouldering four newly invented rebreathers and carrying them back through the portal.

"Look, you're still alive," Elsa said brightly, accepting the lab book back from Porzia.

"Alive and bored," she said, taking the fourth rebreather off Leo's hands. "Oof, this contraption weighs a ton. You call this quality engineering?"

Leo replied, "I swear, you could find something to complain about in paradise."

"The oxygen balance is going to be high at first, so shallow breaths," Faraz warned. "We don't want anyone hyperventilating and passing out down there."

Elsa adjusted the oxygen tank's strap across her shoulders, held the facemask over her nose and mouth, and took an experimental breath. Everything seemed to be in working order, so she tied the facemask in place. She exchanged a nod with Faraz, who detached Skandar from his shoulder and—with some difficulty—convinced the beast to wait for them in the courtyard. Then the humans took the stairs down again.

"So what now?" Leo said, looking around the cavern. His voice came through the facemask, muffled but still audible.

Porzia said, "We investigate until we find another clue, like we did above."

The cavern floor had the smooth but uneven feel of water-eroded rock. With the help of stalactites, the string of gaslights around the perimeter cast strange patterns of light and shadow on the ceiling. The unevenness of the stone and insufficiency of the lighting made it difficult to say if there was only one cavern, or if there were passages leading away to a network of caves.

Elsa walked forward, trying to get a better feel for the space, and a wave of nausea flowed through her. Her face flushed hot and her stomach clenched. She checked her air supply but found nothing amiss. So what was that feeling? Another kind of trap scribed into the world? She turned to warn the others and saw something exceedingly strange.

Her three companions were still there in the room, but they were moving so fast their features blurred and she could barely tell one from another. Then one of them sped toward her, resolving into Leo as he approached. He held one arm back, connected to the blurs that were Porzia and Faraz, and threw his other arm toward her, still moving faster than a person should.

She reached out—he was gesturing at her impatiently—and took his hand. He yanked roughly on her arm, and she winced. As he drew her closer, though, the nausea washed over her again, and everyone slowed down to normal speed.

"What—" Elsa said, baffled.

"Temporal pockets," Porzia explained. "You were stuck in there for ten minutes—we weren't sure how to get you out safely."

Elsa blinked. "Felt like seconds. Good thing I stopped walking when I did."

"If we're not careful, we could spend centuries down here and not even know it. Montaigne does seem to love nested security measures, doesn't he?" Porzia set her hands on her hips and glared at nothing in particular.

Leo adjusted his facemask. "There must be a way through to wherever the book is. Montaigne got out, after all."

An idea occurred to Elsa. "Leo, do you have your pocket watch on you?"

"Of course," Leo said, taking his out. "Name me a mechanist who leaves home without a pocket watch."

Elsa declined to point out that she, obviously, did not own one; otherwise she wouldn't have asked. Instead, she explained, "Hold it out in front of you at arm's length. If the second hand slows down, we know not to walk in that direction."

Leo did as she instructed. The progress was slow, but after a few minutes they had mapped out the pattern of temporal dilation in the cavern. The bubbles of slow-time were everywhere around them, with only one invisible passageway large enough to admit a person.

"I suppose it's this way, by process of elimination," Leo said. "Watch your knees and elbows, everyone."

He inched forward, sweeping the pocket watch left and right to detect the curves of the passageway. Elsa and the others followed single file, carefully watching where Leo stepped and matching his route exactly.

At the front of the line, Leo stopped suddenly, and Elsa nearly crashed into him. They were close to one wall of the cavern, but other than that, nothing seemed odd about the spot.

"What is it? Another temporal bubble?"

"No," Leo said, lowering his pocket watch. "I think we've arrived at our final destination."

He stepped aside to give her a clear view. Set into the stone wall were four large, faceted wheels, each facet carved with a different number, zero through nine. A combination lock. Beside the wheels was a single lever, presumably to be pulled once the proper combination was entered.

"Four digits," Porzia observed. "Possibly a year, but which one?"

Elsa reached out and thumbed the first wheel, setting it to the number one. Then, figuring that Montaigne wasn't much of a historian, she set the second digit to eight. She withdrew her hand, considering what to do next.

Leo ran a hand through his hair, frustrated. "Even assuming the code is a date from this century, we still have ninety-one possible combinations. We don't have enough oxygen left to try them all."

"Hold on." Elsa thought hard, trying to imagine this from Montaigne's perspective. Even after everything that had happened with Jumi, Veldana was still his greatest accomplishment—the victory that Jumi had wrenched from his grasp. Could he really be so egotistical?

Elsa set the last two numbers. "1873," she said. "The year he completed the Veldana worldbook, and made history as the first scriptologist to create sentient people."

Porzia asked, "Are you sure?"

"One way to find out." She pulled the lever.

From deep within the wall there was a *click click click click*, and a whirring of gears, a grating of stone, and on the floor two stone panels swung upward. Elsa had to back up hastily to get out of the way. When the hole in the floor opened, a pedestal rose out of it, and upon the pedestal was a large leather-bound volume. The spine was marked in Jumi's elegant script.

"Careful," Faraz warned. "Could be yet another trap."

"Mm," Elsa agreed.

She circled the pedestal, examining it from all angles. No hidden weapons compartments, no pressure plates, no suspicious-looking materials, no electrodes. She tapped the front cover with one finger and quickly withdrew her hand. Nothing.

Leo fiddled with his pocket watch impatiently. "Oh, just pick the damned thing up, already."

"Fine," Elsa said, "but if the ceiling caves in, I'm blaming you."

Still, she hesitated. This was her mother's secret creation, part of the legacy she was born to inherit. Jumi had chosen to hide it from her, and that knowledge pinched like a thorn between her ribs.

Elsa placed both hands on the worldbook. Even through the cover, the pages seemed to sing to her. The air close to the book vibrated, as if it were made of butterfly wings instead of paper. And Elsa found that she did want to pick it up—deeply yearned to, in fact.

She lifted the book.

The ceiling did not collapse, though Elsa might not have noticed if it had.

No one wanted to cut it close with the oxygen, so Leo led them back through the minefield of temporal pockets. As they climbed the stairs, Elsa cradled her mother's book in her arms the way another person might hold a young babe.

"Don't just hug it," said Porzia, stepping out into the court-yard. "Let's crack that cover and give it a read, shall we? Find out what sort of weapons are inside."

An anxious tentacle tugged at Elsa's skirt, but she had her hands full with the book. Faraz lifted Skandar to his shoulder while Elsa opened to the first page.

As she read through the text, she could feel the weight of their gazes upon her. She didn't need to look up at Leo to know the wait was killing him.

"So?" he finally said. "What kind of worldbook is it?"

"It's . . . not." Elsa scanned the front pages a second time, but the usual properties—gravity, land, air, heat—remained stubbornly absent.

"Not what?" Porzia leaned closer, scowling at the Veldanese text as if she could understand it by force of will alone.

"Not a scribed world at all. You see these references here?" Elsa pointed to a particular section; though Porzia couldn't read the words, she might recognize the structure and formatting. "The text is linked to Earth, like my doorbook."

"Really? Oh, I see . . . but it's so much larger than your doorbook."

Elsa flipped through a few more pages, her heart sinking as she read further and her suspicions were confirmed. Dread settled in her stomach, and when she spoke again, her voice came out hoarse. "That's because it's not meant for traveling."

Leo said, "What does the damned thing do, then?"

Elsa looked up to meet Porzia's waiting gaze, but she could tell the other girl—for all her scriptological talents—had not guessed what the book could do. Elsa cleared her throat. "It makes . . . changes. It doesn't contain a weapon, it *is* the weapon: this book is designed to *edit* Earth."

All the color drained from Porzia's cheeks.

Faraz said, "But—but that's not possible. Is it?" On his shoulder, Skandar fanned its wings anxiously, picking up on the sudden change in mood.

"It's preposterous," Leo protested with a sudden, blustering confidence. "You can't edit the real world! It's the *real world*—it wasn't made with scriptology."

"There is precedent," Porzia said quietly. "A person born in the real world can be changed. Think of Simo—he was textualized by a bad script. There's no theoretical impediment preventing someone from designing a book to make intentional changes to reality."

Faraz held his hands up in a steadying gesture. "Okay, okay. Let's assume for the moment this . . . *editbook*, or whatever you want to call it, actually works. What's Garibaldi planning to do with it? How dangerous is this thing?"

"It's not just that he could edit the world to make Italy a single, unified state," Elsa explained. "He could edit the world to force everyone to *want* unification. Of course if he tried that and mucked it up, he might accidentally textualize the entire population of southern Europe."

Porzia sucked in a breath between her teeth, horror written all over her face. For her own part, Elsa struggled to hold down the nausea roiling in her gut. How could her own mother have given birth to such a diabolical invention? She felt unclean by association.

In a dazed voice, Faraz recited, " 'The world has entered a time of flux. Much depends on the choices you make.' "

"What?" said Leo.

Faraz wrung his hands. "That's what the Oracle said to me. At the time I didn't understand how our choices could affect the entire world, but now . . ."

Elsa exchanged a weighted glance with Faraz, remembering the rest of the Oracle's prophecy. *The waters writhe with eldritch horrors. A plume of ash ten thousand meters high blocks out the sun.* She said, "We can't let Garibaldi get his hands on this book."

Porzia planted her hands on her hips, moving on from horror to decisive practicality. "Garibaldi thinks he has the advantage because he is willing to hurt Jumi—or whoever else, I'd imagine— to get what he wants. We have to beat him at his own game."

Leo snorted. "How, hold a knife to my throat? He threw me away, remember."

"Don't be ridiculous, I'm not suggesting we threaten *you*," she said.

"Then what?"

"We threaten to destroy the editbook." A small, devious grin pulled at the corner of her mouth. "Or render it useless, at least. We don't need the editbook to be functional, but he does. Garibaldi may not have realized it yet, but we'll have a hostage, too."

It took them much less time to find their way out than it did to find their way in. The walls seemed to have stopped shifting around, and they knew to keep to the southeast quadrant to avoid the giant pit in the floor. A good thing, too, since Elsa's attention was focused more on the book in her arms than on the ground in front of her feet.

"So," Porzia was saying, "we'll take it back to Casa della Pazzia first. Agreed?"

Elsa nodded. "I'll need a minute with it, before we go after Jumi."

Leo said, "Best not to show it to Gia, though."

Porzia's mouth tightened into a grim, unhappy line. "With any luck, Mamma will be too busy repairing the house to even notice we're back."

Elsa shrugged, deferring to their judgment on the matter of Signora Pisano. Her natural inclination was to hide everything from everyone, so this seemed a perfectly reasonable approach. "Here we are, this should be the corridor where we came in," she said, turning around the last corner.

Elsa stopped short. There was someone leaning in the entranceway of the labyrinth—dark hair, amber eyes, insouciant slouch. Aris.

"Took you long enough," he said, smirking. "I was about to send in a search party."

19

Leo went cold at the sight of his brother. It took him a moment to find his voice. "What are you doing here?"

Aris pushed away from the wall and strolled closer to them. "After our conversation in Nizza, I was concerned you might be getting ideas. Might try to trick Father—leave with Jumi and the editbook."

It was disorienting, meeting him here so suddenly. Leo hadn't had the chance to prepare himself for seeing Aris again. "But . . . but how did you—"

"Relax, little brother," Aris interrupted. "I'm here to protect you. Protect your friends. You don't want to find out what happens to people who cross our father."

Beside him, Elsa's eyes narrowed. "You tracked us."

"Better. I tracked your portals," Aris gloated.

That, at least, remained the same. Aris had always been one to brag about his accomplishments, to bask in praise of his brilliant inventions.

"Is that so," Elsa said. She had a careful, calculating look about her, as if she were already running through scenarios in her mind. Leo could only be grateful that someone was—he felt too blindsided to think clearly about their next move.

Instinctively, the four of them huddled closer, forming a united front in the face of Aris. Porzia was doing something behind her back. Leo didn't dare look at her, lest he draw Aris's attention as well.

Instead, he stepped forward and reached for his rapier. Aris registered the motion and drew his own, and the tips of their rapiers met in the air with a *clack*.

Aris grinned. "Been a long time, brother. Do you remember how we used to practice in the ballroom in Venezia?"

"I remember beating you on more than one occasion," Leo replied.

They exchanged a few lunges and parries experimentally, each trying to gauge the other's skill. Every fencer's fighting style evolves over time, and there had been plenty of time since their last match. Leo feinted right, forcing Aris to circle him. He didn't need to win; he only needed to hold Aris's attention.

He drew Aris farther into the corridor, away from the labyrinth's exit, always careful to keep himself positioned between his brother and his friends. He played just well enough to keep Aris's rapier away from any vital organs, but let him believe he had the upper hand. He even allowed the sharp tip to graze him once, and tear his sleeve another time, all the while making room for the others to inch their way closer to the Edgemist.

"You're out of practice, brother," Aris crowed, slicing dangerously close to Leo's cheek. "Pisa has turned you soft."

"Or maybe I don't believe you're willing to skewer me just to get the book," Leo countered.

"I'm confident I could patch you up afterward." He flicked his wrist, the rapiers knocking together with a *clack*.

Leo deflected. "Emphasis on 'confident.'"

Finally, he heard the sound he'd been stalling in anticipation of: the whoosh of a portal opening behind him. Leo glanced over his shoulder to see Elsa hesitating at the mouth of the portal. "Go!" he cried.

For once, she went without argument. Thank God for small mercies. Leo pushed in with a quick combination—riposte, counter-parry, counter-riposte—unbalancing Aris and buying enough time to disengage. Then he turned and dove for the portal just as it began to close.

Elsa skidded to a stop along the inlaid tile floor of Casa della Pazzia's grand foyer. She glanced around. They'd all made it without any pursuers following them through, and the portal was already winking closed.

Faraz held a protective hand up to Skandar. "Is Aris coming after us?"

Porzia said, "If he could track our portals to Amsterdam, he can track us here."

Faraz said, "But how is that even possible?"

"A recently opened portal leaves a residual weakness in the fabric of reality, even here on Earth, it seems." Porzia spared a second to throw a rueful look Elsa's way. "Aris must have invented some sort of device—like our tracking worldbook—that detects and locates these weak spots. He'd also need some way to exploit the weak spots, to link up his departure point with our destination portal."

"You mean . . . like Elsa's doorbook, except it reopens old portals instead of creating new ones. Did he find out about the doorbook somehow?" Faraz turned his confused frown upon Elsa.

"No, he never saw it." Elsa reluctantly added, "Though he may have inferred its existence from how freely we've been hopping around the continent."

Porzia's hands found their usual position on her hips. "One way or another, he's invented a way to follow us. The question is, will he follow us here?"

Everyone looked at Leo. He'd been disturbingly quiet since they'd arrived back at Casa della Pazzia.

"I . . . I don't know," Leo said, sounding shaken. "We have to go back to Nizza for Jumi, and he knows it. He may wait for us to come to him."

Anxiety roiled in Elsa's gut, and she could not honestly say how much of it was for Leo and how much for herself. "I have some work to do, and fast. I'll be in my study." The editbook clutched in her arms, she took the stairs at a run.

Behind her, Porzia was already planning for the worst. "Casa, set all monitoring systems to high alert. What's the status of your defenses?"

Elsa didn't linger long enough to hear the house's reply. Up in her rooms, she took a portal to her scribed laboratory. It was at best impossible and at worst extremely dangerous to make alterations to a worldbook while inside that same world, and she guessed the editbook worked the same way with Earth. She cleared a space on her workbench and threw herself into her chair. Sucking in a deep breath, she opened the cover with a combined feeling of reverence and dread.

Inside, the paper tingled with anticipation beneath her touch, as if the editbook yearned to be used. The more she looked over the text, the more beautiful it seemed, and she marveled at Jumi's ingenuity. Elsa could not help but admire her mother's grand accomplishment. At the same time, she was terrified of how drawn she felt to the editbook, of her own insidious desire. Terrified that her mother had been capable of creating such an instrument of potential destruction—what need or hatred or desperation had led Jumi down this path?—and equally terrified that she herself might contain those same cold capabilities.

Elsa hesitated, pulling her hands away from the pages like a guilty thief. But her beloved Veldana was in peril, cut off from Earth if not entirely destroyed. She needed to muster her courage. She needed to trust in herself.

She flipped past the core text, which defined the nature of the book, giving it power to alter the real world. Toward the back she found a section describing the one small change Jumi had made; Elsa focused all her attention on that text, trying her best to ignore the flash flood of relief that threatened to carry her away as her suspicions were confirmed.

The chamber inside the wall of Montaigne's library, where the Veldana worldbook resided, was a scriptological addition to Earth. A tiny pocket universe, latched onto the real world like a barnacle to a whale's hide. Which meant there was a chance—even a reasonable probability, Elsa dared to hope—that Veldana had survived, attached to Earth but unaffected by the fire, still there-but-not-there even now. Her heart fluttered against her ribs at the thought.

Toward the end was an unfinished line of text. At the time of her abduction, Jumi had had the editbook open on her writing table . . . apparently with the intention of scribing access privileges for Elsa, so her daughter could also open the Veldana worldbook's hiding place.

Elsa's throat stung with the pressure of unshed tears. Jumi might have hidden the editbook, but she entrusted Elsa with something even more precious to the both of them: the text of their own world. Jumi had meant to give Veldana to her daughter that very day in their cottage.

Her hands unaccountably steady, Elsa took out a bottle of scriptological ink along with a pen. Her pulse quickened as she dipped the nib. The words must be chosen with the utmost care—specific enough that, in effect, only she would gain access privileges, yet vague enough that it could theoretically refer to someone other than Elsunani di Jumi da Veldana. It would be all too easy to accidentally render herself textual.

Looking over Jumi's half-finished work, she discerned her mother's intent: change the permissions from *the protector of Veldana* to *the protector of Veldana and his or her descendants*. Elsa dipped her pen and cautiously completed her mother's changes.

She held her breath as the ink dried, irrationally afraid despite the confidence she had in her own work. But as the text settled in and the real world subtly altered, Elsa remained self-aware and free. She had not turned herself into another Simo. Letting out a sigh of relief, she set the pen aside.

There. Now, no matter what happened when they confronted Leo's father, at least she would be able to find out if Veldana had survived the fire. She did not dare to hope for it, but perhaps she and her mother would soon be returning home together.

Elsa brought the editbook back to her real-world study, where she discovered that dawn had come and gone while she'd been working. She hurried into her bedroom to wash up. There, on the bed, the outfit Porzia had made for her was carefully laid out, and a little handmaid bot stood idle off to one side, waiting to help her change. She still felt resistant about the trousers, as if that one small detail would mean she'd turned her back entirely on the traditions of her people. But she had to admit her current dress was in need of changing—dirty and torn in a few places from her mishap with the chasm—and if recent experience was any indication, dresses weren't the wisest choice of clothing to begin with.

She quickly wriggled out of the old clothes with the bot's help and scrubbed her hands and face at the basin. Then it was time for the gray trousers, linen shirt, leather bustier with all its attachments. She was buckling the tall boots when Leo knocked twice and let himself in.

"Elsa, are you ready? We—" Leo's eyes went wide as he took in her new outfit. "Wow, you look . . . uh . . ."

"I'm not trying to look pretty," Elsa interrupted, feeling acutely self-conscious about the trousers. "I've done just about all the running in skirts that one person can stand to do. Porzia's right—it's time I dress the part."

"I was only going to say that you look different. Good different. More like yourself." His cheeks turned a little bit pink.

Finished with the boots, Elsa scraped her damp palms against her thighs and stood. "You were about to say we need to talk about what we're going to do. Right? Does that mean you don't like Porzia's plan?"

Leo grimaced, as if his next words pained him. "Elsa . . . what if we just . . . gave my father what he wanted?"

"We can't," Elsa said, looking away. "Jumi created the edit-book. It's a part of my inheritance. This book confers a great and terrible power, and if Garibaldi were to misuse that power, as he almost certainly would, I would be responsible."

Leo shook his head. "He was a madman long before you came along, Elsa. It isn't your job to police his actions. You should take your mother and escape his sphere of influence while you still have the chance to."

She took a deep breath and let it out, wondering how to explain it to him. "I have always despised Earth and its people—mostly for their sense of superiority over Veldanese," she began. "I resented the idea that because our world is scribed, it isn't real. So when I came here, nothing mattered to me but Veldana, and I would have happily scorched the Earth in return for Jumi's freedom and Veldana's safety. But don't you see? Protecting Veldana is a duty I claim for myself, not a task I am obliged to, for I did not scribe Veldana and neither did my mother. Protecting your world from the editbook is a responsibility I cannot shirk, because that *is* Jumi's creation."

The conflict cleared from Leo's expression, and he gazed at her with respect. He nodded once and said, "Of course you're right."

"Good," she said. "Now that that's settled, let me just grab the book—"

"Elsa, wait," he said, stepping closer. "There's . . . there's something I have to tell you."

"Yes?" she breathed. His proximity was distracting. She could see the faint line between his drawn-together brows, and the way a tense muscle pulled at the corner of his mouth.

His lips parted as if to speak, but the words caught in his throat, and instead of saying whatever it was he wanted to say he leaned in and kissed her. Cautiously at first, but when she reached for the back of his neck, his arms snuck around her waist and pulled her in. She closed her eyes and the world faded away to nothing but the heat of their bodies touching, like the void between portals, only warmer, infinitely warmer. And she smiled against his mouth, because it was funny that she'd just finished fastening all those buckles and laces, and now he'd have to unfasten them again.

But Leo pulled away too soon for that, and he stared at her breathlessly. Up close in the light, his eyes had the color and depth of amber. "We have to . . . There's no time, but I . . ." He looked away, raked a hand through his already mussed hair. "I needed you to know."

His other hand was still on her waist, and the warmth of his touch only worsened the temptation to fall back together like a pair of magnets. Softly, she said, "We need to go. They'll be waiting on us."

Elsa pulled away, breaking contact, and busied herself with fetching the editbook from her study. Her hands were still shaking a little from the exhilaration of kissing Leo, and she laughed at herself. Who would have thought, Jumi da Veldana's daughter quivering like a lovestruck girl? But then, perhaps it was time to acknowledge that her mother might not be the best authority on love.

When they left her rooms to rejoin Porzia and Faraz, Leo hesitated in the hall. "What's wrong?" she said over her shoulder.

"Nothing," he said. "Nothing. I'll be down in a minute."

Elsa searched his face for clues, but his expression was well schooled. If something was bothering him, he chose to hide it. Reluctantly, she nodded, and carried the editbook downstairs alone.

Porzia and Faraz were waiting in the foyer. Porzia cradled a little glass bottle of ink in her hands, and Faraz was attending to Skandar.

Elsa joined them, the editbook propped against one hip. To Skandar and Faraz, she said, "What are you two doing?"

Skandar raised its tentacles cheerfully in response to her attentions. It was holding five little vials of Faraz's gooey sleeping potion.

Elsa laughed. "Don't drop those, or you'll find yourself without your favorite perch."

The beast solemnly blinked its one enormous eye at her, as if to assure her of how seriously it took its new responsibilities. Elsa pressed her lips together, trying not to laugh again.

Porzia seemed less amused. "Apparently we're arming the tentacle monster now," she said sourly. "Not that it's going to solve our new problem."

Elsa knew what she meant. "Getting away when Aris can track our portals wherever we go."

Leo finally came down the stairs behind her, at which Porzia said, "Nice of you to join us. Now—what are we going to do about Aris?"

Elsa said, "I've been thinking about that. Once we have Jumi, we can open a portal to my laboratory"—she took a deep breath, steeling herself for Porzia's reaction—"and carry the laboratory worldbook through with us."

"Have you gone insane?" Porzia screeched. "That would sever our connection to Earth! We'd be stranded in your laboratory world with no way back."

"In theory, the doorbook should still be able to link back to

Earth. The core text of the doorbook references Earth specifically, in a manner not unlike that of the editbook."

"*In theory?*" Leo said.

"See? Aren't qualifications just infuriating?" Elsa smirked at him. "In any case, we have to take the chance. If we port somewhere on Earth, Aris will be able to trace our destination. But if we wait off-world for a while, we can slip back undetected."

Leo frowned. "You think that'll work?"

"His device may be able to detect the energy signatures of portals, but they all look the same. He can find us *only if* he knows the precise time a portal opens, or if he keeps an eye on a particular location, like Casa della Pazzia. But we won't be going there. We'll be lost in the background noise of all the other scriptologists porting back to Earth."

Porzia pursed her lips thoughtfully. "We'll have to hide the editbook somewhere before returning here."

Elsa nodded. "I was thinking of the old castle near Corniglia. It's well hidden." She paused. "If that's all right with you, of course."

Porzia gave her a thin smile. "We don't have the luxury of time. Let's use the ruins for now, until we can come up with something more secure. I'll grab the keys."

When everything they would need was collected together, they took a minute to shuffle the objects. One portal device was set for Nizza and the other for Elsa's laboratory, and Porzia took the doorbook. Leo drew his rapier and held it at the ready. Elsa opened the editbook to the early pages—the most critical part of the core text—and Porzia pressed the bottle of ink into Elsa's other hand.

"Ready?" Porzia made eye contact with each of them in turn before flipping the switch on her portal device.

Faraz and Leo stepped through first, with Elsa and Porzia quickly following. The portal opened directly into the room where Jumi was being kept. Elsa had only a second to absorb the scene—Jumi lying prone inside the machine, one guard leaning in the corner—before it started.

"Skandar, quick—the guard," Faraz urged.

The beast launched into the air on a collision trajectory with the guard's face. At the last moment, Skandar released one of the vials and angled sharply upward, skimming over the guard's head with mere inches to spare. The vial, however, met its mark, shattering on contact to coat the guard in bluish ooze. He made a surprised noise and then collapsed, unconscious.

The sound of a grown man hitting the floor was enough commotion to draw attention from the other room, but they were ready. Skandar hovered over the doorway and hit another two of Garibaldi's highly trained ex-Carbonari guards with sleeping bombs dropped from above. The third person through the door—Aris—ducked to the side, narrowly missing his own dose of blue ooze. Aris, glowering up at Skandar, reached for his rapier, and at that point the beast had the good sense to retreat back to Faraz's shoulder.

"Don't!" Leo said to his brother. His own rapier was already free of its sheath and aimed in Aris's direction. "Leave it."

Aris released the hilt and held his hand open in a show of compliance, though he grinned as if the situation amused him.

At last Garibaldi stormed through the door, nearly tripping over the prone forms of his men. "What in hell is going on here?"

"Not a step closer," Elsa said, holding up the clear glass bottle of scriptological ink. "Make one move, and I'll ruin the editbook."

Garibaldi's eyes widened, and Elsa let herself feel a grain of pleasure at surprising him. Whatever he'd expected they might try to do, he hadn't considered this. "You wouldn't," he said.

"Wouldn't I?" Elsa shook the bottle menacingly. "Do you know me so well you can be sure?"

"That book is your mother's magnum opus, her greatest achievement, and you'll throw it away?"

"My mother," Elsa said, "wouldn't want her greatest achievement falling into the wrong hands."

"Disposing of the editbook in the wrong manner could damage the real world," Garibaldi said with growing confidence. He took one step toward them.

Elsa narrowed her eyes and added some steel to her voice. "What do I care for Earth? I am Veldanese. I'd burn your world to the ground if I had to."

Those words seemed to give Garibaldi some pause. She could see the indecision in his face as he considered the veracity of her performance. On her left, there was a click as Porzia flipped the switch and opened a portal to Elsa's laboratory world.

"I'll have the code now, if you please," Elsa said.

Garibaldi ground his teeth, but gave it to her. "Up down down, up down up."

Elsa held his gaze with her own as she said, "Faraz, if you would . . . ?"

In the periphery of her vision, she saw Faraz nod and move toward the stasis machine. He flipped the switches, and there was an audible click as the lid unlatched. "I think we're good," he said, checking Jumi's vitals.

"Get her through the portal," Elsa told Faraz.

The whole apparatus was on wheels, though it proved so heavy that Porzia had to throw her weight in, too. Together, the two of them wheeled her mother out of her field of view while Elsa and Leo stood facing Garibaldi.

There was a scrape of wheels against the wood floor and a soft whoosh, and then Porzia and Faraz were through the portal with Jumi.

Elsa allowed herself the luxury of a triumphant smile. "A pleasure doing business with you. Don't expect to hear from us again." Then she backstepped toward the portal, Leo following at her side.

On the brink of the portal, Leo sheathed his rapier and turned to her, whispering, "Hand me the book."

"What?" she whispered back, holding on to the editbook.

His hands moving almost too fast to see, he reached forward and neatly wrenched the book from her grasp.

"What are you doing? We had a plan!" she hissed.

"I'm sorry, Elsa," he said, "but this was always the plan."

He grabbed her upper arm and shoved her, sending her flying backward. The cold of the portal hit her like water and swallowed her whole.

Elsa fell out the other side, losing her footing and sprawling across the wood floor of her lab. The ink bottle flew from her grasp and shattered against the leg of a table. She scrambled to her feet, ready to lunge back through the portal, but it was already closing. "Ugh!"

"Oh my God," Porzia said, taking in the scene. "Where's the editbook? *Where's Leo?*"

"Open the portal, we have to go back!" When neither Porzia nor Faraz replied, Elsa yelled, "What are you *waiting for?*"

Recovering from her shock, Porzia fumbled with the device, rushing to enter the coordinates. A black portal irised open halfway, then snapped closed again.

"What's wrong?" Elsa shot over her shoulder as she ran to her mother's side.

"I don't know!" Porzia tried again with the same result. "They must be blocking the connection somehow."

"Keep trying!" Elsa checked the rise and fall of Jumi's chest, the slow but even pulse in her wrist.

"She's stable," Faraz assured her.

Elsa turned her attention back to Porzia, who was flipping the switch again. Another nascent portal aborted itself. "Elsa, what happened to the editbook? And . . ." She swallowed. "And to Leo?"

This wasn't happening. This couldn't be happening. They had to get back and fix this and make everything right again. Shock warred with anger inside her, and Elsa's jaw worked for a moment before she managed to squeeze the words out. "He grabbed the editbook and pushed me through the portal."

"What!" Faraz shouted, looking up from Jumi's medical readouts. "That's not possible!"

"Well, that's what happened!" Elsa shouted back. She couldn't remember ever hearing Faraz raise his voice before. She took a deep breath. Her hands were shaking, and she flexed her fingers in an attempt to steady her nerves. "We have to . . . we have to think, we have to get it back." *Get him back.*

Porzia was staring at the portal device. She looked up, giving Elsa a stunned look. "Even if they weren't planning to immediately move the editbook to a secure location, we have no leverage left. How would we, you know, avoid getting shot on sight?"

Faraz raised a finger in the air. He seemed to have regained his usual composure. "I, too, am somewhat concerned about the getting-shot-on-sight scenario. Also, I don't fancy the notion of crossing swords with Leo."

Elsa cast him a scathing glare.

"I'm sorry, are we avoiding the topic of how my closest friend decided to abandon us and join the evil side?" he said mildly, eyebrows raised. But there were cracks in his calm facade, lines of pain etched around the eyes.

Porzia stepped closer to Faraz and put an arm around his shoulders. More than anything else could have, watching them struggling to process Leo's choice drove home for Elsa that he was gone. Something inside her—her drive, her certainty—seemed to deflate. She could still feel the imprint of Leo's hand on her arm, and she put her own hand over it, wrapping her fingers down to cover the ghost-grip he had left behind.

No, no, no. Desperately grasping at her last shreds of hope, Elsa said, "Try it again."

Porzia made no move to comply, so Elsa wrenched the portal device from her grasp and set the coordinates again herself. The seconds slipped away like water running through her fingers, each failed attempt distancing her from the possibility of catching them.

No, there was still a chance. She tried again. Reset. Tried again.

"Stop," Porzia said softly. "It's not going to—"

But on the next try the portal stayed open, widening enough to admit a person. Elsa did not hesitate to dive through, Porzia swearing behind her as she went.

The portal deposited her in the small room that had housed her mother's stasis machine. The unconscious guards were gone from the floor. Elsa bolted down the narrow hall, barely aware of Porzia's footsteps following her, and she burst through the door into the main room of Garibaldi's stronghold.

It was empty. No Garibaldi, no ex-Carbonari agents; even the long table had been hastily cleared of its jumble of paperwork. No evidence that someone had been planning a revolution here, nor any indication they'd ever return to this location.

No editbook. No Leo.

Elsa sank to the floor, her legs suddenly too weak to hold her up. Leo was gone. She felt as if she were watching herself from a detached perspective, floating dreamlike above her body. Was that silence the sound of a heart breaking?

"Well, there's no corpse," said Porzia. "That's good, right? That means he's still alive, at least?"

After a moment, Elsa mustered the will to reply, though her voice sounded hollow even to her own ears. "Why would they harm him, now that he's joined their side?"

Porzia sighed, looking around the room as if she half hoped to see him wounded and left behind rather than accept the truth. "He always did love his secrets."

No power on Earth could stop me, he'd said. Elsa rubbed her face with one hand. "I've been such a fool. He told me—he *told* me he'd do anything to be with his family again, and still I didn't see it coming. How could I not know?"

"None of us knew," Porzia said, her voice turning tight with contained anger. She rested a hand on Elsa's shoulder. "Come along. We have to see to your mother."

Porzia helped her stand, and then they left the place where he'd left them.

20

BE HAPPY FOR THIS MOMENT. THIS MOMENT IS YOUR LIFE.
—*Omar Khayyam*

Elsa waded through the rubble that was all that remained of Montaigne's house. It had rained at least once since the fire, and the runnels of ash-dirty water had dried in patterns of swirled black and gray. Another section of roof had collapsed since last she'd seen the ruins, which added to the difficulty and disorientation of trying to navigate her way back to where the study once had been.

She spun a slow circle, getting her bearings. Yes, the bookshelves had stood over there on the right, and the big windows were behind her—one broken, one warped by the heat. So this section of empty air used to be the wall where the Veldana worldbook was hidden.

Her stomach flip-flopped with anxious nausea. She lifted a shaky hand, holding it up to the air. How would she know exactly where to place her palm, with the wall gone? Slowly, she swept her hand back and forth, tracing over the nonexistent surface where she estimated the wall had once stood. Nothing.

Barely breathing, she pulled her hand back a little and tried again at a different depth. At shoulder height she felt a sort of gentle tug, as if the air had turned the consistency of honey. She leaned into the feeling.

The air shimmered and dissolved, revealing a dark compartment floating where the wall had been. The rectangular opening was visible only from the front, making the whole compartment appear two-dimensional, but when Elsa stuck her arm inside she confirmed it had depth to it. She laid her hand gently upon the cover of the worldbook inside and stood there for a moment before lifting it out.

Veldana. Untouched by flames. She could go home.

Elsa had worried about how she would manage to relocate her mother, but her concerns proved to be unfounded. In the end she had more help than she knew what to do with. Faraz and Porzia brought Jumi to Casa della Pazzia while Elsa retrieved the Veldana worldbook, and then they all went through—not just the three of them, but Gia and several of the children besides.

Everyone wanted to see Veldana. Burak and Porzia's brother Sante ran ahead down the path to announce their arrival, and so the villagers met them partway. Elsa and Jumi's homecoming became something of a carnival procession, dozens of voices chattering in Italian and Veldanese, children shouting with excitement and chasing one another. It felt like centuries since Elsa had last laid eyes on them all.

Then there he was, striding like a shark through a school of minnows: her oldest friend, Revan. He cut a line straight for her and fell into step at her side, and she felt suddenly, unaccountably shy. He had to be angry she'd disappeared with no explanation.

"Hi," Elsa hazarded. "How's . . . how's things?"

He shook his head, half-disbelieving. "That the best you can do?" he said, but when she looked at him, there was amusement crinkling the corners of his eyes.

"You'll have to cut me a little slack. I was rather occupied, saving the world and all."

He laughed. "We've never been very good at cutting each other slack, have we?"

Elsa showed a tentative smile. "I suppose not."

Impulsively, she stopped walking and pulled him into a hug. He froze for a second, surprised, then hugged her back fiercely.

"I'm glad you're not dead," said Elsa.

"Same to you, dummy," he replied. "Same to you."

When they all arrived at the village, Baninu—Revan's mother and Jumi's oldest friend—helped Elsa make up a bed in the main room of her mother's cottage. It might be a while before Jumi could manage the ladder to the loft. With Faraz's supervision, they disconnected Jumi from the stasis machine and tucked her in, and Elsa settled down to wait for her mother to wake.

When the sun dipped low in the sky, the villagers built a bonfire and brought out the drums and reed flutes. Elsa watched from the open doorway, her own people and the Italian guests making joyful attempts at communication. Faraz slipped away from the light of the fire, and as he approached, Elsa recognized him only by the height of his rail-thin silhouette.

"Hey," he said, his voice pitched low. "Has your mother woken up yet?"

Elsa shook her head. "Still unconscious."

"Ah, well. Slow victories are still victories."

"I'd prefer not to tally our gains and losses," she answered wryly. "I doubt we'd come out ahead."

"Your fellow Veldanese seem to think there's reason enough for celebrating," Faraz said with his usual tone of careful neutrality.

Elsa watched the festivities while she puzzled over his words. Was this what victory felt like? On the far side of the bonfire, Porzia was attempting to converse with Revan, a feat that apparently required much wild gesticulation.

"How's she doing?" Elsa said.

Faraz followed her gaze to Porzia. "She's angry. She tries to hide it, but she's angry."

"And you?"

"I'm . . ." His jaw worked as he struggled for words. "He's like a brother to me, you know? Disbelieving is how I am. I cannot accept this."

"I've been such a fool." Elsa clenched her fists against the turmoil inside her; it felt as if denial and fury were two snakes wrestling inside her gut. "I was warned, and still I didn't see it."

Faraz tilted his head to look at her, his eyes catching the firelight. "What do you mean?"

Elsa shook her head. Leo had worked so hard to earn her trust, only to leave in a spectacular act of betrayal—just as Jumi had always warned her men would do. A part of her wanted to tell Faraz, *I will never trust again*. Lesson learned.

Instead she told him, "Nothing, I . . . I was thinking of the Oracle. That's all."

Behind her in the cottage, Jumi coughed and groaned. "Elsa? Where are you?"

"Oh!" Elsa said with a start. "I'd better . . ."

"Yes, of course," Faraz said, motioning for her to go back inside.

Elsa bid him good night and moved to her mother's bedside. Jumi's complexion was still wan and her forehead damp with sweat, but her eyes were clear. Relief swept through Elsa like a new tide, washing away the hurt and confusion. Her mother keeping secrets, hiding the editbook, even scribing it in the first place . . . none of that seemed to matter now.

She said, "You're awake."

Jumi coughed again, and when she spoke her voice grated in her throat. "What in the world is all that racket?"

Elsa sat on the edge of the cot and took her mother's hand. "The whole village is celebrating your safe return. Welcome home, Mother."

The festivities wound down and the Italians went home, but the next day Elsa looked outside to see the lanky, familiar form of Alek de Vries picking his way slowly down the path. She could tell even at a distance that his hip was bothering him. When was he going to give in and start carrying a walking cane?

When had Elsa become the one who took care, and Jumi and Alek the ones who needed taking care of? Strange.

"Darling, where are you going?" her mother said.

Jumi hadn't called her *darling* since she was a little girl. The word—and the raw need with which her mother said it, so uncharacteristically defenseless—made her heart ache inside her chest.

"You're not going back for that boy, are you? The one who betrayed you," Jumi said disapprovingly.

"I never would have found you without *that boy*," Elsa snapped. The phrase irritated her, as if Leo in all his complexity could be reduced to *that boy*. "You don't know what you're talking about." Though even as the words left her mouth, she knew Jumi wasn't really the one she wanted to yell at. She was just mad at Jumi for being right, and mad at herself for being so gullible.

Jumi sighed and leaned back against the pillows. Her voice softer, she said, "I don't know how it started, but I was with you at the end. When I was sick, I could still hear things."

Elsa wanted to say, *It's not over yet*, but the doubt twisting in her gut kept the words from forming. What if Leo truly was beyond her reach? He'd chosen a side, after all, and it wasn't the same as hers. She should never have trusted him.

"I was only looking," Elsa finally said, by way of explanation. "Alek is coming down the path."

She left the door standing open and returned to Jumi's bedside.

Jumi took her hand in a firm grip. "I know you, daughter. I didn't raise you to give up so easily. But this is my fight, not yours, do you hear me?"

"You can't go back to Earth," she said. "The restorative properties only function in Veldana—if you went back, you'd fall ill again. Mother, you could die."

Jumi looked as if she wanted to argue, but instead she released Elsa's hand and said, "Tell me, what became of Montaigne?"

"The Order of Archimedes has him in custody."

"So he's to be locked up. As traitors ought to be," Jumi said suggestively.

Elsa gave her mother a sidelong look. Were they still discussing Montaigne, or had they returned to the topic of Leo? But she never got the chance to clarify—that was the moment when Alek came shuffling up to the open door, and his arrival ended the argument.

Elsa tried to step aside, not wanting to intrude on their reunion, but Alek drew her in and they all huddled close, talking much longer than they should for Jumi's sake. Three generations of scriptologists, mentors and students to one another but also something more. Family. Elsa had more of it than she'd once thought.

Later, when it was time for Jumi to rest, Elsa drew Alek aside to speak with him privately. "Will you stay with her? She needs time to recover, whether she likes it or not. And she won't like it—you know how difficult she can be."

Alek gave her a wry look. "How difficult *she* can be?"

"She needs someone to look after her," Elsa persisted.

"And who's going to look after you?" he said.

She wanted to snap, *I can look after myself,* but that would hardly be the reassurance he needed. Instead, she settled for saying, "There's Porzia and Faraz. I believe I can still count on them, even with . . ." She swallowed the words, *Leo gone.* "In any case, my work's not done. We must retrieve the editbook."

Alek frowned, and for a moment she thought he'd argue with her. Perhaps insist that the Order take over the battle with Garibaldi after her spectacular failure. But he voiced no words of criticism, only nodded. "Very well. I'll stay."

She nodded. "And I'll go."

Elsa took the shortcut up the steep hill, weaving her way around rocks and trees. She didn't want to be seen on the main path, didn't want the villagers making a production out of her departure. After weeks of fearing she might never return to her world, it would be hard enough to leave Veldana without a reminder of the people staying behind. *Her* people—she saw now that they truly were.

At the Edgemist, Elsa paused to check her supplies: doorbook and laboratory book, revolver in its holster, stability glove, portal device. The instruments of her craft. She suspected she would need them all.

She set the dials and flipped the switch. The portal irised open before her—cold as betrayal, black as uncertainty, edged in swirling chaos. The portal, so like the future that lay beyond it.

Elsa stepped through.

EPILOGUE

Leo balanced on the narrow platform between cars, his knees slightly bent to buffer against the rocking and swaying of the train. Behind him, the access door creaked, but he didn't turn to see who it was.

"There you are," Aris said, his voice raised to be heard over the noise of the train's passage.

Leo shut his eyes and focused on the feel of the wind whipping by, the clattering of wheels over the rails. He'd grown so accustomed to Elsa's doorbook that now it felt almost like a luxury to travel the slow way through reality.

"That was quite a performance," Aris continued, seemingly unbothered by Leo's lack of response. "I wouldn't have guessed you had it in you."

Sourly, Leo wondered if he meant the performance he'd given Father, or the earlier one—the one for Elsa. Now Leo turned, wanting to gauge his brother's response as he said, "At least one of us got what he wanted."

Aris regarded him mildly, though there was a flicker of calculation buried deep under that expression of innocence. "You're the one who made the deal: the editbook for Elsa's freedom. Isn't that what *you* wanted? We both know Father would have pursued her if she'd escaped with the book."

"I did what I had to do. There were no good choices." He'd only wanted to protect her, even if that meant protecting her from her own sense of responsibility. Now the memory of the moment he'd betrayed Elsa was like a sore tooth—painful, but he couldn't stop prodding it. Her shocked expression played over and over in his mind. Leo swallowed, his throat tight. "You're the one satisfied with this outcome, not me."

Aris looked away, and for once there seemed to be a vulnerability about his smile. "I won't pretend to be unhappy to have you back, brother. Do you fault me for being pleased at our reunion?"

Leo knew what he'd done was unforgivable. His life in Pisa was gone now. Faraz and Porzia, Burak and the rest of the children—his surrogate siblings. Gia and Rosalinda, who had both been mothers to him in their own ways. Elsa. He could never go back to them.

Aris put a gentle hand on his arm. "It's cold out here. Come inside with me, little brother."

"In a minute."

Aris nodded, acquiescing, and left Leo alone again with his

thoughts. It *was* cold, but Leo welcomed the numbness of the wind against his face. He wished it could numb him all the way through to the ache buried in his chest.

He had stolen the editbook; he had robbed Elsa of her chosen agency as the protector of Earth. So it was his burden, now, to prevent the editbook from ever being used. Yes, he would have to stop Ricciotti. Somehow.

Leo took a deep breath, pulled open the access door, and stepped inside the train car like Heracles entering the underworld. It was time to face his family—once the source of all his joy, and of more grief than his heart could hold.

Time to face his father.

AUTHOR'S NOTE

The political conflicts presented in this book are based on real nineteenth-century conflicts, but this fictional history diverges significantly from the true events of Italian unification. In real life, Archimedes mirrors were never successfully deployed for military use. So Giuseppe Garibaldi—an actual Sardinian general—landed his ships without incident in Marsala in 1860 and then led a famously successful campaign against the Kingdom of Two Sicilies. His battles in the south were supported by the highly dissatisfied local populace, including the real-life Carbonari rebels.

Garibaldi was passionately devoted to the idea of a unified Italy, and he went on to pursue multiple campaigns in other regions. By 1871, the modern borders of what we now know as Italy were established. Garibaldi did have a son named Ricciotti, but he led an ordinary life, always in the shadow of a famous father. In this alternate history, I've posited that Giuseppe's untimely death would not only have delayed unification by several decades, but also have a profound effect on his son.

Any similarities to real life are because Italian history is awesome; any inaccuracies are my own.

ACKNOWLEDGMENTS

First and foremost I have to thank my literary agent, Jennifer Azantian, for her unwavering enthusiasm and hard work bringing this project to fruition. I'm deeply grateful to the whole team at Imprint, but especially to my editor, Rhoda Belleza, and my publisher, Erin Stein, for helping to bring forth the best possible version of this manuscript. Thanks also to Natalie C. Sousa and the rest of the design team for transforming my words into such a beautiful physical object.

The support and critiques of my beta readers got me through the early drafts, so thanks to: Dan Campbell, Gwen Phua, Cynthia Tedore, Erin McKinney, and Athena DeGangi. More generally, I learned so much about the craft and business of writing from the Codex online writers' group and from my Triangle area critique buddies, Dan, Kim, and Natania. I wouldn't be where I am today without y'all.

Lastly, a shout-out to the local cafés of Durham, NC—especially Guglhupf and Mad Hatter—who kept me fed and caffeinated while I wrote this novel.